RIDES A DREAD LEGION

RAYMOND E. FEIST

RIDES A DREAD LEGION

HARPER
Voyager

HarperCollins*Publishers*
77–85 Fulham Palace Road,
Hammersmith, London W6 8JB
www.voyager-books.com

Published by Harper*Voyager*
An Imprint of HarperCollins*Publishers* 2009
1

Maps by R. M. Askren

A catalogue record for this book
is available from the British Library

ISBN-13: 978 0 00 726470 4

Set in Janson Text by Palimpsest Book Production Limited,
Grangemouth, Stirlingshire

Printed and bound in Great Britain by
Clays Ltd, St Ives plc

Mixed Sources
Product group from well-managed
forests and other controlled sources
www.fsc.org Cert no. SW-COC-1806
© 1996 Forest Stewardship Council
FSC

FSC is a non-profit international organisation established
to promote the responsible management of the world's forests.
Products carrying the FSC label are independently certified
to assure consumers that they come from forests that are managed
to meet the social, economic and ecological needs
of present and future generations.

Find out more about HarperCollins and the environment at
www.harpercollins.co.uk/green

NORTHLANDS

The Great Northern Mountains

Stone
Mountain

The LAKE
OF THE
SKY

Elvandar

Crydee

THE FAR COAST

THE
GREEN
HEART

The
Grey
Towers

Carse
Jonril

Tulan

THE
ENDLESS
SEA

THE STRAITS OF
DARKNESS

Tyr-Sog

Yabon

LaMut   Loriél

Zūn

Hawk's Hollow

Walinor
Hush   Natal   Ylith
Bordon   Quester's View

Port
Natal   Queg

Margrave's
Port
Lan   Palanque   THE
KINGDOM
OF QUEG

THE FREE CITIES

SORCERER'S
ISLE

Sarth

Calastius Mountains

THE
KINGDOM

DIMW

Sethanon •
THE GREAT

Darkmoor

Krondor

Dorgi

Landreth
SEA OF
DREAM

LiMeth   THE
BITTER SEA   Land's End

Durbin

Ranom

Elarial

Caralyan   Trollhome
Mountains   JAL-PUR DESERT

Shamata   VALE OF
DREAMS
(DISPUTED BORDER)

The
Pillars
of the Stars

THE
SCAR

The

THE EMI

MIDKEMIA

th of the World

•Ironpass

•Northwarden

•Highcastle

VOLD

THE BLACKWOOD

•Dolth

Rodez

Ran

Euper•

•Romney   •Tiburn

OD

Bas-Tyra   Sadara

•Silden   Cheam

Rillanon•

•alac's Cross

udor
ony's Vale   •Timons

The
rey
nge

THE KINGDOM SEA

THE
KINGDOM
OF
ROLDEM

GREEN REACHES

Deep Taunton•

Mallow Haven

The Peaks of Tranquility

•Pointer's Head

E OF GREAT KESH

CHAPTER ONE

Warlock

*T*HE DEMON HOWLED ITS OUTRAGE.
Amirantha, Warlock of the Satumbria, reeled backwards from the unexpected explosion of mystic energy hurled at him. Had his protective wards not been firmly established, he would have died instantly. The demon responsible was powerful enough to force through the barrier and slam the magic user hard against the cave wall behind him. The blow Amirantha took on the back of the head was going to raise a nasty bump.

Demons always carried a large amount of mystic energies, enough to destroy any unprepared mortal standing nearby as the monsters entered this plane of reality. It was one of the reasons for erecting wards, beyond merely confining the demon to a specific location. This one had arrived with a much more impressive explosion than the Warlock anticipated, and had surprised him.

Amirantha incanted a single word, a collection of otherwise meaningless syllables that together formed a key, a word of power that activated a much more complicated enchantment; a trick taught to him years before that had often meant the difference between controlling a summoned demon effectively and dismemberment at its hands. The word strengthened the ward spell that now confined the creature.

Amirantha regained his feet as the demon continued to howl at discovering itself summoned and confined. Experience had taught the Warlock that demons rarely objected to being summoned as they found this world easy to plunder, but they hated being trapped and controlled. Their hate was the one thing that made Amirantha's area of study problematic; his subjects kept trying to kill him.

He took a deep breath to calm himself and studied the enraged conjuration. The demon was not a type he recognized, though obviously a battle demon of some sort. Amirantha knew more about demons and their nature than any mortal on Midkemia, but still possessed only a tenth of the understanding he wished for. This specimen was new to him. He did not have exhaustive knowledge of every demon in the Fifth Circle, but he recognized its basic type: massive upper torso, roughly human in design, with a bull's head, or at least something that resembled a bovine; long, forward-arching horns, giving weight to its minotaur-like appearance. As he began to conjure a spell designed to immobilize any demon, Amirantha wondered if such a monster had been the basis for the ancient myth of the Minotaur.

Its legs were almost goat-like, but there anything remotely familiar about the creature ended. Its body was covered in some black substance up to its waist, though it was no wool, hair, or fur that Amirantha recognized. Its upper body looked like it was made from black leather, but slick and shiny, as if its skin had been tanned, dyed, and highly polished. Its horns were blood red, and its eyes burned like hot coals.

From the howls shaking the cave, Amirantha could tell that the demon's disposition was getting nastier by the second. The creature even looked on the verge of rending its way through wards that should be impenetrable, though Amirantha knew better than to place too much stock in the world 'should' when a demon was involved.

He finished strengthening his spell of confinement and saw the demon step back a moment, shudder, then return to battering the wards, accompanying its renewed efforts with even louder bellowing.

Amirantha's eyes widened slightly, his only outward concession to surprise. The demon had just shrugged off a spell designed to immobilize any conjured entity. Looking at the raging demon, the Warlock of Satumbria stroked his chin whiskers and considered what he observed. He was a vain man by any measure, and had his servant trim his beard and hair weekly, knowing exactly how it should look each time. His receding hairline had caused him to let his dark hair fall to his shoulders, and his dark brows and pointed chin beard gave him an appropriate cast for his calling in life: a summoner of demons. Or at least made him look the part for those willing to pay gold for his services.

Adjusting his purple robe, covered with fine silver needlework at the collar and upon the sleeves, he muttered a reliable invocation and watched. The demon should have instantly knelt in abject obedience, but instead he could sense the summoned creature's rage intensifying at the command. Amirantha sighed in a mixture of frustration and confusion, and wondered what he had conjured this time.

Ignoring the ringing in his ears, the Warlock reached into a large belt pouch. He had sewn this pouch years ago, patiently weaving magic into the threads under the supervision of a master artificer named Leychona, in the great City of the Serpent River, his one and only attempt at fabricating magic cloth. He had been pleased with the results, the confining bag let him carry many stones of power without provoking disastrous consequences. He was proud of the needlework, but had found the entire process so tedious and exasperating, he now paid artificers and tailors to fashion what he needed in exchange for his skills or gold.

Amirantha's finger rubbed lightly against a series of embroidered knots, each indicating a pocket he had fashioned. Swiftly, he found the one he sought and withdrew the stone he had prepared for a time such as this. Holding it aloft, he incanted a spell that drew forth the power stored in the stone and directed it to the hastily reinforced barrier. As he did, he felt the shock reverberating through the ward as the demon hurled itself against the mystic defence.

Then the creature paused, and looked at the space in the air where the barrier stood *as if it could see it*. Pulling back its massive right fist it unleashed a blow that could shatter a bull-hide shield. Amirantha imagined that he felt the shock from it travel through the air to strike him. Then the demon struck the wards even harder, and Amirantha raised his hand to reinforce the barrier with even more power. To his astonishment, this time he could feel the demon's energy translated into a blow that ran up his arm. He stepped back, until he stood hard against the wall. 'What do I do now?' he muttered absently.

Again the demon hurled itself at the barrier and Amirantha, Warlock of the Satumbria, decided it was going to get through. Pushing aside a sudden urge to laugh – the unexpected and dangerous often affected him this way – he drew another object from his belt pouch and smashed it on the floor.

A noxious gas erupted from its ruin and as it spread, Amirantha fled from the deep cave in which he had conjured the monster. It was a summoning area he had especially prepared for this ritual, protected by multiple wards and other safeguards he had erected against such a mishap. He hurried along a narrow tunnel, muttering, 'What next?'

Reaching a large open cavern, closer to the entrance of the stone warren, he cursed himself for a fool. All of his most powerful items had been stored in the smaller cave. He had been so surprised by the conjuration, that he had left them on the floor. He had thought himself ready for any eventuality surrounding demon summoning; it never occurred to him that one he hadn't summoned might appear unexpectedly.

Shaking his head at his own stupidity, he stopped. He had at least stored a lantern here; although such forethought had simply been intended to indicate the way out, rather than in anticipation that he might be forced to flee for his life, having abandoned his other lantern. Muttering to himself, he said, 'Sometimes I wish I was as clever as I claim to be.'

Amirantha turned back towards the tunnel, realizing that if he didn't stop the demon here, the creature would be free to choose from exits. Not only would that be bad for anyone living within the demon's reach, almost ten thousand people by the last census, it would also prove disastrous for Amirantha's reputation.

The Governor of Lanada waited for him near a particular cave mouth, accompanied by a sizeable retinue of soldiers, but nothing that could stop this monster should it come their way. Not only would the Maharajah's Court look down upon an itinerant Warlock responsible for the disembowelment of a regional governor, he was almost certainly not going to be paid for performing this banishment.

Pulling a long wand of ash from his belt, the Warlock readied himself. The device had been commissioned from the finest wand maker in the Kingdom of Muboya, and was capable of seven effective theatrical stunts, each designed to illicit 'oohs' and 'aahs' of wonder from onlookers. But it also possessed four very powerful enchantments that could inflict significant damage should the need arise. Amirantha was fairly certain the need had arisen.

He was greeted by the stench of the gas moving through the corridor from the summoning cave. It was designed to weaken and eventually incapacitate demons, and was not at all pleasant for humans to inhale. He knew that probably meant the demon was through the wards and coming towards him. Then Amirantha winced.

It wasn't the odour that made him shudder, but a sudden cave-rattling sound; a combination of tones and vibrations that made his heart jump and cringe at the same time. The angry shriek made his skin crawl, as if he were listening to a smith sharpen a sword on a turning wheel. If nothing else, the Governor of Lanada was receiving a better performance than the one Amirantha had originally planned for him.

Then the demon came straight at him.

A voice from behind Amirantha said, 'Need any help?'

'It would be appreciated,' the Warlock said to Brandos. His

companion had been waiting outside the cave mouth, reinforcement for eventualities such as this, and to make sure that the Governor became curious enough to send in his guards to 'help' the Warlock banish the demon.

Amirantha gripped his ornately carved wand and spoke a single word in a language known to very few men. A searing burst of heat washed over the two men as a massive fireball exploded away from them through the tunnel, sweeping over the demon and forcing it back.

'I'm going to need a few moments to banish it.'

The old fighter was still powerful, though nearing fifty years of age, and he had more experience in confronting demonic opponents than he wished for. This creature looked as if it might be the most dangerous he had faced so far. 'Where are the rest of your toys?'

'Back in the summoning cave.'

'In the cave?'

'Yes,' said Amirantha quietly. 'I realized that myself, just a moment ago.'

'Well then, we'll have to do this the difficult way, won't we?' He wore a buckler, a small round shield, on his left arm, and he pulled a broadsword from its scabbard that hung from his hip. 'It's times like this I wish I had taken up baking.'

Brandos knew he did not need to defeat the demon, only delay it long enough for Amirantha to banish it back to the demon realm. It was only a matter of gaining a minute or two, but the old fighter knew that even a few seconds could be a very long time. 'Let's go in before it comes back here. I don't welcome trying to keep it from those side tunnels. Best to keep it confined.'

Amirantha stayed behind his friend as Brandos moved up the tunnel, stopping only a few yards from where the demon had retreated. The stench of the gas filling the cave was nearly overwhelming, but it had the desired effect. The demon approached them cautiously, halted and then stood motionless for a moment, regarding the two humans.

Then it opened its mouth and issued sounds; not the inarticulate sounds of rage and anger, for they seemed meaningful, with rhythm and distinct pronunciation.

Brandos said, 'Is it casting a spell?'

Amirantha hesitated, his curiosity overwhelming his need to rid this realm of the demonic visitor. He listened for only an instant before he realized that Brandos was correct: the demon was a spell caster!

'We should interrupt that, I think,' said Amirantha. He uttered a single word, another cantrip release he had prepared for such dangerous encounters. The word acted as a mystic placeholder for a long, complicated spell, and its utterance instantly released the full force of the enchantment. As a result, the raging demon was suddenly unable to speak. The efficacy of the spell was dependent on several factors, but most importantly upon how powerful the targeted magic user was compared to Amirantha. The average village enchanter could be rendered silent until Amirantha chose to lift the spell. A powerful magician would be silenced only for a minute or two. A more powerful magician could shrug off the spell with little effort. This demon was an unknown quantity.

Amirantha began the spell of banishment and was only halfway through the incantation when the demon again found its voice, and resumed its own incantation.

'Bloody hell,' muttered Brandos as he darted forward, starting a slow, looping overhand strike at the demon's head; at the last moment, he moved his blade, dropped to one knee and unleashed the blow upon the demon's left leg. Shock ran up his arm as if he had struck the trunk of a massive tree, but even so, the demon howled in pain and retreated back up the tunnel, its spell casting interrupted. The creature was injured and it knelt for a moment, nursing its leg. Years before, Amirantha had paid a magician in Maharta to enchant the sword, to inflict additional pain on demons. Now he wished that he had paid for the spell to cause real injury, instead of a mere distraction.

As Amirantha finished his spell, the air seemed to come alive with hissing energy. The demon screamed defiantly, and the stone beneath their feet vibrated for a moment.

'It's still here,' observed Brandos.

'I can see that,' countered the Warlock. 'It's using its own magic to remain here.'

'What next?' asked Brandos.

'A more powerful spell of banishment, obviously. But we're going to have to wear it out.'

'Wonderful,' said Brandos shaking his head. 'So I bleed and you chatter.'

'Try not to bleed too much.'

'I'll see what I can do,' said Brandos as Amirantha drew a large gem-like object from his pouch and smashed it on the floor.

A hazy curtain of ruby-coloured energy sprang up, bisecting the tunnel. 'Back through the wards!' commanded Amirantha, and Brandos did not hesitate. He had been through too many of these confrontations to ignore the Warlock's instructions.

The magic user's deep voice resonated in the narrow confines of the tunnel as he quickly strengthened the new wards with a cantrip and reached into his pouch once more. A tiny light pulsed on his palm as he held out his hand. He cradled the light as it quickly grew into a throbbing crimson orb, and threw it at the demon just as the creature moved purposefully towards the two men.

The demon was instantly engulfed in a scintillating web of crimson threads, which caused tiny explosions of white heat as they touched its skin. It howled and the stone tunnel shook from the sound, dislodging fine soil and small rocks that fell on Amirantha and Brandos.

Brandos took a quick look around, to see if the entire hillside was about to come down on them, but satisfied that things were relatively stable, returned his attention to the enraged demon. 'I think it's annoyed,' he said dryly.

'What made you notice that?' asked the Warlock.

Brandos swung again as the creature advanced, giving Amirantha a moment longer to prepare the complex spell of banishment. As a safeguard, the Warlock quickly placed another set of wards behind the first, as an emergency measure. The demon recoiled from the blow, but Brandos wasn't trying to attack it, only slow it down. 'Back!' commanded Amirantha, and the old fighter retreated behind the next invisible threshold.

The Warlock uttered an invoking word and a wall of pulsing violet-coloured energy sprang up to encircle the demon in the tunnel. The sizzling cylinder of light was shot through with rose and golden colours, and when the demon struck its surface, it recoiled as if it had hit a stone wall. Smoke coiled from its flesh and its wounds were charred.

Brandos knew that demons expended energy to heal themselves, so each time they were injured they were weakened. But demons also had an exasperating ability to feed off other sources of energy given the chance, so it was wiser to weaken them as fast as possible so that the summoner could quickly banish them back to the demonic realm. 'Do I need to hit it a few more times?'

'Wouldn't be a bad idea,' said the Warlock as he readied another set of wards.

Brandos feinted high and wide, causing the demon to raise his hands above his head; then the fighter crouched and thrust, taking the creature's left leg out from under it again. With another stone-rattling bellow the huge monster fell back, crashing onto the floor as its dark blood spurted into the air. It smoked and emitted a foul sulphur stench as it splashed onto the stones. Brandos pulled back.

'That was a good strike,' observed the Warlock.

'I strive for the greatest result obtained from the least effort; I'm getting old, you know,' said the fighter as he retreated back to where Amirantha had erected the next set of confounding wards. Taking a deep breath, as perspiration flowed down his face, he added, 'One day you're going to get one of us killed.'

'More than likely,' agreed the Warlock.

'Or both of us,' added Brandos, raising his buckler and holding his sword ready against any new, unexpected problem.

The demon healed its latest wound slowly, and both men took that as a good sign. It required time without distractions to repair itself, and the more damaged it was, the more time it required. Lacking that space, it consumed its own magic essence to heal faster, leaving it less magic to use against Amirantha and Brandos.

'We're wearing it down,' observed Brandos.

'Good,' said Amirantha, 'because it's wearing us down, too.'

'Can you banish him?'

'Just a minute more, perhaps two.'

'Very well,' said Brandos, and he stepped forward again, reading the boundary of the wards and striking hard at the demon. It was an easily anticipated blow, and the creature raised its hand to sweep Brandos's blade aside. But the old fighter had expected such a move, demons were predictable when it came to non-magical combat. In their realm, the bigger, stronger demon almost always triumphed simply by physically over-powering their smaller, weaker opponent. Rarely did demons of similar stature confront one another. In the mortal realm their size and savage nature gave them a decided advantage against any but the most powerful creatures. A greater dragon would make short work of such a foe, but a simple swordsman would have to overcome brute strength with intelligence. Brandos turned his wrist as the demon tried to brush aside his blow, and let his blade slide along the creature's raised left arm, inflicting a series of cuts and causing the demon to retreat half a step. Then the demon lashed out with its uninjured right arm, almost dislocating Brandos's shoulder from the blow taken on his buckler.

Brandos retreated across the ward threshold again and braced himself for another onslaught. The demon hesitated for only a moment, then charged. As it crossed the ward barrier, it shrieked in agony, but continued towards Brandos and Amirantha. Three strides from where the old fighter stood ready, the demon paused to gather magic. Amirantha felt a spell of some consequence begin to manifest.

'Damn,' said Brandos. 'More magic.' He lowered his shoulder and charged.

The demon's spell casting was interrupted as Brandos drew his buckler up against his left shoulder and rammed it into the creature's chest. It felt like hitting a stone wall, but it threw the demon backwards a few feet and allowed Brandos just enough time to pull away before a massive clawed hand decapitated him.

Brandos lashed out with his sword, striking the demon's exposed arm. Again, the touch of enchanted steel caused a smoking wound and the demon cried out in rage. As he pulled back to stand before Amirantha, Brandos shouted, 'It's a first-time visitor to Midkemia; no protection spell in place to prevent harm from cold metal.'

With practised fluidity, Brandos let go of the hand-grip on his buckler, and allowed it to dangle on his arm; then he tossed his sword from his right hand to his left, catching it with his now free hand, as he drew a dagger from his right hip. He threw the blade with as much force as possible, impaling the demon's right foot and pinning it to the floor. Black smoke and a sulphurous stench filled the cave and the conjured creature screamed. Then it fell silent, regarding the two humans with its glowing red eyes, and calmly resumed its incantation.

'Now would be a good time to finish,' said Brandos, flipping his sword back into his right hand as he slipped his left back into the strap on his buckler. 'This fellow is bloody determined!'

Amirantha had less than a moment to make his choice; he could continue his spell of banishment and risk Brandos being struck with a potentially lethal blast of magic, or abandon it and employ a spell he had prepared against such dangers.

His affection for his friend overcame the desire to finish in an orderly fashion and he ceased his conjuration, shouting, 'Close your eyes!'

Brandos did not need to be told twice. He immediately crouched behind the small protection of his buckler as well as he could, and covered his eyes.

Amirantha closed his eyes as he incanted a five-syllable word, and unleashed a very powerful and destructive energy bolt. The warlock knew, from painful experience, that the energy carried within the crimson bolt, which flew out of his upraised hand to strike the demon, would pour into the creature through its skin, and set it alight from within.

They felt a sudden flash of searing heat, lasting mere seconds, but hot enough to scorch the hair on Brandos's arm. The stench of something foul cooking filled the tunnel and assaulted their nostrils. Then it was silent.

Brandos let his arms drop to his side as he let out a long sigh. 'I wish you didn't have to do that.'

'So do I,' returned Amirantha. 'An orderly banishment is so less taxing—'

'—And painful,' interrupted the fighter, as he inspected his singed arm.

'And less painful,' agreed Amirantha, 'than destroying the demon.'

Shaking his head and letting out another long sigh, Brandos said, 'Have you ever considered that conjuring demons so you can be paid to banish them might not be the best use of your talents?'

Smiling ruefully, Amirantha said, 'Occasionally, but how else can I earn the coin necessary to broaden my knowledge of the demon realm? I've learnt as much as I can from those creatures we're more familiar with.'

'Speaking of which, why didn't one of them show up?'

Amirantha shrugged. 'I don't know. I sought to conjure Kreegrom . . . He's almost my pet now.'

Brandos nodded. 'Ugly as sin. Have him chase you a bit where the Governor's men can see him. Let him follow you back inside, give him a treat and send him back. Good plan.' He fixed his friend with a scowling gaze. 'If it had worked!'

'I didn't think I was conjuring a battle demon.'

'A magic-using battle demon,' corrected Brandos, as he sheathed his sword.

'A magic-using battle demon,' echoed Amirantha. He looked into the tunnel, now filled with noxious, oily black smoke. Charred demon flesh decorated the walls and floor of the tunnel and the smell was enough to make a battle-tested veteran vomit. The creature's left leg lay on the floor only a few feet away from them. 'Let us collect our fee from the Governor, remove ourselves from this quaint province and return home.'

'Home?' asked Brandos. 'I thought we'd head north for a bit, first.'

'No,' said Amirantha. 'There's something about this that is both familiar and troubling, something I need ponder in my own study, with my own volumes for reference. And it's the safest place for us to be right now.'

'Since when did you concern yourself with safety?' asked the old fighter.

'Since I recognized a familiar . . . presence behind that demon.'

Brandos closed his eyes for a moment, as if weighing what he had just heard. 'I'm not going to like this next part, am I?'

'Probably not,' said Amirantha inspecting the contents of his belt bag to note what would have to be replaced. 'When the demon exploded, a series of magic . . . call them signatures, hall-marks of spellcraft, tumbled away. Most were my own, from the wards and spells I had fashioned, save two. One was the demon's, which I expected, alien and unfamiliar, but the last belonged to another player.' He was silent for a moment, then said, 'A player with a signature as familiar to me as my own.'

Brandos had been with Amirantha for most of his life and had heard many stories from the Warlock. He could easily anticipate what was coming next. Softly, Brandos asked, 'Belasco?'

Amirantha nodded. 'Belasco.'

'Bloody hell,' the old fighter swore quietly. His face was a map of sun-brown leather, showing years of privation and struggle. His hair, once golden blond, had been grey for more than two decades, but his startling blue eyes were still youthful. Shaking his head, he said, 'The one thing about travelling with you, Amirantha, is that things are always interesting.'

'You find the oddest things interesting,' said Amirantha.

'Comes from the company I keep,' said Brandos.

Amirantha could only nod. They had been together for a long time. He had found Brandos as a street urchin in the city of Khaipur, nearly forty-two years ago. Now, despite being years older than his companion, the warlock looked twenty years his junior. Both men knew that the magic user would outlive the fighter by a generation, yet they never spoke of it, except upon occasion when Brandos quipped that Amirantha's proclivities would end up getting him killed before his time. Despite appear-ances, Brandos looked upon Amirantha as a father.

How a practitioner of a particularly dark form of magic had come to play the role of foster father to an illiterate street boy was still a bit of a mystery to Amirantha, but somehow Brandos had insinuated his way into the magic user's affections and they had been together ever since.

Amirantha led Brandos past the charred remains of the demon to the summoning cave and picked up two large leather bags, handing one to the fighter. Both men shouldered their burdens. Looking around at the overturned ward stones, the burning pots of incense, and the other accoutrements of demon summoning, the Warlock said, 'I'm not criticizing, but what brought you into the cave?'

'You were taking a bit longer than normal and the Governor was getting restless. Then that noise erupted so I thought I'd best go and see what had gone awry.'

Shaking his head slightly, the Warlock said, 'Good thing you did.'

They exited the cave, a deep recess in the hillside a few miles away from the village of Kencheta. Waiting astride his ornately saddled horse was the Governor of Lanada, who said, 'Is the demon dead?'

Raising his hand in an indifferent salute to the ruler of the region, Amirantha said, 'Most efficiently dead, Your Excellency. You will find his remains scattered around the tunnel about a hundred yards within.'

The Governor nodded once and signalled to one of his junior officers, 'See that it is so.'

Amirantha and Brandos exchanged glances. Local rulers were usually content with their word. On the other hand, they usually caught a glimpse or two of the monster, and not just heard howls and bellowing from within a dark cave.

A short time later, the young officer returned, his face pale and sweating. Amirantha said, 'I should have mentioned the peculiar stench—'

'You should have,' agreed Brandos.

' —takes some getting used to.'

'Well?' asked the Governor.

Nodding, the officer said, 'It is so, Your Excellency. Most of the creature was strewn around the tunnel, bits here and there, but one leg was intact, and it was . . . nothing of this world.'

'Bring it to me,' instructed the Governor.

Again, Brandos and Amirantha exchanged questioning looks.

This time the officer motioned to two of his older soldiers and said, 'You heard the Governor. Go and get the leg.'

Eventually the two soldiers emerged from the cave carrying the huge charred limb between them. The reek caused even the strongest stomach to weaken and the Governor backed his mount off slightly, holding up his hand. 'Stay,' he instructed.

From his distant vantage point he could see the top of a thigh covered in burned hair, down to the foot with its three massive toes ending in razor-sharp claws. Whatever it might be, it was not of this world, and at last satisfied, the Governor nodded. 'We had word from the Maharajah's Court of charlatans preying on the gullible, promising to rid outlying villages of non-existent demons, dark spirits, and other malefactions. Had you been such, we would have hanged you from that tree,' he said, pointing to a stout elm a few yards away. 'As this is without doubt a demonic limb, I am now convinced that your timely arrival so soon after word reached us of this demon, is but a lucky coincidence, and shall convey my opinion to my lords and masters in the city of Maharta.'

Amirantha bowed his most courtly bow, and Brandos followed suit. 'We thank His Excellency,' said the Warlock.

As the Governor began to turn his mount,' Amirantha said, 'Excellency, as to the matter of payment?'

Over his shoulder, the Governor said, 'Come to my palace and see my seneschal. He will pay you.' With that, he rode off, followed closely by his men-at-arms.

'Well, at least it's on the way home,' the Warlock said.

Shrugging, the warrior picked up his companion's shoulder bag. 'There are times one must settle for small benefits, my friend. At least this time we get paid.

'Maybe it was a good thing that new demon showed up. Kreegrom is fairly hideous, but for a demon he's about as menacing as a puppy. If that Governor had caught on that he was only playing "chase me" and not really trying to kill you . . . well, I don't particularly relish ending my days hanging from an elm.' He glanced at the tree as they walked past it. 'Though, I must confess it's a handsome enough tree.'

'You do always see the good in a situation, don't you?'

'Someone must,' said Brandos, 'given the usual nature of our trade.'

'There is that,' agreed Amirantha as they started down the road that would take them to the Governor's Palace in Lanada, and then on to their distant home.

The village had been the only home Amirantha had known in the last thirty years. For about five months each year, he resided in a stone tower on top of a tor a mile north of the village. The rest of the time he and Brandos would travel.

His tower was on top of an ancient hill, Gashen Tor, highest of the hills overlooking the village of Talumba, two days' ride east of the city of Maharta. The small farming community had come to appreciate the presence of such a powerful magic user, even if his area of mastery was considered to border on evil by most people. They believed that the warlock had wandered to Talumba from another land, and had come to his lonely hill to avoid persecution. It had been said that he built the single tower in which he resided using demons for the labour, and that he had placed wards about the tor to prevent intruders from troubling him.

The truth was far more prosaic; Amirantha had used magic, though not his own, to build the simple tower. A pair of magicians, masters of geomancy, had used their arts to manoeuvre rocks in such a design that when they were done, Amirantha had only to employ a local carpenter to install the two wooden floors, hang doors, and build some furniture; including the large table now before the magician and the heavy chair in which he sat.

He examined an old text he had written nearly a century before, letting out a long sigh of regret as he pushed it aside. Looking out of the window of his study, at the village below, now caught in the reddish glow of sunset, he considered how almost idyllic his life had become during the last twenty years – if he didn't give too much thought to the occasional mishap like the one three days ago, near Lanada.

He remembered when he had first come here, with a young Brandos and his wife, and how he had decided, almost on a whim, to take up residence. He looked above the village at the distant sunset and wondered how much of his decision came from his affection for these views. A sunset was, he thought, an odd thing to be drawn to, but then so much of his life had been a series of choices that seemed arbitrary, even capricious, at times; such as giving a home to an uncouth street boy who had tried to rob him more than thirty years ago.

This village was the only home he had known since his child-hood, a time so distant he often had to concentrate to remember much about it. The villagers had at first been frightened of the Warlock on the Hill, as they called him, but he had since then protected the village from marauders on more than one occasion, and had even kept the army of the ambitious Maharajah of Muboya from occupying the settlement when the region was annexed into that burgeoning nation. He took pride in having used only ruse and guile with no loss of life. While absent of the everyday concerns of most people, Amirantha did scruple over crossing certain boundaries.

Some of his dilemmas were practical in nature, dabbling in the darker arts brought scrutiny that could lead to persecution. However, most of his moral concerns were for his own well-being; often he had seen that travelling down a certain dark road to knowledge cost a magician far more than the disapproval of others. Although not a pious man, Amirantha still wished to face Lims-Kragma, certain that he had no major stains on his escutcheon; he could accept having to explain a minor blemish here and there. Some, because of his chosen art, might not consider him a good man, but he had his principles. Besides, he had seen better men fall prey to the lure of the dark arts. It was a drug to most magicians.

He moved slightly in his seat and determined, as he had almost every day for the last two years, that he needed to take a trip to the city and purchase new cushions. He glanced around his study. The fire burned as it always did during the cold weather, casting a warm glow across the room. The sleeping quarters below were often draughty in the winter, and the Warlock often slept up here next to the fire. He was convinced the problem had something to do with the way the chimney was fashioned, but never could find the time to have anyone look at it, so for three months each year he endured blankets on the floor.

Brandos trudged heavily up the circular stone staircase, which hugged the interior of the round building, and entered the room. 'What did you find?' he asked without preamble.

'What I feared,' said the Warlock, standing up. With a wave of his hand he indicated the old tomes on the table. 'I think we need to undertake a journey.'

'Going shopping in Maharta, are we?'

Amirantha regarded his oldest friend. At nearly fifty years old, the warrior was still a powerful looking man, even if his grey hair was now bordering on white. His sun-worn, leathery face spoke of years of campaigning, and he bore an impressive number of scars. 'Well, yes, for I do need a new seat cushion, but that will have to wait.' He gazed at his old tomes and said, 'I think something very bad is happening, and we need to speak to someone about it.'

'Anyone specific in mind?'

'Tell me about this Kaspar.'

Brandos smiled and nodded. He sat down on a small stool near the fire and said, 'Here's what I know: About a month or so after General Alenburga disappeared, which was ten years ago now, this Kaspar of Olasko arrived at the Maharajah's Court along with a small army of soldiers from the Tsurani world. The young ruler of Muboya gave Kaspar the title of General of the Army, announced that Alenburga had retired to some distant place, and turned his attention to consolidating his territory and preparing to conquer more.

'But, this is where it gets interesting. Kaspar seems to have earned the Maharajah's trust, and has come up with diplomatic solutions for two conflicts, set up a very difficult relationship with some of the clans ruling the City of the Serpent River, and has annexed two city states to the north without bloodshed. After a long war, he's also achieved an alliance with Okanala through a couple of well-crafted royal marriages, effectively ensuring that his and the King of Okanala's grandchildren will eventually rule a combined empire. He helped Okanala put down two rebellions, and now Okanala and Muboya will combine to move against those murderous little dwarves who live in the grasslands to the west.'

'A prodigious list of accomplishments for so short a period of employment.' Amirantha tapped his chin with his right index finger, a nervous gesture that Brandos had seen since childhood. 'Now, what else?'

'Speculation and rumour. Kaspar is an outlander, from far across the sea to the northwest, a nation called Olasko, so I have been told. He was a ruler there, before being deposed, and has been absent for some years. Somehow he became close to General Alenburga, but little is known of that. It is also rumoured that he often vanishes from Muboya's new capital city of Maharta for a week or so, simply to show up again as if he had always been there.'

'Magic,' said Amirantha. 'He goes somewhere, but no one sees him leave or return.'

'Or he enjoys very long naps in the privacy of his quarters,' quipped the old fighter. 'Perhaps with friends; he's reputed to have quite an eye for the ladies.'

Tapping his chin as he weighed his options, Amirantha was silent for a long time. Brandos knew his foster father preferred silence when he was reflecting, so the old fighter got up and left the study, trudging down the stairs.

The tower was a simple cylindrical keep with three levels, the middle held two large rooms, one for the Warlock and one for Brandos and his wife, Samantha. Brandos crossed the tiny hallway separating the two sleeping rooms and moved down the stairs to the bottom floor, where the kitchen, storage room, and guarderobe were housed. The kitchen smelled of freshly baked bread and something bubbling in a cauldron above the fire, Samantha's well-regarded chicken stew if Brandos guessed correctly.

Brandos paused for a moment to observe his wife. A stout woman, she could still spark a fire in her husband with just a whisper in his ear, though the years had taken their toll on the former tavern girl from the Eastlands. She wore a simple green dress with a blue cloth head covering, arranged in her native style. Brandos had met her in the huge tavern at Shingazi's Landing, on the Serpent River where it bends near the Eastern Coast, less than a mile west of the Great Cliffs, overlooking the Blue Sea. With the aid of a lot of flirtation, and a lot of good wine, she had eventually agreed to come to his bed.

But rather than forget her, as he had so many before her, his mind kept returning to the pleasant-looking, plump young woman from the Eastlands. After months of incessant mooning over her, Amirantha had given his foster son leave to visit her.

He had returned a month later with his new wife. Despite Amirantha's original reservations, he had come to understand that Brandos had found something very rare with his tavern wench from the Eastlands. Brandos knew the Warlock envied them, even though he had never spoken a word.

Brandos knew his foster father better than any man alive, and knew that only once in his life had the old magic user succumbed to a woman's guiles. Remembering the encounter still made him smile; if it weren't for Amirantha's genuine pain over how that liaison had ended, it would have been worthy of a bard's most ribald tale.

Samantha looked up at her husband and smiled. 'Ready to eat?'

'Yes,' he said returning the smile.

As he sat at the table, her smile turned to a frown. 'Very well, when are you two leaving?'

Brandos shook his head and smiled ruefully. She could read him like a proclamation posted on a wall in the city square. 'Soon, I think. Amirantha is very troubled by what happened up in Lanada.'

She only nodded. One of her talents was ignoring how her husband and his foster father made their living, by summoning demons in distant lands, then banishing them for a fee. They did occasionally do real work, dangerous work, for those willing to pay, but those were rare callings, the rest of the time the pair behaved little better than a pair of confidence tricksters.

Still, there were some matters that she and Brandos were willing to argue about, and some things best left unspoken; it was why their marriage had lasted for twenty-three years.

'Is there any point to me asking why?' she said coolly. 'It's not like it was when the children lived here.' She stopped and looked at her husband accusingly. 'Bethan is at sea, sailing who knows where. Meg lives with her husband up in Khaipur.'

'Donal is down in the village with the grandchildren. You can walk down to visit them any time you wish,' he quickly countered. He knew where this was heading.

'And his wife just loves having me around,' she said.

'What is it about two women under the same roof?' asked Brandos rhetorically.

'She'll come around when the new baby is born and she needs another pair of hands, but until then, she sees me as an intruder.' He was about to speak, but she cut him off, her vivid blue eyes fixed on him as she absently pushed back a strand of grey hair trying to escape from under her head covering. 'It's lonely here, Brandos, with you gone for weeks, even months at a time . . .' She let out a theatrical sigh. 'When you returned early, I can't tell you how happy that made me.

'When are you going to stop all this travelling? I know how wealthy we are. You don't need to do this any more.'

'That would be true if Amirantha wasn't always worried about what he might have to spend on one of his . . . devices, or an old libram of spells, or whatever else takes his fancy,' countered her husband. 'Besides, it is his wealth, isn't it?'

'Yours, too,' she shot back. 'It's not as if you sat around doing nothing.'

He knew there was no avoiding the subject. 'Look, most times I would argue with him on your behalf, I would agree with what you're saying: We just got home, we've been gone over a month; but this time, well, we have to go.'

Samantha put her hands on her hips and said, 'Why?' Her tone was defiant and bordering on anger, and Brandos knew he must tell her.

'It's Amirantha's brother.'

She looked stunned. She blinked and then asked, 'Belasco?'

He nodded once.

She said, 'I'll prepare a travel bag. Enough food to take you to the city. You can buy the rest as you go.'

Her sudden change in mood and manner were entirely under-standable. Over the many years they had been together, she had listened to the same stories as Brandos while Amirantha chatted over supper. She knew that Belasco was a magician of mighty arts, easily Amirantha's equal, and that he had been trying to kill Amirantha since before Brandos or Samantha had been alive.

• CHAPTER TWO •

Knight-Adamant

*S*ANDREENA SAT MOTIONLESS.

She focused her mind on the seemingly impossible task of thinking of nothing. For seven years she had practised this ritual whenever conditions permitted, yet she never reached the total vacancy of thought that was the goal of the Sha'tar Ritual.

Despite her eyes being closed, she could describe the room around her in precise detail. And that was her problem. Her mind wanted to be active, not floating blankly. She resisted the urge to sigh.

On her best days in the Temple, she found something close to nothingness, or at least when the ritual ended she had no memory of thinking about anything and felt very relaxed. But she was still not entirely convinced that having no memory and possessing no thought were the same. Her concern always caused

Father-Bishop Creegan some amusement, and the fact she was moved by the thought was another reminder that today she was far from attaining a floating consciousness.

She was still aware of every single object in the room around her. Without opening her eyes, she could recount every detail; her ability to recall it all without flaw was a natural skill honed and refined since joining the Shield of the Weak. Her vows required her to protect those unable to protect themselves. Often, there was little time to ascertain the justice of a claim, or the right and wrong of a dispute, so she relied upon making quick judgment in deciding where and how to intervene. Attention to detail often gave her an advantage in not making things worse, even if she couldn't make them better.

The smell of the wooden walls and floor, rich with age, and the faint pungency of oils used daily to replenish them, tantalized her, recalling memories of other visits to this and other temples. She could hear the faint hissing of water on hot rocks as the acolytes moved almost silently through the room, bringing in hot rocks from a furnace outside. They managed to carry a large iron basket full of glowing basalt and place it quietly on the floor, then they ladled water over its surface, a sprinkling that caused a silent steam to rise. She remembered her days as an acolyte spent concentrating on moving through a room much like this one without disturbing the monks, priests, and occasionally a knight like herself. It had been her first step on the path towards serving the Goddess. As many as a dozen men and women would sit silently, their clothing folded neatly on benches along the rear wall, and it had been her job to ensure the tranquillity of the room. At the time she had wondered whether a more difficult task existed; now she knew that the acolytes had the simpler role, and those seeking a floating consciousness the more rigorous challenge.

She felt perspiration drip down her naked back, almost but not quite enough of an itch to make her wish to scratch. She willed her mind away from the sensations of her flesh. Sitting with crossed legs, eyes closed, and her hands resting palms up on her knees, nothing was supposed to distract her; yet that drip of perspiration felt almost as if she were being touched. Her annoyance at being distracted by it began a cycle she knew well. Soon she would be as far removed from a floating conscious-ness as she would be during combat or enjoying a lover. She found a spark of irony in that thought, since in both those cases, she was probably closer. Other parts of her mind seemed to predominate when fighting or loving, and the ever-questioning, ever-critical part that made her difficult for most people to be with, detached.

Like all members of her order, Sandreena was always welcome at any temple of Dala, the Patron Goddess of the Order of the Shield of the Weak. Being a member of an errant order, she wandered where the Goddess directed her, often providing the only authority or protection for small villages, tiny caravans, or isolated abbeys. She adjudicated disputes and dispensed equity by reason, but she was well equipped to do so by force of arms if necessary.

The drop of perspiration had now reached the top of her tail-bone, and as it pooled there for a moment, she focused her mind and dived into it, seeking to float within it. She took slow, deep breaths, enjoying the sybaritic pleasure she took from the hot steam, the silence, and the total absence of threat. She found her quiet place within that drop of moisture on her spine. A light breeze made the brass wind chimes outside ring softly, heightening the calming experience. Then Sandreena caught a hint of something unwelcome, a musky male odour so slight it was almost unnoticeable.

She knew the ritual was over. This was not the first time her presence in the sanctuary had brought unwelcome results. There were only two other women partaking in the ritual, neither young nor attractive by any common measure. Such considerations should have been of little consequence in the service of the Goddess, but human beings were imperfect by nature and those considerations often became relevant. Sandreena shifted her weight, tensing and relaxing each muscle in turn as she ended her meditation. Now she was very aware of her nakedness, the perspiration running down her back and between her breasts, and her matted hair. One young acolyte waited near the door to the bathing room, holding out a coarsely woven towel for her use.

She stood in one fluid motion, like the dancer she had been in another life. She knew that one of the young brothers watched her depart, examining her every movement as she quietly left the room. She also knew what he saw, a young woman of exceptional beauty, with sun-coloured, shoulder-length hair, and a pair of heroic battle scars, but no other obvious flaw. She knew that she possessed many flaws, but carried them within; her own beauty was a curse.

With long legs, strong buttocks, trim hips and waist, and some breadth in the shoulders, she was at the height of her physical power. But nothing could change her face, her straight, perfect nose, the set of her slightly slanted pale blue eyes, and her full mouth and delicate chin. She was even more stunning when she smiled, though that happened rarely. Even in her armour, men still turned to watch her pass.

She resisted the temptation to turn and see which of the young brothers had been aroused by her presence; that was his burden to bear and if he was wise in the teachings of the Goddess, he would know it was his weakness to overcome, a lesson put before him to instruct and make him stronger.

She hated the idea of being someone else's lesson.

Sandreena took the towel and entered the bathing room, sitting on a bench before a bucket of cold water. She picked up the bucket and tipped its contents over her head, embracing the sudden shock of cold and the clarity of thought it brought. As she dried herself off she revelled in the quiet privacy of the bathing room. She had experienced very little solitude during her lifetime. Above anything else, her calling had brought her time alone on the road, when all she could hear was the wind in the branches, birdcalls, and animal sounds; she prized those moments.

After her travels, she had come here, to the Temple in Krondor. It was the only real home she had known. Sandreena had been raised in the streets by a mother addicted to every known drug, but she favoured Dream, the white powder that when smoked induced intoxicating images and experiences, more vivid than life itself. Her mother had protected her, as much as her weaknesses permitted, until she had become a woman. The body that Sandreena considered a curse, that stole the breath of foolish men, developed early in her eleventh year. By her thirteenth Banapis celebration she had become a beauty. Her mother had taught her some tricks, staying dirty, cutting her hair short, binding her breasts to look boyish, that had kept her safe until the age of fourteen, until one of the bashers had seen through the disguise.

The Mockers of Krondor were a criminal organization under the control of the Upright Man, but not so tightly controlled for the wellbeing of one street girl to be of any consequence. The basher took her while her mother was in the throes of delirium induced by a gifted vial of Bliss. After that he had come for her on a regular basis. He always brought Bliss, or Dream, or one of the other narcotics sold by the Brotherhood of Thieves.

Sandreena finished drying herself and went in to the dressing room. The monks detailed to care for visiting Sisters and Brothers of the Shield were tending her travel-worn armour. She quickly donned her preferred raiment: baggy trousers, a loose-fitting tunic, both made of unbleached linen cloth, heavy boots, and her sword belt. As she dressed, she remembered that her first man actually hadn't been such a bad fellow. He had eventually professed his love for her, and she recalled him being almost gentle when taking her, in a clumsy, fumbling way. It was the men who she experienced after him who had taught her what it was to be truly cruel.

She was fifteen years old when her mother died. Too many narcotics, or one bad drug, or perhaps it was a man who took out his anger on her; no one knew the cause, save that she was found floating in the bay near Fisher's Dock at the south end of the harbour. It was strange that she was found that far from her usual haunts, but not strange enough for the Upright Man or any of his lieutenants to look into the matter; what concern had they over the death of another addicted whore? Besides, she had given the Mockers a daughter who was worth far more than the mother had been.

Sandreena had then been removed from a particular bruiser's crib, and installed in one of the city's finer brothels, where she began to earn gold. For a while, she had known how it felt to wear silks and gems, have her hair cleaned every day, and to be given good food regularly. She had become an expert in the use of unguents, oils, scents, and all manner of makeup. She could appear as innocent as a child or as wicked as a Keshian courtesan, depending on the client's need. She was schooled in deportment and how to speak the languages of Kesh and Queg, but more importantly, she learnt how to speak like a well-born lady.

Because her captors had taught her languages, to read and write, and even simply how to learn, she had forgiven them enough to resist hunting them down and delivering a harsh punishment. The Goddess taught forgiveness. But Sandreena vowed never to forget.

What she could forgive them for was awakening an appetite for things better avoided: too much wine, many of the drugs her mother had craved, fine clothing and jewellery, and most of all, the company of men. Sandreena had left that profession with a profound ambivalence: she only craved the touch of men whom she also despised, and hated herself for that perverse desire. Only the discipline of the Order kept that conflict from destroying her otherwise strong mind.

Sandreena left the dressing room to find a young acolyte waiting for her. 'Father-Bishop would like a world with you, Sister.'

'At once,' she responded. 'I know the way.'

Dismissed, the boy hurried along on another errand, and Sandreena let out a barely audible sigh. The Father-Bishop had managed to grant her only two full days of rest before finding her something to do. As she started towards his office, she amended that thought: finding her something dangerous that only a lunatic would agree to.

She reached a corner of the temple and looked out of a vaulted window. To her left she could see the Prince's palace by the royal docks, dominating the city. To the right, close at hand, lay Temple Square, where the Order of Sung and the Temple of Kahooli were housed. Other major temples were also nearby, but those two were especially close. She wondered, not for the first time, how her life would be had Brother Mathias been of a different order.

He had been the first holy man she had encountered, and the first of the two men in her life for whom her feelings were not dark; she had loved Brother Mathias as a daughter loved a father. After three years in the elegant brothel, one of them lost to the very drugs that had claimed her mother, the Mockers had sold her to a very wealthy Keshian trader; he had become so enamoured with Sandreena that he had insisted on buying her and taking her back to his home in the Keshian city of Shamata. Because he was as proficient in illegal trading as he was in honest business, the Mockers considered him a valuable associate and while not in the habit of selling their girls – slavery was not permitted in the Kingdom – they gladly vended her services for an unspecified duration in exchange for a prodigious sum of gold.

It had been Brother Mathias who had saved her life and changed it. She could not recall their first encounter without becoming distressed, and now was not the time to show such feelings, not before seeing the Father-Bishop. She turned her mind from the memory back to the matter at hand.

She reached the modest office wherein worked the single most powerful man of the Order of the Shield of the Weak. Only the Grand Master in Rillanon ranked higher. But although he retained his ceremonial responsibilities, age had robbed the Grand Master of the ability to perform his real duties and the seven Father-Bishops directed most of the Order's business. There was a persistent rumour that Father-Bishop Creegan was the prelate most likely to succeed when the Grand Master's health finally failed him.

To the surprise of almost everyone who visited the Father-Bishop, his office had no anteroom, no clerk or monk waited to attend him outside, and the door was always open. Those who resided in the Temple of Krondor knew the reason: the Father-Bishop's door was open to anyone who needed him, but for the sake of the Goddess's mercy, their reasons for disturbing his work had better be good.

She stood outside the door, waiting to be bid to enter. She remembered the first time she had come here, fresh from her training at the temple in Kesh. She had returned to Krondor with a mixture of anticipation and fear, for she had not been back to the city during the five years since her sale to the Keshian. But just one minute in the Father-Bishop's presence had made all of her concerns about returning to the Kingdom's Western capital vanish.

He noticed her standing and waved her in. 'I have something that needs investigating, Sandreena.' He didn't give her leave to sit in one of the four chairs placed around the room, so she moved closer but continued to stand.

His desk was simple, a plain table with a stack of woven trays in which to file documents for his staff to dispose of. He kept them very busy.

He should be considered a handsome man, Sandreena considered not for the first time, but there was something about his manner that was off-putting, a quality that could be considered arrogance, if he wasn't always proved right. Still, he had been instrumental in helping the former Krondorian whore find a meaningful life, and for that she would always be grateful. And, she had to concede that he always found for her the most interesting tasks. 'I am ready, Father-Bishop.'

He glanced up, then smiled, and she felt a strong surge of pleasure at the hint of approval. 'Yes, you always are,' he said.

He sat back, waving her over to a chair. She knew that meant a long discussion, or at least a very complex set of instructions. 'You look well,' he observed. 'How have you been since last we spoke?'

She knew he was already aware of what she had been doing in the year and a month since she had last been in his office. She had been sent to investigate a report of some interference with lawful Temple practices in the Free City of Natal – which proved false – and she had then travelled on to the far Duchy of Crydee, where an isolated village was suspected of harbouring a fugitive magician, by the name of Sidi, which had also proved false. But she gave the Father-Bishop a full report anyway; of her encounter with a mad sorcerer who had dabbled too far into what were called the Dark Arts, and how she had saved the villagers from his depredations. His small band of dark spirits had completely sacked the settlement, leaving the survivors without any means to endure the coming winter. She had interceded with the younger son of the Duke of Crydee, who had agreed to send aid to the village – his father and elder brother were away from the castle at Crydee, but the boy had easily turned the castle's reeve from ignoring the villagers' pleas to sending immediate help.

In all, it had been an important but prosaic burden, once the mad magician had been disposed of. The Duke's second son, a boy of no more than fifteen summers old, namesake of his father, Henry, had impressed Sandreena. He was called Hal by most, and had showed both maturity and decisiveness when acting as interlocutor between his father's surrogate and the itinerant Knight-Adamant of the Temple of Dala. The outlying villages often seemed more a burden than a benefit to the local nobles, producing little in the way of income from the land, but requiring a disproportionate amount of protection from marauding renegades, raiding goblins, dark elves, or whatever other menace inhabited the region.

Sandreena had spent the better part of the past year in Crydee, and had only left when she had seen the village back on a firm footing. On the way back to Krondor she had intervened in half a dozen minor conflicts, always taking the side of the outnumbered, besieged, or beleaguered as her calling dictated, attempting to restore balance and work out a peaceful solution, always mediating where she could. She was often struck by the irony of how violence was usually needed in order to prevent a more violent outcome.

'What are your orders, Father-Bishop?'

His brow furrowed slightly. 'No time for pleasantries? Very well then, to your task. What do you know about the Peaks of the Quor?'

Sandreena paused for a moment before answering. The Father-Bishop had little time and less patience for overblown attempts to impress him, so she finally said, 'Little that is germane to what you're about to tell me, I suspect.'

He smiled. 'What do you know?'

'It's a region of Kesh, south of Roldem, isolated and sparsely populated. Rumour suggests that smugglers put in there from time to time, seeking to circumvent Roldem and Kesh's revenue ships, but more than that I do not know.'

'A race of beings live there, called the Quor. Hence the region's name. They are in turn protected, if that is indeed the correct term, by a band of elves.' Sandreena raised an eyebrow in surprise. To the best of her knowledge, elves only resided in the lands north of Crydee.

'We have a little information beyond that, but not much. This is why I have decided to send someone down there.'

'Me, Father-Bishop?'

'Yes,' he replied. 'There is a village on the eastern side of the peninsula, named Akrakon, the inhabitants are descendants of one of the more annoying tribes of the region, but were long ago subjugated by Kesh. They mind their manners, more or less, but lately they've been troubled by marauding pirates.' The Father-Bishop's tone changed. 'We've had sporadic word of these pirates for over ten years. We have no idea who they are or why they bother to trouble the coastal villages. . .' He shrugged. 'All we know is that they seem to have a liking for black headgear, hats, scarves, and the like. Where they come from, what they want, who they serve . . . ?' Again he shrugged. 'Be cautious, Sandreena; occasionally they number a magic user or two in their crew. Our first report involved a demon, as well.'

She nodded. Now she understood why she had been chosen. She had faced down more than one demon in her short tenure with the Order.

'As Kesh's Imperial Court is occupied by far weightier concerns, it has fallen to us to investigate this injustice.'

'And if I should also happen to discover more about these people in the mountains, the Quor, all the better.'

'All the better,' he agreed. 'But be careful, for there is another complication.'

Dryly, she said, 'There always is.'

'Very powerful people are also interested in the Quor and the elves who serve or protect them; people who have influence and reach, even into very high office.' He sat back and said, 'The Magicians.'

She didn't need to ask whom he meant. The Magicians of Stardock were looked upon with deep suspicion by the Temples of the Kingdom and Kesh. Magic was the province of the gods, granted only to their faithful servants to do the work the gods intended. Magicians were seen as expropriators of power intended for only a chosen few, and as such were considered suspect at best, untrustworthy at worst. Many magic users became seduced by the darker arts, several having been marked for death by the Temple's leaders due to past wrongs.

Sandreena had encountered several magic users over the years, most with unhappy outcomes, and those that weren't had still been difficult. It was a sad truth that even the most depraved had believed they had some justification for their behaviour. She recalled one particularly ugly incident with a group of necro-mancers, a trio of maniacs who had been so overcome by madness that the holy knight had no alternative but to see them dead. She still carried a puckered scar on her left thigh as a reminder that some people were incapable of reason. One of the magicians had thrown a dark magic bolt at her before he died, and while the initial injury had been minor, the wound would not close, festering and growing more putrid by the day. It had taken a prodigious amount of work by the Temple healers to keep Sandreena from losing her leg, or worse, and she had been confined to her bed for nearly a month because of it.

'I'll be alert to any sign that the Magicians have a hand in this, Father-Bishop.'

'Before you go, have you paid a courtesy visit to the High Priestess yet?'

Sandreena smiled. No matter how devout the members of the Order might be, there was always politics. 'Had you not summoned me from my meditation and cleansing, I would have made that call first, Father-Bishop.'

Creegan smiled ruefully. 'Ah, just when things are going smoothly, I cause a fuss.'

'That fuss was caused long before today, Father-Bishop.'

He shrugged slightly. 'The High Priestess is . . . steadfast in her devotion, and not well pleased that one of their brightest students choose the Adamant Way. We both agree that you would have risen high in the Order as a priestess, but, it is not for us to question the path upon which the Goddess has placed you.'

Sandreena's smile broadened. 'Not to question it, perhaps, but apparently it still permits some to demand a degree of clarification.'

Father-Bishop Creegan laughed, which he rarely did: 'I miss your wit, girl.'

She resisted the urge to reflexively sigh at the word. He only called her girl during their private conversations, and it reminded her of a time when their mentor and protégé roles had come very close to becoming something far more personal. The Orders of Dala were not celibate; although the demands of the calling made marriage and family a rare occurrence, liaisons did occasionally take place. However, for a man of the Father-Bishop's rank and stature to become intimate with an acolyte, or even a Squire-Adamant, would have been inappropriate, and Sandreena's natural aversion towards men had made it difficult for her to trust his more personal interest in her. So they had never managed to confront the tension between them. Still, both were painfully aware of the attraction. Forcing down disturbing feelings, Sandreena said, 'If there's nothing else, Father-Bishop?'

'No, daughter,' he said formally, apparently recognizing his previous choice of words. 'May the Goddess look over you and guide you.'

'May she guide you as well, Father-Bishop,' said Sandreena. She quickly departed and made her way down the long corridor that dominated the south side of the huge Temple. Directly to the north lay the huge central Temple yard, holding the worshippers' court and several shrines around its edge. Unlike other faiths, there were few occasions for the public worship of Dala, but there were many times when suppliants came to offer votive prayers and thanks for the Goddess's intercession. There was a constant coming and going through the main gates of the Temple, at all hours of the day and night.

As a result, most business within the Temple took place in the offices along this southern corridor. The residences and guest quarters, servants' quarters, and all the requisite function rooms, kitchen, pantry, laundry, as well as the baths and meditation gardens, lay on either side of the great courtyard. The sleeping quarters of the clergy and those, like herself, of the martial orders, were situated in a basement hall, below the one she now walked through.

At the opposite end of the hallway stood the office of the High Priestess. The fact that the offices of the two Temple leaders lay as far from one another as was physically possible was not lost on many. Unlike the Father-Bishop's office, the High Priestess's had an antechamber, in which sat her personal secretary, one of the Temple priestesses. She looked up as Sandreena entered the room. If she recognized Sandreena from previous visits, she didn't reveal so.

'Sister,' she said softly in even tones. 'How may I assist you?'

Fighting off a sudden urge to turn and walk out, she said, 'I am Sandreena, Knight-Adamant of the Order of the Shield. I am paying a courtesy call upon the High Priestess.'

The slender, middle-aged woman stood up regally. She wore the plain robes of her order, a brown homespun bleached to a light tan. Around her neck she displayed the Order's sign, a simple shield hung from a chain, but it was not lost on Sandreena that they were made from gold and were of fine craftsmanship. A gift from the High Priestess no doubt. 'I will see if the High Priestess has a moment for you.'

Sandreena quietly prayed that a moment was indeed all she had to spare, for she knew that an invitation to sit and 'chat' meant a long and tedious inquisition. A moment later Sandreena's worst fears were justified when she was ushered into the main chamber and found two chairs flanking a table with a fresh pot of tea.

High Priestess Seldon was a robust-looking, stout woman in her fifties. She had rosy cheeks and hair so light a grey it bordered on white, which made her dark sable eyes all the more dramatic and penetrating when she fixed her gaze upon Sandreena, as she had on more than one occasion. 'Ah, Sister,' she said beckoning Sandreena to take the empty chair. The High Priestess was also an ample woman, who seemed to grow in girth each time Sandreena met with her. 'What brings you to Krondor, child?' she asked.

Sandreena almost winced. If 'girl' meant the Father-Bishop had put aside his authority, 'child' meant the High Priestess was asserting hers. Despite the fact that Sandreena had served for four years as a Squire-Adamant in the Temple, had been trained in every weapon blessed for use by the Order, and for the last three had been wandering the Kingdom and Northern Kesh as a weapon of the Goddess, the High Priestess was ensuring that she remembered who held the authority in Krondor, and reminded her that she was a traitorous girl for giving up the path of the Priestess and preferring to take up arms to bludgeon the unworthy.

As Sandreena was about to answer her, the High Priestess said, 'Tea?' and without waiting for her guest to answer began to pour the hot liquid into fine porcelain cups.

Sandreena examined the cup handed her by the High Priestess and said, 'Tsurani?'

Her hostess shook her head and said, 'From LaMut. But it is of Tsurani design. Real Tsurani porcelain is far too costly for us to use here. The Goddess provides, but not to excess, child.'

Even that tiny explanation felt like a reproach to Sandreena. 'So, again, why are you in Krondor?'

Sandreena knew she did not have to explain. She could claim it was mere happenstance that had brought her to the capital of the Western Realm of the Kingdom of the Isles. But she was certain that the Mother Superior already knew of her summoning to the Father-Bishop's office. She would not trust coincidence when a conspiracy was possible.

'I was in Port Vykor, High Priestess.'

'Visiting Brother Mathias?'

Sandreena nodded. He had brought her to the Mother Temple in Kesh where she had been tutored and expected to become a priestess. He had come into her life again in Krondor when she had changed her calling from that of a novitiate in the priesthood to a Squire-Adamant of the Order of the Shield of the Weak. Mathias had stepped in to take her as his squire when the debate between the High Priestess Seldon and Father-Bishop Creegan had grown contentious. Sandreena now knew that she was a useful tool for Creegan and whatever personal affection or desire he might possess for her, was easily put aside. Seldon saw her as a stolen possession, another setback in her endless struggle with the Order and those associated with it, especially the Father-Bishop. It was rare for anyone to rise from the martial orders to a position of authority within the Temple proper, but Creegan was a rare man.

'He is . . . content,' said Sandreena slowly. 'The illness that takes his memory has not lessened his pleasures in most things. He's content to fish when allowed, or to walk in the gardens. He sometimes remembers me, sometimes not.'

'He is well otherwise, then?' asked High Priestess Seldon and for a brief moment, Sandreena saw a hint of genuine concern and affection. Brother Mathias had refused rank and position over the years, but had gained great respect in the Temple.

'The healers at the retreat say he is healthy and will abide for years. It's just difficult . . . to not be remembered by him.'

45

'He was like a father to you,' said the High Priestess in a flat, almost dismissive tone, and whatever spark of humanity Sandreena had glimpsed was gone. Sandreena was Creegan's creature, and the High Priestess would never forget that, or forgive her betrayal. Sandreena knew that much of the friction between the High Priestess and the Father-Bishop was because Seldon believed Creegan had usurped too much authority in Krondor, rather than being caused by losing a talented novitiate to the Order. It was rumoured that the High Priestess saw herself as a viable candidate for the most holy office in the Temple when the current Grand Master's health failed. And if that were true, Creegan would be her biggest barrier to the office of Grand Mistress.

Sandreena resisted the temptation to remind the High Priestess that she had no idea what a father was like, given that her mother had no idea who her father had been; and that from what she had seen of other fathers while growing up, they were generally poor at best, and drunk, abusive, womanizing, brutal monsters at worse. No, Brother Mathias had been closer to a saint than a father. He had become, and remained to this day, the only man she trusted without reservation. Even Father-Bishop Creegan was viewed with some reservation, because his needs always trumped hers or indeed anyone else's.

She simply nodded and made non-committal noises.

'So, what is next for you, my child?'

Sandreena knew it was best not to equivocate. The High Priestess would have sources in the Temple. Yet, she didn't have to tell the complete truth. 'Word has reached the Order that pirates are troubling a village along the Keshian coast. It seems that the imperial court is too busy to be bothered with the problem, so as I am the closest Knight-Adamant to the village,

I'm to go.' Using her title reminded the High Priestess that despite her rank and former position of authority Sandreena visited her only as a courtesy, nothing more. Draining her cup, she rose and said, 'I should be on my way, High Priestess. Thank you for taking time from your very busy day to seem me.'

She stood waiting for a formal acknowledgement, as was her right, and after an awkward moment, the older woman eventually inclined her head in consent. She could expect any priestess or novice to remain until dismissed, but not a knight of the Order. As Sandreena reached the door, the High Priestess said, 'It is a shame, really.'

Sandreena hesitated, then turned and said, 'What is a shame, High Priestess?'

'I can't help but feel that despite the work you do for the Goddess, you've somehow been turned from the proper path.'

Sandreena instantly thought of a dozen possible replies, all of them unkind and scathing, but her training with Brother Mathias made her pause before speaking. Calmly she replied, 'I always seek the path intended for me, High Priestess, and pray daily to the Goddess that she keeps my feet upon it.'

Without another word, she turned and left. As she strode furiously down the long hall she longed for something to hit, a brigand or goblin would do nicely. Lacking one, she decided it was time to go to the training yard and take her mace to a pell and see how fast she could reduce the thick wooden post to splinters.

Sandreena stood panting, having taken out her bad temper on a pell for nearly an hour. Her right arm ached from the repeated bashing she had given the stationary wooden target. Like all members of her Order, she carried a mace. The tradition of not using edged weapons was lost in time, but believed to be part of her Order's doctrine to strive for balance. Those she fought were given every opportunity to yield, even to the point of death. Edged weapons spilled blood that could not be given back. She had wondered on more than one occasion whether the original proponent of the tradition knew how much damage could be done to a body with a well-handled mace. A broken skull was as fatal as bleeding.

A girl wearing the garb of the Order, someone's squire, or a page, approached her. She was very pretty, and for a moment Sandreena dryly considered that she was probably on the Father-Bishop's personal staff. Sandreena nodded a greeting. 'Sister.'

The young acolyte held out a small, black wooden box. 'The Father-Bishop asked me to give this to you. He said you would understand.'

Sandreena laughed. She was on his staff.

The girl looked slightly confused and Sandreena said, 'Sorry, just an idle thought after a long practice. Are you training for the Order Adamant?'

She shook her head. 'I am a scribe and cleric,' she answered. 'I serve in the Temple library.'

'Ah,' said Sandreena. The Father-Bishop had one of his little spies where she could monitor all comings and goings; as well as being the repository for all the Order's valuable volumes, librams, tomes, and scrolls, the library was where all of the scribes did their superior's bidding. She took the box. 'Thank you.'

She watched the slender girl walk purposefully away and for a fleeting moment wondered what her life story had been before coming here; did she have a loving father and a mother who wished for grandchildren? Was she a fugitive from a harsh and uncaring world? Putting aside such pointless thoughts, she opened the box.

She understood immediately what the contents of the box heralded. Within lay a dull, pearl-white stone set within a simple metal clasp and hung from a plain leather thong. She lifted it out with a resigned sigh. It was a soul gateway. Before she departed on her assignment, Sandreena would now have to endure a very long and difficult session with one of the more powerful Brothers of the Order, preparing her stone, so that in the event of her death, her spirit could be recalled to the Temple, and questioned by those who could speak to the departed. If the magic used were strong enough, she could even be resurrected in the Temple. This act was the most powerful magic available to the Temple, rare in the extreme and most difficult to execute. She wondered if her scars would reappear in the event of her resurrection; the scar on her thigh had a habit of itching at the most inconvenient times. Then she considered the stone.

Its presentation meant that whatever she was being sent to discover was important. So important that even if she didn't survive, the discovery must still be reported to the Temple, even if that report came from her ghost, kept from Lims-Kragma's Hall for a few additional hours. Or, should the need be great, and if Lims-Kragma were willing, she might escape death entirely.

Despite the heat of the day and her exertion, she felt a chill and a need to cleanse herself.

From a window high above the marshalling yard behind the Temple, Father-Bishop Creegan watched the girl regarding the soul gate he had sent to her, and said, 'She's young.'

The man standing at his shoulder said, 'Yes, but she's as tough as any Knight-Adamant in the Order. If Mathias were still sound, or Kendall still alive, I'd say either of them would do, but right now she's the best mix of skill, strength, and determination you have.'

Creegan turned to face his companion, a man he had known for most of his life, though only well over the last three years. He was dressed in the garb of a commoner, and a rather dirty one at that, his hair was scruffy and his chin beard surrounded by days of stubble. Even his fingernails were dirty, but the Father-Bishop of the Order of the Shield of the Weak knew that this was but one of several guises employed by James Dasher Jamison.

'Are you acting on behalf of the Crown?'

'In a manner,' said the most dangerous man in the Kingdom from Creegan's point of view. Not only was he the grandson of the most important Duke in the Kingdom of the Isles, he was also reputed to be the mastermind behind the Kingdom's intelligence services, and even, according to some, in control of the criminal brotherhood known as the Mockers.

Jim Dasher looked out of the window for a moment longer, then said, 'An impossibly beautiful woman, that one.'

'As dangerous as she is lovely,' said Creegan.

Jim Dasher looked the cleric and said, 'You two . . . ?'

'No,' said the prelate. 'Not that the thought hasn't crossed my mind upon occasion.' He waved his guest to a small table with two chairs. 'If I have one flaw, it's my love of beautiful women.' The room was not utilized for any specific reason, but Creegan had long ago claimed it for his clandestine meetings and other moments when he felt the need to be away from the

High-Priestess's army, or when he wanted a few undisturbed minutes to think.

'I knew her,' said Jim, 'when she was a whore.'

'You?' asked Creegan.

Jim Dasher laughed, a single bark of embarrassment. 'No. Not that way. I may not be first among those she would wish dead, but I am high on that list, no doubt.'

'Really?'

Dasher nodded. 'I sold her to the Keshian trader.'

Creegan let out a long sigh, and shook his head. 'The things we do in the name of the greater good.' Then he asked, 'But it was you who arranged for Brother Mathias to intercede and rescue her from the Keshian, wasn't it?'

'I wish I could claim that were so,' said Jim. He looked out the window again, this time into the distance and said, 'My plan was for her to endure the company of that fat monster for a month, then I would have made contact with her and turn her to my purpose; I was going to promise her safe passage back to the Kingdom from Shamata and enough wealth to start a new life if she provided me with certain documents that were in the merchant's possession.'

'I never knew that,' said Creegan. 'I always thought it was all some elaborate plot to rid yourself of a Keshian spy and that Mathias just happened to recognize the girl's quality.'

Jim barked out another laugh. 'Zacanos Martias was as much a Keshian spy as you are. What he was, however, was a choking point for certain . . . .' He paused. 'Let's just say that since his demise it's been a lot easier for me to get certain things in and out of Kesh. I now deal directly with those whom Zacanos previously distanced me from.' He drummed his fingers on the chair arm. 'Still, I wish I had been able to get those documents from him. By the time my people got to his home in Shamata someone else had already been through his effects, leaving nothing of importance.'

'Who, I wonder?' asked the Father-Bishop.

'The Imperial Keshian Intelligence Service,' said Dasher. 'Which, of course, doesn't exist.'

'What?'

Jim waved his hand. 'Old family joke.' He sighed. 'As long as the Emperor is smart enough to leave his spies in the control of Ali Shek Azir Hazara-Khan, I have my work cut out for me.' He sat forward, as if in discomfort. 'That family has been responsible for more trouble between our two nations than any other single group of people.'

'Why not simply have them removed?' asked Creegan.

'Well, to begin with it would constitute an act of war, and we need an excuse to bloody our noses against Kesh's Dog Soldiers like a house fire needs a barrel of pitch. Secondly, it's not how things are done in the espionage game; death is the last choice in all circumstances. And lastly, I really like Ali. He's very funny with some wonderful tales, and he's a very good gambler.'

'Your world is one I can barely understand,' admitted the prelate.

'As is yours to me, Father, but sometimes the greater good demands that we trust one another.'

'Obviously, or else you wouldn't be here.' The Father-Bishop stood. 'I need to return to my office.' As he walked his guest to the door he said, 'If you didn't engineer that encounter between Brother Mathias and the Keshian merchant, who did?'

'You'd have to ask Sandreena what she recalls; if there was another player in the game, I have no idea who it might be.'

'Perhaps it was simply the Goddess's plan,' said Creegan and Jim saw he was not being facetious.

Jim said, 'I've seen too much in my life to believe anything involving the gods to be out of the question.'

Jim Dasher glanced out of the door and said, 'I'll try to be as inconspicuous on my way out as I was coming in.'

'Then goodbye,' said the Father-Bishop as Jim Dasher hurried down the short hallway that led to the southernmost stairs. Creegan knew there was a good chance, despite the busy Temple throng, that the agent of the Crown would manage to get cleanly away with no one noticing the scruffy looking commoner.

He sighed; things were becoming far too complex and he worried that the enormity of their undertaking was going to prove too much, even for the combined resources of the Crown and the Temple. He put aside the thought as best he could; there was no point in wasting time and energy on matters beyond his control. Better to trust the Goddess and move on to the day's needs.

Creegan followed Jim Dasher down the stairs and as he had suspected, saw no sign of the man in the massive, open court-yard when he reached the door.

CHAPTER THREE

Taredhel

*T*HE AIR SHIMMERED.

A light breeze blew across the valley as heat waves rose from the warmed rocks on the hillside and larks flew overhead. The afternoon sun chased away the night's chill and bathed the grasses in a warm blanket as spring arrived in Novindus. A fox sunning herself raised her head in concern, for she smelled something unusual. Springing to her feet she turned her head left and right seeking the source. Curiosity soon gave way to caution and the vixen darted off, bounding into the shadowed woods.

The cause of her fright, a solitary figure, made his way carefully through the thinning trees. At this altitude, the heavy woodlands below gave way to alpine meadows and open reaches providing easier transit.

Any observer would think him barely worth notice. A large hat masked his features. His body appeared neither overly stout nor slender, and his garb simple travelling robes made of grey homespun or poor linen. He carried a sack across one shoulder and used a gnarled black stave made of oak.

The man paused and looked at the peaks to the north and south, noticing their bald crowns above the timberline. They were known by those who lived nearby as the Grey Towers, but he put aside his appreciation of their majesty and instead considered them in a complex evaluation of the valley's defensibility.

A people once lived here, but invaders had driven them out. Then the invaders eventually departed, but the original inhabitants of the valley never returned. There were signs of their settlements scattered throughout this region, from the deep northern pass, beyond which a large village of dwarves resided, to the south where the high ridges gave way to the sloping hills that led to bluffs commanding the strait between two vast seas.

Like all of his race, the traveller knew little of dwarves to the north, or the seemingly numberless humans. Of those who had lived in this valley before he knew only lore and legend. What little he had pieced together had provided him with more questions than answers.

He had travelled this continent for three months, and was barely noticed by most as he passed; even when seen or spoken to, he was barely remembered. He was an unremarkable being, who may have been tall, or just average; a man of some circumstance, or perhaps of modest means. His hair could have been described as brown, or sandy, or sometimes black. The guise, created by the arts and employed by the traveller, made him difficult to notice or remember.

Looking around, to finalize his sense of the place as much as to ensure he was not being watched, the traveller reached within a belt pouch and withdrew a crystal. It was of no intrinsic value, but it was his most precious possession; his only means of returning to his people. He held tightly to the crystal and let his glamour slip away, revealing his true appearance before his return. Had he stepped through the portal in his magical guise, his death would have been immediate.

The traveller considered it strange that while he did not change physically he felt as if he were casting off clothing that was too small. He took a moment to stretch his long arms before incanting the brief spell that activated the crystal.

There was a sudden sizzling sound, like a small crackle of lightning, followed by a rip in the air that looked like a tall curtain of heat shimmer, then a portal formed above the ground: twelve feet high and nine feet across, a grey oval of nothingness. An instant later the traveller had stepped into it and vanished.

Up in the trees, a motionless figure observed the departure. It was by only the most strained of coincidences that he was in this valley at all, for it had been unoccupied since the Riftwar, but the game trails and pathways along the more northern ridges gave faster access to his destination than the more frequently used routes through the Green Heart Forest to the south. Like most of his kind, solitude or anticipation of danger didn't bother him, but an appreciation of swift passage was keen in the messenger. Of all the mortal races, only the elves had better woodcraft skills than the Rangers of Natal.

He was a tall, lean man, with skin burned dark by the sun,

though his brown hair showed streaks of red and blond from the same exposure. His eyes were dark and hooded, his high cheekbones and narrow eyes, and his straight nose gave him an almost hawk-like countenance. Only when he smiled did he lose his grim visage, something that rarely occurred outside the comfort of his home, in the company of family.

Ranger Alystan of Natal was undertaking a service for a consortium of traders in the Free Cities, in negotiation with the Earl of Carse. He carried a bundle of documents that both parties considered vital. His sun-darkened features were set in concentration, his dark eyes narrowed as if willing himself to see every detail. His dark hair was still free of grey, but he was no youth, having spent his life serving his people with stealth, speed, and sword.

He had chanced upon the newcomer's trail just an hour earlier, spotting his fresh tracks in the spring-damp soil. He had first thought little of the traveller, perhaps a magician from the look of him and his heavy staff, but he had followed. His usually limited curiosity over a solitary nomad wandering the wilds of the Grey Towers – even should he be prove a magician – was piqued not when he first glimpsed the traveller, but rather from the first moment he had taken his eyes from the man.

Alystan could not recall what the man looked like. Was his cloak grey or blue? Was he short or tall? Each time he took his eyes from his quarry he could not recall the details of his appearance. Alystan was certain that the man was a magic user, and that he was using some glamour to hide his true visage. To his consternation, the ranger found it easier to follow the magician's tracks than watch him. Something about doing so made him wish to turn his attention away and go about other business, so he forced himself to stalk this mysterious figure.

Then he saw the change.

In that instant every detail of the creature's true appearance was etched into the ranger's memory. Upon witnessing its sudden departure, he knew he now had a more important task. The last time that strangers had appeared through a rift in this valley, their arrival had heralded the coming of a twelve-year-long, bloody war. And from the creature's appearance, history could be repeating itself.

To Alystan, it looked as if an unremarkable man had transformed himself into the tallest elf he had ever seen. He wished he had been able to move closer and note more detail, but the traveller disappeared too quickly.

From what Alystan had seen the creature stood nearly seven feet in height, with massive shoulders, but a surprisingly narrow waist, giving his upper physique a startling 'v' shape. His legs were proportioned like those of an elf, though more powerfully muscled. A decorative band secured his grey-shot red hair on top of his head, the rest falling below his shoulders. But it was the creature's startling shade of red hair that had surprised him: it was not a natural reddish-brown or even the orange-tinged red sometimes seen among humans and elves alike, its hair was a vivid scarlet colour. Its brows were the same vivid hue, and seemed to have been treated with wax as they swept out and up, mimicking a butterfly's antennae.

Alystan moved cautiously, in case other creatures waited close by, though he doubted it, this valley had remained unoccupied during the century since the Riftwar. The dark elves who had once abided here were content to remain far to the north, and Alystan had only seen the trail sign of one man. Or elf, he amended.

He continued to think about what he had seen as he made his way back up to the higher game trails. Like other elves whom Alystan knew, the newcomer had shown effortless grace as he had stepped through the magic portal. But, unlike the elves known to the ranger, this one trod with heavy feet, as if it was ignorant of wood-lore or simply didn't care. No elf of even modest experience would have left tracks so easily followed.

There had been something else about the creature. Alystan had only caught a briefest glimpse of the creature's face, as it had looked around before disappearing, but it had been long enough to notice the creature's eyes. They were deep set and so pale a blue that they were almost cloud coloured. There had been something malevolent in its face; Alystan couldn't express how he knew, but he was certain it was no Midkemian elf, previously unknown to the Rangers, but something else. It was obviously intelligent enough to use magic to pass as human, no mean feat for even the most powerful of the magic-using creatures, the great dragons. Not only was this elf creature a magician of some fashion, it was possibly a very powerful one.

Alystan was also troubled by the creature's attire. Upon its brow, it had worn a delicate circle of gold set with a large polished ruby in the middle. Elves occasionally wore jewellery, but only during festivals; the rest of the time they were content with garlands or other natural adornments. And then there was the manner of his clothing.

The elf had worn finely made robes, and the circlet upon his head was also of exceptional craftsmanship. While striking in countenance and massive in body, he did not look like a warrior or scout, and given his human disguise, the creature was intent upon stealth, not conflict. Alystan knew him some manner of magician, but his garb and illusion set him apart from the Spellweavers of Elvandar, or the Loremasters of the Eldar. Their magic was as much a thing of nature as mind and will; this conjuration had been worn around the shoulders like a cloak, and was too much like dark human arts.

The strange elf obviously hailed from a people who enjoyed material splendour as much as humans did, for his robes had been made of a shimmering weave, pearl-white satin or silk perhaps, and their hems were decorated with ruby and azure threads. His staff of oak, which had seemed to be a simple walking stave, had in that instant shown itself to be a thing of magic, adorned at its top by a large glass orb, which glowed even in the bright sunlight. Alystan was certain that no human – certainly no Ranger – had encountered this elf's kin before.

As he picked up speed, Alystan wondered why he was here. He knew that once his business was concluded in Carse, rather than return to Bordon, he must hie to the dwarves of the Grey Towers, in the village of Caldara, and take counsel with them. They knew more of elf lore than any this side of Elvandar, and it was upon their borders that this elf trod. Perhaps the dwarves knew why such a being was scouting this region, although thirty years of experience tracking in these mountains and forests on both sides of the peaks told him that no one in the Free Cities or the Kingdom of the Isles would like the answer.

Demons howled in rage and pain as they assaulted the barricade. A shower of arrows rained down on them striking dozens as they sought to climb the barricade using the bodies of their fallen comrades to crest the defences.

Undalyn, Regent Lord of the Clans of the Seven Stars, pointed to an oncoming wave of the creatures on the right, near the top of the barricade, and shouted, 'There! Pitch!'

Two Conjurers waited nearby, far enough behind the battle-front to be relatively safe, flanked by a dozen archers detailed to bring down any flyers who might target them. A massive cauldron of burning pitch waited on top of a blazing mound of logs, and the two magicians acted in concert. Well practised in their arts, they closed their eyes, needing no sight to manage their task.

The cauldron, so large that a dozen men and two draught animals had placed it on top of the pyre, rose into the air as if gently lifted by an invisible giant hand. It floated over the heads of the defenders and poured its contents over the demons below.

Flaming death rained down on the demons near the top of the barricade, while those below hung back for a moment as waves of heat washed over them, singeing hair and eyebrows. The usual stench of demon was made even more noxious by the burnt odour. The creatures fell back, but the Regent Lord knew they were still hard pressed in the centre and on their left.

He turned away from the pile of writhing demons and assessed his position. His warriors fought valiantly, as their fathers and grandfathers had before them. For one hundred years the Clans of the Seven Stars had struggled against the Demon Legion, and for a hundred years they had made the monsters pay dearly for every inch of ground they gained, for every village they sacked, and for every life sacrificed.

Still, he knew that his resources were dwindling and theirs seemed without limit. In the distance, on the horizon, he saw a dark cloud yet knew there was no rain in the air. Before he could speak one of the lookouts on the tower above shouted, 'Flyers!'

Knowing his command was gratuitous, as his magic users already conjured their defence, he still felt the need to give the order. 'Shields!'

It was part of Undalyn's nature to be wary of ceding too much authority to others. He knew this could easily be a failing, but another part of him took pride in knowing that every one of his warriors, priests, and magic users understood their task and answered him without hesitation. The more desperate his people's struggle became, the more proud he felt of them.

He was Undalyn, leader of his people by lineage and law, Regent Lord of the Clans of the Seven Stars. He was the most powerful elf among his kind.

His features were typical of his people, though his skin tended towards a darker tone than most, due to his passion for hunting and spending years under the sun. His blue eyes were the colour of the ocean, containing flecks of green, and his brow was unlined, despite his more than three hundred years. A white leather circlet decorated with five perfect rubies set in gold tied his snow-white hair above his head in a noble's knot and left some free to fall in a long cascade down his back. He was handsome, but nevertheless had a dark and dangerous aspect to his features that was revealed at odd moments, though he rarely raised his voice in anger. It was his eyes that held the fury within.

The Clans of the Seven Stars, the *taredhel* in the old tongue, accorded him the utmost respect, for it was his burden to guide them, as it had been his forefathers' before him. But no Regent had faced a burden such as his, and the responsibility was taking its toll. Dark circles under his eyes told of many sleepless nights, endless worry, frustration, and ultimately a sense of doom.

He felt rather than saw the energy barrier go up, as the remaining magic users employed one of their more powerful spells. The demons had encountered this barrier before, yet they hurled themselves against it, time and again.

Archers waited at the ready against the possibility that one of the creatures breach the mystic defence. Those on the walls peppered the retreating horde of demons that appeared to be marshalling for another assault on the wall should the flyers break through. The Regent Lord took a deep breath and pulled out his sword again to be ready. He glanced at his hands and saw they were free of blood. His shoulders ached and he felt as if he could sleep for a week, yet he had not struck one blow against the enemies of his people.

His soldiers had kept the demon horde at bay for another day and he had been free to oversee the defence of the barrier and not put himself at risk. Other days he had not been so fortunate and had killed his fair share of demons, returning to his palace at night covered in their evil black blood.

He watched without emotion as the flyers struck the barrier. The sky above scintillated in rainbows of colour as the winged horrors of the Demon Legion bounced off the shield. The Regent Lord knew some of the monsters were clever, but the ones who assaulted his defences every day seemed without any spark of intellect. Had the demons possessed half the guile of the elves, they would have overwhelmed the Seven Clans years ago. But even without organization, they were grinding the Clans of the Seven Stars to nothing. Entire worlds had already been abandoned and now here on the home world – he shook his head, for this wasn't their true home world, only the capital of his nation – but here they were making a final stand. He knew that no matter how valiantly they struggled, eventually they would fall.

The flyers beat furiously against the barrier, but it held. Lately demons capable of magic had appeared from time to time, costing the elves dearly, but this day at least it seemed that victory would go to the Clans.

The demons eventually withdrew and the Regent Lord surveyed the barrier. As the flyers retreated and the sun lowered in the west, Undalyn knew the battle was over for today.

He removed his helm and almost instantly an aide appeared at his side to take it. Another came over to him and said, 'My Lord, we have a report that the Conjurer Laromendis has returned.'

The Regent Lord didn't ask what news he carried, for the Conjurer had been under strict instructions not to divulge his findings before reporting directly to the palace. Undalyn could not afford for rumours to be racing through the capital until the truth was known. The fate of the Clans of the Seven Stars rested on this report.

'I will return to the palace at once.'

'He is being transported to the palace, my lord,' said the aide, a youth who bore a striking resemblance to one of his sons, lost years before. The Regent Lord pushed his feelings aside; too many sons had been lost to too many fathers, and fathers lost to sons. They all shared in the tragedy of this war.

With a dismissive wave of his hand, the Regent Lord shooed his aides to one side and alerted the portal guardian that he was returning to the capital. The magician whose sole responsibility was to manage the portal nodded and activated the gateway with a simple spell. His job also was to destroy the gate should the demons breach the barrier, and give his life to keep them away from the capital for a few more days.

The Regent Lord stepped through the portal and found himself in the marshalling yard of his palace. Two companies of warriors stood ready to answer the call should reinforcements be required. The Regent Lord motioned to the Officer of the Yard and said, 'How go our other struggles?'

'Well, my lord,' he answered. The old elf was still robust looking, though he had sustained enough injuries that his fighting ability was severely diminished; but his mind was still as keen as ever and he was among those most trusted by the Regent Lord to act in his absence. Jaron by name, he was given full responsibility to decide where reinforcements were sent and when. Men lived or died on his order, and that trust had been hard won over many years of service. 'They've fallen back on all fronts, and so for another day we hold.' Glancing around, he repeated, 'Another day.'

'We live another day,' echoed the Regent Lord.

'Rumour has the Conjurer returning,' said Jaron in a low voice.

'Best not to repeat that to anyone,' said the Regent Lord, walking away without further comment. He knew he would reach his chambers before the magic users and he wanted a few moments to compose himself in private, lest the news was ill. He also needed to be composed should the news Laromendis carried be good. Walking silently towards the large doors into the palace, Undalyn cursed hope.

The Regent Lord of the Clans of the Seven Stars sat quietly, trying to enjoy one moment of solitude and peace in a day dominated by violence and noise. The enemy battered the Barrier Wall every minute of every day, yet here, in the heart of the capital, he could indulge himself in the illusion that his city was as it had been since he was a boy. Deep within, he felt weak for longing for days by, gone beyond reclaim, but it calmed him and gave him hope that someday the People would find a haven as tranquil as this world once was.

Large open windows granted the sun, wind, and rain admittance into the room. The Regent Lord would always meet guests in the open, so that the People and the Spirits of Ancestors might witness it, such was the law. The only adornments to the room were the battle standards of the Host of the Clans hanging from the ceiling, providing a moving reminder of the People's history as they stirred in the wind.

The tall warrior rested on a simple wooden chair that had been his nation's seat of power since memory began.

The People, his race, were dying and there was nothing he could do to save them as long as they remained here.

Despite the heat of the day, Undalyn's shoulders were covered in white fur, as a mark of his rank; it was the pelt of a snow bear he had killed during his manhood rite high in the mountains of Madrona. He rested his hand upon the hilt of his father's sword, Shadowbane, absently caressing it.

Below his mantle of fur he wore a light tunic and trousers of a dark green cloth, simple but for the gold thread at the collar and cuffs; his feet were clad in fine brown leather boots, still covered in dust from his morning walk inspecting the city's defences. The same dust covered his nearly-white hair, and he wished for time to bathe, but knew much needed to be accomplished before a relaxing bath was possible.

He looked out the window at the blue sky and felt the warmth of the sun on his arms and face, and felt the heat under his furry mantle; he welcomed the sensation, trying to drive out the cold that gripped his very soul.

Then a scout, his hair tied in a hunter's queue, entered. 'He's here, m'lord.'

Waving away the courtier, Undalyn spoke in a deep, commanding voice, 'Show yourself, Conjurer!'

The magic user strode into the throne room, his white robes bright and his staff aglow with power. He bowed and said, 'I am here, my lord.'

'Show me,' ordered the Regent Lord.

Raising his staff, the magic user moved it slowly through the air, and as he did a scene appeared, as if painted on an invisible wall, but moving and alive. When the shimmering ceased, it looked as if a new window had been created by magic, but while the windows of the chamber overlooked the sun-baked table-lands of Andcardia, the magic window showed a completely different landscape.

The Regent Lord scanned the scene before him. It appeared they stood on a hill's ridge, and it was late afternoon from the angle of the sun behind them. Across a vast valley he could see more peaks. Everywhere he looked he saw natural abundance. The trees were old, heavy with growth, and he could see two large meadows in the distance below. White clouds floated above, pregnant with rain, and the wind carried exotic scents mixed with those more familiar to him: balsam, pine, fir, and cedar. The forest sounded rich with game and in the trees birds sang without concern. 'This seems a hospitable land,' observed the Regent Lord. Fixing his gaze on the magic user, he asked, 'Is it Home?'

Knowing his life, and his brother's life, probably hung on this answer, Laromendis, Supreme Conjurer of the Circle of Light, hesitated, then said, 'I must speak with the Loremasters m'lord.' As the Regent Lord's expression darkened, he hastily added, 'I'm being cautious, but yes, I believe it is Home.'

The Regent Lord's expression betrayed a tiny flicker of relief. If this was their ancestral homeland then there was still hope. 'Tell me more of it, our ancient Home.'

'It is a fair world, my lord, though not without problems.' He moved the staff and the scene disappeared.

'Problems,' repeated the leader of the Clans of the Seven Stars. 'Is there ever a day without problems, on any world?'

The Conjurer said nothing at the rhetoric.

'Name them,' said the Regent Lord just as another figure arrived through a portal, his hand on his sword. He was a warrior nearly equal in stature to the Regent Lord, and he seemed on the verge of speaking until he saw Undalyn raise a gauntleted hand, indicating that he wanted silence.

'This world is rich in game, crops, and metals. But it is home to others.'

'Others?'

'Dwarves,' he almost spat.

'Dwarves,' said Undalyn. 'Is there a world to be found without those mud grubbers?'

'I fear not,' said the Conjurer. He had in fact located several worlds without dwarves in the last ten years, but none of them was habitable; this was not the time to engage in petty debate over the fine points. Since the discovery of the translocation magic and the search for the homeland, all hopes for the survival of the People had turned to locating their mythical Home; a search that the Conjurer had thought futile. Finding any world into which they could flee, be it ancient or new, that was the survival key for a race now reduced to a relative handful by thirty years battle with the Demon Legion.

His discovery of their Home was a happy accident, nothing more, or at least that's how he saw it; his vanity almost equalled the Regent Lord's and so it was unthinkable for him to admit that someone without any knowledge of the arts might have been right. Laromendis, Master of the Arts of the Unseen, would settle for the Regent Lord simply being lucky.

And lucky for his People and for Laromendis and his brother, he quickly amended.

'There are also humans. They thrive there like flies on dung. Their cities are ant hives, with thousands in residence.'

'Our People, do they abide?'

'Yes. But they have . . . fallen.'

'What do you mean?' asked the Regent Lord.

As if needing to emphasize his point, Laromendis moved to stand before the northernmost window, which provided a vista of the city outside. Tarendamar, Starhome, capital of the Clans of the Seven Stars, and for generations a monument to the majesty of the People. The Regent Lord came to stand beside the red-haired magician. Still untouched by the brutal war to the north, the city remained much as it had been since Undalyn had been a boy.

The Hall of the Regent's Meeting was a short walk from the Regent's palace, and this very hall, ancient and honoured, had been among Undalyn's earliest memories. His father had ensured the next Regent Lord would understand the responsibilities of his heritage.

He knew this precinct well, as he had played in every alleyway and garden, swum in every pool and brook, climbed the holy trees to the outrage of the priestesses, and had come to love this city as if it were a living being; it was a living being, it was the heart of the Clans of the Seven Stars.

Built by magic and sweat, Tarendamar was the crown jewel of the People. Seven great trees formed a massive ring around the heart of the city, one mystic tree for each of the sacred stars in the heavens. Even in the harsh light of Andcardia's sun, the deep shadows within their bowers glimmered with fey light.

It was from those seven trees, the 'Seven Stars,' as they were called, that the power of the taredhel was drawn. Each tree had been grown from a sapling carried from Home to this world, the first refuge of the taredhel, the 'People of the Stars,' as they called themselves.

They had fled their birth world, ages before, and found refuge on this dry, inhospitable world, with its small oceans and lakes, scorching hot save for in the middle of their short winter. This world had grudgingly yielded to the magic of the original Spell-weavers, and the seven magic trees, carried from Home had been the anchor that had allowed them to survive. The survival of those saplings had been paid for with the very blood of the taredhel. If the soul of the Clans of the Seven Stars resided anywhere other than Andcardia, it was, and could only be, Home.

When the trees began to flourish, so did the taredhel, providing them with magic they called Home Magic. They had at first used it to bludgeon Andcardia into submission, then they had refined their magic, blending it with the natural harmonies, until a tune native to both the taredhel and this planet emerged. Over the following centuries, it had changed both the world and the elves.

Lush forests now hugged the mountainsides, still halted in the lowlands by blistering hot tablelands and vast deserts. Yet even they were slowly retreating as the Water Gatherers found ways to use the translocation magic to bring water from other worlds. During his lifetime, Undalyn had seen the sea level gradually rise and lakes expand. Once where his grandfather had hunted the great scaly lizards of the Rocky Flats, now an orchard of red fruit trees sheltered the melon vines, and streams ran through the heart of the flats all the way to the sea.

Undalyn was impatient for Laromendis to continue, but remained composed. He knew the Conjurer was trying to make a point. Finally the magic user spoke. 'They have nothing like this.'

The Regent Lord inclined his head and said, 'No cities?'

'Only for the darkest among our kind, the lore speaks of them as the Forgotten.'

The Regent Lord glanced around. Only one servant waited near the door and he was out of earshot; what the Conjurer spoke of was approaching heresy. Lowering his voice, he said, 'The . . .'

'They are called *moredhel* on the homeworld.'

'The dark people,' nodded the Regent Lord. 'They have a city?'

'It is rumoured.' He moved away from the window as he gathered his thoughts. 'In the north, in slavish imitation of the Masters, they built a twin of the city of lore. It was called Armengar by the humans, and was destroyed according to the tales. Our people's name for it I did not discover, but I've heard the story enough times to judge it has some truth to it.

'I spent most of my time with the humans, for it is easier to guile them. The humans thrive. In some ways they are like us, but ultimately they are inferior, like the other short-lived races. And like the others, they breed like mice. They are everywhere. What they know of our People borders on myth and legend.

'I travelled across one of their larger nations, learning the language as I travelled; fortunately, there are many nations and languages on this world, so someone who spoke oddly barely brought notice.

'We know so little of these creatures, these humans . . . I found them fascinating.'

The Regent Lord looked at the magic user, his gaze narrowing. While the ancient Spell Weavers were venerated and honoured for their work transforming this harsh world, those like Laromendis and his brother Gulamendis were viewed with caution approaching fear. Anything connected with the dark arts, or indeed anything that those Conjurers and Demon Masters found 'fascinating' was likely to be viewed with suspicion. 'Why?' He asked.

'There are many reasons, m'lord. But foremost is their magic. It is varied beyond calculation; they seize the power of the world and bend it to their will in so many ways, it staggers the mind.

'There are those who use arts much like our own; I wondered at first if elves had been their first teachers, but there are others . . . called Greater Path magicians, who have no subtlety, no . . . grace in their craft, yet possess vast power. It is difficult to explain to one not given to magic.'

The Regent Lord nodded. By nature elves were at one with the natural magic of their race, but circumstances had forced the People to adapt, to change their ways. Now among the taredhel there were those, like the two brothers, who hungered for power. And there were those, like the Regent Lord, who had sacrificed any understanding of the arts so that they might bend their will instead to serving the People in other ways.

'Tell me of the humans later,' said the Leader of the Clans of the Seven Stars. 'Tell me more of our people now. You said the . . . the Forgotten exist there?'

'So it would seem,' said the magic user. 'Humans know so little about our kind, but I could piece together some understanding of how our brethren fare.

'Humans call the Forgotten "The Brotherhood of the Dark Path".'

The Regent Lord nodded. 'An apt name if the secret lore is true . . .' He hesitated, realizing he had inadvertently uttered a blasphemy.

'There have been many debates among the Farseeing over whether the secret lore is literal or metaphor.' With that simple remark, he let the Regent Lord know he understood the comment and would make no issue of it. Given the current situation among the People, any hint of disorder brought swift and harsh punishment; it was why his brother currently languished in a dark cell. Then again, Laromendis's younger brother always had a tendency to speak first and think later; a bad trait in one who immersed himself in demon lore at a time when demons threatened to obliterate the People.

'What did you learn of the Forgotten?'

'Little, to the humans the Brotherhood is almost a myth, though I did encounter a traveller from Yabon, a city far to the north of a realm known as 'the Kingdom,' and he swore that he had once seen those . . . unspeakable beings.

'The Forgotten war against our brethren,' said the Conjurer, his tone betraying a hint of his anger and disgust. 'I walked the land listening to gossip in taverns, buying drinks for sailors, speaking with priests and anyone else who might know ancient lore. In one place I found an abbey dedicated to a god, but their wards were two strong for my guise to endure, so I could not enter. But I encountered one of their members on the road and questioned him. He was a monk and his mind was disciplined, but eventually it yielded most of what I learned of their ancient lore, which I now share with you.'

'Did you kill him?'

'Of course,' said the Conjurer. 'He was merely a human, after all.'

'No dishonour,' agreed the Regent Lord. Killing a prisoner would only be dishonourable if they were of the People or of a race considered equal.

'The Forgotten war against the ones most like us, who abide in a forest grove they call Elvandar.'

At the utterance of that word, the Regent Lord's eyes shone with emotion. He said the name softly, 'Elvandar.' It meant 'Home of the People,' but echoed with deeper meaning.

In ages past, the People had served another race, the dreadful Valheru, and had endured slavery and degradation. Then came a great upheaval, a war in which the very fabric of time and space was rent and chaos reigned.

The ancestors of the taredhel, called *edhel* in their own tongue, were among the mightiest of the servants of the Valheru. They were the spellweavers, the masters of the groves, the keepers of the land, and the librarians of their masters' power. Many of those who had served with their masters had perished on other worlds, though it was thought that a few had escaped and found refuge. It was the faint hope that there were others like them, out among the stars, that had driven a band of edhel to escape the Valheru through one of the tears in space and time.

To Andcardia they had come, a band of no more than two thousand magic users, hunters, and their families. It was a harsh land, but eventually they made it their own. As centuries passed, they prospered and eventually numbered in millions.

In the past few centuries, they had learned the secrets of translocation magic, tearing the fabric of the universe. No fewer than a dozen magic users had died mastering the art, but they could now stabilize the rifts and explore new worlds; some were inhospitable, others barely able to support life. A few had showed promise and upon them the Clans of the Seven Stars had established colonies. Some of those colonies had grown and were even flourishing.

The People had thrived, and when they encountered other races, they tolerated them as long as they did not oppose their will. If they did not comply, the other races were crushed. All had been glorious, until they found the world of demons.

'Those in Elvandar serve a Queen . . .' continued the Conjurer.

The Regent Lord's eyes went wide. 'She dares!'

'She outlived her king,' said the Conjurer, quickly. 'He . . . may have been of the line.'

The remark hit the Regent Lord like a physical blow. His eyes filled with even more emotion. Among the most ancient, sacred lore of the taredhel was the story of the first king and queen of the People, a couple who had shepherded them safely through the early chaos of the war that had driven the *eldar* from Home.

Little was known about them, save their deeds and names,

which would never be mentioned aloud, lest their spirits be disturbed; but they had been recorded in the annals, and read by every lorekeeper and regent lord. 'Her name?'

'They say it is Aglaranna.'

'The Gift,' said the Regent Lord.

The Conjurer said, 'It also means "Bright Moon," for the largest of the three moons on that world is known by that name, the Gift.'

The Regent Lord shouted, 'Send for the Loremaster!' To the Conjurer, he said, 'Continue, but do not speak of this or the Forgotten until I summon the Meeting.

'What of these humans who thrive like mice? Have they a ruler?'

'The humans live in many nations, with many rulers. They war amongst themselves on a regular basis, it seems.'

'That is good,' said the Regent Lord calmly. 'What else?'

'The dwarves live at peace with their neighbours and are content to do so as long as they remain untroubled. There are also goblins and other such creatures.'

'Goblins?'

'*Lea Orcha,*' said Laromendis.

Shaking his head in near disbelief, he said, 'My father raised me to be a pious man, like all of our line, yet I will confess to have been guilty of doubt.' Lea Orcha, or goblins, were nightmare creatures, conjured as bedtime stories to frighten children into being obedient.

'They worship dark, ancient gods and spill blood in sacrifice. They consort with trolls and other inferior races.'

'Goblins . . . how have they never been exterminated?'

The magic user shrugged, a human gesture he had picked up

and which caused the Regent Lord to frown. 'I don't know,' he said softly. 'There is so much discord and warfare among the human tribes, they hardly seem to have time to deal with goblins.'

The Regent Lord indicated he should continue.

'This world is known by several names in different tongues, but most commonly it is called Midkemia: a human word.'

'The land I showed you in my vision is a valley in the mountains called the Grey Towers. This valley was once home to the Forgotten. A human tribe called the Tsurani drove them northward, and they have never returned. To the south live dwarves, but there are natural barriers between the valley and the dwarves' territory. Some ancient mines still link them, but they have been abandoned and are easily defended. To the north there are paths and trails leading where our evil kin abide.

'Once established in this valley we may range far and wide. To the east live humans in a federation called the Free Cities. They are poorly organized and ripe for conquest.

'The danger lies to the west, for there lies the outpost region of perhaps the mightiest human nation—' He stopped speaking as the Regent Lord raised his hand.

An elderly male dressed in flowing robes entered the room carrying an ancient tome, inside which the history of the People had been recorded since the Time Before. His eyes were dim with age and behind him strode a younger male, his heir, who when not assisting the Loremaster studied, preparing himself for the day he would assume the responsibility of that office.

Both bowed before the Regent Lord, who said, 'Midkemia. Do we know that world?'

The Loremaster paused for a moment as his assistant leaned

over to whisper something. 'Speak aloud!' demanded the Regent Lord. 'No one hides a word from me in my court.'

The younger elf looked abashed, and said, 'I beg my lord's forgiveness. I meant no slight. It is just that I have studied some of the earlier passages more recently and recall seeing that name.'

The Loremaster waved away his apprentice's apology. 'His name is Tandarae, Regent Lord; he is young, and perhaps a little rash, but his memory is as keen as mine was in my prime.' The older historian's face was wan and his eyes watered. 'Soon this office shall be his, and I recommend him to you.'

The younger historian bowed low before his master and the Regent Lord.

'Very well,' he said to Tandarae. 'What do you know of this world?'

'In the time before time,' began the younger historian reciting the ritualized words of the most ancient of myths, 'before fleeing the Wrath, the People abided.

'Slaves were we in our Home, ruled by cruel masters, the Lords of Power, the Dragonriders.

'Then came the Wrath and the skies were torn, and the Dragonriders rose to contest a great war. Many of the People perished and many were lost among the stars, left behind when our masters returned to the Home to struggle with the Wrath. As the war continued,' said the young Loremaster closing his eyes as if he read from the ancient text in his mind, 'many lesser beings, Dakan Shoketa, Dena Orcha, and Dostan Shuli, came to Home across a golden bridge, feeling the Wrath as it descended on the world.'

He stopped and said, 'Midkemia is a word used by the Dakan

Soketa, my lord, the ancient word of our People for humans. The humans called our home world, "Midkemia".'

The Regent Lord closed his eyes, as if praying silently. Then he said, 'It is Home!' To Laromendis he said, 'Tell us more of this valley, the one you showed me.'

The magic user nodded. 'To the west lie the westernmost garrisons of that nation I spoke of, the Kingdom. The humans there mostly reside in three small cities, barely larger than our towns, Tulan, Carse, and Crydee. They are well fortified. We can isolate them by land, but they have a vast navy and can be sustained by sea. We shall need to strike all three fortresses quickly to seize them.

'At the right time. But first we need a secure bridgehead on the Home world and devise a plan to give us more time.' He thought about how the great Barrier Spell, the sphere that stalled the advancing Demon Legion, was weakening to the north. It had been breached three times in the last ten years, and in the last report had failed to the far west for a short time. The fighting had been brutal and many of the People had paid a terrible price while the magicians repaired the breach. It would fail everywhere eventually, so time was not an abundant commodity. Guile and wit would have to serve until other forces could be brought to bear. Looking at Laromendis, he said, 'The plan for conquest will be considered, and perhaps an accommodation with those already in residence upon Home is in order. But that is for others to consider. Upon you I must place different burdens.'

'I will serve, my lord,' answered the magic user.

'We are hard pressed. Our enemies have driven us out of Thandar Keep, so Modaria has fallen.'

The Conjurer said nothing, but the slight tension around his eyes asked the question. 'No one survived,' the Regent Lord said softly.

Modaria was the last of the outpost worlds, so now the entirety of the People remained on Andcardia. 'We made them pay dearly, but as it has always been, for each of them we lose three warriors.' His deep voice took on an almost plaintive tone as he said, 'We need a safe haven, Conjurer. Is this such a place?'

There was a moment's silence, and Undalyn demanded, 'Speak! Is this a safe haven?'

'There are demon signs. Not recent, but . . . demons have been there.'

The Regent Lord threw back his head in rage and torment and let forth a howl of pure barbaric anger and pain. 'Is there no refuge?'

'Only signs, my lord,' said the magician. 'I found no demons.'

'How can that be?' said the Regent Lord as he fixed his dark gaze on the magician.

'In my travels I saw many lands, heard many stories. A century ago, a demon lord reached this land, but he was without a battle host. He took the guise of a woman, a queen of the humans, and conquered a third of that world before he was stopped.

'A magician of vast power, aided by other magicians and a human army, defeated the demon and threw him down.'

The Regent Lord sat back, his head cocked to one side as he listened, and he shook his head slightly as he said, 'Just one demon. That is unusual.' He was silent for a moment, then said, 'But even one means more may follow.'

'I bring hope too, my lord. For there are hints in the stories that the demon did not come to that realm by conjuration, but rather through . . . a gate.'

'The demon gate!' spat the Regent Lord. 'That tale grows old, Conjurer. It is but a fantasy to explain the demons' presence among the mortals and absolve those like your brother. Every Master of Lore since the time before time has avowed that demons cannot come to this realm unbidden! I will hear no more of this blasphemy, lest you wish to end up with the same fate as your brother!'

At the mention of a brother, the Conjurer's face went rigid.

Lowering his voice, the Regent Lord's expression calmed. 'He still lives.'

'In your dungeon, my lord?'

The Regent Lord actually smiled. 'In a cage I had placed in a small courtyard. I thought the dungeon overly deleterious to his health, with no sunlight. I wanted him still alive if you returned, as you have. It must become a little uncomfortable in the afternoon heat, but otherwise he is well enough.'

A slight flicker of anger crossed the magician's face, but he remained silent.

The Regent Lord said, 'Your brother's continued survival depends on your obedience, Conjurer.'

The magician inclined his head. 'Gulamendis and I serve at your pleasure, my lord. It has always been thus.'

The Regent Lord's mood darkened. 'Do not be glib with me, Conjurer.' He pointed to the west. 'The Plains of Delth-Aran are covered with the bodies of warriors who "served at my pleasure", and I count each loss as an affront to our people. There are children here in Tandamar who will never know their fathers' faces.

'Across five worlds we have battled the Demon Legions, and each world we leave behind is littered with valiant fighters who

"served at my pleasure"; and their females, and their young.'
Behind the anger in the Regent Lord's eyes, the Conjurer could
see genuine pain. 'My grandfather, and his father before, all stood
with defiant resolve, and each warrior serving "at their pleasure"
gave their full measure and left us poorer for their sacrifice.

'I would not dishonour their memory by forgiving those
responsible for this horror. Now they are here, on the World
of the Seven Stars, and we have nowhere left to go.' Then his
voice softened and he almost whispered, 'Except Home.'

The Conjurer said nothing. It was an old argument, one that
he had experienced many times before. Laromendis and his
brother were practitioners of the mystic arts, a calling barely
tolerated at the best of times, and this was hardly the best of
times. Laro was a Master of Illusion, a Conjurer, who could kill
a warrior using his will and imagination, conjuring up illusions
so real to the opposing fighter that a killing blow would even
end his life. Gulamendis was a Master of Demons, and among
those who were blamed for the terrors now visited upon the
People. Laro and his brother had been raised by their mother
in a remote village; she had known her sons had inherited great
and terrible gifts, the ability to use magic.

The Regent Lord said, 'Now, is this world safe?'

'I think so, my lord.' He paused, choosing his words carefully.
'As I have said, the knowledge I have gathered tells me that this
world has powerful protectors, men and women who could serve
to stem the coming of those with whom we battle.' He paused
again, then carefully said, 'We may have found allies.'

'Allies!' shouted the Regent Lord. 'Dwarves, lesser elves,
humans! Perhaps we should treat with the goblins as well? Would
you have me be the first ruler of our people to parley with those

we have warred against since time immemorial? Would you have me seek succour from those who are fit only to be conquered and bent to our service?'

Laromendis said nothing. He knew this was an argument that would take the leaders of the Regent Lord's Meeting weeks, even months to debate. And he also knew that if he was to save his brother's life, he must ensure that when the Regent Lord's Meeting was called, the Loremasters and priests were his allies; the fate of the People hung in the balance, and in order to save itself, this once proud race had to start making accommodations with those who had always been counted as enemies.

The Regent Lord asked further questions for an hour, insightfully pulling out details needed for his next plan. Finally he said, 'We shall move two clans into this valley, have them occupy the fortress at the north end.' Laromendis nodded. The dark elves had left everything intact. While overgrown and falling apart after a hundred years, it still would provide a safer place from which to muster, and could quickly be reclaimed as a highly defensible position.

'Have the Solis and Matusic ready themselves,' the Regent Lord ordered, and the herald bowed and departed. Laromendis kept his face expressionless, but inside he smiled. The Solis were under the command of Sebottis, Undalyn's favourite surviving son. That unexpected decision gave Laromendis a tiny advantage, for when the time came the Regent Lord would be less inclined towards conquest as the only solution if the heir to his throne stood at risk. Like his brother, Laromendis knew the People had to change to endure. Undalyn would favour conquest to reclaim Midkemia as the rightful home of the taredhel. He might reach an accommodation with those living in Elvandar, could even acknowledge their Queen as the true ruler, giving up his line's power – though Laromendis counted that unlikely. But he would insist that she govern a people who ruled the Home, not shared it with lesser beings.

Laromendis knew that such thinking had done nothing but destroy the lives of millions of the People over three generations. To survive, the People would need to put aside dreams of conquest and come to terms with the dwarves and humans. His way required planning and luck, for the two brothers were barely tolerated and hardly trusted, yet it fell to them to change the mind of the Regent Lord.

A messenger appeared at the door, breathless from the dash up the long flight of stairs from the stable yard below. As he fell to his knees before his ruler, he lowered his head and held out the scroll.

The Regent Lord's expression darkened as his worst fears were fulfilled. 'Garjan-Dar has fallen. The demons are through the breach.'

Laromendis knew two things; the demons would be repulsed and the Barrier Spell would be re-established, but at great cost. But how many more times could they repair the barrier, for each time warriors were needed to hold the ground while magic users spent their lives to maintain the spell. Once more, twice perhaps, but eventually the Barrier Spell would fail entirely, and soon after the city would be besieged. The walls of Tarendamar would prove little obstacle for the Demon Legion. Masonry and magic might keep them at bay for a week or two, perhaps a month, but the city would fall and with it, the heart of the Seven Stars.

The Regent Lord put his boot against the shoulder of the kneeling messenger and pushed him away. 'Get out!' he shouted, and the messenger appeared glad to obey, obviously relieved the Regent Lord's wrath had been limited to an impolite kick. In days past his head might have adorned a pike at the entrance to the keep.

The Regent Lord moved back towards the window and stared out. He took a deep breath then he asked, 'Which is your birth world, Conjurer?'

Laromendis said, 'This one, my lord. Far to the north in the snowlands, at the foot of the Iron Mountains.'

The Regent Lord said, 'I was born here, as well, but my eldest son was born on Utameer.' The Conjurer knew this, but if the Regent Lord felt the need to belabour the point, the magician was not fool enough to interrupt. 'When he was but ten seasons, I took him hunting bovak and longhorn greensnouts in table-lands to the east of the city of Akar. It was hot, all day, every day. Rain came rarely in those lands, and when it did it thundered and came down in a deluge. Children and small animals were sometimes washed away in flash floods. Lightning would rip through the sky as if the gods themselves were at war.' He turned to look at the magic user. 'We are going to lose this world, Conjurer, as we lost Utameer.' He leaned against the window's ledge, staring off into the distance. 'As we lost Katanjara, and Shinbol and the others.

'In my grandfather's grandfather's time, we conquered the stars. The Clans of the Seven Stars ruled worlds!' He added sadly, 'Now we have come to the end of our reign. Now we must become refugees.'

Turning away from the Loremasters and the magician, he moved back to the chair and said, 'We must return Home. It is our only salvation.'

Turning to Laromendis he said, 'Eat, rest, then return at first light. You shall conduct our battlemaster and a company of scouts to Home. We will begin preparing the way.' He frowned at Laromendis and said, 'Go!'

The Conjurer bowed, turned and hurried from the hall. He had a great deal to do between now and the morning, and had no illusions he would get any rest. It took a great deal of energy to plot treason.

CHAPTER FOUR

Harbinger

*T*HE RIDER RACED UP THE HILLSIDE.

It had taken Alystan three days of hard running to reach the Keep at Carse. He had paused in Carse only long enough to deliver the merchant's response to the Earl's request, eat a hot meal, sleep in a warm bed, then leave again at first light. As the negotiations had ended on good terms, the merchants could wait for another to return with the agreement. He had bid farewell to the Earl and his household that evening, for he left as dawn approached, accepting the loan of a sturdy gelding, and promising to return it on his way home.

The Ranger kept his own counsel on the matter of the elf, not wishing to involve the Kingdom unless it became necessary. At the moment the only evidence he had was what he had seen, and there might still be some explanation that would remove his foreboding. Yet, there was something in the manner of that elf, the way he carried himself, something that communicated menace. If nothing else, he was dangerous.

The quickest route to the dwarven stronghold at Caldara was through the Green Heart, the thick woodlands dominating most of the Duchy of Crydee. For the first ten miles inland, the coastline was dotted with small hamlets and solitary farms, trails and roads, and three towns of some size, Tulan, Carse, and Crydee. Light woodland occupied some of the land between them, but once a traveller moved farther inland, heavy forest was all one encountered.

The Rangers of Natal were second only to the elves in their ability to move swiftly and quietly through the heavy woods, but when it came to the open road, they had no difficulty in letting a horse carry them swiftly. They were a close-knit society, the inheritors of a unique birthright. Their ancestors had been Imperial Keshian Guides, the elite scouts of the Empire's army who had come to the region when the Empire of Great Kesh had expanded northward. Like Kesh's Dog Soldiers, they stood apart from mainstream Keshian society. When Kesh withdrew from the northlands, abandoning their colonies, the Guides became the de facto intelligence and scouting arm of the local militia. The cities had become autonomous and had bound together in a loose confederation, the Free Cities of Natal. And the Guides became the Rangers.

Rangers lived in large camps, moving as it suited them, always vigilant for any threat to the Cities. They felt more kinship with the elves of the north than the citizens they protected, and felt their only equals to be the present Keshian Guides and the Krondorian Pathfinders, also descended from the original

Guides. The three groups shared a traditional greeting, 'Our grandfathers were brothers,' which was to them a bond.

Many Rangers had died beside soldiers from the Kingdom and the Free Cities during the Tsurani invasion, and because their numbers had been small, it had taken a devastating toll. Alystan remembered his grandfather's stories of the Riftwar, and now he feared another threat of that magnitude was approaching; he knew another such invasion might mean the end of the Rangers.

Alystan was newly wed and as he rode through the dark pathways of the Green Heart he thought of his young wife, staying with his own mother and father as they broke winter camp down near Bordon and prepared to move up into the mountains for spring and summer. They had spoken of having their own child someday, and while they had yet to conceive, Alystan now feared that he might never see that child should his worst suspicions prove true.

The Ranger rode through the first day without incident, the patrols from Carse had kept the King's Road clear of bandits and other troublemakers. He had seen game sign, bear and elk, so he knew few hunters were nearby.

In years past, the moredhel, the Brotherhood of the Dark Path, had roamed these woods and the Grey Tower Mountains making such a ride suicide without a company of soldiers as escort. Now times were more peaceful and the worst a traveller might face was a small band of poachers or the occasional outlaw. Still, goblins roamed the Green Heart from time to time, and more than three or four could prove dangerous to a solitary rider.

Alystan made a cold camp on the first night, not wishing to

draw attention to his presence with a fire. He staked out his horse and moved some distance away, lest the animal draw unwanted attention. He risked losing the horse that way, but gained the advantage of not being surprised.

The night passed without incident.

Alystan quickly saddled his horse after inspecting it to ensure it was sound. The animal was one of the best the garrison at Carse had to offer, a solid gelding, well trained and fit. Not the fastest mount available, but one capable of long journeys at a good pace. With luck he would reach the dwarven stronghold at Caldara within three days. He mounted and returned to the road.

Three days later an exhausted rider and horse approached a gap in the mountains across which a large wooden palisade had been erected. Two dwarves stood on either side of the road, dutifully taking their turn at watch, though for years it had hardly been necessary. They waved him through, recognizing him from previous visits, and Alystan entered Caldara.

The village looked lovely in the morning light, nestled in a cosy valley. Trails led up to the high alpine meadows that were used for summer grazing, and down to lower valleys where the cattle and sheep were kept during the winter. Alystan remembered that beyond well-tended fields, a small stand of apple trees in an orchard marked the eastern boundary of the holding.

The wooden buildings were heavily thatched and plastered to keep out the winter cold. They shone pristine white in the morning sun, save for the massive longhouse that dominated the community. The King and his retainers lived there, with a large part of the local population. The longhouse was the hub of dwarven activity and on most nights any member of the community was as likely to be found sleeping on the floor of the great room before the huge fire as he was to be found in his own bed. Unlike the plastered walls, this building had been constructed in the old way: the boles of huge trees were stacked in cradles, forming the outer walls that defied both the elements and attacking enemies. The floor was made of stones laid upon the earth, flattened and smoothed so one could barely feel the joints when walking over them. But they were as impenetrable from sappers tunnelling up from below as the walls were from assaults above ground. The dwarves were miners and understood the uses of tunnels in warcraft as well as in mining.

Alystan pulled up his mount before the entrance to the longhouse and dismounted. He unsaddled his horse, and put the tack over the hitching log, then quickly wiped down the animal with a rag from his saddlebags. It would have to do until he had time to take the animal to the stables and tend to it properly. Dwarves were not horsemen, and the only horses they did keep were draught animals, all of whom would be out in the fields this time of day pulling ploughs as the dwarves readied the ground for the spring planting.

As he finished, a dwarf emerged from the building. 'Alystan of Natal!' he said with pleasure. 'What brings you our way?'

'I come to see your grandfather, Hogni. Is he inside?'

The young dwarf's grin split his long black beard. The dwarves were small compared to humans, but still broad of shoulders and powerful of frame, averaging a little over five feet in height. Nearing five feet, five inches tall, Hogni was especially tall for a dwarf. He had a merry light in his eye as he said, 'Grandfather refuses to take his rank seriously, as always. He says he's still "new to this King business" as it's "only been a little over a hundred years or so".'

'He's down in the fields ploughing. Come along, I'll take you there.'

He waved over a dwarven boy and said, 'Toddy, take that horse to grandfather's stable and see to him, will you?'

Alystan took his longbow off his shoulder and returned it to the familiar grip of his left hand. He wore a dubious expression: the horse had rendered stout service and deserved to be well treated and the boy barely reached three feet in height, topped with a shock of red-blond hair and an apple-cheeked grin; but if Hogni was confident that Toddy could somehow reach the gelding's withers and groom him sufficiently, he wasn't going to argue. The urgency of his news kept him from properly tending to the mount before seeing the King.

They quickly made their way through the village to the eastern fields where a half a dozen draught horses pulled ploughs. Crossing carefully over the new furrows, they approached a dwarf with a grey head of hair and a long grey beard. He was perspiring heavily as he wrestled the plough's iron blade through the hard soil, compacted by a winter's weight of snow and the morning's frost. The horses, like their masters, were powerful but diminutive. They looked more like broad-chested ponies than true horses, yet Alystan knew that they were a special breed of horse, used by the dwarves for centuries.

Dolgan, King of the Dwarves and Warleader of Caldara, reined in the gelding pulling his plough and waved a greeting. 'Alystan of Natal! Well met!'

'Greetings, King Dolgan. Have you no liegemen to plough your fields?'

'I do, but they're busy ploughing their own at the moment, and I wish it to be done right the first time.' He took a long, well-worn briar pipe out of his pocket and a contraption of flint and steel, a clever device traded from the Free Cities. A big spark ignited the tobacco in the pipe, and Dolgan took a long pull. He made a face and said, 'This is a useful enough gadget, but that first taste of burning flint I could do without.' He puffed again, looked more contented, and asked, 'What brings you to Caldara, Alystan?'

Alystan held his bow with the tip on the ground, a mannerism that Dolgan knew meant the Ranger was choosing his words carefully. The gesture always allowed him a moment to think. 'I bring word of something strange and troubling. I seek your wisdom and counsel.'

'Well, that sounds serious.' He tossed the reins to Hogni and said, 'Finish up here, boy, and then go help your father. I'll be in the longhouse with our guest.'

'Yes, Grandfather,' said the young dwarf with a resigned sigh. The King might prefer that the ploughing was done correctly the first time, but he also enjoyed chatting with travellers in the longhouse over a flagon of ale. The youth smiled, it was barely two hours past breakfast, hardly the time his mother would approve of her father-in-law tapping the ale keg, despite his royal station. Putting the reins over his shoulders, Hogni flipped them and shouted, 'Ha!' The horse threw one impatient glance backwards as if questioning the young dwarf's seriousness; another flick of the reins told the animal it was indeed time to return to his labours, and the animal reluctantly returned to dragging the plough through the rich mountain soil.

*   *   *

Dolgan listened carefully as Alystan finished his narrative. The old dwarf was silent for a very long time, then said, 'This is troubling news.'

'You recognize this newcomer?' asked the Ranger, before taking a long pull of the marvellous dwarven ale the King's daughter-in-law had provided. She seemed irritated to the point of saying something, but held her silence before a stranger.

Dolgan shook his head. 'No. Although I would not have recognized the so-called "mad elves" from beyond the Teeth of the World before they ventured down to Elvandar.' He turned and shouted, 'Amyna!'

Hogni's mother appeared a moment later and said, 'Yes, Father?'

'Send Toddy to find Malachi. Have him join us here, please?'

She nodded once and departed.

Dolgan said, 'Malachi is the oldest among us.' He chuckled. 'He was old when I was a boy and I'm nearing three hundred years, myself.'

Alystan barely concealed his surprise. He knew that the dwarves were a long-lived race, like the elves, but he had no idea they lived that long, or stayed as robust as they apparently did. The old dwarf seemed content to smoke his pipe, drink his morning ale, and chat of inconsequential matters, such as how his human acquaintances fared along the Far Coast and in the Free Cities, or the news from Krondor, or further afield. It was clear to the Ranger that Dolgan was keenly interested in matters outside his own small demesne, which given the dwarves' long history was understandable.

An independent people, the dwarves nevertheless found their fortunes tied closely to those of their human neighbours and to a lesser degree, the elves in the north. Twice in the last hundred years, war had visited the west; first came the Tsurani invaders in the very valley where Alystan had seen the stranger, and later the armies of the Emerald Queen, from a land across the sea. The second struggle had involved the dwarves only indirectly, but its repercussions had echoed through the land for a long time. The west had been almost forgotten by the Kingdom for a decade, trade had been reduced to a trickle, and banditry and piracy had risen. Alystan's grandfather had claimed that now things were back to the way they had been before the coming of the Tsurani; in fact, he had insisted life was better now, as the dark elves no longer hunted the Green Heart or the Grey Towers. Given the bloody history between the Rangers and the moredhel, Alystan was inclined to agree that his grandfather's view had merit.

Time passed, but Alystan, like all Rangers, possessed patience born of generations of woodcraft and hunting skill. A fidgeting hunter was a hungry one, his father had told him many years before on his first hunt.

At last Toddy returned, slowly escorting the oldest being the Ranger had ever encountered. The dwarf moved with tiny steps as if he feared losing his balance. He was shrunken with age, so he barely stood a head taller than the boy, and he was slight of frame. In contrast to the robust stature of the other dwarves the Ranger knew, his appearance was startling. His skin was parchment-white and almost translucent, so the veins of his hands stood out over his swollen knuckles. He used a cane with his right hand, and the boy held him firmly under his left arm. His receding hair fell to his shoulders, whatever colour might once have graced his ancient pate now fled, leaving snow-white wisps.

Cheeks sunken with age were marked with small lesions and sores, and Alystan knew this was a dwarf nearing the end of his days.

The old dwarf looked about the room, and the Ranger realized that he must be blind, or his vision so poor that he might as well be sightless. Those in the room remained silent as he found his seat.

Then he spoke, 'So, what reason have you, to rouse an old man from his nap?' he demanded. His voice was surprisingly strong and deep for so frail a figure.

Dolgan said, 'Malachi, this is Alystan of the Free Cities.'

'I can see he's a Ranger, Dolgan,' said the old dwarf, and Alystan reassessed his previous judgment on his eyesight. 'Well, you have something to say, else they wouldn't have required me to come here, so say it,' instructed Malachi.

Alystan retold his encounter with the strange traveller. The ancient dwarf said nothing, but leant forward slightly as if paying closer attention when the Ranger began describing the creature's true appearance.

When Alystan was finished, Malachi leaned back and let his chin drop, in thought. The room remained silent for several minutes, then the ancient dwarf said, 'It's an old tale, told by my grandfather's grandfather, from the time of the Crossing.'

Dolgan said nothing, but he glanced around the room at the other dwarves who had gathered there while Alystan had spoken. There were now perhaps twenty dwarves, most of whom Alystan recognized as being part of the King's Meet, Dolgan's council of advisors.

Malachi paused then said, 'At the end of my days, I am, but I remember this tale as if it were told to me yesterday.

'My first raid was against the dark elves to the north, who had been troubling our herds in the lower meadows when calving was underway. We had chased off a band and my father, and—' He pointed at Dolgan, '—and your father, though he had not the title of King, only Warleader, decided we needed to chastise the miscreants and let them know there would be no stealing of calves from the dwarves of Caldara!' He took a breath, and said, 'We followed the thieves for two days, and as we camped on the night before the raid, my father told me a story told to him by his grandfather.

'He said that before the Gods warred, dwarves lived on a distant world and fought long and hard against the great goblin tribes, Lea Orcha, the orcs. Our people also defended their crops and herds from gryphon and manticore and other creatures of myth. Father spoke of ancient legends, of great heroes and deeds, their truth lost even to the Lorekeepers, for he spoke of a time before the Crossing.'

Alystan said, 'The Crossing?'

The old dwarf nodded. 'A madness consumed our world, a war visited upon us by beings of power beyond our most puissant Lorekeeper's art. We know them as Dragon Lords.'

'The Valheru,' said Dolgan, thinking of his time spent with Lord Tomas during the war against the Tsurani. He had learned much Valheru lore while he watched the boy from Crydee grow into a being of unimaginable power; but he knew there was far more untold knowledge.

'Aye,' said Malachi. 'So the elves call their former masters. My father told me the very masters of that world drove us here, by design or chance no one knows. But flee our home world we did.

'Great tears opened in the heavens above and earth below, swallowing up those nearby. Some, it was said, went to other worlds, but most of us hunkered down and tried to withstand the forces of chaos on all sides.

'There were races of men on our home world, along with the great goblins and our people. It was they, these masters of magic, who constructed bridges to flee from the destruction visited upon us during the Chaos Wars.

'We lost almost everything, but this much knowledge remained: in ancient times others ranged across these lands, kin to those we warred with, but they were not those in Elvandar with whom we were at peace. He told a tale of a time when the wars on the ancient birth world forced dwarves, humans, even the magic users of the *Dena Orcha*—'

'Orcs!' spat Dolgan, as if the very word was an insult.

The Ranger looked at the old man.

'Dena Orcha in the old tongue,' said Malachi. 'The true enemy of our blood. The great goblins. None live on this world.'

'But they live in our memory,' said the Dwarf King.

Malachi waved away the comment. 'The magic users of many races banded together to save entire worlds in the time of the Mad Gods and raging Dragon Riders. They formed the Golden Bridge and many of our ancestors came to Midkemia.

'But the elves and some others, the serpent men and the tiger men, already lived here and we were met with more war and magic.

'The fighting on both sides of the Golden Bridge continued for a time without time, for the very nature of the universe was twisted and fluid.

'Then, it was over,' said the ancient dwarf, quietly.

'In days after the Crossing, but before the line of Kings was named, in the dim mists of memory, the elves told our ancestors that many of their people left this world as we had fled our own, and to the elves they were known as the Lost Elves.'

The old elf sat silently for a minute and then said, 'I can only guess, but perhaps one has returned to this world, for never have I heard of such a being before. You'd best ask the elves, for this much I know at least; many things can be said of elven magic, but I have never in my long life heard tell of them using illusion as a guise.' He said, 'If I may leave, King?'

His tone left no doubt the request was only a formality, as he turned before Dolgan waved permission.

As the old man was about to leave the chamber, Dolgan said, 'Malachi, one more question. Why did my father not speak of this to me?'

Malachi shrugged. 'You would have to be able to ask him. Your father was a quiet, thoughtful leader. He spoke very little.' Dolgan nodded. 'Unlike my father, who liked to tell stories.'

'I remember something else,' said Malachi. 'Three great bridges were built on our birth world, or so my father said his grandfather told him. Two were built by humans and dwarves, and one by the orcs. One bridge led to the Tsurani world. If any of our people crossed, no memory of them remains with the Tsurani. The second came here, and it was on that bridge that humans and dwarves came to Midkemia. The orc bridge went to another world, and so from the time of the Chaos Wars we were no longer plagued by that ancient hate. It was said that some humans and dwarves crossed with them. Perhaps,' posed the old dwarf, 'the Lost Elves built their own bridge to escape their masters?' And without waiting for an answer, Malachi left the hall.

Dolgan and the others remained silent for a long while, then Dolgan said, 'What if the Lost Elves built their own bridge to escape their masters, indeed.'

'But now one returns,' said Alystan.

'Apparently,' said Dolgan.

'Know this, wielder of Tholin's hammer,' said a voice behind them. Dolgan and the others turned to see Malachi standing in the hallway. 'One last thing,' he added, pointing a frail finger at the Dwarf King. 'It was your ancestor who led our people here, making these mountains our home. His brothers led other bands to Stone Mountain and Dorgin. Our people were once as numerous as the leaves on trees, but where one dwarf crossed the bridge from our home world, five remained to fight the madness that came to destroy our home. No one knows what that madness was, save that it shattered the world.' The old dwarf seemed fatigued from telling his story. Then, catching his breath, he began again. 'If the Lost Elves are coming to this world, you must call The Moot and prepare for the possibility of war! Since we've come to this world we've found enemies, Dolgan, and if these are the Lost Elves, and kin to our friends in Elvandar, they are also kin to the dark elves.' Dolgan nodded to Toddy to take him back to his quarters.

As the boy led Malachi away, several of the dwarves in the room nodded at his words. Hogni, Dolgan's grandson, said, 'When the Tsurani first came, when we first heard of them that night in the cave when you, Father and uncle Udell found Lord Borric hiding from the goblins, Father told me he felt an icy cold in the pit of his stomach.'

Dolgan nodded. 'I, as well; and I feel it again.'

The Ranger said, 'I can only tell you what I saw. I could put no name to that creature until this very hour. I had not heard of the Lost Elves until today.'

Dolgan said, 'It could be a coincidence. The creature might have been some other kind of being that merely looks like our own elves. After all, don't the Tsurani look like other humans? Or perhaps it *was* a human you saw, and he was simply putting on a magical guise for a mission on the other side of the rift.' He puffed on his pipe and was silent for a moment. 'Still, if it is the return of an ancient race of elves . . .'

'Caution urges you to prepare as if they are coming,' said the Ranger. 'I'm for Elvandar and the Queen and Lord Tomas.'

Dolgan fixed the Ranger with a stare, then said, 'And I'm with you. If anyone remembers those days, it will be Tomas. He often can't recall his distant past until prodded by events, and if there was ever a time for prodding a Dragon Lord, it's now.'

'You'll ride?' asked the Ranger.

Dolgan grinned. 'No. I'm old, but I'm not dead. Thick woodlands lie between here and the River Crydee, and I've yet to see a horse I couldn't run down. I'll keep up, have no fear.'

Hogni fidgeted and cleared his throat.

His grandfather fixed him with a barely hidden amused expression and said, 'What is it, boy?'

'You said that when next you went to Elvandar, I could come as well, Grandfather.' Dolgan feigned a scowl and then said, 'That I did. Get ready. And tell your father he gets to play king for a while, until I return. We leave in an hour.'

Hogni grinned and hurried to gather his travelling gear. Dolgan sighed. To Alystan, he said, 'He's very young; not quite forty years old yet.'

The Ranger, who was only a few years older, suppressed a chuckle. Then the moment of mirth passed, and the grim prospect of what they were facing returned. The room seemed colder, despite the brisk fire.

• CHAPTER FIVE •

Exodus

LAROMENDIS BEGAN HIS SPELL.
Across the vast courtyard sat a huge iron cage in which his brother rested as best he could in the blistering afternoon heat. The soldier who guarded the cage hadn't yet noticed the Conjurer's presence, so when Laromendis finished his spell and approached, the man saw not one, but two figures: the Conjurer accompanied by a guard captain.

The sentry looked quizzically at the pair, unaware that one of them was a phantom of his own imagination, and when they stopped before him, he heard the officer instruct him to draw away and give the brothers a moment of privacy. The guard nodded once, and followed the order.

Gulamendis looked up at his brother and smiled, though it

obviously pained him to do so: his lips were cracked and bleeding from the heat. 'How fare you, brother?'

Laromendis shook his head as he thrust a small water skin through the bars of the cage. 'Drink slowly,' he warned. 'I'm faring better than you, by all appearances. What happened?'

'Our master, the Regent Lord, became most vexed by the news that we had lost the outpost at Starwell and turned his wrath upon me. He already held me in the dungeon, and since he couldn't kill me and keep your service, he decided a little torment might serve to show his wrath,' Gulamendis said. He glanced at the sun, which was now lowering towards the keep. 'In an hour the shadows will cover me and I'll be all right.'

Pointing to the skin, Laromendis said, 'Hide that; it should last for a few days.' He glanced over his shoulder at the distant guard. 'I don't think they'll completely forget to give you food and water, but they may decide to let you suffer for a while. It's the mood of the times.'

'Not a lot of joy to be found,' agreed the Demon Master. Gulamendis moved the stale straw that was his bedding and hid the remaining water. 'I'm better than I look. I send Choyal into the kitchen at night to fetch me extra food and drink.' He chuckled but it came out dry and rasping. 'But imps are so stupid. One night he delivers me a delicacy from the Regent Lord's own larder, another night it will be rotten vegetables.'

'I'll do what I can to get you out.' He paused, looked his brother in the eyes and said, 'I found Home.'

His brother's expression stilled. The resemblance between them was staggering, but Gulamendis was slightly shorter, a little thinner, and had lighter, almost orange, red hair.

'What?' asked Laromendis.

'If you have found Home, what need has the Regent Lord for us?'

'There are problems,' said Laromendis, standing. 'I must leave as the guard is returning and I can't be here if a true officer arrives. The Regent Lord needs me for a while longer, and because of that you will be safe, if not comfortable.

'And I have a plan.'

The younger brother smiled. 'You always do.'

'We need to get you to Home, because not only will you be safer there, the People will also have need of your knowledge.'

'Demons?'

'Perhaps, I can say no more. If you are questioned, ignorance is your best ally.'

He turned and hurried away from the cage, nodding once at the guard who returned to watch over Gulamendis. Leaving the courtyard as quickly as he could, he made his way to his quarters. The Regent Lord had grudgingly admitted to the Conjurer's usefulness by providing him with a modest suite of two rooms, one for sleeping and the other for his study.

Laromendis kept little of value here, save for a volume of notes he had prepared before departing on his latest exploration, the journey that had taken him to Home. He sat on his bed and thumbed through the journal. Reaching the last page, he reached over to a small table, expecting to find his quill and ink. They had been moved. Someone had been in his quarters and they had read his journal.

He withheld a smile, as he expected nothing less from the Regent Lord. He wrestled with what he had heard of his distant kin on Midkemia and what his own people had become. There was much to admire about the achievements of the taredhel, but in truth, there was much apparently lost as well.

A trapper from Yabon had told Laromendis long stories about the elven forests to the west of his home, so long as the stranger paid for the ale in the tavern in Hawk's Hollow. The stories he told painted a picture of a people at one with the forest, content if not happy with their lives, and able to come and go effortlessly through the woodland. He spoke a little about elven magic, but his small amount of knowledge revealed volumes to Laromendis: The great Spellweavers and the older eldar endured!

He had left that fact out of his report to the Regent Lord, for two reasons. First he had no proof that the trapper's tale was remotely accurate, even if he felt in his bones that it was. Second, he needed to discover for himself how many of the magic users of Elvandar there were and what capabilities they possessed. A great deal of their ancient lore had been lost at the crossing of the Starbridge.

So much of it had been rooted in their spiritual links to the very soil of Home, the energies that rose from the heart and soul of the planet had been coaxed and finessed into serving the edhel, the People. Their new world had held different magic, and it had been difficult to blend that which had been brought with them and that which they found already here. The seven great trees, the Seven Stars, had been their anchor to the old magic from Home. But their new soil had been alien soil, from a world with its own rules and nature, and from the blending had come the majestic force that the taredhel had first struggled to control, but eventually had come to master.

The taredhel Spellmasters were most likely the equal of all

but the very best human and elven magic users on Midkemia, but there were so few of them left; many had paid for the survival of the People with their blood. They were honoured and remembered in the annals, but each loss weakened the People beyond measure.

More students were sent to fight the Demon Legion every year, each class less ready, less practised, and less able to withstand demon magic. If there had been any other way for the Regent Lord to find Home without utilizing 'outlaw' magic users like Laromendis and Gulamendis, he would have put them to death years ago.

The relationship between magic users in the Star Guild, the legatees of the original Spellweavers who fled from Home, and those outside that organization, had always been strained at best, and outright hostile at worse. Wild magic, broken magic, or any number of other terms had been used to describe those who came into their power without the training of the Star Guild.

The Star Guild had tended the Seven Stars for generations, seeking to bring the wild magic of Andcardia under control, and to prevent the destruction of the People. Their labour had earned them a place at the tables of power, and the most gifted among them – the Chief Magister of the Guild – sat second only to the Regent Lord in prestige and power.

In times past those like Laromendis and his brother were hunted down and murdered, or captured and indentured to the guild as 'dirt magicians' or some other demeaning epithet. But now 'dirt magicians', like Laromendis, and 'demon lovers', like his brother, were too valuable to be squandered away by bigotry. This Regent Lord wasn't a great deal more forgiving of deviant practices than his forebears, but he was a great deal more pragmatic about using talent whatever its origins.

Laromendis put away his journal, certain it would be read as soon as he left the city. He had made sure that nothing he had written would be found to be inconsistent with his report to the Regent Lord.

He stood up and looked out of the window. He was unable to see the portion of the courtyard where his brother sat imprisoned, but knew that by now the shadows covered the cage. *Just a while longer, little brother. The Regent will be reading my journal within an hour after I depart, and no matter what he may think of our arts and us, he needs us. You will be free soon*, he said, silently.

Putting away his pen and ink, he placed the journal on the small table and sat back on the bed thinking. He should try to rest, but his mind was racing.

There was so much that he hadn't told the Regent Lord, so much he had wished to share with Gulamendis and a handful of others; for this world *was* Home. Moreover, every fibre of his being sensed that somewhere to the north of that valley lay all of the answers that the People sought; if they were proved wise enough to recognize their salvation.

Though Laromendis believed that he was as dedicated to saving the People as the Regent Lord, he was aware that Undalyn suspected him of having a different agenda. Glancing at the journal once again he resisted the urge to smile; let the Regent Lord and the High Magister, and the other members of the Regent's Meeting suspect him. Let them believe his ambitions to be personal: power, glory, wealth, and the freedom of his brother; those goals they would understand. Just as long as they didn't suspect what his real aim was. His real purpose would be as alien to them as the nature of their terrible enemies to the north.

Sighing despite his iron resolve, Laromendis stood up and left his quarters. He must eat something, then be about his business quickly, for by dawn tomorrow a thousand taredhel warriors, magicians and scholars would be moving through the translocation gate into that lovely valley long ago abandoned by the Forgotten, and where the Clans of the Seven Stars would return to their ancient homeland on the world humans called Midkemia.

Laromendis stood next to the leader of the Clans of the Seven Stars as he surveyed the valley below. The Regent Lord's face was a fixed mask, but the slight sheen in his eyes and the softening around them told the Conjurer all he needed to know: the trap was sprung. Any thought of somehow saving Andcardia fled, as the ruler of the taredhel looked upon the ancient homeland of his race: Midkemia.

Undalyn waved his warleader over to his side and softly said, 'Begin.'

Warleader Kumal stood silently for a moment beside his ruler, experiencing the intense emotions that had struck every elf like a hammer's blow after they stepped through the translocation gate. Then he nodded once, turned and walked back through the portal. The Regent Lord stepped aside. Behind them a humming sound filled the air, more resonant than before, like the sound of heavy stones being dragged across the ground, producing vibrations in the soles of the Conjurer's boots. He knew his brethren on the other side of the portal were employing their arts to widen it so that the numbers waiting on the other side might pass through with more haste.

Pointing down the game trail that marked the edge of this clearing in the hills, the Conjurer said, 'My lord, in the vale below stands a vacant stockade of familiar design. I judge the Forgotten once lived within it, and with little effort it can be made to serve us now. Beyond this immediate area are more campsites, for the stockade will only serve temporarily as your court, and no more than a thousand can occupy the vale until more shelters are built. I have marked the trails so that the trackers can lead bands to those campsites. They will serve as a defensive perimeter until the city walls can be erected.'

To the warleader, Undalyn said, 'Let them begin. I want lookouts posted in the hills above us, sentries in the passes below. Let the workers build signal towers so the outer settlements can be summoned when needed. Send out hunting parties and let it be known that no member of the Clans must be spied by human, elf, or dwarf, or I will have his head on a pike before my throne. Any who discover us must die before word can spread to others that we have returned. We shall decide when our cousins to the north and the lesser races discover that the true masters of this world have returned.

'The day will come when we will rid this land of our enemies,' he said, looking back at the portal as it ceased its expansion and the first soldiers came through. Each wore the Clans armour: a heavy metal breastplate, pale yellow in hue, with peaked shoulders. The pale golden colour came from the metals used to forge them, a blend that the taredhel smiths guarded closely, and which provided their warriors with protection stronger and lighter than steel. Each breastplate was trimmed in the clan colours, one hue for each of the Seven Stars, one for each colour in the rainbow. Upon the heads of the standard-bearers rested crested helms, more ornate than functional and topped with a plume dyed in the colour of their clan. The infantry carried their more functional helms tied to their belts.

The first hundred soldiers hurried away from the portal, splitting into squads, each led by a tracker who led them to various positions around the valley. Within hours, camps and watch stations would be in position and a secure perimeter would be thrown up around the valley. The taredhel bridgehead would be established.

Laromendis watched patiently as heavy-bodied horses pulled massive wagons through the gate, laden with females and the young. These were refugees from the outer villages and strongholds that had already fallen before the demon horde.

The children were silent, but their eyes were wide with wonder. There was something in the very air of this world that called to each elf as they returned to their ancestral soil; the Conjurer could only liken it to a reawakening of something deep within their souls that had been dormant for generations.

The Regent Lord knelt, removed his gauntlets and picked up a handful of soil. He lifted it to his nose, sniffed and said, 'This land is rich with life. We shall reclaim our home, no matter what.' He fell silent, reflecting for a moment, then he turned to Laromendis. 'This is our world,' whispered the Regent Lord. 'Our world.' He looked at the first ragged refugees, and shook his head. Those in the city would be the last through, with the defenders who still held the demons at bay, giving their lives to save the last of their kin. A play of emotions flickered across the ruler's face, before he again composed his mask. He said, 'We must rest, recover and grow, for we have lost too much in recent years.'

Removing his fur mantle, as the day's heat grew, he took a deep breath. 'The air here is sweet, despite the dwarves and others using it.' He chuckled at his own joke.

Moving closer to his ruler's side, the Conjurer lowered his voice so that those emerging from the portal would not hear him over the wagons' rumble, 'Sire, there is but one other troubling matter.'

'Tell me,' said the Regent Lord.

'As I said before, there have been rumours of demons . . .'

The Regent Lord's eyes closed as if he was in pain. Softly, as if he could hardly bear to utter the words, he said, 'I had put that out of my mind.' He regarded Laromendis and asked, 'Here, as well?'

'They are only rumours. I have seen no demon sign personally; and as you know, I have diligently searched for any hint that they are here. Still, I lack certain arts that others possess, which would ensure the demons were absent.'

The Regent Lord looked at the wagons as they continued to rumble through the portal, more warriors appeared as well, flanking the caravan of taredhel females and young. There was hardly one fighter without a wound or damage to his armour. The People had been battling the Demon Legion for almost one hundred years; millions had perished. At one time the taredhel ruled the stars, travelling through magic gates from world to world. But the demons had reduced their millions to thousands and now the very last of their kind sought refuge on a world known only through ancient lore, a world upon which they had abided in hallowed antiquity, before the time the gods warred and chaos reigned.

The Conjurer smiled. 'Yes, my lord. It is rich with life here;

and much of it is familiar. There are deer and bear, lions and wyverns; game is plentiful. The corn tastes oddly sweet, but not unpleasantly so, and the dwarves, for all their despicable flaws, sell their brews to any and all. The humans and dwarves have herds of cattle and sheep, and the seas are abundant as well. Here lie riches beyond what we've known in a century.' Then he fell silent.

The Regent Lord stood and said, 'You have something to say. Say it.'

'My lord,' said the Conjurer, 'if I offend you, take my head, but as I am sworn to serve, I must speak only truth: If the rumours are true, or if the demons follow us here, we will be left with two choices: to flee and leave the humans, dwarves and our primitive cousins to battle the Legion, yet again seeking another world—'

'Where?' injected the Regent Lord. 'I read every report. You have found no alternative, only harsh, barren places where life scarcely survives . . . no, there is nowhere else for us to go.'

'—Or we stay and fight.'

The Regent Lord said, 'When my father was a boy, the Seven Clans numbered two million swords, Conjurer.' He watched as more wagons and beasts of burden emerged from the portal. Livestock was now being driven through, a herd of razor-spine hogs, herded by wolf-like dire dogs. An especially large canine loped through the portal and came to the Regent Lord's side, licking the monarch's hand while wagging its bushy tail.

Roughly patting the beast's massive neck, the Regent Lord almost crooned as he knelt and said, 'Sanshem, my good companion.' He looked fondly upon the animal, perhaps the only being in all creation for whom the Regent Lord felt genuine affection.

Looking back at the Conjurer, he continued, 'When my father took the throne, four hundred and twenty thousand swords could answer the call of the taredhel battle horn.'

'When I took the crown from my father's brow, *after demons had ripped his still-beating heart from his chest*—' He almost shouted '—I had less than a third of that number to call upon!' He stood up, patting the dog on its massive head. 'Since our last battle, we have less than half that number again, and not all are full warriors.' He shook his head in open regret. 'We have trained our young to fight; children barely more than babes have smelled our blood and the stench of demons since their birth!'

He gazed down into the lush forest below and said, 'I am torn, Conjurer. The Demon Legion seems endless. No matter how many we kill, more appear. If they were to follow us, how could we stand here in this valley, behind wooden walls calked with mud, when we could not hold the massive walls of Starwell, or keep them at bay with the death towers along the Gap of Doom? The Pamalan Dome soon collapsed and their flyers descended on the city like an evil hailstorm. All of the magic known to the taredhel defends Tarendamar, its defences are unmatched in our history, yet the demons keep coming.

'I thought perhaps we might linger for a while upon this world, while we sought another refuge, but then I came to see it.' He looked around the valley as the trees rustled in the breeze and birds darted across the sky. The only other sound was the rumbling of wagons and the tread of boots on the soil. He took a deep breath. 'No, this is where we shall stand; if they follow, we have no other choice. Here we shall live or die as the Goddess wills it.'

The Conjurer nodded. It was not the right time to say what

he must. Soon, but not today. Not after fleeing the Demon Legion across the tundra of Mistalik, being hounded for months by creatures so foul and powerful that only the mightiest warriors could delay them and only the most powerful magic could destroy them.

As the line of refugees continued to issue from the portal, the Conjurer knew one thing above all else: for the People to survive in this new land, no matter how abundant and hospitable, they would need allies. Which meant that generations of making war upon those not of the People would need be forgotten, and aggression as a way of life needed to be set aside.

The Regent Lord nodded to one of his heralds standing near the portal. The servant bowed slightly and darted through the magic opening. A moment later he returned, followed by a dozen older elves dressed in the guild cloth of the geomancers.

Laromendis knew that they were needed to repair the damage to the city defences on Andcardia, and he knew what their presence here meant: these few remaining masters of earth magic would begin to build a new city, in the heart of this valley. The repairs to the last bastion of Andcardian defence had been left to the lesser masters and apprentices. It was an admission of defeat that the Regent Lord had yet to voice.

A group of elders made their way through the small crowd and came to stand before their Regent Lord, bowing as one. To the oldest of them Undalyn said, 'Oversee the creation of our new home. Begin at once. Defend the valley and start down there.' He pointed to a distant rise that overlooked the small lake at the centre of the valley. 'Around that lake we shall plant the Seven Stars. On that rise you shall build a new palace.' He looked around, as if fixing the sights of Home in his mind. 'All who can be brought here will arrive within the month, and then we shall seal this portal behind us.

'I shall return to Andcardia to oversee the fighting. We will hold the demons at bay for as long as possible.' To the Conjurer he said, 'What do you need to discover the truth about demons here?'

Taking a breath, he simply answered, 'My brother. No one among the People knows more of demon lore than he, my lord—' As the Regent Lord was about to object, Laromendis hurried to cut him off, '—I know there are many who see him as the cause of the demon invasion . . .'

'If that were true,' said the Regent Lord, 'he would already be dead. I do not think that he personally summoned the Demon Legion, Conjurer. But I do believe it was the meddling of those like him and yourself into realms prohibited by the Spellcrafters that caused the magic barriers to be breached.' The Conjurer almost winced at that, for he knew there had been no breach; somewhere a gate had been opened between the realms, and if that could be found . . . He quickly turned his mind back to the Regent Lord, who said, 'No. I must hold him against your good behaviour.'

'You have my pledge, my lord.'

Breathing deeply, the Regent Lord looked around once more inhaling the sights, smells, and sounds of Midkemia in his memory before he returned to the struggle.

'Very well,' he said finally. 'Return with me and change places with him, Laromendis. You shall be his guarantee.'

'Ah—' began the Conjurer.

Smiling, the Regent Lord said, 'When the very last of the People are through the translocation portal, then shall I free you to be with your brother. Until then, you are going to use your talents to defend against the Demon Legion.'

Laromendis nodded; there would be no dungeon or cage in the courtyard for him; he would be at the battlements sending demons back to whatever hell they came from. 'Very well, my lord. I wish to serve in whatever way you judge right.'

The Regent Lord stepped around a wagon and through the magic curtain. Keeping his features still, the magic user followed his ruler, satisfied that his plan was almost underway. He knew he had to steal one minute alone with his brother, no more, and then he could gladly give his life to save the People. But he prayed to an ancient goddess that his sacrifice wouldn't be necessary, for to truly safeguard their future, his particular arts, those of his brother and of many others who were considered less than elven by the Regent Lord, would be needed.

And to do that, changes needed to be instituted, and quickly.

And that required a little treason.

He stepped through the portal and vanished.

• CHAPTER SIX •

Premonition

*P*UG CAST HIS SPELL.

The assembled students watched in rapt attention as a column of energy rose above the master sorcerer, speeding upwards unseen. They could still sense the energy, and some, more attuned to the magic arts than others, could almost feel it radiating on their skin. He was teaching them a basic skill, one usually left to those whose time was less valuable to the Conclave of Shadows, but Pug felt the need to be in the classroom from time to time. The lesson was a simple one: how to feel the presence of magic, and locate it when it was employed nearby. Over the years he had been astonished to discover that many magicians and magical clerics didn't realize a fireball had been cast until the flames had singed their hair.

Young men and women from many nations, and a few from

alien worlds, had gathered here to study under the tutelage of the greatest practitioner of the arcane arts on Midkemia. Today's lesson was on perception and reaction to changes in magic, and the first step was mastering the ability to recognize when magic was being deployed. The skill might seem rudimentary to most of the students, but the three people who observed the lesson from a short distance away knew better: it was the first step in learning how to react to hostile magic; instant recognition of changing magic often kept a magician alive.

Magnus turned to his brother and mother and said, 'He seems to be fine.'

Miranda shook her head. '*Seems* is the operative word. It's another bout of melancholia.'

'Nakor?' asked Caleb.

Miranda nodded. 'I don't know; maybe. It's been almost ten years, and he hides it well, but those black moods come upon him still.'

Caleb, Pug and Miranda's younger son, said, 'Marie notices it, too.' His wife was a perceptive woman and in the ten years since she had arrived on Sorcerer's Island, had become something of the mistress of the household, a position Miranda was more than happy to cede to her, as she had her magical studies to conduct.

Magnus said, 'I was there, and no one could have done more than Father did. Nakor chose his fate.' Quietly, he added, 'As much as any of us can choose.'

Miranda's dark eyes showed a mixture of distress for her husband's pain, and irritation, an expression both sons knew well. A tender-hearted woman at times, but she could also be as impatient as a child.

'Nakor?' asked Caleb again.

'He misses him,' agreed Miranda. 'More than he'd like anyone to know. That bandy-legged little vagabond had a unique mind and even when I was furious with him he could make me laugh.' She paused and turned away, motioning for her sons to follow her down the hill and back towards the main villa. 'During the ten years since his death, your father has uttered Nakor's name once or twice a month. But he has mentioned him half a dozen times in the last week. Something is on his mind, something new and troubling.'

Villa Beata, 'the beautiful home', had grown over the years. The large square house still commanded the heart of the vale in which it nestled, but along the ridge, other buildings had been constructed, providing housing and study space for the students whom Pug had recruited. Miranda, Caleb and Magnus made their way down a long winding path towards what had once been the perimeter garden on the original property; it was now flanked on the north and south by barracks-like student housing.

Magnus said, 'If Father is anticipating some new trouble, he's not mentioned it to me or anyone else, as far as I can tell.'

Caleb said, 'I've seen or heard nothing to suggest that our present tranquillity is in peril.'

Miranda said, 'There's always peril. Sometimes we simply don't see it coming.'

Caleb smiled and said nothing. He had been given the responsibility, along with his brother and a pair of younger magicians, of coordinating the intelligence gathered by the Conclave of Shadows' numerous agents, many of whom were placed in high offices throughout the major nations of Midkemia. There were reports of political rumblings in the Kingdom of the Isles, but they were so frequent that it wasn't seen as a major concern. Kesh was unusually tranquil, and Roldem's nobility continued to sit comfortably on their island, secure in their own sense of superiority.

They reached the villa and once inside, walked to the family's quarters, now occupied only by Pug and Miranda since their sons had grown to manhood. Caleb lived nearby with his wife in a small house that Miranda had built for them when her son had first brought Marie to Sorcerer's Island. Magnus still lived in the heart of the students' wing on the large estate, to be on hand should the need arise when his father was absent.

Sitting in her favourite chair, a large wooden one with upholstered seat and back, Miranda said, 'Something more than Nakor's death has been haunting your father for years.' She glanced at her 'boys'; only Caleb looked his age, now well into his middle years, while Magnus still looked much as he had in his twenties, despite his snow-white hair and seniority. Neither son betrayed any hint that they knew of what she spoke.

'No one knows your father like I do,' said Miranda. 'Yes, he's a man of deep feelings and convictions, as well you both know.' She pointed first at Magnus then at Caleb. 'But what you don't know is what happened to him before you were born, during the war with the Emerald Queen's army. He nearly died when the demon's magic took him by surprise.' She looked away as she remembered. 'I can't persuade him to tell me much about that time, he lay near death and every healer we could find worked frantically to save him, but something in him changed after that.

'Nakor's death . . .' She stopped and said, 'Of course he was saddened by it, but this is not . . .' Again she paused, choosing her words carefully. 'It's more than wistful regret. Your father is the most complex man I've known. He sees things, considers options, and makes choices before most men even understand what it is they are seeing. 'His mind works in ways that I can't begin to fathom. Oh, most of the magic disciplines—' she glanced at Magnus, '—I recognize, but beyond that. . . .'

She caught her breath, realizing that she was no closer to sharing her concerns than she had been minutes before. It was Caleb who said, 'He's waiting for the other boot.'

Magnus said, 'What?'

'The old expression, "waiting for the other boot to drop".' Still his older brother didn't seem to understand. 'Comes from you wearing sandals, I suppose,' said Caleb with a smile. 'When you're at an inn and someone in the room above kicks off a boot before going to bed, you hear the first one hit the floor and you wait until you hear the second before your mind can return fully to what it was doing before.'

Magnus nodded. 'He does appear distracted from time to time.'

'Preoccupied,' said his mother. 'He just hides it well from everyone, but me.'

'Perhaps Father is anticipating something?' Magnus said. He glanced out the window at the warm afternoon sun, 'Well, as you said, he masks it well.'

Caleb shrugged at his mother. 'Why don't you ask him what he expects?'

'You think I haven't?' She stood up and walked over to her younger son. Looking into his eyes, she said, 'He is adroit at not telling me what he doesn't want me to know.' She smiled ruefully. 'I always tell him to mind his own affairs and leave me alone. He's more diplomatic in his avoidance.' With an aggravated sound she added, 'I hate it when he does that!'

Her sons laughed. Their parents loved one another deeply, but both Magnus and Caleb were aware that their parents' marriage was occasionally tense. Their mother was a strong-willed woman and older than her husband, though when both parents were over a century, the age difference became mostly academic. Still, they both knew that something else was bothering their father.

Pug had assumed a huge amount of responsibility over the years since he had returned to Midkemia from his life on the now extinct world of Kelewan. First he had ended the terrible war between the Tsurani and the Kingdom of the Isles, and then he had founded the colony of magicians called Stardock.

Magnus said, 'He has been visiting Stardock more often than usual.'

When Stardock had become rife with political intrigue, he had quietly started his school here on Sorcerer's Isle. The outside world considered the island a damned place, and ships from all nations gave it a wide berth; an attitude that Pug encouraged with deftly planted rumours and the occasional frightening display should a ship venture too close.

Pug was close to achieving his dream, creating the place he originally intended Stardock to be: an academy where magicians could study and practise their arts, exchange information and leave a legacy of knowledge to be passed on to future generations of magic users. This was the mandate he wished to leave as his personal legacy; Pug wished to perfect a haven for those who wished to be free of petty politics, the bigotry of superstition, a place where students were inculcated with the desire to serve and benefit others, rather than use their talents for personal aggrandizement, gain, or dominion.

Miranda said, 'I count that as another sign he's worried. He rarely bothers to visit them, unless he's summoned. He's fairly pleased with the current political situation.'

'He had good reason,' said Caleb. 'That envoy from the Kingdom who offered some nonsense . . . What was it?'

'As soon as Father learned that it once again involved us pledging fealty to the Kingdom, he rejected it,' reminded Magnus.

Miranda nodded. 'He wouldn't even hear the man out. He didn't tell me, the last time I was at Stardock one of the students took evil delight in explaining how the envoy from the Kingdom suddenly found himself in the lake, about a hundred yards off the docks at Landreth.'

Caleb laughed. 'I assume the poor man could swim, else we'd be at war with the Kingdom by now. Drowning their envoys doesn't sit at all well with kings.'

Magnus said, 'They would never start an open war with Stardock. They still fear magic too much, and with that many spell casters . . .' He left the thought unfinished.

Miranda said, 'The King's men are often stupid, but rarely are they suicidal.'

Pug had learned some bitter lessons from the Academy. He had eventually bequeathed daily control of Stardock to those who lived there, angering the Kingdom of the Isles who had considered the island in the middle of the Great Star Lake to be one of their minor holdings, though its elevation to the status of Duchy simply served their own political ends.

To the south, the Empire of Great Kesh had sought to ensure

their interests were served by persuading many young practitioners of magic to seek refuge at Stardock, while retaining
their loyalty to the Empire. The two brothers, Watoom and
Korsh, had almost succeeded in convincing the majority of
students that Kesh's claim to the island was legitimate. Only
Nakor's time at the Academy, and his formation of a third faction,
which he had mirthfully called the Blue Riders to honour the
gift of a beautiful horse and blue cloak from the Empress herself,
restored a precarious balance and stopped the brothers, who Pug
was now convinced long after their deaths had been Imperial
agents.

He had visited the Academy occasionally, always with two
aims in mind; first he wished everyone there to remember he
still held official title to the island, even though he had renounced
his claim to Kingdom nobility. Secondly, he wished to maintain
contact with a handful of Conclave agents and keep an eye on
whatever nonsense the ruling triumvirate – the current leaders
of the three factions – were up to.

The 'Hands of Korsh' were the most conservative group, but
they were as opposed to becoming a province of the Empire as
they were of joining the Kingdom. But they also perceived all
non-magic users, and anyone outside their faction as possible
enemies.

'The Wand of Watoom' were more moderate in their policies
towards general outsiders, but decidedly pro-Keshian in their
world-view.

The Blue Riders continued to delight Pug, for their leadership always seemed to reflect Nakor's slightly mad and manic
views on magic. Many of them had adopted his notion that there
really wasn't any magic, but only some mystical "stuff" that could

be manipulated by anyone once they managed to achieve a certain level of familiarity with it.

They were the group almost entirely responsible for recruiting new students, while the more conservative factions waited until someone who met their more rigid standards of acceptance arrived at Stardock. Pug was always grateful for their closed-mindedness, for it allowed the Blue Riders more opportunity to keep the island's population in balance.

Caleb said, 'If Father's spending more time there, something is undoubtedly wrong. Either he's alerting our agents to be on the watch for something, or they've told him that something's already happening.'

Magnus said, 'No, he would have said something to one or all of us.' He glanced out of the window, as the breeze rustled the leaves of the old trees sheltering the building from the afternoon heat. 'No, it's something else.'

The mother and her two sons were silent as they pondered what could be disturbing Pug so deeply that despite his attempts to disguise his distress, they all could see it. Miranda finally stood and said, 'Well, we can be certain of one thing: when your father judges it time to share his worries, he will be totally forthright, and whatever he's worried about will be a very big problem.'

She left the room and the brothers exchanged nods, for they knew she was probably making an understatement. Whatever worried their father was likely to be more approaching disaster than problem.

Pug dismissed his class and gathered up the few items he had used to demonstrate the lessons of the day. He knew his family had been observing them for a while, and was nearly certain of the reason. He had attempted to conceal some grave concerns from them, but had obviously failed. Still, today he was reluctant to assume things worse than he already knew them to be; today he would finally come to grips with the cause of his worries: a summons from the Oracle of Aal.

But it was more than the missive, it was also the way in which it had arrived; one moment Pug had been alone in his study, writing notes late into the night, and the next a figure in a white robe had appeared at his side. As soon as he saw the man, he had recognized him as one of the consorts or companions of the Oracle. Conventional human concepts were only an approximation. For the Aal, gender was a function of legacy, their bodies were human, so their physical makeup was familiar, yet their spirits and minds were alien. Pug had felt cautious at first, for the Oracle had taken the dying body of a great dragon, her golden scales fused with a riot of gemstones welded by furious magic unleashed in the heat of battle, as the dragon and its rider, Tomas, heir to the power of the Valheru, had confronted the most dangerous of creatures: a Dread Lord.

That battle had been fought over a century before, yet for Pug it might as well have been yesterday. He could still conjure vivid memories of the chaos that had surrounded him, of Macros the Black, and the two Tsurani magicians who had joined him in trying to stem the return of the assembled host of the Valheru, the Dragon Lords, to Midkemia.

That battle beneath the long-abandoned city of Sethanon had been but the first of many encounters with agents of the Nameless One, Nalar, God of Evil; the agent behind the Chaos Wars and the subsequent battles waged by Pug and his allies.

He paused to gather his thoughts. The strangest thing about

the summons wasn't its personal delivery, but that he hadn't been asked to come at once. He had been summoned to appear before the Oracle upon a date nearly a month away. And now the day was upon him.

Pug considered letting Miranda know what was occurring, but for some reason he felt it best to hear the Oracle first, then deal with his wife's moods. She would certainly wish to come with him, but neither her name, nor Magnus's had been mentioned.

Besides, his previous encounters with the Oracle had tended to be short, the longest lasting barely half an hour. He would be back before the evening meal.

For ten years he had been practising the art of transporting himself without the use of the Tsurani orbs. They were becoming increasingly rare as the years passed since the destruction of Kelewan. A few artificers from Kelewan had immigrated to LaMut, but most who survived the destruction of their home planet now lived on New Kelewan.

Though he would never admit it, Pug hated the fact that his wife was able to transport herself effortlessly to places she barely knew, while he had to muster all of his concentration.

Still, the chamber of the Oracle was unique and he had been there many times over the years. It should present him little difficulty to move there now. And now was the time to go.

Pug closed his eyes and willed himself to the chamber; as he appeared, he heard the voice of the Oracle within his mind.

Welcome, sorcerer. Your timing is perfect.

As Pug turned to regard the majesty of the gem-encrusted great golden dragon, a screech loud enough to make her companions cover their ears tore through the room.

Something appeared between Pug and the Oracle, a shadowy form at first, which rapidly resolved into a figure. A demon, at least twenty feet in height, stood motionless for an instant, disoriented by the magic that had brought it to this place. But its confusion lasted but a moment. It quickly surveyed the room, judging the little figures around it as scant risk, then it turned its attention to the Oracle.

With a bellow that echoed in the vast chamber, the demon launched itself at the great golden dragon.

CHAPTER SEVEN

Prophesy

P UG UNLEASHED A SPELL.

As the demon took a step towards the Oracle's dragon form, a searing hot band of energy lashed out at it, wrapping around the demon's torso like a lasso. Evil-smelling black smoke erupted where it touched the creature's skin.

The demon towered over everyone in the cavern, save for the Oracle. It had scales like a lizard or serpent, mottled red and violet. Its shoulders were massive and the creature's arms ended in huge black talons; its ape-like face wore a mask of hatred and rage. It let forth with a roar that caused the walls of the cavern to shake, loosening soil that rained down on everyone.

Huge fangs protruded down from an exaggerated upper lip, and the demon's head was adorned with two long black horns tapering backwards, like those of an antelope. It shook its head in frustration and howled in outrage at being confined and injured.

Pug had limited experience with demons, and all of it bad. He did not hesitate to follow his confinement spell with the most powerful assault he could muster.

Tendrils of flaming white and purple energy shot forward, waving like the tentacles of a squid as they latched on to the creature's body. As each touched the demon's hide more acrid black smoke was released and a tiny flame of dull orange shot upwards.

The demon trembled as it fought against its confinement, then howled again in outrage and burst the binding spell. The shock that reverberated back through the tether struck Pug's mind like a physical blow.

The Oracle's mystic powers were nothing like the battle magic the greater dragons of Midkemia possessed, but she was still a force to fear. She lashed out with claws and teeth, sinking them deep into the demon's shoulder at its neck. Fountains of steaming black blood erupted and flowed down its back and chest as it lashed out over its shoulder with the opposite claw, raking her muzzle, aiming to blind her.

Pug recovered from the shock of the magical backlash and sent out a spear of energy. This was one he had never employed before save in practice in an isolated part of his island.

The invisible energy filled the cavern with a hissing noise, counterpoint to the shouts and screams of the Oracle's companions as they hurled themselves at the demon.

They were not without their own magic and strength, and although the first companion to reach the demon was eviscerated with one claw, the next two were able to cause some injury. The dragon's maw held fast on the creature's shoulder, while Pug and the companions inflicted as much damage as possible.

The invisible energy spear struck the demon full in the chest; it stiffened, as if it had been run through by cold iron. The creature's mouth moved, and Pug suspected it was attempting some type of incantation. But the spell was too much for it; its eyes rolled up into its skull and the demon fell limp.

For a moment the Oracle held fast to the creature, now as limp as a child's doll, then it released its hold. Pug saw gashes in the dragon's snout, blood flowed freely to drip upon the still carcass, but the wounds looked relatively trivial.

'Stand back!' instructed Pug as the Oracle's companions continued to attack the fallen demon. 'Back!' he commanded as calm returned to the room.

As he anticipated, the demon's body began to smoke and smoulder and then a sudden flash of crimson flame, gone almost as soon as it was perceived. A stench of brimstone and putrefaction filled their nostrils and several of the remaining companions fell back, physically repelled by the odour.

Pug turned towards the towering form of the Oracle of Aal and asked, 'You wanted to see me?'

Over the years Pug and the Oracle of Aal had forged a trusting relationship, though Pug had never been convinced their aims were always the same. The Oracle, despite appearing as a mighty dragon, was more alien to the world of Midkemia than any creature he had ever encountered.

The Aal were rumoured to be the oldest life forms in the universe; no other race could trace their lineage back as far. Even the Dragon Lords at the height of their power gave the Aal a wide berth and left them in peace.

When Pug had first encountered them, they were a doomed race, as the world upon which they resided was nearing the end of its long life. He had offered those who remained safe passage to Midkemia, and through a series of circumstances the Oracle had found a host in the mindless body of Midkemia's single greatest creature: a golden dragon.

Her companions found willing hosts among men and women of diverse backgrounds. They were sought over the years by arcane arts that even Pug didn't understand, and offered the unique chance to hold a place in this world, as a servant and companion to the Oracle.

Pug allowed himself to believe that the selection involved no coercion, that those who were here had been willing; it let him sleep better at night. But whatever their reasons, the beings in this cave had been willing to sacrifice their lives to protect this unique creature.

Pug had visited this cavern many times, yet he still had only a vague idea of their history and place in the order of things. His direct questions were always answered vaguely, and eventually he came to accept that he would only find out what the Oracle wished him to know. He was content with that, for she had proven to be a valuable ally in the defence of his world upon more than one occasion. He could have believed her aid to be born of self-interest, for if this world perished, she would die along with it, but he judged her motives to be loftier than that; she seemed genuinely concerned with helping Pug and his Conclave re-establish a semblance of order in this part of a very big universe.

All this ran through Pug's mind as he waited for the Oracle to reply. She laid her head down on the floor so that her companions could tend to her wounds. Two lay dead and would be disposed of as soon as she was healed.

Pug watched fascinated as magic he barely recognized, let alone understood, was employed. He had seen enough clerical magic to recognize the healing arts, but this manipulation was unlike anything he had witnessed before.

Each companion tending a wound seemed to encourage the dragon's body to repair itself, but at an accelerated rate. But the price was dear; those ministering to the dragon aged before Pug's eyes, their faces becoming sallow and haggard, the weight melting from their bodies. They were giving her their life essence. As he watched, her wounds healed, after five minutes their mistress was left looking as she had before the attack. They, however, had aged years in minutes.

'Impressive,' said Pug.

'We are an old race with many gifts.' Indicating the bodies of her fallen companions who were being carried off, she added, 'But we have limits, too.'

'Can I assume this encounter was the reason you specifically requested my appearance today?'

'What is, is as it should be, as it was, and as it will be again.' Slowly she rose up, and stared distantly into space as she received visions that no other could witness.

'Even for you that's unusually cryptic, my old friend,' said Pug.

The Oracle stood silently for a long time.

Finally Pug said, 'Ah, I see. I must ask. What else troubles you?'

'Much, sorcerer. I see a nexus approaching, a blending of time and probability, a place of many outcomes. Beyond that I can see nothing, too many possibilities flow from that moment. Or an end, should the worst outcome occur.'

'Worst for you or for all of us?'

'They are one and the same. Should I fall, this world will have fallen with me.

'I see havoc and destruction and the deaths of many, on a scale which dwarfs all that you've endured; and I see the tipping of a precious balance, one which will cause the gods themselves to tremble in fear.'

'I'm listening,' said Pug quietly. Already his skin crawled in anticipation of having his suspicions confirmed. Summoning demons as powerful as the one he had just faced required prodigious magic. Confining one was difficult enough, but to be able to subdue, then send a creature like that by magic means into this cavern, required a Demon Master of unmatched skill and power.

'A legion comes this way, Pug of Sorcerer's Island. It rides hard and brings chaos and death in its wake. Others battle it already, and they yield grudgingly, but they will soon be overwhelmed.

'The Dark One, he whose name cannot be uttered, sleeps restlessly, and in his fevered dreaming he reaches out with the power of a Greater God. He has envisioned a passage between the realms, and as he dreams, it is so. He dreams of home and wishes to return.

'The other Greater Gods soothe his restlessness, and stem his dreams, but they are overmatched. Only she who balances him can stop the madness.'

Pug felt a cold tightening in his chest. 'And she is dead,' said Pug.

'She is,' said the Oracle, 'yet even in death she provides, for her legacy lives on, in the hearts of those who serve good.

'Find allies, Pug. Find those whom you have never sought out. Seek strength where you are weak, and find those who have knowledge where you are ignorant. Understand what comes soon.'

The Oracle's head lowered again to the floor and Pug knew from experience that her vision had drained her. He had time for one, perhaps two more questions, and then she would enter a slumber which could last for days, even weeks. Once she had awakened, those visions would be lost.

Pug's mind raced as he thought of a dozen things he wished to ask. He finally said, 'Tell me of the legion that approaches.'

'Demons from the Fifth Circle, Pug. The demons are coming.'

The hair on Pug's neck rose; after the many things he had seen in his very long life he was surprised to find that he could still be shocked. The attacking demon had not been the minion of some powerful human agency, it had been a scout, an assassin from the demon realm, sent to rid their target world of their most powerful ally: forewarning.

Pug had fought demons before; one had almost killed him. He had also witnessed the final struggle between Macros the Black and the Demon King Maag. Imagining a legion of such creatures numbed his mind, visiting upon him a sense of despair that he rarely experienced. Even during the darkest moments of his life he had retained hope, and had always sought to survive until he could seize an opportunity. But this was an onslaught beyond imagining.

Even the danger posed by the Dasati paled in comparison to the denizens of the Fifth Circle. The grass wilted under their heels, and their touch would burn flesh. Only demons with powerful magic could contrive to exist in this realm, and the scope of that magic was majestic. Pug knew that for a legion of demons to enter this realm meant that they faced a repeat of what happened on the Saaur home world: utter and complete destruction.

'Who do I need to seek out—' Pug began, but then saw that the dragon eyes were closed.

He glanced around the room and saw the silent companions watching him. They could provide no further aid, so he merely nodded a farewell and transported himself back to his study.

His wife was waiting. When he appeared she said, 'Oh, there you are. I felt you depart and was about to get very angry with you.'

He could tell Miranda was making light of her worry, she exhibited genuine concern. 'I went to see the Oracle,' said Pug, flatly

The tightening of her eyes communicated she understood that he had heard nothing good.

'We need to find someone who knows a lot about demons,' said Pug.

Magnus and Miranda stood while Caleb sat opposite his father. Pug had just finished recounting the Oracle's warning and Miranda said, 'You're right. We need a Demon Master.'

Magnus shook his head. 'They are . . . difficult to find.'

Mastery over demons was one of the forbidden arts, others

included necromancy and arcane life. All existed outside the bounds of respectable magic, requiring misery and pain at their least malignant, death and the rending of the very soul at their most terrible.

During his life, Pug had encountered three magic users who used the precious life force of others for their own dark purposes. Leso Varen, also known as Sidi, Pug's long-time adversary, had been a necromancer, as had a magician named Dahakan whom Nakor had encountered, and the false dark elf prophet, Murmandamus. Animating the dead to do their bidding had been the least of their offences. Stealing fleeing spirits as bodies died created disharmony of staggering proportions in the universe.

Arcane life was the distortion of living creatures, modified to the magician's whim. Humans were sometimes given bestial powers, or animals blended into improbable creatures. Only necromancy was more evil.

Demon Masters were more of a mystery, for often the advantages they gained from their practice came at a high price. Controlling demons was not seen as inherently evil, but it was still considered a dark art, as little good ever came of keeping a demon minion.

Pug sighed. 'We need to send word to our agents to start reporting any rumours of demons or summoners.'

Caleb rose and said, 'I'll do so at once.' As he started towards the door, he paused and said, 'I think I remember something . . .' He returned to his father's desk, which he occupied when Pug was not at the school. Riffling through papers, he said, 'Yes, there was a report from Muboya; about a magic user banishing demons for a fee.' He smiled ruefully. 'They appear and then the magician arrives fortuitously.'

Magnus said, 'A confidence scam, no doubt.'

'We should still investigate it,' said Pug. To Caleb he said, 'You are in charge. I'm going to see to this myself.' He turned to Miranda and Magnus. 'If you don't mind, Miranda, can you see if there's anything at Stardock on demon lore?' To his elder son he said, 'And you should talk to the monks at That Which Was Sarth.'

Both nodded agreement and Miranda vanished.

Pug turned to both his sons and said, 'I was about to add, "after lunch."'

They chuckled, but in the wake of what their father had just told them, it was false mirth.

• CHAPTER EIGHT •

Demon Master

*G*ULAMENDIS FROZE.

The feeling that greeted him as he stepped through the portal to Midkemia was unexpected. He stood silently drinking in the vista, his travel bag thrown over his left shoulder and his brother's staff in his right hand. He knew the Regent Lord had ordered some geomancers away from repairing the bastions of Andcardia in order to construct a new city on the ancient world they thought of as 'Home'.

When his brother had told him about finding this world, Gulamendis had been half-convinced that Laro was either feigning the discovery or perhaps deluding himself, but one breath here and he knew: this was Home.

There was a resonance in the air, a feeling of solidity under-foot, of being in touch with something fundamental, a faint but almost palpable energy that seeped into the core of his being. This was the world upon which his race evolved, the very core of their existence began here. Emotions he thought he no longer possessed rose up and threatened to sweep him away. It took him a moment to take another breath and step away.

'It strikes everyone that way,' said a voice to his right. Gulamendis saw a magician named Astranour standing beside the gate. He was an aremancer, one who specialized in creating and controlling the translocation portals and transporting devices employed by the taredhel. 'My wife wept when we arrived.' Looking out over the valley, he said, 'It is . . . remarkable.'

Gulamendis nodded, saying nothing as he looked down the trail – now a road – to the walls of the city. He remembered his brother's brief description of the valley, but what he saw now was something entirely unexpected. With a cursory farewell to Astranour, Gulamendis moved purposefully down the hillside.

Massive walls had been erected, already encompassing a third of the vast valley floor. The geomancers would have exhausted themselves and their apprentices to accomplish so much in so little time. Not too far away, at the end of the wall, he witnessed half a dozen geomancers enchanting massive piles of rocks, moving them into place with their minds; others readied spells that would cause the stones' fundamental essence to flow into a liquid, be coaxed into any shape the magicians desired, and then re-hardened. The magic was complex, requiring decades of study, and the force it required and the artistry employed always impressed Gulamendis. Basic rock was not simply turned into building material, it was lent a beauty and elegance that was the hallmark of the taredhel. The wall was an off-white colour, topped with a parapet, but the merlons between the crenels were a deep yellow. From a distance, they looked white and gold. Barely a tenth complete, and their new city already spoke of its future splendour. It would be the new capital for all elvenkind on this world.

In less than a week the outlines of the new settlement could be seen. He had heard people call it, 'e'bar', home in the ancient language, and suspected that might come to be its official name, no matter what the Regent's Meet might decide. As he walked, Gulamendis could sense the magic everywhere, a faint vibration in the fundamental fabric of this space, what the mancers called 'the loops of being'. All around him, elven will was being imposed on rock and mud; vast boulevards were being cleared, with flashes of blinding white light, and he could only imagine the heat as the incendiari, the magicians specializing in fire magic, burned away acres of undergrowth and detritus. Arboris had already worked their arts on the trees, commanding them to uproot and walk to their desired locations.

Gulamendis understood the scope of his people's power, he had seen evidence of it all his life, but never before had he witnessed so many practitioners of the arcane arts expending their skills so vigorously at the same time. It was positively intoxicating.

As he watched, Gulamendis saw a team of drovers divert their carts down a pathway towards a levelled patch of land. The building pad had been fashioned with magic only hours before; the geomancers completing in minutes what picks, shovels, and drags would have taken hours to accomplish.

The massive horses were urged forward slowly, while the cleverly contrived carts gently tipped, depositing large rocks on the ground in a roughly straight line. Gulamendis lingered, fascinated by the unfamiliar magic. These masters of the arcane controlled the very stuff of the world: the rock, soil, crystal and sand.

Three young magicians walked to a point halfway along the line of rocks and together incanted a spell. The stones grew soft and began to flow together before the Demon Master's eyes. Then two master geomancers, supervised by a Grand Master, moved between the three younger spellweavers, and began to control the flow. A wall of stone rose before them, liquid like runny clay. When it reached the appropriate height, the Grand Master began to apply his arts. First he smoothed the surface until it became an unbroken, almost eggshell white, then along the top decorative designs appeared, carvings that would have taken artisans months to achieve with chisels and hammers. Gulamendis understood the theory behind this craft; his own spells were often designed to layer other spells, patterns such as this were combined and then unleashed in series simply by incanting the master spell. Still, it was a wonder to behold.

Then the Grand Master added the crowning touch as patterns transmuted on top of the wall, in a reddish-gold colour that the Demon Master presumed to be a blend of copper and gold. He knew it was not paint or gilt, and that this Grand Master's power allowed him to refine the rock into a patina of metal.

The taredhel were unmatched when it came to the arcane arts, their control over the very elements of the world was breathtaking. Centuries of inherited craftsmanship had resulted in this spectacular creation. It was more than a splendid wall, it was its effortlessness that stunned the Demon Master; the legacy of scholars, artists, and magicians in action. Like all of the taredhel, these magic users took quiet pride in their accomplishments, they sought no praise, for to do less than their best was to court personal shame.

Gulamendis turned away. To one who usually laboured in solitude, whose expertise lay in darker arts, there was something almost too bright here, something that could cause sun blindness if one stared too long. Not for the first time, the Demon Master wondered at his people's appetite for power. Unlike the Forgotten, who had lusted after their ancient master's might in a vain attempt to raise themselves up to the stature of the Dragon Host, the taredhel sought knowledge for its own reward. They were descendants of the eldar, the true Keepers of Lore. Still, the Demon Master wondered if there was much difference between the taredhel and the moredhel.

Gulamendis was first required to report to the senior magician at the site, Grand Master Colsarius, but after that the Regent Lord's mandate directed him to discover if demons were present on this world.

Gulamendis didn't need to do much investigation; there was demon scent in the very air, but muted, so distant that only one as sensitive as he would recognize it. Magic had flavours and signatures, and if you knew the spellweaver well enough, you could recognize his handiwork as easily as spotting a master's mark on a sword blade or fine piece of jewellery.

Still, this very faint sense of demon piqued Gulamendis' curiosity. He would have to travel some distance from this place, as so much surrounding magic would make detecting the exact location of the demons more difficult. Once he was alone, far from here, he could deduce where to begin his search. Besides, it was a good excuse to get away.

He had his own agenda, one that he, his brother and a handful of others had sworn to see fulfilled, even should it mean their death, for they understood the destruction racing headlong towards the taredhel only too well.

Andcardia was lost, no matter what anyone still defending it might wish; the fervour with which the Regent Lord threw his remaining resources into building this city at the expense of defending Andcardia was proof that he knew that the Demon Legion would overwhelm them eventually. It was as inevitable as the surge of the ocean tide, and like the ocean tide, relentless. Still, much had been revealed and more could be learned, for Gulamendis knew one thing above all else: somewhere out there lay a portal, a gate between worlds, a path from the Fifth Circle to this one, and while it stood open demons could be summoned easily, or worse, find their way into this realm unaided.

He reached a huge gap in the first section of wall, through which this road passed. Gulamendis had no doubt that the Regent Lord would spend time with the fabricators of its majestic gates ensuring that their design and execution were as precise and ornate as they had been back on Andcardia. The Regent Lord fancied himself as a tasteful man and had taken an interest in the design of everything the taredhel had constructed over the last two centuries. Every façade was framed with ornate mouldings and cornices, rooftops were peaked, and every one topped with a spire. Gulamendis was forced to concede that though his people had a taste for ostentation, he was in the minority, preferring simpler, more elegant design.

He considered what he knew about the demon gate. He and others of his calling had faced scorn and ridicule over their assertion of its reality, accused of seeking to avoid complicity in the demon assault. No matter whom he tried to convince, only a handful of magicians, almost all practitioners of the darker call-ings, had believed him. One ally had proven a surprise, an ancient priest, the elta-eldar. Gulamendis had simply made one passing observation that had sent the ancient Loremaster rushing to the archives.

That priest had later sought out Gulamendis when he had been imprisoned. He had asked questions and offered his insights, eventually leaving the prisoner alone to sweat out his days and shiver through the nights.

It had been his apprentice, Spellmaster Tandarae, who returned at last to speak on his master's behalf. Gulamendis saw the younger priest approaching.

'Gulamendis,' he said in greeting.

'Fare you well, Tandarae?' answered the Demon Master.

'As well as one might expect, given our current circumstances.' He glanced around to make sure no one was listening, then walked over to Gulamendis and put his left hand on the Demon Master's shoulder. Lowering his voice he said, 'I suspect you have much to do and need to be about your business; I'll walk with you, for I also am hard pressed by duty.

'I just wanted you to know that what you have brought to the attention of myself and others has not gone unheeded. You have our thanks.'

Not entirely sure where this was leading, Gulamendis said, 'I only serve.'

'Yes,' said Tandarae with a slight smile, lowering his voice even more, 'and yet there are those among the Lorekeepers, Loremasters and priesthood who would happily see you burned as a heretic.'

Gulamendis said nothing.

146

'Like yourself, I have witnessed the fall of our great race.'

Gulamendis kept quiet as they walked past a circle of priests who were enchanting a Star Stone. Having been raised by his mother in a small town on the frontier of the Empire of the Stars, he had never before seen one created. Their fabrication was rare, yet seven were being fashioned in this, the People's new home. He paused to observe the wonder, then finally said, 'No one has escaped being witness to tragedy.'

Tandarae nodded and remained silent for a moment.

The priests finished their spell. A dull grey object, like a large piece of unfinished lead or tin ore, hovered in the air. It began to glow, slightly at first and with a pulse. Over the next minute the glow brightened and the pulse quickened. In less than an hour it would glow with the brightness of a star and to gaze upon it for more than a moment would blind you. But the magic prepared the ground for the most holy of the People's artefacts, their living breathing heart, one of the seven great trees known as the Stars.

Quietly Tandarae said, 'I could be burned at the stake for saying so, but all of this is unnecessary.'

Gulamendis turned to study the Lorekeeper. He looked much like any young male of the People, tall and regal, with broad shoulders and a haughty expression. His features were unremarkable: a straight nose, deep-set eyes, a strong chin and high cheekbones. His hair however, was unusually dark, almost deep auburn in colour. 'Unnecessary?'

Tandarae knelt and gently rubbed his hand over the dirt of the valley floor, as if stroking a pet. He then picked up a loose clot of soil. 'This is Home, Gulamendis.' He raised it to his face, sniffed, and said, 'The magic is already here.'

Standing again, he looked at the Demon Master. 'We needed the Star Stones in the past to prepare the soil of an alien world and allow the Seven Stars to flourish.' He took a long, slow, deep breath, and said, 'The magic here is in the air. I know you felt it when you first came through the portal.'

Gulamendis nodded. 'It was impossible not to.'

'We could excavate the Seven Stars, wrap their mighty roots, magic them through the portal and plant them without the stones and they would thrive here. This is their home, too.

'But the People are wed to tradition.'

Gulamendis nodded in agreement. Entrenched beliefs were difficult to challenge. Those in power were so certain that a Demon Master had caused the invasion that it was only by fortune's favour he still lived.

Looking around to make sure no one eavesdropped, Tandarae continued. 'You and your brother have lived on the fringes for too long, my friend. Masters of Illusion are treated with indifference, they have no place on the Council of Magic. Over the centuries, the builders, geomancers, aremancers—' he nodded at the group of priests and magicians who were now leaving the site where they had created the Star Stone, '—and especially the tarmancers, have convinced the People that they alone should be entrusted with advising the Regent. Overcoming their bias . . .' He left the thought unfinished.

Quietly, Gulamendis said, 'Why are you saying these things to me?'

With a slightly sad smile, Tandarae said, 'I have no magic, Gulamendis. My only gift is a prodigious memory. I speak without false modesty when I say that no Lorekeeper before me has been able to recall, word for word, every passage in every tome he has read. I know the history of our People better than any living elf, better than any who came before me.

'And I can see a pattern.'

'Pattern?'

'We have much to talk about, but first you must find us a demon.'

'I don't understand?'

Taking Gulamendis's arm, the Lorekeeper gently turned him towards a distant gate. 'We both know that your obligation to report to the Grand Master is a formality. You're a free agent, under direct orders from the Regent Lord. You have two tasks . . .' He squinted a little as he studied the Demon Master's face. 'No, you have *three* tasks,' he said softly. 'You have one of your own, I see.'

Gulamendis stiffened slightly, but didn't break a stride. 'I am to seek out demon sign,' he said. 'If I find none, I rejoice.'

'Oh, I suspect you'll find some . . .' He again studied the Demon Master while they walked. 'Perhaps you already have.' Gulamendis stopped, and Tandarae smiled. 'My other gift is reading expressions.' He waited for the Demon Master to speak, but when he did not, the Lorekeeper said, 'Too long have we glorified power, Gulamendis. When it serves us, it is a grand thing, but to seek power for its own sake makes us little different from those we call the Forgotten.'

For a brief instant Gulamendis wondered if the Lorekeeper could read this thoughts, for his words echoed them. Weighing his response carefully, he asked, 'What do you advise?'

Tandarae started moving towards the distant gate. 'I will speak to Grand Master Colsarius, who will discharge your obligation to report. He will consider it a blessing to be saved from meeting

a demon lover.' He gave a wry smile and Gulamendis understood he meant the insult to be humorous. 'There's always the
risk that he might take it upon himself to augment or extend
the Regent Lord's instructions, and I'd rather you weren't
distracted from your tasks.'

Gulamendis saw they were approaching the gate opposite the
one through which he had entered the burgeoning city, and said,
'What do you know of my tasks, Tandarae?'

'I know the Regent Lord wants you to ensure we are not
troubled by demons. And I'm guessing he will send someone
with a great deal of experience to skulk through dark places to
investigate a few other things too, such as how our kin on this
world fare.'

Gulamendis was impressed. His meeting with the Regent Lord
had been private, and held over the first good meal the Demon
Master had been given in months. The Regent Lord had been
adamant that Laromendis would remain hostage against his
brother's good behaviour while Gulamendis carried out two tasks;
firstly to see if they were free of demon taint in Midkemia, and
secondly to travel north and discover what he could about the
elves living there, especially the so-called Elf Queen. Gulamendis
suspected that the Regent Lord was in no hurry to surrender
his authority to another, no matter what her lineage might be.
She could claim to be descended from the true kings of the
edhel, but it would take more than a garland crown and some
rustic, leather-clad attendants to convince him to bend his knee
before her.

Tandarae said, 'And there's something else, but I can't tell
what it is . . .'

Gulamendis preferred it that way. This young Lorekeeper was

too adept at discerning truth from fragments and glimpses. He might prove to be a powerful ally, but he would make a deeply dangerous enemy. Still, Gulamendis wasn't without his own talents in seeing a larger picture when enough information was available. He studied Tandarae and said, 'You have great ambitions, my friend. Is not Master of Lore enough?'

The young elf smiled, but it was a pained expression. 'I am a loyal friend. But the needs of my people come before any single elf's desires.'

Gulamendis nodded and turned to walk through the gate. He understood completely. The young Lorekeeper meant to be the next Regent Lord. It now made sense why he had sought out the Demon Master. He wished the Elf Queen to know there were those within the ranks of the taredhel who were ready to acknowledge her as the rightful ruler of all the edhel. And they would aid her in exchange for certain considerations, such as being named her Regent Lord in Elenbar.

Gulamendis turned just as Tandarae was about to return to his other tasks, and said, 'Why have this conversation? You already knew of my mission, yet you expose yourself, even if only slightly, by talking as you have. Why?'

The Lorekeeper turned back towards Gulamendis and said, 'Do you know the Tome of Akar-Ree?'

'I grew up in a tiny village on the frontier. As you can imagine, my education was not a formal one. I am self-taught.'

'Impressive,' said the Lorekeeper. 'Your studies are among those forbidden for centuries, Gulamendis. What little we know of demons is either taken from ancient lore or won through bitter recent experience.

'The Tome of Akar-Ree is a recounting of a great battle during the Chaos Wars, when gods and mortals struggled to seize the very heavens. Much of it makes obscure reference to things the reader is supposed to already know, but it holds some imagery that is open to a myriad of interpretations.

'But there is one passage without a hint of obscurity, as clear as a clarion ringing in the cold dawn air: demons, beings of the deeper realms, were summoned to fight in that battle, and in answer, beings of light, from the higher realms, appeared. They came unbidden, for when a creature from the depths transcended, his counterpart would seek him out. When they met, they were both destroyed, or returned to their home realm, we don't know which.'

'I didn't know that,' whispered Gulamendis. He knew he was hearing something very important.

'These higher beings, those in opposition to the demons, have many names, but they are most commonly called angels. Their glory is blinding and their power equal to their opposing demons.'

Gulamendis's mind raced; he had summoned demons for years, yet this was the first he had heard of other beings, these angels.

Tandarae smiled. 'You see the obvious question, don't you?'

Gulamendis nodded. 'Where are the angels?'

Tandarae shrugged. 'Unless this ancient tome is a work of a master storyteller, then it suggests that the balance of our universe has been skewed since the time of the Chaos Wars. The host of demons who have destroyed our worlds should have been stopped by an equal number of angels, and the taredhel should have continued to live in peace.'

'Why do you tell me this?'

Tandarae shrugged. 'There may be no answer, or the tome may be apocryphal at best. But what if it is true?' He placed his hand on Gulamendis's shoulder and gently turned him back towards the gate, indicating the conversation was at an end. 'You are about to travel widely, while the rest of us labour to build our glorious new city and plan our conquest of this world. You may meet all manner of beings on your travels, some may be wise, or powerful, or have access to ancient knowledge, and you need to know the right question to ask. Journey safely.' He walked away from the stunned Demon Master without another word.

Gulamendis left the nascent city, unsettled by what he had just heard, and by what he knew was coming. He sighed to himself as he trudged up the hill, unsure if his tasks had just got easier or more difficult.

• CHAPTER NINE •

Warning

*B*RANDOS PACED.

Amirantha sat patiently in an anteroom, expecting a summons that seemed never to come. This was his fourth day spent waiting for an audience with General Kaspar, Chancellor to the Maharajah of Muboya. The new palace in Maharta was an exercise in ostentation, something Amirantha had come to expect from royalty, but he was forced to admit that the ostentation around him came with a fair dose of beauty. Some of the décor was actually tasteful, a rarity among those whose first priority was usually to display how much gold it cost to build something.

They had arrived at last in the capital of the vibrant new Kingdom of Muboya. The Maharajah had ended over twenty years of campaigning and annexation when he reached the sea, having united all of the city states along the River Veedra, from the western grasslands to the City of the Serpent River in the east. It was now the largest political entity on the continent of Novindus, and like all young and sprawling nations, was comprised of diverse cultures, nearly impossible to govern.

While waiting, Amirantha had gained some sense of the size of the tasks set before this Lord Kaspar. Nobles from many parts of the nation, envoys from other states in the Westlands and even from across the sea, paraded through his antechamber into his reception hall or private chambers or whatever was behind those massive wooden doors.

He and Brandos had presented themselves four days earlier, both wearing their finest clothing, so there was nothing of the vagabond or poor petitioner about. They had simply told the secretary, a fussy and self-important little man, that they wished to speak to Lord Kaspar on a matter of some urgency and importance to the Kingdom.

And for three days they had been soundly ignored.

Brandos sat down next to his friend for about the fifth or sixth time, although Amirantha had lost count, and said, 'Do you think we need to bribe the secretary?'

'Tried it yesterday and almost got us arrested.' He turned to look at his companion and in low tones said, 'It seems that what we've heard about this Kaspar of Olasko is true; he's running a very principled state.' He leaned back against the wall carefully, conscious of the need to keep his white robes free of dirt, and said, 'Given the rogues and mountebanks who pass as government agents in most places, it's a surprise, but I'm not sure if it's a pleasant one or simply unsettling.'

'Well, since you can't bribe our way in to see this General, and we seem to be growing moss just waiting for something to happen, do you have any other ideas? Not that I mind doing nothing for days on end . . .'

Amirantha said, 'Very well. I suppose I could send him a more compelling message.'

The Warlock sat up and closed his eyes. He barely raised his right hand, but Brandos instantly recognized a summoning. This was hardly the time or place to call forth a demon, but the old fighter trusted Amirantha's instincts; they had come close to getting him killed on a number of occasions, but had saved his life countless times.

A faint 'pop' heralded the appearance of a tiny figure, about knee-high. It was the imp Nalnar, oldest of the Warlock's summoned creatures. When persuading the gullible to part with their gold, Brandos and Amirantha had relied on half a dozen summoned beings, all possessing different abilities to amaze and terrorize, but few who posed any real danger.

The dark-skinned imp – his hue shifting from deep blue to purple depending on the light – was the most intelligent. His bright yellow eyes with their black irises regarded Amirantha from under flame-red brows. He grinned, revealing an array of razor-sharp teeth, and pointed one taloned finger at the Warlock. 'You have summoned me, Master. I waiting your bidding, Master.'

The secretary looked up from his desk at the unusual sound of the imp's voice, and his eyes widened. Amirantha pointed to Kaspar's office and said, 'Beyond those doors resides a man of importance. He is General Kaspar, Chancellor to the Maharajah of Muboya. Bear to him a message, that I, Amirantha of Satumbria, seek an audience, for I bring a dire warning and need to speak with him now.' Lowering his voice, he said, 'Can you remember that, Nalnar?'

'I remember, Master,' said the imp as it leapt away, reaching a window in two bounds.

The secretary at the desk stood and shouted, 'Guards!'

Instantly, the guards from the corners of the large antechamber and by the doors raced to see what the problem was, as Amirantha calmly sat back down on the bench. Brandos looked on with some amusement as the secretary tried to explain how he saw the two men now sitting quietly on the bench conspire to make a tiny blue man appear who then leapt out of the window.

Unsure what to do next, the secretary ordered the guards to subdue the men on the bench, which confused the guard sergeant even more, as the two men hardly appeared in need of subduing. It was then that the secretary realized that the next window provided access to the General's offices, and said, 'Quick! Inside! Protect his Excellency.'

The guards hurried through the door, the frantic secretary only a step behind them. Brandos and Amirantha exchanged glances, stood slowly and followed the excited man into the General's meeting room.

Kaspar of Olasko, General of the Armies of Muboya, and the King's Chancellor, sat behind his desk, while the imp Nalnar sat quietly eating baked corn wafers and cheese from a large plate. The General had pushed his chair back, obviously startled at first, but now calmly observed the imp at his meal.

The guards stood uncertain, while the secretary shouted, 'Excellency, are you safe?'

'Safe enough it appears,' said Kaspar. He was a round-faced man but otherwise slender and fit. His hair had turned steel grey over the years, but he once again affected the chin whiskers he had sported in his youth, keeping his upper lip and sideburns shaven. His mouth was set in a tight, slightly amused expression that conveyed his annoyance at the interruption, but also that he found the novelty of it intriguing.

It was clear he saw nothing remotely threatening in the situation. 'It came in the window a moment ago and leapt upon my desk. Then it started eating my lunch.'

Amirantha and Brandos exchanged knowing glances. Nalnar had a particular weakness for cheese.

As the imp ate with single-mindedness, Kaspar waved away the guards. 'I think I'm safe,' he observed.

The secretary, still hysterical, shouted, 'Arrest those men!' pointing at Amirantha and Brandos.

With a single wave of his hand, Kaspar aborted their attempt. 'Is this yours?' he said to Amirantha, pointing at Nalnar.

'In a manner of speaking,' replied the Warlock.

With another wave, Kaspar dismissed the guards and secretary. After they left, Amirantha and Brandos noticed a man cowering in the corner. Kaspar rose to address the man. 'Lord Mora, perhaps it would be best if we continued our discussion on another day.'

The man stood slowly, nodding vigorously but still unable or unwilling to speak. He quickly exited the room, leaving Kaspar alone with the imp and two strangers. 'Now,' said Kaspar, 'what am I to make of all this?'

Amirantha's eyes closed in exasperation. 'Nalnar!'

The imp jumped at his name. 'Master?' he hissed.

'The message?'

Abashed, the imp lowered his head and said, 'Amirantha of

the Satumbria seeks an audience, for he has a dire warnings and needs speak with you now.'

'You forgot?'

'He had cheese,' pleaded the imp.

Brandos shrugged. 'It could have been worse. It could have been a plate of muffins.'

'Muffins,' agreed Amirantha.

'Muffins!' shrieked the imp as he started to look around the room.

Amirantha held out one hand and said, 'Thou art dismissed, minion!'

The imp faded out of view and the Warlock said, 'My lord Kaspar, I apologize, but I've been waiting outside those doors for three days—'

'Four,' corrected Brandos, 'if you count today.'

Shooting his companion a dark look and a silent warning not to interrupt again, Amirantha said, 'We thought it likely to be days more, unless I resorted to something more dramatic.'

Kaspar nodded, sat back down, and finally said, 'I'm listening.'

In efficient style, Amirantha told Kaspar of his encounter with the summoned demon, leaving out the issues of why they were undertaking to summon a demon in a cave in the first place. Still, he left out nothing critical, stressing how dangerous the creature was and that its appearance was a warning of far deeper dangers.

After he finished, Kaspar was silent for a while, then said, 'Let me see if I have the right of this. You are the two mountebanks who have been fleecing the locals east and north of here by banishing demons you summon.' When they didn't deny it, he continued. 'But this danger is great enough for you to risk coming to see me, even though you knew I might decide to employ harsh judgment against you for your confidence tricks?'

Amirantha glanced at Brandos, who stood motionless. 'Yes,' he said finally. 'This issue is dangerous enough that I felt the need to carry word of it.

'Magic has a signature, each unique to its caster, but only the most accomplished among us can discern that difference. The man who distorted my magic in order to summon that battle demon is well known to me.'

'Who is he?' asked Kaspar.

'My brother, Belasco.'

'So, this is a family problem?' said Kaspar, his eyes narrowing as if this was not the sort of answer he had expected.

Brandos shifted uneasily and said, 'It's . . . an odd family, really.'

'Apparently so,' said Kaspar, heaving himself out of his chair with a sigh. He moved to the window. 'I travelled a lot in my day, to places even you would be surprised to hear of . . . Warlock?'

'It's a title among my people,' said Amirantha, 'the Satumbria.'

'I've never heard of them,' said Kaspar.

'They no longer exist,' said Amirantha, and even Brandos looked surprised to hear that. 'They were obliterated years ago by the armies of the Emerald Queen.'

Kaspar nodded. 'I've heard tales of that time.' He didn't think it necessary to explain how he had served with men who had fought against that army. He paused, then said, 'Very well, Warlock. Let us say for a minute that I believe your tale. I am still not clear on why you are so concerned.'

'I thought I had explained,' said Amirantha, and a note of impatience seeped into his voice.

'Think of me as a slow student,' said Kaspar dryly, as he sat on the edge of his desk, looking at the two men. He motioned for them to bring over chairs and then returned to sit behind his desk.

Amirantha sat and stared at Kaspar of Olasko, the second most powerful man in the Kingdom of Muboya. He recognized at once that he was no ordinary courtier, but a man who had seen much, and who could be very dangerous. Amirantha had no fondness for danger, preferring to give it a wide berth. Avoiding this man's displeasure was the safest course.

Slowly he said, 'I was born in a village far to the north, one of many inhabited by a people called the Satumbria. I suppose we had been nomadic at some point, like the tribes to the east of us, but for many generations we had occupied a particularly nice valley and its surrounding meadows.

'We paid tribute to whichever city state or local robber baron claimed us, but for the most part we were left to our own devices and did as well as any poor farmers could expect to at that time. We even had a town hall and a ruling council of sorts, which was more of an excuse for the men to sit around, arguing and drinking.

'Our women were the caretakers of the children and our ancestors, and we worshipped our forebears as diligently as we served the gods.' He paused. 'In fact, we probably stinted in our devotion to the gods and paid more attention to our ancestors.' He glanced at Brandos who was paying close attention; he hadn't heard parts of this story before.

'My mother had the vision, or second sight, as it was called. That made her both revered and feared. As was our custom, she was made to live apart, in a hut on a hill outside the village, but she was provided with food and other necessities. She was expected to endure isolation, yet be our eyes into the next world, providing guidance and wisdom whenever she was called upon.

'She was also supposed to have lived a chaste existence, but as you can see by my presence, that was not the case. She was a beautiful woman and men sought her out.

'She bore three sons. I was the youngest. None of us knew our father, or fathers. My mother was adamant about never mentioning who he or they might have been.

'In the end, we three were raised and taught by our mother.' He shifted his weight in his chair, as if speaking of this made him uncomfortable.

If Kaspar was impatient to get to the point, he didn't show it, merely saying, 'Go on.'

'None of us could read, we came to that later. We were taught magic. All three of us had inherited some of her gifts, though they manifested in different ways.

'We were all practitioners of the dark arts, for my mother was a woman of dark secrets. I suspect her gifts came at a price, perhaps she made a pact with dark powers, but I can only speculate now.

'As a child, I could sense presences, things I could not see, and I longed to call them to me. Nalnar was the first to answer, and while he is not overtly malicious, he has no natural sense of constraint. He injured me severely before I could subdue him. Once I bent him to my service, he became a lifelong companion. I can now summon him with a single word, and his obedience to me is absolute. Of all those I have summoned from the demon realm he is my most reliable servant.'

'You have others?' asked Kaspar.

'Yes,' said Amirantha. 'Several, most of whom are fully controllable.'

'Most?'

'There are a few I have only lately come to dominate, upon whom I would not rely,' said the Warlock, shifting his weight in his chair, uneasy about discussing his craft with a stranger.

Brandos raised his eyebrows and in a gently mocking tone said, 'They tend to try and bite off your head until you get to know them better.'

Kaspar was silent a moment, then said, 'This is beyond me. There are other people with whom I would have you speak, but until then, I will hear the rest of your tale.'

Amirantha let out his breath slowly, uncertain what to say next, then shrugged and said, 'It's difficult to know how to explain. We were left to our own devices much of the time; mother was a little mad, I'm certain, but she was also a woman of remarkable gifts.

'There were three of us; I was the youngest, as I have said. Perhaps her madness was passed along to my eldest brother for he was ... different. At an early age he became obsessed with death, or more precisely, the moment of death, when life flees, and was fascinated by the meaning of that transition. He would often kill things just to watch them die.

'Our middle brother wasn't as mad as the eldest of us, but that didn't make him sane. He had his own madness: it was rage. He was born angry and he stayed angry. We used to fight all the time, for he was too frightened to challenge our elder brother. So I became the target of all his ire. Only my mother prevented him from severely injuring me several times.

'Ironically his beatings are why I became a Warlock of Demons. One day as my brother was administering a thrashing I called to Nalnar to come and help me, and he appeared. He's small, but he can be very nasty and has enough flame magic to burn down a house if he's of a mind to. He drove my brother away and left him with a nasty set of scars. That's when Belasco's anger turned to cold hatred.

'He's been trying to kill me ever since.'

'And other people think they have family problems,' Kaspar said dryly.

Amirantha studied the General for a long moment, then smiled. 'It does appear absurd when narrated, doesn't it?'

'Somewhat, but then I have seen many things in the last twenty years that I would have once scoffed at.

'Still,' added Kaspar, 'you haven't explained why your family difficulties concern the Kingdom of Muboya.'

'It's difficult to explain in a short time—'

'Oh, take all the time you need,' said Kaspar, as he glanced through the doorway where his guards stood ready to answer his call. 'Even after all the trouble you've caused to gain my attention, after what I've heard it would be foolish of me not to give it to you. After all, if you don't provide a compelling enough reason for unleashing your odd little friend in my offices, you'll have ample time to contemplate your folly chained to the wall of my king's dungeon.

'So, please continue,' said Kaspar agreeably.

Amirantha and Brandos exchanged glances, but said nothing. Then the Warlock said, 'After the fight, when Nalnar scared my brother, we spent as much time apart from one another as we could, especially when we reached a certain age.

'I spent a great deal of time in some caves near our hut, calling up Nalnar and learning as much as I could from him about the demon realm. It took a great deal of luck, frankly. I almost got killed a number of times until I began to puzzle out the creatures, how they respond to being in our realm, what drives them.'

'This is all very interesting,' said Kaspar. 'Go on.'

'My brothers meanwhile became immersed in their own areas of . . . interest. My eldest brother was probably the least talented among us, but was the most driven. My second brother had flashes of brilliance, but no discipline. Yet he's quick to learn, and has mastered many things. I fall somewhere in the middle, I suppose. I am very good at what I do, but what I do has narrow limits.' He looked at Kaspar. 'I really don't understand much about other types of magic, if you must know.'

'Your brother?' Kaspar prodded.

Amirantha sighed. 'I'm having difficulty coming to the point because I want to impress upon you just how difficult the task my brother achieved was.'

'Which brother?'

'The middle brother, Belasco.'

'Continue.'

Amirantha said, 'I say with no false vanity that I know perhaps more about demons than any living man. My knowledge is hardly exhaustive, as I discovered rather recently when I met the battle demon my brother conjured instead of the one I was expecting.

'That's the point of it, my lord Kaspar; not only did my brother find me – and I have been successfully avoiding him for nearly fifty years – he found me in the middle of a conjuration that should have been far beyond his ability to understand, let alone influence. Moreover, he introduced a component to my magic of which I was unaware at the time, bending it to his will – alone no small feat – and almost got me killed, which I suspect was his intention.

'If he has become that powerful he could have used far simpler means of disposing of me, but instead he chose to kill me in a fashion that was both ironic and insulting. He wanted me to recognize that he was the author of my death at the last instant, and meant me to know that he controls my craft better than I.'

Kaspar sighed. 'So, your brother hates you and wishes you dead. But we still haven't reached why I need fear for the safety of this kingdom.'

'The demon my brother conjured was of a type I've never encountered before.'

'So?' asked Kaspar, not seeing the significance.

'By our measure, demons tend to be stupid, their existence one I can scarcely imagine, and I have more knowledge of them than most men. It's a lifetime of combat and struggle, where guile serves better than reflection. The idea of a reflective demon is . . . laughable, really.

'They can be cunning; but the demon that I faced was not only cunning, he was intelligent. Once he realized his physical power was ineffective, he changed his approach and began to use magic.'

'I know nothing of demons, but I have heard stories from those who encountered one in the past,' began Kaspar.

Amirantha looked intrigued. 'I would like to speak to them if possible.'

'More than possible,' said Kaspar. 'But I'm still not clear on why an intelligent, magic-using demon is something I need worry over.'

'There is a demon realm, General, a world apart from our

own. I've read a few ancient records, and there is no certain
knowledge of what that place is like, but we do know a few things:
If demons could, they would happily invade our world, for our
abundant life intoxicates them. All life is helpless against them.
The stoutest warrior I know—' he indicated Brandos '—could
only keep that demon at bay for a few moments, just long enough
for me to effect its destruction.

'Imagine if you could, a dozen such creatures appearing inside
this palace at any time. I am the most powerful Demon Master
I have encountered, and there are not many of us anyway, and
I could only best two, perhaps three such creatures given the
most perfect of circumstances.'

'Life rarely provides perfect circumstances,' offered Brandos.

'Yes,' said Kaspar. 'I think I see where this is going.'

'Yes,' said Amirantha. 'Now, imagine an army of such creatures . . .'

Thinking of his past encounter with the Dasati Deathknights
on the now destroyed world of Kelewan, Kaspar said, 'I think I
can imagine.' He sat lost in thought for a moment, then asked,
'How would you control such an army?'

Amirantha took a deep breath, the rise and fall of his shoulders communicating what he said next. 'I have no idea. Perhaps
they have rulers, or some sense of loyalty; my dealings with those
I have mastered lead me to believe everything in their realm is
predicated either on power or usefulness. A demon will serve a
greater demon rather than be destroyed; a demon will spare a lesser
demon if he can be useful. Beyond that I have no notion of how
an army of such creatures might be controlled.'

Kaspar was silent and then said, 'Yes, you most certainly need
to speak with some friends of mine.'

He moved towards the door and signalled for his secretary who had been hovering outside the room with the guards, waiting for his master's command. 'Secure quarters for these two and give them a good meal. Tomorrow I will take them on a journey with me.'

'Sir?' asked the secretary. 'A journey?'

'Yes,' said the General. 'I'll inform the Maharajah personally, tonight.'

'A journey by sea or land?' asked the secretary.

'By land,' said the General. 'I'll need half a dozen of my personal bodyguards.'

'Only half a dozen?'

'Six will do. Have horses prepared for these two,' said Kaspar, pointing at Amirantha and Brandos. 'We'll need enough provisions for a week of travelling overland to the east. That will be all,' he finished, waving the man away.

Returning to his desk, he sat down. To Amirantha he said, 'Belasco, you say?'

'Yes,' said the Warlock.

'He was your middle brother?'

'Yes,' said Amirantha. 'He's become something far greater than I imagined.'

'Your eldest brother,' asked Kaspar. 'What of him?'

'I don't know,' said Amirantha. 'He was, as I said, obsessed with death and dying. He was a powerful necromancer by the time I left home. By then my only reason for being there had gone. My eldest brother had become fascinated by a necklace mother had found. He'd remove it from the small cache of her most treasured things at every opportunity, bringing down her wrath.

'He claimed it spoke to him. Finally, one day, he murdered Mother for it.' He spoke almost dispassionately, though there was still a hint of feelings behind his words. 'It was a particularly gruesome and messy murder, but it provided him with a very powerful burst of magic.

'I glimpsed him covered in her blood, invoking some dark power as he stood wearing that necklace.'

'Glimpsed?' asked Kaspar.

'I was running for my life at the time,' said Amirantha. 'Belasco had already fled using some translocation or invisibility spell, or something of that sort. I was forced to outrun my eldest brother, who was fatigued from killing our mother; else I think he might have overtaken me.

'I was desperate and summoned a demon named Wusbagh'rith, who carried me off. He's a foul creature, but he has massive wings. Fortunately, I had enough control over him to get miles away from Sidi before the demon tried to kill me.'

Kaspar's eyes widened. 'What did you say?'

'I said I had enough control to get miles away from my brother before the demon tried to kill me.'

'No, the name? What was your brother's name?'

'Sidi. Why?'

Kaspar took a deep breath, then let it out slowly. 'Do you know the name Leso Varen?'

'No,' said Amirantha. 'Should I?'

Kaspar regarded the warlock. 'You never saw your brother Sidi again after he murdered your mother?'

'No, I saw him twice, once in the City of the Serpent River, and once across the sea in the town of Land's End, in the Kingdom of the Isles.'

'I know the place,' said Kaspar.

'Both times I avoided him before he saw me; I never spoke with him again, if that's what you're asking. If I could, I'd happily cut out his heart and feed it to one of my demons. She may have been a crazy witch, but she was our *mother*.'

'Your brother is dead.'

'You knew him?' asked Amirantha, showing the most emotion he had since entering the palace.

'I had the unfortunate luck to have him guest with me for a while. He used the name Leso Varen and caused me . . .' Kaspar stopped, as if weighing his words. Finally he said, 'He caused me great personal injury; and was identified as a necromancer named Sidi by someone I trust implicitly. He is dead beyond reclaiming.'

'General,' said Amirantha, 'please, I must know how he died.'

Kaspar nodded and quickly recounted the role Leso Varen had played in the war with the Dasati. He glossed over the Conclave's part, deciding to let Pug decide how much to trust this Warlock and his companion. Kaspar was a good judge of men and thought the pair reliable enough if watched closely, but it wasn't his decision to make.

Ten years after the event, knowledge of what befell the Tsurani home world had spread throughout the land; many of the survivors had sought refuge in Muboya, a large cadre of Tsurani warriors even served as the Maharajah's core troops. But the exact details were shrouded in rumour and speculation, for even those who had lived through the horror of the Dasati invasion knew little of the truth about that war, that an army from another plane of reality had attempted to obliterate all life on Kelewan in order to make it their own.

Kaspar told the story as best he could, surprised at the long-buried emotions that threatened to rise, for it had been one of the most difficult and horrific experiences of his life. 'At the end, we think your brother perished on the Dasati home world at the hands of some horror attempting to enter our realm, or that he was obliterated with the utter destruction of Kelewan.

'More than one witness can confirm his presence on Kelewan near to what we called the Black Sphere, the gateway to the Dasati home world. I have friends who are convinced that had he possessed one more soul vessel with which he might flee his death, it would have had to have been hidden on Kelewan, and was therefore also destroyed with the planet.'

A mix of emotions played across Amirantha's face. 'I ... I accept what you say, General, and put aside ... old hatred.'

Brandos said, 'That's one hell of a tale, General.' He looked down, shook his head slowly and said, 'You hear stories ... the entire world destroyed?' His expression told Kaspar the old fighter didn't want to believe this.

Kaspar just nodded, remaining silent.

Amirantha looked away for a moment then turned and looked Kaspar in the eyes. The pain and regret had been replaced with a clear-eyed certainty. 'It doesn't change anything. I must stress this: whatever troubles Sidi caused you, are nothing compared to what Belasco is capable of.'

'Are you sure?' asked the General.

'Absolutely. Belasco had a prodigious curiosity; he would pursue his interest with single-mindedness until he mastered it. And while Sidi was insane, Belasco is insane and brilliant. Of the two, he's far more dangerous.'

Kaspar was silent while he weighed the warning. He sighed.

'Leso was the most dangerous I've met, so to hear you say your other brother is more so . . .' He fell silent for a moment. Finally he said, 'I'll have you escorted to your quarters. We leave at first light.' He walked out of the room, leaving Amirantha and Brandos sitting in their chairs.

After a moment a court page appeared, flanked by two soldiers-at-arms. Brandos rose and looked at his friend. 'Well, I guess we're going on another journey.'

'Apparently so,' said Amirantha.

• CHAPTER TEN •

Threat

SANDREENA SWUNG HER MACE.
 The massive weapon took the other rider in the stomach – he had been coming in high and she had ducked under his blow and struck him hard – lifting him out of his saddle. She knew her art well enough to know he was done for the time being. If he hadn't passed out from lack of breath, he was likely to be lying on the ground stunned from the fall.

She had happened on a wagon being attacked by bandits, four roughly-dressed thugs with surprisingly good weapons. The merchant and his two sons battled the more experienced brigands with a poor assortment of weapons; one battered shield and an old sword, two clubs and a lot of determination. Still, they gave a good account of themselves and had held the bandits at bay for a few minutes before Sandreena had ridden over the rise and seen the conflict.

The three remaining riders saw one of their own drop suddenly and a fully armoured knight riding at them. Without a word they turned their horses and put heels to their sides, galloping off. Sandreena weighed giving chase, then decided the struggle was over; they were heading into the hills and her heavier mount would soon fall behind. They knew the terrain and she didn't; while she had no doubt that she could best the three of them, given what she saw of their fighting skills, but she didn't relish fighting her way out of an ambush.

She paused for a minute to ensure the bandits hadn't doubled back on her, then turned to see the two boys strip the bandit on the ground. She judged that meant he was dead.

She rode over to the wagon, where the man sat regarding her suspiciously, holding his very old and battered sword at the ready, in case one brigand had merely driven off others. Raising the visor of her full helm she said, 'Stay your weapon, sir. I am a Knight-Adamant of the Order of the Shield of the Weak.'

His suspicious expression didn't change. 'So you say,' he said in strangely accented Keshian. He turned to the boys and shouted something in a language she didn't understand, then turned back to her. 'Well, if you expect thanks or reward, you're mistaken. My boys and I already had things well in hand.' The boys had taken everything, including the robber's filthy small clothes, and now left him lying nude in the road as they ran off after the brigand's horse, which was cropping grass a short distance from the road.

'Looks like a good horse,' said the man on the wagon and Sandreena couldn't tell if he was addressing her or talking to himself. He seemed intent on inspecting the contents of his wagon, against the remote possibility that one of the bandits had somehow managed to pilfer an item or two while the conflict was underway.

Finally happy that nothing was missing, he shouted to the boys who were having a little trouble corralling the horse, which seemed to like cropping grass better than the idea of having another rider on her back. Finally one of the boys grabbed up a long clump of grass and held it out for the horse to sniff while his brother gently reached out and snagged the reins. If the horse objected, she hid her disappointment well and came along quietly.

The driver shouted more instructions to the boys in their strange language. When they had at last tied the horse's reins to the back of the wagon, and climbed in, the driver turned and sat down to find a patient Sandreena still looking directly at him.

'What?' he demanded. 'I'm not going to pay you.'

'I'm not asking for payment.'

'Good, then get out of my way. I have business.'

Sighing at the man's impossible rudeness, Sandreena said, 'One question. Do you know the village of Akrakon?'

'Yes,' he answered, then with a flick of the reins he started his team, deftly moving the horses to skirt around Sandreena.

As he rode past, she shouted, 'Where is it?'

'You said one question, and I answered it,' was his reply and the boys burst out laughing.

Suddenly impatient, Sandreena turned and urged her horse on, quickly overtaking the wagon. With one swift motion she reached over, grabbed the man by the collar, hauled him off the seat and deposited him in the mud.

'Try again,' she said, her voice hissing with menace.

'All right,' said the man, rolling to his feet in one deft move. With three strides he was back alongside his wagon and then back on the seat. 'Akrakon is down the road, maybe five miles. You'll be there by supper.'

'Thank you,' she said, putting heels to her horse and urging it into a lazy canter. She wished to put as much distance between herself and the annoying man as quickly as possible.

Then she remembered what the Father-Bishop had said about the villagers being from one of the more annoying tribes of the region. She had thought he meant fractious and rebellious, but perhaps he simply meant they were rude.

As the man predicted, Sandreena rode into the village of Akrakon near suppertime. Two boys ran past her through the centre of the village, perhaps returning from overseeing a flock, or fieldwork, and now intent on reaching the day's final meal. She overtook and pulled up her mount before them. 'Has this place an inn?'

Neither boy answered her, but one pointed over his shoulder as he darted around one side of Sandreena's mount, his companion dodging around the other. Shaking her head at the lack of civility so far demonstrated by these people, Sandreena wondered how much information she would be able to extract about the goings-on in the mountains above the village. She might have to club it out of them.

She had never seen a region like this one. Since leaving Krondor she had passed through miles of coastal lands, but none like this.

Both the Kingdom of the Isles and Roldem held claim to the

long strip of coastal land running between the southern shores of the Sea of Kingdoms and the mountains called the Peaks of Tranquillity.

She assumed the tranquillity was reserved for those who lived south of that massive barrier, for the region between the Kingdom city of Timmons and Pointer's Head was anything but tranquil. Two other cities rested between them, Deep Taunton and Mallow's Haven, neither of which properly acknowledged either kingdom. The local nobles and merchants had enjoyed playing one kingdom off against another for decades, building their own alliances and keeping free of close supervision.

Only the mountains kept Great Kesh from also laying claim to the region; they tried in the past, but their attempt to annex the area had resulted in Roldem and the Kingdom putting aside their differences in order to drive Kesh south again.

Sandreena vaguely recalled from her history studies that the last battle had been fought over a century before, when a Kingdom duke from Bas-Tyra had driven Kesh out of Deep Taunton. That land was rich with forests and farms, this side of the Peaks of the Quar had little to covet. Since riding north from the port city of Ithra, she had seen nothing but rocky bluffs and stone-strewn beaches. It was a difficult road cut through in a dozen places by swiftly running streams hurling down from the peaks above. The woods towering above her looked dark and uninviting, and the only villages she encountered were small fishing enclaves, where the inhabitants scraped out a harsh existence.

Sandreena expected to find a few farming communities, else those fishing villages would have vanished ages before, yet she saw no gardens or fields. She deduced that they traded their catch for vegetables, fruits, and other necessities. If there were farming enclaves in the region, she didn't encounter them; but there were occasional trails and pathways leading up into the hills, some with recent wagon tracks.

But what was strangest to Sandreena was there was no authority in the region. If Kesh claimed this part of the peninsula they invested nothing; gone were the usual outposts and patrols, governors or minor nobles, it was as if this rocky coastline had been forgotten by the Empire.

She rode through the village, the most prosperous place she had seen since leaving Ithra, and judged it poor at best. There were no recognizable shops; only a smithy at the end of the street whose huge chimney was belching smoke, and another stall that appeared to belong to a woodworker, probably the local barrel maker, cartwright, wheelwright, and woodcarver all in one. It was a very strange place and it was too quiet, as if everyone strived to be about his or her business inconspicuously. Even the few children she saw were sullen and stared at her with suspicious eyes.

Reaching the marked building, she could scarcely believe it was the inn; a large, ramshackle house, perhaps. Still, there was a hitching rail in front, with two horses tied to it. She rode around the building leisurely, looking for anything that might resemble a stable, finding only a large corral where a tumble-down shed stood, one side of it completely collapsed. Her mount had endured worse.

Sandreena dismounted and untacked the animal. She put her saddle and bridle on a rail – it still was slightly sheltered by what remained of the roof and the three walls. She quickly brushed down her horse and picked its hooves. A well provided clean water, and she used grain from the sack she carried behind her saddle.

Ensuring everything was as secure as it was likely to be, she turned her attention to her own needs. She expected a bath would be out of the question, and instead vowed to bathe at the first stream, lake, or river she found, but hoped that at least the bed was something more than a bag of straw.

She didn't worry about her tack, as her mount was a well-trained warhorse. Anyone foolish enough to approach her would be in for a very rude shock.

Sandreena made her way around the modest building to the entrance and entered. The interior of the inn was no more promising than the exterior. The low ceiling made it feel cramped and the long narrow bar and one table provided all its accommodation for eating and drinking and Sandreena assumed large gatherings never occurred.

A single door to the back seemed the only other passage and when no one appeared after a minute, she shouted, 'Hello! Is anyone here?'

Quickly a woman's voice answered: 'Who's there?'

'Someone in need of a meal and a room,' and muttering more to herself than to the disembodied voice, she added, 'and a hot bath if that's possible in this hovel.'

A pinched-faced woman of middle years appeared from the door at the rear of the building. She wore plain grey homespun, a stained faded yellow apron and a blue scarf over her greying black hair. 'What do you need?' she asked curtly.

Sandreena felt a sudden urge to turn round, ride back to Krondor and strangle the Father-Bishop. Biting back a frustrated and angry retort, she simply said, 'Something to drink. Ale?'

'No ale,' said the woman. 'Beer.'

Sandreena nodded. The mug appeared before her and she took a drink. It was weak and sour, but it was wet. 'Food?' she asked after she had drained a third of the mug.

'I have some homush cooking. Should be ready in a few minutes.' Sandreena had no idea what *homush* was, but she had eaten a wide variety of things in her travels and knew that if the locals ate something, it probably wouldn't kill you. 'I sometimes have mutton, but there was no one here to slaughter a sheep this week. I'm waiting for my husband and sons. They are due back from trading in Dunam.'

Sandreena nodded. She had ridden through Dunam on her way from Ithra. It was a small trading town with a small harbour. She assumed it was where the locals had their goods shipped, which seemed likely if that's where the innkeeper and his sons went for supplies. She had seen other towns like it, ancient communities left over from the days of coastal sailing, before the big deep-water ships started plying their trade, leaving the smaller stops along the once prosperous trade routes to wither away.

She looked at the older woman and said, 'A two-horse rig, with a bay and a dapple grey pulling it?'

'That's my Enos,' said the woman. 'Did you see them?'

'They should be rolling in any time now,' said Sandreena. 'I came across them on the road a little while back. They were fighting off some bandits.'

'Bandits! Black Caps?'

Sandreena said, 'I don't know about any black caps, but they were a scruffy lot. One of them died and the others rode off. Your man and the boys are fine.'

The woman didn't lose her strained expression, but relief

showed in her eyes. All she said was, 'Food is almost ready. It is four coppers for the beer. The meal is two.'

Sandreena reached into her belt purse and pulled out a silver real. Kingdom silver was as good as Keshian in this part of the world. 'I need a room.'

The woman nodded as she scooped up the silver coin. 'I have one through there.'

'Bath?'

The woman shook her head. 'You can bathe down in the creek. No one will bother you.'

Sandreena rolled her eyes, but said nothing. The bed was probably filled with straw and bugs. Well, it was better than sleeping on the ground next to her horse in the run-in. 'You have any fresh hay or grain for my horse?'

'When my husband gets here,' was the reply. 'He went to buy supplies. We were running low on many things.' There was a hint of concern in the woman's otherwise stern tone and Sandreena wondered why, especially since she had been assured her husband was close to arriving safely. Sandreena had been in dozens of villages like this one over the years and had developed a good sense of when things were normal and when they were not. Something was very out of place here, and she wondered if it was related to her mission.

'Well,' she said, 'I'm for a quick rinse. Will you ask one of your boys to see to my horse when they get here?'

'That will cost extra,' said the woman without hesitation.

'Why am I not surprised?' muttered Sandreena. She took another silver coin out of her purse and put it on the counter. 'I may be here for two or three days. If there are more costs, let me know.'

She walked out of the building and past the shed. She retrieved a bundle from her saddle kit and moved through the small southern meadow. No one had to tell her where the creek was as she had been north of the stream for the last five miles along the road into town.

She quickly found it and noticed with some satisfaction it was isolated and private. She removed her cloak, and the Order's tabard, letting them both fall to the ground. She removed her heavy leather gauntlets and tossed them onto the cloak. Taking off her helm, she set it down on the ground next to the cloak. The coif and mail shirt were annoying to untie alone, and she knew she must look ridiculous bending at the waist and shaking them off. There was one advantage to being a Temple knight rather than a Knight-Adamant, and that was having a squire at hand to help you. Some errant knights had squires, just as some mendicant friars of her order had begging acolytes, but she preferred her solitude.

Stripping off her head covering, tunic, trousers and under-clothes, she waded into the stream.

Each time she bathed outside, Sandreena was revisited by the conflicts and contradictions her body raised within her. At the cloistered Temple baths, or in the privacy of a tub in an inn, she felt confined and protected from them, but outside she felt more exposed, yet more fundamental and almost primitive in nature.

She enjoyed being a woman, yet she always felt it to be a burden. She despised the men who had used her when she was young, but occasionally she longed for a gentle man's hands on her body. She knew men found her beautiful, so she hid under armour and arms, rejecting the allures of her former trade. Gone were the unguents and colours, the soft silks and jewellery. Her face remained hidden behind a faceplate, and her body under armour and tabard.

She sighed as she scrubbed at her hair with the very costly Keshian soap she had purchased the year before. She paused and luxuriated as much as possible in the cool breeze and the faint scent of lilacs that the soap maker had instilled in his product. The bar was almost gone; she resolved to purchase another on her way back to Krondor; it was her only indulgence in an otherwise austere existence.

Feeling an unexpected twinge of sadness, she wondered if her life would end in bloodshed and pain, or if she might find another life after this one, perhaps with a good man, and children. She shook her head in frustration and pushed aside the familiar feeling of futility. The Goddess often tested her faithfulness and doubt was to be expected; the priests and priestesses had prepared her for these moments, yet it was difficult.

She put aside her worries and set about pounding her trail-dirty clothing on a flat rock, using the method Brother Mathias had taught her: thoroughly soak the article, twist it as much as she could into a rope, and slam that twisted cloth as hard as she could against the rock; keep soaking, twisting and pounding until the garment was clean. She had no idea why her clothes ended up cleaner for it, but they did. Then she conceded that she was equally ignorant of how soap cleaned anything, she was content to just accept that it did. She spent a few more minutes pounding, then hung her clothes to drip on a nearby tree branch.

Sandreena ignored the breeze off the mountain raising goose-flesh on her body, and waited patiently to dry enough to don fresh clothing. This was the part she hated most, for now she could do nothing but let the air caress her. She wished for a towel and realized she really would have preferred being sent somewhere with at least a tub and hot water.

Finally, she climbed into her clean underclothes and pulled on a fresh tunic, some leggings, trousers, and wrapped a clean head covering under her mail coif to keep her hair from becoming tangled in the metal links.

Once she had dressed, she sighed audibly and put on her boots. Again she wondered about taking a squire as she struggled to get the stubborn things back on.

By the time she was dressed, the washing on the tree was no longer dripping, though it was still thoroughly soaked. She gathered it up and carried her load up the hill to the inn, her helm under her arm and her mace in her left hand.

Reaching the door, she saw another horse in the run-in next to hers and recognized it as the bandit's mount. She then found the wagon at the back door, being unloaded by the two boys she had encountered earlier in the day. She shouted, 'One of you see that my horse gets a bag of grain and I'll give you a copper.'

Both boys looked at one another, as if weighing the offer against what their father might do if they left off the unloading. Silently they nodded. They then raised their fists, pumped them up and down twice and on the third pump, one of the boys shouted 'Odd!' as the other shouted 'Even!'

The one who had shouted 'even' smiled and leaped down from the wagon, lifting a bag of grain off the ground and carrying it to the run-in shed. The other boy glowered at Sandreena but said nothing as he continued his work.

Inside the inn, Sandreena spread her cloak out over the back of a chair closest to the fire and put her wet tunic, trousers, leggings, and small clothes down next to it on the floor.

'Supper is ready,' said the woman as she came out of the kitchen. If she had any objection to the guest drying her clothing before the fire she did not voice them.

Sandreena put her bag and weapons under the table, but kept them close at hand.

Glancing around the room, she reaffirmed there were only two entrances, one at the front and the one from the back of the building, where she assumed both her room and the kitchen lay, as well as the family's quarters. As inns went, this wasn't the worst – that honour had been claimed by a hovel in Kesh – but this inn was only marginally better.

When the woman appeared, her husband and their two boys followed her in. As food was placed before Sandreena, the man said, 'You. From the road.'

She nodded, not entirely sure if that was an accusation or a question.

'You said you'd pay my boy a copper to feed your horse.'

'Yes.'

'Give it to me.'

Sandreena didn't argue, but pulled out a coin and put it on the table. The man snapped it up. 'That is for his work. The oats are two more.'

She put a silver real on the table and said, 'For today and tomorrow. If I stay longer, I'll pay in advance.'

The man nodded. 'I'm Enos, this is Ivet, and my boys are Nicolo and Pitor. Your room is at the end of the hall.'

Sandreena nodded. 'My Temple received reports of bandits. I see they were true.'

Your Temple know about us? Who

The man paused as he started to turn away, and then turned back towards her. 'Why does your Temple know about us? Who told them?'

Sandreena was a little surprised by the questions. The man seemed more concerned with how the information reached the Temple of Dala, than the fact that someone had arrived to help.

'Does that matter?'

Enos shrugged.

'I don't know. I was simply ordered here by my Father-Bishop. It seems the Empire is too busy elsewhere to protect you.'

'Protect us?' said Enos with a bitter, barking laugh. 'They are worse than bandits, the tax men. They come, they take, and they leave. They do nothing for us.

'Pirates and bandits; smugglers and . . .' He stopped himself. 'We don't need help. We manage.'

Sandreena weighed her words carefully. She said, 'I'm sure you do, and I'm not here to help you.'

The man's eyes narrowed, as if he didn't understand, but he said nothing.

'I'm here to gather information to take back to my Temple.'

'What sort of information?' asked Enos suspiciously.

Sandreena said, 'Why this out-of-the-way village is being ravaged.'

Enos and Ivet's look of alarm was barely hidden, but the boys positively went white with fear. Something here was far from ordinary and she felt as if she had just stuck a stick into a hornet's nest.

She didn't need the sudden look of panic that swept over the family to warn her something bad was about to happen. She had had too many unpleasant encounters in the last few years to be taken completely unawares, but she had let her attacker get too close.

She stood, and in a single fluid motion, kicked her chair straight back, as she lifted the table and turned it over. Kneeling, her mace was in her hand before she turned. The chair had struck a man in the legs, slowing him just long enough for her to be ready when he swung his sword at her, aiming to remove her head from her shoulders.

He didn't expect her to move so quickly, and was shocked for a brief instant as he tried to regain his balance – just before her mace slammed into the side of his head. The blow propelled the man sideways, landing him in a heap on the floor. It also knocked off his black leather hat.

Sandreena had seen many bodies hit the ground; she knew this man wasn't going to answer any questions. She hadn't intended to kill him, but her battle-honed reflexes had taken over.

She inspected the body. Her would-be assassin wore a dark maroon tunic, black trousers, and black leather boots. His black cape was fastened with a golden clasp that looked more suitable for a gentleman's garb than for any sort of serviceable travel wear, so she assumed the man had stolen it.

The side of his head was caved in, blood ran from his nose and ears, and his eyes were set in an expression of surprise. They had once been a vivid blue, but there was something about the eyes of the dead that always made them look greyish to Sandreena, no matter what their original colour.

She knelt down and inspected him. There was no belt purse, no sign of who he might have been, only an ordinary dagger. The other personal item she discovered was a chain around his neck, from which hung a black balled fist made out of iron or some other base metal.

She picked up the man's leather hat and turned to Enos and his family. 'A Black Cap, I presume?'

Enos's eyes were wide with terror and he seemed unable to speak. He merely nodded.

Sandreena stood, righted the table and chair, and sat down ignoring the body on the floor. 'I think you need to tell me some things,' she said.

Softly, in a whisper, Enos said, 'We are all going to die.'

CHAPTER ELEVEN

Upheaval

*G*ULAMENDIS HOWLED.

A primal sound erupted from his throat as he threw back his head and unleashed his frustration in the only way he could. The pounding of waves upon the rocks quickly engulfed the sound. The Demon Master of the taredhel knew this moment was coming, but had laboured on in hope of seeking the source of the demon signs he had encountered.

An emotional people, the taredhel were restrained when it was required. On the rocky bluffs of this wilderness, miles from any habitation, human, dwarf, or anything remotely intelligent, Gulamendis felt no such requirement. He raised his hand and conjured a seething mass of energy, a writhing ball of mystic black tendrils within a dark purple sphere, and hurled it down at the rocks below.

The ball struck a massive boulder and exploded in a satisfying display of blindingly brilliant pyrotechnics. It released clouds of dark smoke and sent a shower of silver sparks in all directions. When the ocean breeze had blown the smoke away, all was as it had been before. The only sign of Gulamendis's outburst was a bare patch of rock, now devoid of moss and lichen. Otherwise the ocean and the rocks below remained indifferent.

Gulamendis chuckled at his childishness and sat down to ponder his next move in this terrible and dangerous game. His original plan had been simple: follow the demon sign long enough to establish exactly what kind it was. He was almost certain that he had detected a conjuration, for the lingering residue had held a different quality, or flavour, to that which was left when a demon entered this realm unbidden. He had noticed that fact the first time he had encountered demons along the Diazialan frontier, when the first conflict had erupted in this long and bitter war.

He was intrigued. Who was this summoner of demons? In his travels, Gulamendis had met very few magic users who could order such creatures into this realm, and none who could match his abilities. He would be first to admit that he had also been lucky over the years, but he took credit alone for learning the lessons his luck brought to him. He was as apt a student as his brother.

He sighed and stood up. The demon was across the sea, and while he couldn't be certain, he suspected that the far shore was a very long way away, perhaps even on the other side of the world. He could conjure demons with the ability to carry him, but none could fly across such a vast distance.

Besides, there were more important matters closer at hand

than satisfying his academic and professional curiosities. Finding this other Demon Master would have to wait.

He now faced the task set before him by the Regent Lord, to investigate the elves in the north, at a place called Elvandar. He felt a strange longing at the thought of finding them, for although the taredhel had established their own order, their own view of the universe, they were still edhel at heart, and ancient ties abided.

Standing on the bluffs overlooking the sea, in a land called the Far Coast, Gulamendis considered what he knew of this region. He believed he was near a city called Carse, just south of another human settlement named Crydee and, if his brother's intelligence was accurate, the Elven Forest lay just north of that town. He weighed what he had in his travel bag and judged it too difficult a journey to make on foot.

He took a long look around, still being cautious, closed his eyes and began a summoning. Within moments a demon appeared before him. Hellspawn it might be, and a lower-caste creature, but it could run as fast as the swiftest horse, and he could ride it. It was, however, a sight to behold.

The creature blinked its huge black eyes against the light of day. It looked around and snorted. It had been summoned by this elf before and knew better than to attack or try to escape, for this was his master. The demon lowered its head and waited.

It looked as much like a huge dog as it did a horse, though its legs were longer and its body more slender. It had a pointed snout, almost lizard-like, and its ears were flattened back against its skull, like an angry cat. The stub of its tail didn't wag in greeting, but trembled slightly, a warning that it was ready to attack.

Gulamendis closed his eyes again and used a spell taught to him by his brother, a glamour that would make any onlooker, save those with exceptional magic ability, see a horse when they looked at the demon. It was akin to the spell Laro had used to disguise himself as a human while he travelled, and it had served him well.

Gripping the creature's scaly hide, the elf leapt onto its back and using his legs, turned it northeast. There was a decent road a few miles in that direction, and it would take him to the human town of Crydee. There he might investigate a little, before travelling north to see his long-lost kin.

Gulamendis moved his demonic mount through the fields. He had taken to riding off the road, and had found a track between the fields of the farms scattered to the south of Crydee. He had abandoned the King's Highway when he saw humans staring at him.

At first he had worried that his mount's disguise was ineffective – he was not the master his brother was – but the second time some human children shouted and pointed at him, he realized the excitement was caused by the fact that he was an elf. Despite this region's proximity to the Elven Forests, it was apparent that its inhabitants rarely ventured south of what was called the River Boundary, which made him the object of much scrutiny and comment.

From what he could understand, these humans perceived no difference in his attire, manner, or mount from those of the local elves. Still, he decided stealth served him better than attempting to play the part of a local, and at the first opportunity he turned eastward, away from the road.

He could ride between the boundaries of these farms, within sight of the road, without attracting too much notice. The crops were ripening, but not yet ready for harvest, so the fields tended to be unoccupied, and on the few occasions when he spied humans, he avoided them. His perceptions were superior to theirs, so he felt no fear of detection.

When he came to a cluster of farmhouses, he rode eastward, into the woodlands that fed into the deeper forest called the Green Heart, and then moved north again. He felt a strange disquiet in these woods, a presence both familiar and yet alien. He wished he'd had more time to speak with his brother on what Laromendis had discovered about this place.

As he returned to the farm track, the sun set in the west providing a brilliant display of red, orange, pink and gold light against the dark grey clouds on the horizon. Gulamendis held back his emotion, for it was the first sunset he had seen over an ocean on Midkemia. When last he looked out over the seascape, the day had been grey and forlorn, haze masking the boundary between sea and sky.

Every day he spent on this world reinforced one thought; this was their Home. But something was wrong.

He couldn't put his finger on the exact nature of the wrongness, he just felt out of phase with this place. And he suspected that the wrongness lay within him. Perhaps he had changed during the generations spent on other worlds, away from the nurturing magic that was Midkemia. He wasn't sure, but he did know that his concerns were academic compared to the immediate need to find his distant kin and discover what sort of ally they might make.

For as he sat on this masked demon, riding along in the

evening's twilight, he knew that only he understood the threat poised to strike at this world. And another certainty rose within him; this would their last battle. If the Demon Legion found its way to Midkemia, if they discovered a path from Andcardia to this world, their Home, then all of the edhel, every last elf born of this soil, would perish.

Crydee had proven an interesting and entertaining diversion for a while. Gulamendis had easily avoided the noisy and ill-organized Town Watch that marched the perimeter of the town with little attention to detail. It was clear this place had been left untroubled for some years now. He had passed quietly through a dark street past one or two buildings with lights on, but attracted no attention to himself.

The harbour possessed a tidy waterfront, and a long neck of land stretching to the north boundary, a stone tower that appeared to be more of a watchtower than a lighthouse. There was a light, but it was little more than a single brazier that gave off only a faint illumination. Gulamendis assumed that ships didn't arrive after dark, and that any unexpected visitors would rest at anchor off the coast to wait for dawn rather than risk entering the harbour under that weak beam.

He turned his mount northeast, away from the harbour mouth and skirted the town along its northern boundary. He was curious about the castle on a steep rise high above the town, but knew that soldiers more professional than the Town Watch whom he had easily avoided would guard it. He knew little about these humans, but he possessed keen observation and sharp wits.

Their social organization showed them to be well in command of the region. Neighbours who might have troubled them in the past – elves, dwarves, goblins, or trolls – had been driven out or disposed of; a fact that made the humans dangerous.

His race had not encountered any humans for centuries, and the old encounters had always ended in bloody war. While some human tribes had been relatively peaceful, a large number had proven relentlessly warlike and aggressive, and after several failed treaties, the stance of the taredhel shifted from peaceful negotiation to pre-emptive obliteration.

The dwarves had proven more troublesome in some ways, less in others. They were much tougher and difficult to root out of their underground communities, but they were also far less aggressive and willing to stay within their own territories without problems. Only twice had warfare erupted with dwarven clans, but both had been protracted bloody wars.

Gulamendis realized with a sigh that those histories were now academic, for the Demon Legion had now overrun those worlds. With a sinking sensation, the Demon Master wondered if he was on a fool's errand. Even if he could find potential allies among the other races on Midkemia, would his own people welcome their aid?

Turning his mount round, he walked past the local inn, which seemed lively. A steady stream of voices, laughter and music, could be heard from the road. If indeed that could be called music. Taredhel musicians typically played soft, lyrical arrangements that were supposed to mimic the lofty emotional experience of a magician, in order to share that bliss with those who had no magic. As Gulamendis's magic contained no lyrical emotion, he had always been as moved by their compositions as the soldiers, farmers, and labourers must have been listening to the great performers on festival days; not that there had been many occasions to celebrate since the coming of the Demon Legion.

The priests also kept traditional songs of prayer and welcoming, as well as other, more primitive music and instruments, as a way to preserve the original culture of the edhel. It was seen as more devout, or academic, depending on one's view of faith, and rarely heard outside the Temple.

The music coming out of the inn was boisterous, loud and dissonant, and it sounded like fun. The singers seemed to be enjoying themselves greatly. He could not understand a word as he spoke little of the human tongue. His brother had possessed several spells that allowed him to understand any language, but there was never the time nor the circumstance for him to teach Gulamendis. Had he not learned the spell of disguise years before, Gulamendis would have had to ride through the forest the entire way.

Leaving Crydee town behind, Gulamendis wondered how his brother fared, and then, more bleakly, if he still lived.

Laromendis pointed his wand at a demon climbing the wall and unleashed a bolt of energy into the creature's face. Clawing at its eyes, the demon fell backwards. A magician named Sufalendel had given him the wand, for which Laromendis would be eternally grateful; his own more subtle magic was next to useless.

He stood on the northernmost wall of Tarendamar, shoulder to shoulder with soldiers, priests and magicians, all attempting to repulse the fourth demon attack this day, as the creatures swarmed the defences, seeking access to the last bastion of the taredhel on Andcardia.

The great barrier had been erected in a massive circle around the city of Tarendamar, over a hundred miles radius. Other defences had been placed around the planet, huge traps designed to obliterate demons by the hundreds, death towers that spewed evil mystic fire at any moving body within a hundred yards, a network of tunnels under the mountains to the north of the city, and all had proven useless.

The demons had scourged the planet, leaving nothing living in their wake. Within a year of finding the portal to Andcardia, they had driven the widely scattered population of the world to Tarendamar, forcing the total abandonment of over four hundred other cities around the planet, and countless towns and farming villages. Entire forests had been defoliated and lakes and seas now churned on silent shores, devoid of life. The demons left nothing alive behind them, feasting on any creature they found, no matter how small. Scouts had reported not even insects abided after the demons departed.

The only advantage the taredhel possessed over the demons besides their superior arts, was the demons' single-mindedness. They had elected to attack the barrier in one location, a canyon that funnelled them into the defenders' strongest position, merely it was assumed because it was the shortest route from the portal to the city. Certainly, early in the war, they had attacked on many fronts. Now they came in a straight line from the gate to the city.

Laromendis glanced upwards, out of habit. Had any flyers been overhead, warning would have been passed. He once again marvelled at this powerful magic, a huge invisible wall of energy, only hinted at when struck by a demon's magic or falling body. The Spellweavers had originally erected a dome, but at huge cost, until it was discovered there was a height above which the demons apparently could not fly. The spell was adjusted and lowered, gaining the defenders weeks, even months, before the magic that fuelled the barrier was exhausted. Laromendis caught his breath and kept his thoughts to himself. Around him grim-faced soldiers, magicians, and priests awaited the next assault, despite to a man sharing the same thought: this was pointless; eventually the city would fall. But the Conjurer wouldn't be the first to speak aloud those words, lest someone turn his ire upon Laromendis. Besides, while the city might fall, each hour here on the wall gave more of the taredhel the opportunity to file through the portal to Midkemia. Thinking of Home, Laromendis wished fervently he were there now, with his brother.

Then a voice shouted, 'Here they come!'

Three times since before sunrise the demons had been beaten back, leaving thousands of rotting corpses littering the plains outside the wall. So high were the dead piled, that the last assault ran up the bodies of their fallen brethren as if they were an earthen ramp, gaining them an additional twenty feet on the wall from which to launch their assault.

Laromendis held a dagger in his left hand, against magic not proving effective, and watched for a moment, catching his breath, as another wave of flyers approached, coming low and fast. These were the most dangerous and unpredictable of the Demon Legion, for it was unclear where they would strike next. Something had changed in the last two days, as the flyers – some of them at least – were now able to pierce the barrier.

Hand-to-hand fighting was now the order of the day, and again the taredhel had the upper hand. Despite each demon being physically the match of any two elven warriors, the elves employed magic arts unparalleled. Not only were magic users able to cast spells that would wither demons in their tracks, or stun and confuse them, many of the weapons used had been enchanted to cause far more damage than would be expected. Swords would cause flaming wounds or festering agony, arrows would stun with mystic shock, and high above, green flames of death rained down on the attackers from death towers constructed over the last month. The demons would eventually take this position, but they paid an unimaginable price for doing so.

The flyers dove. In the previous onslaughts they had struck the top of the wall, trying to create a breach in the defences so that the crawlers – as Laromendis had named the scampering demons that climbed the stone wall like spiders – could reach the top of the defences, make their way to the gates and open them. Once the flyers overshot the wall and landed in the open bailey between the defences and the outer city, presumably to mount an assault on the gate's defenders. The few demons that survived the transit through the barrier had been quickly dispatched by 'flying' companies, squads of the best soldiers who stood ready to reinforce any position.

The death towers began to spit at the approaching flyers, and Laromendis watched in fascination. Necromancy was an art so dark that no respectable magic user admitted to having an interest in it, yet this device was so anti-life that only necromancy could have conjured it into existence. The forbidden volumes and tomes must have been taken from the vaults of the Regent's library. No sane being could imagine these hideous engines of death, let alone design one.

The huge black towers had been erected along the wall, each topped with a crystal so black it seemed to drink the light.

Nothing reflected off their surfaces but each pulsed with wicked energies and could unleash bolts of green energy, which flew towards the flyers. The green light only needed to get close to the creatures to suck out their strange energies. Silver lights, like tiny bolts of lightning, flew from their bodies into the green beams as the flyers stiffened in mid-air and then fell to their deaths. Those farthest from the death bolts kept coming, but only to meet with death from the elves on the city walls.

The fighting was the bloodiest of the war so far. Every effort was being made to hold the monsters outside the city walls for as long as possible. The translocation portal in the centre of the city was transporting the Seven Stars and every magician who could be spared from that task was already here on the walls.

A crawler came up the wall so quickly Laromendis was almost taken unawares. He flicked his right hand but the bolt of energy from his wand missed the creature entirely. Quickly he sliced at its neck with his dagger. It was as tough as a tree-trunk and he barely cut into it, but it caused the demon enough pain to distract it; it lost its purchase and fell backwards onto another crawler. Laromendis wondered if others had noticed what he did, but the flyers were now breaching the energy barrier at an alarming rate.

'We can't keep this up for much longer,' he said to no one in particular.

A veteran soldier next to him grunted, which he took was an agreement. The warrior was too busy cutting off the head of a flyer that breached the death tower defences to speak. He was also ignoring a gash in his left shoulder, a wound that would cause him serious blood loss if he didn't get it tended to quickly.

'Get that shoulder dressed!' he shouted. 'I'll hold them!'

He conjured up an illusion, one of those he had prepared against this sort of contingency. A creature appeared in the air above him, a regal wrathbird. It had a seventeen-foot wingspan and was built of anger and muscle. Talons so sharp they could sever a torso, and a beak so strong it could snap through any armour suddenly confronted the demons remaining on the wall. The illusion was so real that they hesitated, which was all that Laromendis had wished for. He aimed his wand at the closest and sent a death bolt to strike it full in the face. It fell clawing its own eyes out in agony before it died.

The conjuration was so lifelike, defenders nearby fell away too. The wrathbird was one of the most feared predators on all of the planets ruled by the Clan of the Seven Stars, and Laromendis's illusion was so vivid, they could smell the carrion stench from its breath, feel the heat of its wings, and see the vivid ruby highlights on its black feathers. The creature's talons dripped with blood and its eyes were alight with rage and hatred. The phantom would remain for at least another minute before it began to waver and dissipate.

The Conjurer cast his wand once more and another demon fell. Archers were now targeting those on the wall, while the heavy engines poured rocks and hot oil, boiling water and flaming refuse upon those at the base of the wall. The corpses already piled high ignited, and the foul smoke that spiralled upwards choked defenders and attackers alike.

The attack faltered, and then the retreat began. Coughing from the rising smoke, the Conjurer moved over to a bucket of water, picked it up and drank from it. He had no idea his throat could become this parched. He ignored the bitter metallic flavour, thinking it wise not to contemplate what made the water taste like that. Catching his breath, Laromendis looked out over the battlefield and saw something new: half a dozen larger demons stood along the battle line, equally spaced and directing other demons. He was no expert, but he had read every report he could, and they had never mentioned the Legion was organized. They usually just came unexpectedly, a flood of creatures that flew, crawled, ran and hopped at defenders in waves. Most of them had no weapons, just teeth and claws, but a few carried swords of some alien metal or wore rudimentary armour.

But these figures looked like field commanders. They wore finer armour and other demons waited at their side, holding a banner of some fashion. The battlefield was too smoky, the light falling, and the standards too distant for him to make out any devices or patterns on them.

He looked around and wondered if he was the only one to notice. He saw no footman officer or soldier of the Regent's Guard or City Watch move to carry word of this to the Regent Lord; nor any magicians or priests make their way down the long stone steps to the bailey below. Most were simply catching their breath, drinking water or tending to the wounded. A few sat, back against the wall, legs outstretched in exhaustion. All were waiting for the next onslaught.

Laromendis looked around again, and finally decided to take matters into his own hands. The officer detailed to watch over him was nowhere to be seen. Obviously other duties had called him away or he was dead. Either way, Laromendis had no one to tell him not to go, so he decided that his time on the wall was over.

Making his way down the long stone steps to the outer bailey, he saw a cluster of officers gathered around a figure Laromendis knew well: Lord General Mantranos, second only to the Regent Lord in command of the army, and a critical force in the Regent's Meeting. He was white-haired and battle-scarred, but still possessed as keen a military mind as the People had ever known. Years of fighting the Demon Legion had brought his skills in the field to near perfection. Although he had never been able to defeat them – no commander of the taredhel had ever won a victory – he had repulsed them, slowed them down, and cost them more blood than any elven commander before him.

He knew better than to attempt to speak directly to the Lord General, so the Conjurer studied the group around him.

Half a dozen senior commanders stared down at a hastily drawn map of the northern defences, covered with marks in chalk. Behind them, ready to carry their commands to any position along the defensive front, was a group of junior officers. Seeing that he was being ignored, Laromendis used his arts to shift his appearance to that of a messenger, covered in blood and nursing an injured arm. He made his way up to a junior officer and said, 'Sir!'

The young commander turned and saw what the Conjurer wished him to see, and said, 'Report!'

'From the wall, sir. I'm to tell you the Legion has officers!'

The Lord General couldn't avoid overhearing. He turned his attention to Laromendis and said, 'What? Repeat that immediately!'

'Sir,' said Laromendis, trying his best to sound faint from his wounds. 'There are half a dozen demon officers upon the field, with standard bearers beside them. They're rallying the creatures for another assault.'

'Who told you to report this?' demanded the Lord General.

Feigning weakness and disorientation, Laromendis said, 'Why . . . it was an officer . . . my lord . . .' He waved towards the outer wall. 'Up there.'

To one of his younger officers, the general said, 'Go see what the truth is.' To Laromendis he said, 'Have your wounds seen to; you're of no use to us as you are. If you're not fit for duty, go to the portal and leave with the others.'

Laromendis bowed as best he could, then moved away. As soon as he was out of sight, he dropped his illusion and hurried towards the translocation portal. As far as the Conjurer was concerned, he had just received permission to leave for Home from the foremost military commander in all Andcardia, and he wasn't prepared to debate the finer points of this with anyone.

He reached the translocation portal and saw something truly awe-inspiring. A massive tree, oak-like in form, but bearing larger shimmering golden leaves, was being carried above ground by magic, floating yards above the earth as it was guided by ropes tied to godos, the massive oxen-like creatures native to this world. It was being pulled through the translocation portal while a stream of refugees moved alongside. The Conjurer got in line with those waiting to go through and watched as the last two of the Seven Stars rose into the air and were tied to the teams of godos. Within an hour the trees would be safely back on their native soil, after being away for millennia, and at that moment Andcardia would become a memory.

The Regent Lord would order the remaining soldiers on the wall to flee to the portal. Those who reached it before the demons would find refuge, and those who arrived too late would die on this world. Two priests watched as the Conjurer and others around him stepped forward. Laromendis knew they would eventually sacrifice their lives, for it was their responsibility to destroy the translocation device. The demons would have to find their own way to Midkemia.

Until this battle, the demons had been clever enough to find and hold gates open to each world they attacked, but this time was different. Or so the Regent Lord and every taredhel hoped, especially Laromendis. For there was only one gate to Midkemia, and despite its massive size, it was easy to destroy. Break the machine, and the gate collapsed. Without the machine, their destination would be untraceable. At least that was the theory.

Stepping through the portal, Laromendis was confronted with a sight that made him falter. When he had last stood on the hill, a pastoral valley had stretched before him. Now, a city was rising, and from the look of things, rather rapidly.

The magic user moved down the road to the newly erected walls that would encircle the city area within a week or so. Few buildings had been erected; mostly wood huts and canvas tents provided the shelter, but as night fell, he saw a veritable tapestry of campfires. He had no idea how many of his people had come through this gate, but they must number in tens of thousands. Watchfires along the upper ridges showed more encampments, and he was certain that the commanders here would have already sent out groups to secure and then occupy the villages he had discovered on his last journey through the region. There was room for at least fifty thousand taredhel in this valley and in the meadows above.

Without a twinge of guilt for deserting his post, the Conjurer counted himself lucky to be alive. He was fairly certain that no one in authority would question his presence, they were otherwise occupied and apparently very busy.

He looked around. 'Now,' he whispered to himself. 'Which way did Gulamendis go?'

Gulamendis rode quietly along the riverbank. He had reached the River Boundary earlier in the day and then looked for a ford. When he found one, he'd felt a strange discomfort and an inability to cross over into the Elven Forest, and so he decided to look for another path.

Now, hours later, he was at the third likely crossing point and still couldn't bring himself to use it. He stopped and dismounted. Perhaps there was a geas or some other conjuration that prevented him from riding his steed into this ancient and sacred forest. He dismissed the demon with a wave of his hand and waited.

He listened. The breeze in the branches sang louder to him than in any other place he had visited, yet there was something odd in the sound, something he didn't quite understand. This land was native to his race, yet he felt alien here, as if he was out of rhythm.

He sighed and sat down on the bank to ponder his next act. He looked at the river, less than one hundred yards away, its water running swiftly over the shallow rocks. It would be easy to walk into the water and make his way to the other side. In his mind he could see himself doing this without any difficulty.

Yet when he tried to step into the water, he could not.

He closed his eyes and used his skills to see if there were wards or a geas in place. There was something, but it wasn't magic as he understood it. This was something more akin to a feeling, as if he listened to an old melody, but couldn't quite remember its name. There was a haunting quality to it that disturbed him as much as it called to him.

From behind he heard a voice ask, 'Having trouble crossing?'

The accent was odd, but he understood the words and quickly came to his feet, his hand seeking the hilt in his belt. Gulamendis stood looking down at an elf who was a few inches shorter than him. 'Yes,' he said slowly. 'I am having trouble crossing.'

The elf tilted his head to one side, puzzled by the manner of Gulamendis's speech. Like the rest of his people, he was patient, so for a long minute he said nothing, then he spoke. 'Nothing about you is familiar to me, yet you are our kin; that I can plainly see. Who are you and from where do you hale?'

'I am Gulamendis, of a modest but ancient line, recently a citizen in the city of Tarendamar.'

'Star Home,' said the elf. 'I have never heard of such a place. Tell me, where is it?'

'On another world.'

The elf shrugged. 'I have met folk from other worlds, but I have never met any of our kin from another world, save those edhel who returned to us from Kelewan—'

'Edhel?' asked Gulamendis. 'Other edhel have come here?'

The smaller elf nodded. He was dressed in green leather, from tunic to boots, and across his back carried a finely crafted longbow. 'Yes. Are you of the edhel?'

'Once,' said Gulamendis, 'my people were, though we now call ourselves the taredhel.'

'The People of the Stars,' said the elf. He smiled. 'I like that. Come, you may enter Elvandar and we bid you welcome. I presume you wish to speak with the Queen?'

'Yes,' said Gulamendis as he walked into the water, now completely able to do so. 'I thought a geas or wards prevented my entrance.'

'More,' said the elf. 'The very woods of Elvandar do not permit anyone to enter without welcome, unless powerful magic is used. Only once have invaders reached the heart of our lands, and they were magicians of very great power.'

Suddenly two other elves appeared from behind the trees, and Gulamendis halted. The first elf introduced them, 'I am Cristasia, and these are my companions Lorathan and Gorandis. We've been watching you for a while.'

The one called Gorandis said, 'Are all of your people as tall as you?'

Gulamendis noticed he was a good six inches taller than Cristasia, the tallest of the three, and he nodded. 'I am about average. Some are taller, but not many.'

The elves exchanged glances and then Gorandis said, 'Well, we are three days from the Queen's court, so we should be off.' To Cristasia and Lorathan he said, 'Continue the patrol, I will guide him.'

They nodded and seemed to melt back into the trees as Gorandis started to run along a trail. Gulamendis hesitated then started to run after the elf. He quickly caught up and said, 'Do you not have mounts?'

'We do, sometimes,' answered the forest elf. 'But we seldom use them unless the journey is long. Three days is hardly worth the bother.'

'I'm not used to running,' said Gulamendis, realizing that he was going to be hard pressed to keep up with this woodland elf.

They wended their way through the woods, moving rapidly

along narrow game trails. Twice Gulamendis faltered and once he fell, and Gorandis said, 'You have no woodcraft, do you?'

'No,' admitted the elf. 'I am city born and my time in the wild has so far been unpleasant.'

The wood elf laughed. 'A city elf! I have never heard of such a thing. Even those who came from across the sea lived on farms or small villages.

'Well, you learn something new every day, as they say.' He turned and started running again. 'We wondered if you simply wanted to be noticed, the way you were trudging along the river bank.'

'You saw me?'

'We'd been watching you for almost the entire day,' he replied.

Gulamendis felt annoyed at being mocked by a rustic. But even more irritating was the fact that the rustic was correct; he had no wood skills, and certainly no desire to gain any.

Sandreena awoke holding her mace in her right hand. Gripping her helmet in her left, she started to rise and was on her feet with her headgear in place before she was completely aware of what had awakened her.

She crawled out of her tiny window and made her way as quietly as possible to bed down next to her horse. From her perspective, there was little difference between the run-in shed and the room she had been given by Enos and Ivet. Both had dirt floors, had been recently used as a privy, only had straw to sleep on and housed a plethora of bugs.

Besides, her horse was well trained and would alert her to any approaching danger, which is what had just occurred. The slight snorting sounds and pawing of the ground would probably not alert anyone else, but to Sandreena it was as alarming as a bell in a watchtower. Someone was approaching the little inn stealthily and they almost certainly planned no good to befall the one guest in residence.

As was her habit when outside, she slept in her armour. It wasn't the most restful way to sleep, but she had grown accustomed to it over the years. Moving as lightly as she could, keeping her shield high on her left arm and her mace in her right hand, she kept her face plate raised, giving her the greatest possible visibility before encountering the enemy.

As she suspected, two figures garbed in black skulked through the open garden behind the house, heading towards her window. She didn't hesitate, she had an instant before they saw her; flipping down her visor, she charged.

They saw her loom up out of the gloom when she was but three steps from her first target. Before he could turn to meet her, the first assassin was cut down with a savage blow to his head. Sandreena doubted he would rise to trouble her again. The other assailant had wheeled round, following her movement as she turned. He lunged at her with a long sword. She caught the sword's point on her shield and expertly turned it so that his blade slid along its surface. The motion carried the man in black towards her and she punched him in the face as hard as she could with her right fist, still clutching her mace. The force of it drove the man backward; blood flowed down his face from his shattered nose and he was blinded for a moment. Sandreena swept her mace downward, catching his heel and causing him to fall over. He slammed his head against the ground and lay stunned.

She calmly stood up and kicked him hard in the side of the

head, and he went limp. She really didn't care if the kick killed him, but she would like to question one of these Black Caps.

Enos and his family had been so reticent that she had threatened to leave them to answer for the death of the man she had killed. That had terrified them even more than being accused of helping her.

She didn't feel sorry for them, they had no way of knowing she couldn't abandon them, despite them being rude and annoying people. She suspected that even under the best of circumstances they'd be hostile to strangers.

She checked and found the first man dead. The second was unconscious and likely to stay that way for a while. She dragged the body under some old straw on the other side of the run-in shed. They might have friends.

She knelt to examine the unconscious man and saw his breathing was shallow and fast. She had done more damage than she intended. Things were difficult to control in the heat of the moment; she might have two bodies to bury come first light.

As she began to rise, she sensed someone behind her and as she spun to defend herself, a blow struck her on the side of the head, glancing down to crack hard into her shoulder. Its force drove her to her knees and only her armour prevented her receiving a broken shoulder or worse. But the glancing strike to her helmet had disorientated her enough to leave her open to another blow from behind. Her last thought before she collapsed into semi-consciousness was: *but there were only two of them!*

There was another hot flash of pain and then her side went numb; she felt another pain somewhere else, but she wasn't sure where, and then darkness swallowed her.

*　　*　　*

After three days of running, Gulamendis was certain that if he never had to set foot in a woodland again, he would be content. He would return to the new city, to Home, and never again set foot beyond its walls. Whatever sense of wonder he had first felt was now gone, replaced by fatigued legs and sore feet. He kept up with his rustic cousin by force of will, and a tiny bit of magic he used when training demons, to dull the pain.

His companion had been less than talkative. At night when they camped, the young elf – Gorandis had given his age as less than fifty years – had been content to sit by their fire and chew on dried fruit and meat, answering Gulamendis's questions with short, non-specific answers. The Demon Master didn't know if Gorandis was especially adept at avoiding conversation or if he was stupid. The second night Gulamendis quickly fell into an exhausted sleep.

Throughout the following day they moved fast and Gulamendis grew used to the gruelling pace. He grudgingly conceded his distant kin possessed impressive skills he had previously disdained. Rustic these elves might be, but they were superb woodsmen, and no doubt excellent hunters.

When twilight approached, he could feel the change around him.

He felt something in the very air of this forest. The same emotional tug, so alien and yet so right, he first felt upon entering this world, Home; a feeling that grew stronger now with every passing minute, as if they were nearing the source of that wonderful sense.

Then he entered the clearing and saw Elvandar.

Across the open meadow stood a huge city of trees, their gigantic boles linked by gracefully arching bridges on which elves could be seen walking.

Gulamendis looked up and saw how the trunks rose until they were lost in a sea of deep green foliage cast almost blue-black in the evening gloom, but somehow alight with a soft glow all of their own. Here and there he glimpsed a tree sparkling with golden, silver, or even white leaves. A soft glow permeated the entire area, and he dropped to his knees, as tears flowed down his cheeks. 'I had no idea,' he whispered.

Gorandis stopped and turned to look at his companion. Whatever emotions played across the taredhel's face, stopped the smaller runner from chiding him. This was a moment of deep, personal feeling.

'The stars,' whispered Gulamendis. 'You have so many.'

'Stars?' asked Gorandis.

He pointed. 'The trees. We call those ... we have seven, brought with us from this world ages ago. They are the Seven Stars. We are the Clans of the Seven Stars.'

Gorandis cocked his head to one side, as if trying to remember something. Then he said, 'Elvandar has always been this way.'

A thicket of massive trees had greeted the eyes of the demon hunter, so many he couldn't tell how far back into the deep forest they stretched. He counted at least twenty, and there were others behind them. Moreover, he saw them leaved in colours he'd never seen before. Of the Seven Stars four had copper bronze leaves, two vivid yellow foliage, and one of them was resplendent in silver. But here he saw blue leaves, deep green, red, orange, silver *and* gold. Their brilliance made the shimmering glow of the Seven Stars pale in comparison.

Pulling himself to his feet, the Demon Master said, 'There are so many.'

Gorandis shrugged. 'I don't know how many, but there are a

RAYMOND E. FEIST

lot of them. We've had babies and they needed room, so the spellweavers planted saplings and the Master of the Green urged them to grow quickly.' He motioned for Gulamendis to follow. 'Come, see for yourself.'

Gulamendis towered over most of the elves he passed, being nearly seven feet in height. His clothes marked him as alien even if his look hadn't. Nowhere did he match the vivid red colour of his hair. He saw dark red-brown, and many blond elves, but most had brown or dark brown hair; their brows were less arched and their features less finely drawn. To his eye, they were a plain, unappealing people.

The rustic elf took him up a stairway carved out of the living wood of a massive tree, and along branches so wide their backs had been flattened to make boulevards. They climbed upwards, deeper into the forest, until at last they reached a massive platform.

The Demon Master then received an even bigger shock than his first sight of Elvandar's heart.

Around the edge of the platform sat the council of elves: the spellweavers, the eldar, and many others, but two thrones dominated the centre. The woman who sat in the higher of the two possessed a regal bearing, though by Gulamendis's standards her robes were simple, and lacked the delicate embellishments he was used to seeing adorn taredhel ladies. Her features were lovely, if a little soft, and she wore a circlet of gold upon her brow.

But it was the being seated next to her who shocked the Demon Master. He sat on a slightly lower throne, but it was clear that he was her Consort. They absently held hands as couples long together do. But he was so much more than that. He was a warrior born, projecting power like no other being

214

the Demon Master had ever encountered. In his bones and to the heart of his being he knew this creature was a Valheru.

'Welcome,' said the Queen. 'We would know your name and from whence you come.'

Softly, without taking his eyes from the man next to the Queen, he said, 'I am Gulamendis, my lady. I am a Demon Master of the Clans of the Seven Stars. I come seeking . . . ' He stopped and looked around, feeling both drawn to these people and repulsed by them. There was something profoundly familiar about them, yet there was so much that he didn't understand. Finally he said, 'I seek your help.'

'How may we aid you?' asked the Elf Queen, but she glanced at her companion.

Taking a breath, Gulamendis said, 'Our lore tells us we came from this place in the days of madness, when the gods fought in the heavens above.' His eyes locked with those of the Queen's Consort. 'We fled from this place, across a bridge to the stars, and we abided there for a long time.'

A robed elf stood and said, 'As did my people, Gulamendis. We were lorekeepers, the eldar, and we abided for centuries upon another world before returning here.'

'Cousin,' said Gulamendis, 'we were once eldar, too, according to our lore. We took the name "The Clans of the Seven Stars" and now call ourselves taredhel.'

Then the Valheru spoke. 'You departed before the war's end?'

Gulamendis nodded, fearful of speaking to him. These creatures of legend were the ultimate masters of the People, and to find one here was terrifying.

'I am Tomas, Warleader of Elvandar,' said the man, standing. When he approached, Gulamendis could see there was something different about him. 'I wear the mantle of one lost ages past, and I bear his memories, but I am more than him. I will tell you that tale at length some other time, but for now you must hear this from me: you are a free people. So it was said at the time of the Chaos Wars, and it as true now. Abide and rest, and share with us your story, Gulamendis of the taredhel, for you have found friends here if you would have us.'

Despite being nearly half a head taller than Tomas, Gulamendis felt small in his presence. He didn't fully understand the meaning of his words, but found them reassuring. If this was indeed a Valheru, he claimed no dominion over these people, or the taredhel.

Then a strange odour registered on the Demon Master's senses. He had also smelled it as he passed though the human town. It was a weed they burned and inhaled. He glanced at the throne and then realized that a small figure stood in its shadow. An old dwarf with near-white hair stepped forward and, fixing Gulamendis with a sceptical look, took a long pull on his pipe.

The dwarf said, 'It's about time you showed up, lad. We carried them word of you nearly a month back; I was growing tired of waiting.'

Tomas smiled and the Queen laughed, her green eyes merry, but the Demon Master was unsettled. They knew he was coming? How? Three weeks ago he was in a cage, as his brother bargained for his life.

Gulamendis hid his confusion and nodded. He couldn't bring himself to smile at a dwarf. He turned to the Elf Queen and said, 'My lady, I am bereft of wits and in need of rest and food. If we could speak tomorrow, I will give a better account of myself.'

'That is fine,' said Queen Aglaranna. She motioned for Gorandis and said, 'Take him to rest and eat and we shall meet again tomorrow.' To Gulamendis she said, 'Rest and be well, for we have ample time to discuss so many things.'

The Demon Master nodded, bowed and allowed himself to be led away by his woodland guide. He wished that the Queen had spoken the truth, for it would mean they had made a clean escape from Andcardia and that the way between the worlds was closed off forever. But in the pit of his stomach he feared it was not so, and that the days before a danger of horrific proportions arrived at this idyllic place were quickly diminishing.

CHAPTER TWELVE

Survival

*A*LL SHE FELT WAS PAIN.
Something vaguely urged Sandreena to do something, but she couldn't quite grasp what it might be. She could barely breathe and pain kept surfacing to cut her like a hot blade. In the distance, someone groaned.

A pain behind her eyes roused her and she thought she felt hands behind her head, lifting it. They were strong but gentle. Water touched her lips.

Thirsty. Her throat was parched and her eyes felt as if sand had been packed behind their lids. She tried to open them, but found the effort to be more than she could manage. A voice murmured softly, 'Ah, I think you'll live.'

Again, a firm but gentle hand lifted her head as water touched her lips. She drank deeply and then the pain returned.

A groan escaped her lips as she again tried to open her eyes, and at last managed to. Her vision swam, images came in and out of focus as she tried to recognize the light and dark shapes before her.

'Slowly,' said a soft, male voice.

Sandreena sipped as more water was brought to her lips. It tasted metallic and she realized it was the flavour of dried blood, most likely her own. She tried to move, and the pain hit her again.

She almost wept from it. There was no part of her that didn't hurt; it was worse than anything she could remember, and she had endured her fair share of wounds. She blinked, feeling a wet cloth cross her face, gently wiping her eyes.

Shapes began to resolve into recognizable images and she saw she was in a dimly lit cave. A single flame, from a floating wick in a bowl of oil, cast yellow highlights over an otherwise grey and black environment. She still could not make out the features of the figure hovering over her, for the flame lay behind him.

Almost whispering, he said, 'Maybe you'll live.'

'What happened?' she tried to say, but the words were little more than a sigh.

'I'll pretend I understand you,' he said, moving to a blanket on the floor of the cave, next to the flame. She could see him, though the vision in her left eye was still blurry. Closing it slightly made it easier to see.

He looked ancient, yet there was an old ironwood quality to his touch that told her this man was still strong despite his age.

His features were craggy; he had a sharp nose and deep-set eyes under a heavy brow; his jutting jaw was covered in a grey beard. There was nothing appealing about him, yet she could imagine when he was young he might have had a certain presence. Some women found that more appealing than a handsome face.

His hands worked quickly as he spoke. 'Someone wanted you very dead.' He paused as he considered what to add next to the bowl of water before him. 'You were stabbed several times, stripped naked, then thrown from the cliffs.'

Sandreena could barely move. Her body was heavily bandaged with what felt like lumpy cloth rags. She reeked of something alien and barely had the strength to speak. 'Who ... are you?'

'Me?' asked the old man, smiling. 'I keep to myself. The people around here don't like strangers.'

'So I have ... discovered,' she said, letting her head fall back and her eyes close. 'I ...'

'You need to rest,' he said. 'I fished you out three days ago. Didn't know if you'd make it.' With a chuckle, he said, 'You are a mess, girl.'

As she felt herself drift off, she whispered, 'You're not the first to say that.'

Time passed alternating dreamless sleep and short periods of consciousness. Sandreena knew she had spoken to the man at least once, perhaps more often, but couldn't remember anything that might have been said. She finally awoke with a clear head, though it still throbbed as she tried to sit up. She was under a pile of skins, seal or otter pelts, lying on a pile of filthy rags. Her bloodstained tabard had been rolled up and used as her pillow. She realized she was nude, save for the mass of rags that served as bandages. She wasn't worried about modesty, the bandages covered most of her body. She ached terribly and did a quick inventory. She had at least a dozen cuts, several of them deep. She lifted one bandage on her leg, and beneath it saw a puckered purple wound sewn roughly together. From the pain in her back she knew she had a deep cut there, and when she coughed, the pain almost caused her to pass out again.

She took a deep breath and it hurt. But rather than the raw stabbing pain of a fresh wound, the pain was the dull, constant ache of healing. She wished, not for the first time, that she had the gift for the majestic healing spells. She could have hurried her healing along if the wounds weren't too bad, but she needed focus and strength, the two commodities she lacked at the moment.

She was alone. She struggled to sit up even more and put a fur behind her back to cushion it against the cave wall. The task was exhausting, but she managed. She was tired of lying down. And she wanted some questions answered.

She dozed off, and when she opened her eyes again, the old man was sitting beside the fire boiling water. He glanced over and grinned. 'Crab!' he said with enthusiasm. 'I thought you might be ready for something besides broth.'

He had fashioned an interesting cooking pot, hard-tanned hides had been stretched over a wooden frame, making a large, shallow bowl. She had never before seen its like, and was surprised it didn't go up in flame when put over the fire, but she could see that as long as there was enough water in the bowl, and the fire didn't reach the wood, the water would steam and eventually boil; the hides would only scorch, not burn.

Weakly she asked, 'Where did you get crab?'

He pointed out the cave mouth. 'There's a pool at the base of the rocks; when the tide is high, in they swim. Some good fish too, when the tide is out, but I have to catch them by hand, so it's harder. With the crabs,' he made a dipping motion with his hand 'you just scoop them up from behind, and they can't pinch you.' He reached into a sack, plucked out a large one and dropped it into the boiling water. With a shrug, he said, 'No butter,' then he started laughing as if it was a very funny joke. As thankful as Sandreena was for her life, it was obvious that her saviour was a little mad.

'How did you find me?' she asked, her voice raspy.

Hearing her tone he stopped cooking, scuttled to her side and took up a water skin. 'I left this here for you, but you didn't find it.' He held it up and she drank eagerly. The water was bitter with minerals and badly tanned leather flavours, but it quenched her thirst.

He sat back, looking at his makeshift boiling pot for a moment, then said, 'I was looking for crabs and found you on the rocks. Almost dead. I carried you back here.'

She narrowed her eyes slightly. He didn't look strong enough to carry her, but she had learned early in life that appearances could be misleading. 'The last thing I remember was killing an assassin, maybe two, and then someone came up behind me.' She fell silent for a moment, then said, 'I was overconfident.'

The old man laughed, a harsh barking sound. 'I have no confidence at all! I'm a mouse! I hide in cracks and crevices, behind the walls, under the floor!'

'You've survived,' observed Sandreena as the old man used sticks to pull the crabs out of the boiling water. He put one on another poorly tanned skin, picked up a rock and smashed the crab's shell repeatedly, until the steaming meat inside was exposed. He carried the makeshift platter to her, and put it on her lap.

'Yes, I've survived,' he said with a note of bitterness in his voice. 'I've survived,' he repeated.

'Who are you?' she asked.

'Who am I?' he responded. He sat back as if considering a difficult question. 'Those in the village call me the hermit, when they admit I'm around.' He looked around as if she could see through the cave's walls. 'I came from over the mountains, a long time ago.'

'How long?'

'A long time,' he said as if that was ample explanation.

'Do you have a name?'

Again he looked like he had to think about this. Finally he said, 'I did, but it's been so long since anyone's used it, I can't rightly remember what it might be.'

She shifted her weight and felt the pain in her side. 'Ribs?'

'I think they kicked you for a while. Ruthia must have been watching over you,' he said, invoking the name of the Goddess of Luck.

She laughed and instantly regretted it. It hurt everywhere.

'No, you should be dead,' insisted the old man, nodding vigorously. 'Six deep wounds, any of which should have killed you, and none did. Lots of other cuts that together could have bled you to death. I think they knocked you out, stripped you naked, then cut you up a bit. I think they were upset with you.'

'Well, I killed one of them, probably another as well.'

'Yes,' he said nodding as if in agreement. 'That would make them upset. After they took your clothing and your weapons, they threw you over the cliff; they must have thought you already dead.

'You should have died on the rocks, but the tide was in and you landed in the only deep pool near the village.' Again he nodded vigorously. 'Ruthia!'

'I'll make an offering at her shrine the first opportunity I have.' She wasn't jesting, as she took her devotions very seriously despite her Order and Ruthia's seeing the world in very different ways; hers sought balance, they accepted chaos and imbalance as natural.

'That would be good,' agreed the hermit. 'The water was very cold and that seemed to staunch the bleeding; you were only there a short while, else you would have drowned before you washed up on the rocks. I found you and carried you here.' He reached over and held up what appeared to be another bunch of skins and furs. 'Look, I made you this.'

Not entirely sure what it was he offered her, she said, 'Thank you.'

'You can wear it when you feel better.'

Then it struck her: she was more than two weeks by horse from the nearest Temple and even if there was a Keshian authority nearby, which there wasn't, they would take no interest in a girl wrapped in ragged skins claiming to be a Knight-Adamant of the Order of the Shield of the Weak. On foot she was a month away from help; even if she grew strong enough to walk, without weapons or coin, her chances of reaching the Temple down in Ithra were close to none.

She lay back and sighed, then started to nibble at the crab. It was surprisingly good, if a little salty.

'What?' he asked hearing her sigh.

'I guess I'm going to have to find those who did this to me.'

He looked at her as if she were the mad one. 'Why?'

'They have my weapons and clothing, and a very good horse. I want them back.'

He laughed, a short barking sound, then stopped, then laughed again, full-throatedly. After a minute of laughter, she heard him say, 'Ah, don't say I never warned you. You're asking a lot of Ruthia after everything she's already done for you.'

'Perhaps,' answered Sandreena. 'But when I'm done, they'll be the ones praying for mercy.' She ate more crab and the hermit fell silent.

Days passed and finally Sandreena's sense of time returned. She had no idea how long she had lingered in the cave, but knew it had been at least three weeks, perhaps a month. She would sport a nasty assortment of scars, for the hermit had sewn her up with some sort of rough fibre, perhaps stripped from some kind of seaweed. She'd been tended by all manner of healers, from the finest magic-using priests in the Temples to village medicine women with their poultices and teas. She found it oddly amusing that she was recovering from her worst collection of injuries, perhaps more severe than all her previous ones combined, and with the most primitive ministrations she had ever received.

As she began picking out her stitches with a fine fishbone – the ones she could reach, anyway – she reminded herself that she needed to thank the hermit, as well as her Goddess – and perhaps she needed to include Ruthia as well. That she was still alive was proof that some benevolent force was looking after her.

By the time the hermit returned she had removed all the

stitches within her reach. She held out the fish bone and motioned to her naked back. He nodded, sat down and quickly took the stitches out. She could feel a little blood welling and some tenderness, but at last she could move without the constant tightness.

She pulled on the rough hide dress he had made for her and said, 'There, that's better.'

'I was going to wait a little longer; some of those wounds were very deep,' said the hermit.

'One thing I know is wounds, and another is my own body,' Sandreena said. 'Those stitches would only start being a problem if we waited any longer to cut them out.' She indicated the cave with her hand. 'You don't have a lot of chirurgeon's tools here.'

He found that very funny and laughed deeply. 'I did once.' Then he stopped. He tilted his head as if listening for something. 'Or did I?'

Whatever had happened to this man long ago, was lost even to him. A tragedy, illness, or a vengeful god, whatever the cause, most of his memory and mind were gone. Still, he had visited kindness on a stranger with no hope of recompense. She wished to repay him, but she lacked even the most fundamental possessions. He had found her as naked as the day she was born, and as helpless.

Still, she felt a debt. 'Once I settle matters with those killers, is there anything I can do for you?'

He was silent for a long time, then he said, 'I would like a real pot.' Then his eyes widened and he sat up. 'No, a kettle!' He nodded vigorously. 'Yes, a fine iron kettle!' His eyes grew even wider. 'And a knife! A knife so I can clean my catch! Yes, that would be wonderful.'

Sandreena felt her heart break. His desires were so modest

and his gratitude for even the possibly empty promise of those minor treasures moved her. 'You shall have them, and more,' she whispered.

There was silence in the cave while he built the little fire he kept banked during the day; the sun was setting and soon it would be very dark. She lay back and closed her eyes. She needed rest. In a day, two at the most, she had to leave this cave; some men wearing black caps had to die.

Sandreena hefted the small branch. The makeshift club was her only weapon, and she felt even more underdressed in the otter skins she wore than she had when she was naked. Sleeping under a pile of rags was one thing, wearing them in place of armour was entirely another.

She was as steady on her feet as she could be on her recent diet of crab-meat, shellfish and the occasional tuber the hermit had cooked up. She could still use a good meal, but knew she wouldn't have one until she put paid to these injuries and got her armour and clothing back. She hoped her horse was all right; it was one of the best mounts she had ever ridden. The mare was dependable, even-tempered and meaner than a tavern rat when she needed to be.

Sandreena approached the back of the tavern, the last place she had any memory of, and the logical starting point for finding her attackers. She hoped Enos and his family were all right, despite them being particularly unpleasant people.

There were no lights. It was twilight and even if there were no guests, Ivet should have been in the kitchen preparing a meal for her husband and sons. By the time she reached the window, she knew in her bones the family was not all right.

She quickly made her way to the one door in the rear of the building. The door was open, and in the kitchen she found the first body. The woman lay sprawled across the floor, her head at an awkward angle. Sandreena quickly deduced that someone had grabbed the woman from behind and broken her neck. Her clothing was intact, so she had been spared rape before she was killed. Sandreena knew that dead was dead, but at least it had been quick and relatively painless.

The Knight-Adamant had no idea why Ivet had been killed, perhaps for offering a room and food to a traveller, or to ensure no one found out who had killed the wandering knight, or maybe they did it for the pleasure of killing. She knew that the father and boys would be dead in another part of the inn. She wondered if some of the pathetic weapons she had seen them use against the bandits might still be around.

She found the three swords and a badly scarred buckler stored in a food locker. The weapons were so inferior that the murderers had left them behind, even though they'd pillaged about every piece of food from the inn. She found one bag of millet. Even the thought of cooking that simple grain caused her mouth to water in anticipation. She inspected the bag in the gloom and found it unroasted. She'd have to find a pan, start a fire, and then boil some water . . . She threw the bag aside and continued her search.

In another corner of the kitchen she found a platter with an apple on it. It was hardly fresh, but still edible and Sandreena devoured it in moments. She sighed. She would probably end up dead some time in the next few hours, but if she did survive, she vowed she'd never be this hungry again.

She returned outside with the buckler and the best of the

three swords – still duller than any sword should be – and went to the window through which she had first spotted the men whom she killed. Given that she had been in the shed when she was struck from behind, she assumed that whoever witnessed her kill his companions must have been standing . . . There! She fixed the point in her mind and hurried over to it. Because of the time between her short fight and being attacked herself, this was the most logical place for her assailants to have stood watching. She studied the landscape in the fading light. Soon the moons would be up and she'd be able to travel but now she had to deduce where to go next.

She waited patiently until the larger moon rose, quickly followed by the middle moon. The small moon wouldn't rise for another few hours, so while it wasn't yet Three Moons Bright, there would be enough illumination for her to find her way. She studied the foothills behind the inn, which swept into the eastern mountains, looking for obvious trails or paths. As the moons rose further over the mountains, the landscape below remained shrouded in shadows. After nearly an hour of searching, she saw it. A cleft between two small hills and a gentle rise into what appeared to be a notch in the mountains. Had there been fog, or rain, or even a heavy mist, she would not have seen it.

She began a steady trot towards the trail, hoping she'd reach it before sunrise. At this time she could not gauge the distance, and her memory was still vague. Things she should remember easily were difficult for her to recall. She'd had the problem before, following a blow to the head, and had most certainly struck it on the rocks in her fall. Those murderous bastards had much to answer for.

She hefted her poor sword and knew that she'd have gone after them, even if that tree-branch club had been her only weapon.

The sun had been up for nearly two hours when she found the tracks of six or seven horses, one most certainly her own. She lacked expertise in the wilds, though she had spent enough time travelling the countryside to be able to read basic trail signs, and she knew she was on the right path. She continued on, having to stop to rest far more often than she wished. Her injuries and lack of good food had weakened her far more than she wanted to admit, and she knew her dreams of walking straight into their camp and quickly dispatching the thugs were just that, dreams. She had her Temple magic, but she had never tried to invoke it when her concentration was this poor. Still, the priests, monks, and sisters of her Order had drilled the spells and mantras into her, and they were not spells to be ignored if she could channel her wrath behind them. She might fail, but if she died, she'd take them . . . The soul crystal! Suddenly she remembered that it was gone, stored among the other items in her belt pouch. She cursed herself for a fool. She couldn't die fighting, at least not yet. Her mission was incomplete and she had no means to send the information back to the Father-Bishop in Krondor.

Sandreena cursed herself for being rash. She had dealt with thugs and robbers many times and should have scouted around for someone holding the horses or standing lookout before she hit the two at the window. She continued her self-condemnation, knowing that had she found her ambusher first, at least she would have been prepared for the two near the house.

With a sigh, she let go of this second-guessing. Regret was a trap and it often crippled, she reminded herself.

She had travelled another hour along the trail when she heard the voices. Before she understood why, the hair on her arms and neck stood up and her skin puckered in gooseflesh. Rather than the usual camp noises she expected – the muffled speech, the sound of horses tied to a picket, perhaps the laughing or the sound of weapons being cleaned – she heard a rhythmic chanting. She didn't recognize the language, but something about the sound set her teeth on edge. It was not native to Kesh or the Kingdom. She spoke a fair number of tongues and could recognize many more, but she wasn't even sure that what she heard was human speech.

The path she followed led into a cleft between two low rocks, and she assumed a small valley or plateau was on the other side. She quickly picked the left side, scampered up it. If there were sentries beyond the gap, she didn't want to run into another ambush. Still, she found it odd no lookouts had been posted on the rocks, for it was the most logical place to put them.

She reached the top and looked down on a horrific scene. There were no sentries or lookouts because no sane man or woman would knowingly approach this place.

A man in a dark orange robe trimmed in black – a magician of some fashion by the look of him – stood holding a huge black wooden staff over his head. The staff was topped by some kind of crystal globe, pulsing with an evil purple light. Just looking at it made Sandreena's eyes sting.

She swallowed back her bile, fighting hard against the urge to retch over what greeted her. Near a pathway leading up into the mountains stood a band of fighters. They were dressed in a variety of clothing, but all had the look of hard-bitten, experienced warriors. Sandreena judged them likely to be well-paid mercenaries and ex-soldiers, not fanatics. Many of them looked away from the carnage before them and those who didn't were pale and shaken by what was taking place.

Around a large, flat stone altar, knelt half a dozen priests and priestesses, their robes thrown back so their chests and backs were bare. Behind them stood others, their backs stripped raw from flails. They were leaning heavily on the backs of those kneeling before them; it was some ritual offering of blood and pain, but to whom?

In the middle of the stone, bodies were piled. At least a dozen men and women, and one small arm that Sandreena was certain belonged to one of Eno's two boys. She realized that had she searched the inn she would have found them missing, not dead as she had assumed. The raiders must have startled Ivet, whom they killed to keep from raising an alarm. Then they must have seized the husband and sons. More villagers had obviously been dragged away, too, judging from the body count.

On top of the pile the last remaining victim lay struggling, his arms and legs held in place by a set of ropes, each held by more monks or priests or whatever those murderous dogs were. Sandreena spat quietly to keep her stomach from churning.

The magician finished his incantation and something appeared in the air above the struggling man. The victim cried out in abject terror as a black form, a thing of long spider-like limbs, a hawk's razor-sharp beak, and huge bat wings, hovered above him for a moment, then dived to land with a heavy thud on his stomach.

Throwing back its head, the demon howled, a sound that set

Sandreena's teeth on edge. She saw several of the mercenaries step further away, while others winced at the noise. The demon cocked its head as it looked at the screaming man upon whom it sat, looking like some bird of prey from a terrible nightmare; then it pulled back one of its long spindly arms, and with stunning speed, it drove it into the man's chest. Sandreena was only too familiar with the sound of ripping flesh and cracking bones, and the man's screams were cut off as his body convulsed when his lungs were ripped out. Before his life fled, he was forced to witness the creature devouring his heart.

Sandreena had seen many horrific things in her life, from the degradation and abuses she endured as a brothel child, to the blood of battle. She had witnessed men dying in their own excrement, put of out their misery by their friends, murdered children and entire villages slaughtered for the meagre goods they harboured, but nothing had felt more evil to her than what she was witnessing now.

The suppliants bowed before the conjured creature and the chanting renewed its urgency. The demon flew to land upon the upraised staff of the magician who staggered slightly under its weight; it must have been heavier than it looked, thought Sandreena. And it can fly . . .

Magic, she thought, counting herself a fool. This thing hailed from some nether region where the natural laws were different. Still, it looked as if the magician was faltering.

Then he fell, and with a shriek of rage, the conjured creature vanished, leaving behind a foul, oily smoke, the stench of which reached Sandreena. The wail that rose from the assembled suppliants was that of a mother who had lost her child.

The magician began to stand, but the worshippers leapt on

him, their bare hands outstretched like claws, or wheeling their flails, and he went down beneath the onslaught. They tore the man apart before Sandreena's eyes. She took a long, slow breath, and wished she could understand what she saw.

From their expressions, the fighting men were also shocked. Many of them had weapons half-drawn, as if they expected to be attacked in turn. Then Sandreena noticed a fact that had eluded her during the chaos of the last few minutes. The men wore an assortment of head coverings, tied bandannas, scarves, flop hats, forager's caps, kepis, cocked hats, and berets, but they were all black. These men were the Black Caps the villagers had spoken of, the men Father-Bishop Creegan had warned her might be in the air. They certainly were more than simple pirates and smugglers.

She sat back, crouching below the top of the rock, so as not to be seen. Why would a band of cutthroats come to this isolated mountain valley? Why would they be in league with a bunch of demonic cultists? And what was the purpose of that bloody ritual she had just witnessed?

She knew she had to find her way back to Krondor, but she also knew that there would be questions. The Father-Bishop would interrogate her for hours and at this moment she could answer few of them. But someone at the Temple would be able to give her some insight into what she had observed, which meant that she needed to push aside her revulsion and continue to watch. Taking a breath, she raised up again.

A quick count put the total number of fighting men at thirty and she could see two dozen cultists. The mangled corpses, including the dead magician, were left on the ground. She moved along the top of the rock, trying to stay in the shadows. The moons overhead made it easy enough for anyone to see her, if they were vigilant. Then again, she considered, they thought her dead and they gathered around several fires, so their vision would be weaker.

The cultists hitched up their robes, ignoring the bloody shreds of flesh on their backs and shoulders. Sandreena wondered if they had some magic to prevent festering, else many of them would be ill within two days. Maybe they just didn't care.

Cults were anathema to the organized Temples. They were almost always predicated on bad doctrine or some half-baked heretical theory. They created distrust and fear. Sandreena, as a Knight-Adamant, wasn't always recognized as a Temple functionary, and even when she was identified as a member of a religious martial order, it didn't occur to people that she could use magic. Priests and priestesses in the Temples in big cities were one thing. Town priests, monks and priors were viewed as part of the fabric of the society. But in the smaller villages in the out-of-the way places, anyone practising any kind of magic was to be feared.

If the Father-Bishop didn't forbid her, she would personally inform the Temple of Lims-Kragma in Krondor of what was taking place here. No one had less patience with evil death magic than the followers of the Goddess of Death; they were content to let people come to their Mistress in their own time. They didn't see any need to hurry anyone along. Most death magic, or necromancy, perverted and twisted the soul energy leaving the dying body, a further insult to the Goddess, as that soul couldn't then find the Goddess's Hall, to be judged and reborn. Sandreena had no doubt that the Temple would dispatch a full company of the Drawers of the Web, their martial order, to come down here and clean up this mess.

Still, she had a duty to her own Temple first.

As she anticipated, the fighters began trudging up the hill, speaking softly amongst themselves, and they kept a discreet distance from the cultists. They were heading to the east of the temple where the carnage had occurred. She waited until she was looking at the backs of the last cultists, then slipped down to follow.

Gripping her poor sword and shield much tighter than necessary, she started trailing the large pack of murderous Black Caps.

Sandreena's legs were cramping; abuse, fatigue, lack of food and water, all were taking their toll, as well as a considerable amount of tension. She had found what she sought: the Black Caps' camp. There were more people there, ten who seemed prisoners, two guards. The prisoners did the menial work, by what she could see, tending the fires, cooking meals, cleaning clothing, weapons and tack. Everyone at the camp was subdued, and if news of the fate of the magician had reached the prisoners, they apparently had no joy in it.

Sandreena found her horse tied to a picket at the rear of the camp. The camp looked as if it had been established for a while: they had built several wooden shacks and even one good-sized cabin. The three fighters who entered it looked to be the leaders of the mercenaries, as Sandreena thought of them. That might be a good thing, as mercenaries often knew when to quit; fanatic cultists never did.

She considered the possibility of reaching her horse and riding out of here, but unless every person in the camp slept soundly, there was almost no chance of that at all. She wished she knew where her belt pouch had ended up. If any of the cutthroats found the soul gem, they might have kept it under the mistaken impression it was a precious stone. It looked similar to a dark ruby or sapphire depending on the light, but if any magic user examined it, they would quickly come to understand that it was holy magic, and would probably destroy it.

What to do? She was torn by the need to report the location of this camp, and the desire to learn as much as possible. Moreover, she was hardly equipped to travel, and needed to replace her missing arms and armour. She might be able to pick off a sentry and take what she needed.

She waited as the camp settled down. It was a restless quiet. The cultists sat sullenly in small groups as far away from the others as they could get. The prisoners who carried food and drink to them cringed when they were spoken to, and the fighters kept a respectful distance. Sandreena had no idea what lay at the heart of this difference, but it was clear neither side considered this a happy circumstance.

Sandreena weighed her options. She decided to wait for the camp to settle in for the night. Whatever else, the smell of cooking was causing her stomach to knot.

Getting information back was paramount, but she could hardly achieve that goal if she died from exhaustion and hunger. Letting out a long resigned sigh, she put her chin on her forearm and tried to get comfortable on top of the rocks.

Hours passed, but as the large moon started to set and the small moon began to rise, the last of the captives bedded down for the night. There was light streaming from the door of the leaders' hut. She had identified one fighter – a black-bearded thug who sported lots of rings, and gold chains around his neck – as the

likely leader of the mercenaries. He and two others had retired
to that hut after eating.

Sandreena carefully made her way down the rocks and through
the camp. The cultists had bedded down in rude leather and
wooden shelters, the evening's slaughter having exhausted them.
The fighters were scattered among a dozen small huts. Reaching
the side of the largest, Sandreena listened through the wall.

'Remember that inn in Roldem?' said a voice.

'Which inn? There's a lot of them in Roldem,' came the answer.

'You know that one. Where we were playing lin-lan and you
got into that fight with that Royal Navy sailor over him trying
to take back part of his bet when no one was looking?' said the
first voice.

'Ya, that one. What about it?' said the second voice.

'They had this lamb pie, with peas and carrots and those little
onions, you know these?'

'Ya, I know those onions.'

'Well, they had this pie, you see, and it had something else
in it, some kind of spice or herb. It was really special.'

'What about the pie?' asked the second voice, impatiently.

'I love that pie, that's all.'

A third voice said, 'You can sit and talk all night about the
greatest meal you've ever had, but it won't change anything.'
This last voice was deep and raspy, and its tone left no doubt
who was in charge. Sandreena would bet her life on him being
the leader. Ironically, she considered that she was probably risking
her life simply being here. Still, a lack of boldness had never
been her problem, and she knew she needed her weapons, armour
and horse to survive the journey back to Ithra.

'Ya,' said the first voice.

The man she now thought of as the leader said, 'I don't see any other way. We need to just kill them all as fast as we can, before they start using their magic, then grab what we can and get out of here.'

The first voice said, 'Ya.'

But the second voice said, 'Even with Purdon dead, the rest of them can still do some nasty things and, besides, there's Belasco. He doesn't seem the type to forgive betrayal. And we did take his gold.'

'We took his gold,' said the leader, 'to keep things around here under control. But what we didn't do was drink the demon's piss. We're not like them. We may be dogs, but we're our own dogs, not his.'

The room fell quiet and then the leader said, 'There's something else. One of the old boys in Pointer's Head told me a story, 'bout a group like us who got sent here ten or so years ago. He said that they sailed all the way around from the Sunsets, and that they'd been provisioned here and that someone said they were heading to the Peaks.'

'Peaks?' asked the first voice.

'This is the Peaks of the Quor, you idiot.'

'Oh, I didn't know,' came the plaintive response.

'How can you be camped in a place for four bloody months and not know what it's called?'

'Nobody told me!'

The leader said, 'This thing with that girl, in the armour. She had Temple Knight written all over her.'

'So?' asked the second voice.

'So, if one of the Temples is sending a Knight to investigate, things here are getting too twitchy.' There was a moment of silence, then he continued. 'I signed on to terrorize some locals, maybe deal with a constable or two from Ithra if they showed up. But I've seen those Temple Knights in a fight. A murder cult surfaced down in Kesh ten years ago, hiding out at the docks in Hansulé. A bunch of Knights from Lims-Kragma showed up and the result wasn't a pretty sight. Magic everywhere, and they didn't take prisoners. Slaughtered every one of those cult fighters like they was lambs.'

'Magic!' said the first voice, like it was a curse.

'The gold is good,' said the second.

'But not if you're dead. Can't spend it here, and Lims-Kragma don't give you a better turn at the Wheel if you brought a little gold with you.'

Silence followed for almost a full minute, then the second voice asked, 'What do we do?'

'This morning, before they wake, I want you to wake Blakeny, Wallace, Garton, and that murderous little rat Allistair, quietly. We hit them hard and fast, and they're all dead before they know it. Then we kill those villagers, grab what we can and ride south. I don't know about you, but then I'm on the first outbound ship, I don't care where it's going. Maybe I'll head down to that other land, Novindus. Or go to the Sunsets.

'But something's coming, something I want no part of, and the faster we get away from here, the better.'

'What about our gold?' asked the second voice.

'Purdon was supposed to have it,' replied the leader.

'The magician?' asked the first voice.

'Yes,' said the leader. 'So if no one's disturbed his kit since he was murdered for failing to bring in the right demon, it should still be there.'

'How much?' asked the second voice.

'Does it matter?' asked the leader. 'It's gold, we take whatever there is. If any of the boys don't like it, they're free to stay and see whom Belasco sends to replace Purdon. They can explain to the next bunch of those blood-drinking whores and pimps why the first batch are dead.'

'OK,' said the second voice. 'It's time.'

'No,' said the leader. 'There's an hour before sunrise. That'll put us in the saddle as soon as the sun comes up and then we head south.'

'How much longer is that?' asked the second voice.

Sandreena glanced at the small moon rising and knew the answer. She had an hour to figure out what to do next.

• CHAPTER THIRTEEN •

Conclave

S ANDREENA TOOK A DEEP BREATH.
She had no love for anyone in this camp, but she had sympathy for the villagers still being used as slaves. She struggled for a long time over her best course of action, but finally rejected all of the choices that didn't involve trying to save the slaves.

She slowly worked her way over to where they were sleeping and gently nudged a young woman. The woman awoke suddenly and was about to shout as Sandreena's hand clamped down over her mouth. 'Shh,' she whispered. 'If you want to live, make no sound. Do you understand me?'

The young woman nodded. 'In a few minutes the guards are going to kill the cultists. Then they'll kill you and your friends. Help me wake them up quietly and escape silently. Do you understand?'

Again the woman nodded and Sandreena let her go. There were eleven other sleeping villagers, all of whom looked exhausted and underfed. They were normally listless but their fear energized them now. The young woman who was the first one Sandreena awoke said, 'What do we do?'

'Go north,' she said. 'Find a safe place to hide for a day. Those cutthroats will ride east to Akrakon; then south to Ithra. After they've gone, it should be safe for you to go home.'

'Who are you?' asked a man standing behind the young woman.

'I'm a Knight-Adamant from the Temple of Dala in Krondor. If I can get out of here alive, I'm going to return with help in case others like those Black Cap bastards come back.'

'Thank you,' said one old woman, obviously frightened.

'Don't thank me yet. I haven't made it out of here alive, yet.' Looking at the young woman she said, 'Remember this, if I don't get out, someone else has to go to Ithra. There's a Keshian garrison there and a shrine to Dala. Go to the shrine first and tell its tenders that Sandreena of the Shield of the Weak spoke to you. Tell them what you've seen and heard, and then tell them that someone named Belasco is behind all of this.' She looked the young woman in the eyes. 'Can you remember that?'

The young woman nodded. 'Sandreena,' she said softly, looking at the Knight-Adamant, as if trying to burn her face into her memory. 'Belasco is behind this.'

'Good. The monk at the shire will talk to the garrison commander and perhaps the Empire will send someone up here. If they don't, my Temple certainly will. Now go!' she hissed.

The prisoners needed no further prodding, they turned as one and began scrambling over the rocks to the north. Sandreena knew that if they could get a half an hour's start, the fighters wouldn't bother to hunt them down. Glancing at the moon, she realized half an hour was about all she had, too.

She hurried to where the horses were picketed. In their certainty that they were under no threat up here in the hills, the Black Caps had become complacent. She approached the horses slowly, for she didn't want their nickering and stomping to alert the three murderers in the big hut or any light sleepers close by.

She reached the side of her mount and found her unharmed. She patted her horse's neck as she looked for any sign of her tack. It lay in a heap nearby and Sandreena quickly gathered it up. She saw nothing that resembled her armour or weapons, let alone the little pouch with the soul gem in it. Most likely her armour had been apportioned to some of the smaller men, one of the leaders had claimed her mace and shield, and the soul gem would be sold to a gem merchant who would have no idea of its true properties or worth.

She pushed aside the regret she was unable to gather more information, and instead considered trying to muffle her horse's hooves, but there was nothing at hand that would easily lend itself to doing so, and she didn't have the time. Sandreena quietly led her horse away from the others and paused a short distance away, waiting to see if the sound of its hooves on the ground attracted notice. When no alarm was raised, she slowly moved through the heart of the sleeping camp and made her way down the trail. Tying her horse to a bush, she hurried back up to the rock from which she'd first observed the camp.

The thirty minutes passed quickly and as she anticipated. She watched as the three murderers from the hut quietly roused their companions. No one seemed to notice the absence of the prisoners, all of their attention seemed focused on the sleeping cultists.

Sandreena felt a conflict; her Order mandate demanded that she should attempt to balance this conflict, which would almost certainly get her killed instantly. Yet it galled her to see cold-blooded murder, even if those being slaughtered were monsters. And she didn't relish the notion of the mercenaries riding off without penalty. Some of those men, perhaps even those in the hut, had sliced her up and thrown her into the sea as food for the crabs.

Without thinking about it for too long, she picked up a rock and threw it hard at the foot of a sleeping cultist, just as the fighters started to cross the clearing to where they slept. In the dark, none of the fighters took note.

But the man whose foot she struck came awake with a cry and before anyone could ascertain what happened, chaos erupted. The waking cultists saw a band of armed men moving towards them and reacted with the only weapons they possessed, their magic.

Green energies shot out and several of the armed men screamed in pain, while the other fighters bellowed their outrage and charged. Sandreena scampered down the rock face, not wishing or needing to witness further carnage. She knew the thirty swords would eventually dispose of the twenty or so cultists, but a lot fewer Black Caps were going to ride safely away from this hellish place.

Sandreena rode down the trail at a nice canter, knowing those fighting for their lives behind her wouldn't hear a thing.

Sandreena worked her way across the rocks to the cave where the hermit had tended to her. She called out, 'Hello! Are you here?' as she entered. It took her some moments for her eyes to adjust to the gloom after riding through the sunrise.

She carried a small kettle and an assortment of cooking items, a knife, ladle, several spoons, and two earthenware bowls. She had raided the inn when passing through town, knowing the previous owners had no use for them anymore. When there was no answer, she moved deeper into the cave.

She found the hermit sitting against the wall, with his eyes closed. 'Wake up, old man!' Sandreena said, for she had no time to tarry, but wanted to make good on her promise. The old man didn't move.

She put down her burden and knelt next to him. She knew before she touched him that he was dead. She quickly examined him and found no wounds. He had simply died during the night while he slept. His face held no expression of pain, and there were no contortions on his body, so he must have never awakened.

Sighing, she reminded herself that sometimes, people just die. He was old, he had lived in a harsh way and it was his time.

She said a quick silent prayer to her Goddess to see him on his way to Lims-Kragma's Hall, and then left the cave. She mounted her horse and turned it towards the south. With one last look around the forlorn seascape and rocky coasts, she wondered if there was anyone in the world beside herself that would note the passing of that strange old man. She put that question aside, for now her only goal was to get to Ithra alive and send warning to the Temple in Krondor.

Pug of Sorcerer's Isle, perhaps the greatest practitioner of magic in the entire world of Midkemia, waved his hand and created a barrier to protect himself and his companions from the blinding, choking smoke. He looked at the elven spellweaver named Temar, and said, 'This is the worst I've seen in a hundred years.'

Temar nodded. 'I've seen a few that match, but not many. Drought and lightning are a bad combination, Pug.'

Temar was from the elven community at Baranor. For ten years Pug and Miranda had visited their enclave in the remote mountain area of Kesh known as the Peaks of the Quor, in an attempt to understand those strange aliens, those they protected – the Sven'gar-ri – and the equally odd race known as the Quor who protected them.

'It wasn't especially dry until a week ago,' said Temar. 'But the undergrowth here is so thick, that only lightning could start something like this.' He glanced around and pointed to the north. 'And an especially dry wind is doing us a double disservice; it's fanning the flames and drying out everything before them.'

'Rain?' asked Pug.

The elf gave Pug one of his small smiles that meant his answer was going to be wry. 'I'm good at weather magic, Pug, but not that good. There's not enough moisture in the air, nor are there any clouds close enough for me to summon. I could attempt it, but I know the effort would be a waste of time.'

A loud pop alerted them to Magnus's arrival. The elf was unfazed by the sudden appearance of the human magician, but Pug was startled to see he was not alone. 'Father,' greeted the tall, white haired magician.

'Who is this?' asked Pug.

'This is Amirantha of Satumbria, someone whom you need to speak with.'

'This cannot wait until I return?'

'I think not,' answered Magnus.

Pug nodded. 'We're concerned about this fire,' he said, pointing to the raging flames on the next ridge. 'It's not likely to reach Baranor, but it might. Conditions here are not good.' Turning to Amirantha, he said, 'Sorry to stint on social pleasantries, but time is fleeting.'

Temar also nodded a brief greeting. 'It's going to get very hot here over the next hour, Pug.'

Magnus asked, 'Can you not turn the wind, blow it back on itself?'

'I can command it,' answered the elf, 'but not over so wide a front. And, like all things with fundamental elements, there is always a price to pay.'

'So rain is out of the question?' asked Amirantha, looking at the rapidly approaching inferno.

'There is no hope of rain,' said Temar.

'Perhaps I can help,' said Amirantha. 'Please stand away from me.'

Pug, Magnus, and Temar moved as Amirantha motioned them to move further back. When he judged them to be at a safe distance, he held up his hand, closed his eyes and incanted a spell. Brilliant white light shot from his hand and burnt a line in the ground. In seconds it encircled the Warlock. He nodded in satisfaction, then stepped out of the circle, being careful not to step on the burned line as he took up a position between it and the people watching him.

He began another spell, this one longer and more involved, and then something huge appeared in the circle. For lack of a better description, Pug saw it as a thing of water, a huge being roughly man-like in shape, but clearly fluid. Ripples across the surface held surging waves within its form, and bubbles and foam seemed to deck its shoulders like a mantle. It cried out in a language that sounded like the roar of rapids or the pounding of waves, and rushed Amirantha. The warlock stood motionless for when the creature reached the boundary of the circle, it recoiled.

Amirantha said, 'Summoned you, I have; and my bidding you will do.' The creature seemed disinclined to agree. Amirantha began another spell, and then it grew quiet. Amirantha pointed to the advancing flames and said one word, then the circle vanished.

The water creature grew. Pug and the others stepped back in amazement as it doubled in size in a few seconds. Amirantha turned his back and walked slowly to where the others stood and said, 'This should take care of the problem.'

The water-being continued to grow and was soon over twenty feet in height; then it sprang into the air. Like a bowshot it was gone, arching high into the sky and then suddenly it vanished. Rain fell.

There was not a cloud in the sky yet rain poured down over the flames.

Amirantha said, 'It won't be enough to extinguish the fire completely, but it should stop the flames spreading this far.' He glanced at Temar. 'And perhaps it will give our friend here the time he needs to select a more permanent solution?'

Temar nodded. 'I can feel the weather changing. In a half-day, there will be enough moisture in the air for me to call the rain. Thank you.'

Amirantha nodded and smiled. Pug said, 'What was that creature? I've never seen one like it before.'

'It was a simple water elemental. A very minor demon. Nasty if you don't contain it immediately as it can fill your lungs with water very fast. My first encounter with one was most painful.' He glanced at the falling water and said, 'Water and fire elementals are natural enemies. Once I made it listen, just pointing out the fire made it eager to kill it.' He chuckled. 'Elementals are not among the brightest of creatures.'

'Will you have any problem controlling it?' asked Magnus, obviously curious.

'No,' said Amirantha. 'The elemental will give itself up to the fire once it runs out of water . . . well, it saves me the trouble of banishing it back to the demon realm.'

'It's a demon?' asked Pug.

'Not entirely, but close in some respects.' He glanced around. 'Interesting place. I don't believe I've ever been here before.'

'You travel a lot?' asked Pug, finding something about this newcomer's manner wryly amusing.

'Many years ago. I have settled down a bit, recently.' He looked around some more and said, 'Given when we arrived at your very interesting island, the time of day we departed, and the position of the sun here, I assume we are many miles to the east of where we were a few minutes ago.' He glanced at Pug and said, 'Somewhere in Kesh.' Then he added, 'Perhaps the Peaks of the Quor.'

'I'm impressed,' said Pug. 'Seeing as you claim to have never been here before.'

'I haven't,' said Amirantha with a friendly smile. 'But given the angle of the sun and the time of day, and the fact we're standing on a mountainside, looking down at what can only be sea coast, there weren't a lot of other likely places. I may not have been here, but I have studied a map or two.'

Pug glanced at his son. 'My demon expert?' His son nodded. 'Where did you find him?'

Magnus said, 'Actually, Kaspar brought him to the island last night.'

Amirantha smiled. 'It was morning when we left Maharta.'

'Maharta?' asked Pug.

'Close to my current home.' He glanced at the other two men and the elf and said, 'If we're going to talk, may I suggest we retire to somewhere less smoky?'

Pug glanced at Temar, who said, 'Go. I can easily return to Baranor from here.' Originally from Elvandar, Temar had elected to come to Baranor with others of his kind to revitalize the dying Sun Elves, the pocket of elven guardians who had been placed in the mountains ages ago by the Dragon Lords.

Duty bound, they had remained even though the toll on them had been terrible. When discovered by Kaspar of Olasko and his men ten years before, the Sun Elves had been barely able to defend themselves against a band of void creatures that had somehow reached Midkemia and taken up residency a few miles away from the elven enclave.

Now, many of those known as the glamredhel, the rustic elves who had once lived north of the Teeth of the World, had migrated to Baranor, swelling the population and revitalizing the community. Temar was originally from the Tsurani world of Midkemia, an eldar Spellweaver who had come out of simple curiosity, liked what he found, and remained. He was as fascinated by the mysterious Sven'gar-ri and their Quor protectors as Pug and the other magicians.

Speaking to the Quor was a frustrating undertaking, for while they appeared primitive, even simple at times, at other times they made observations that hinted at a deep, perhaps even profound understanding of things beyond Pug's own considerable intellect. He had come to speak with the Quor and the Sven'gar-ri over one hundred times, and although each time he felt as if he had gained a tiny bit of insight, no whole picture emerged. He was convinced the Quor were not native to this world, but nothing they said indicated that directly. They spoke without regard for time, being content to live in the moment, and their only concerns revolved around protecting the Sven'gar-ri.

Those alien beings were most certainly not of this world, yet they were somehow connected to Midkemia in a vital way, perhaps essential. They didn't communicate in any fashion Pug understood, but rather filled the air around them – or the minds of those with whom they spoke – with music. Sven'gar-ri music was unlike anything Pug had encountered over the years, it was pure distilled feeling.

He had planned to remain and study the Quor and Sven'gar-ri, but it was clear that his son thought the arrival of this stranger a more pressing matter. And, he had asked Magnus to find him an expert on demons.

Pug said to Temar, 'Farewell. I will return again, soon.'

'You are always welcome,' said the elf, who bowed slightly to the others, then turned and began descending towards the pathway that would lead him home.

Both Pug and Magnus reached out and gripped Amirantha's arms. Suddenly they stood in Pug's study. Amirantha said, 'That is the most wonderful thing a magician can achieve! To go where one wants with just a thought!'

Magnus and Pug exchanged glances. In their experience no

practised magician was unaware of the ability to transport either via a Tsurani orb or through spells that take years to master. Even if he had never utilized the talent, he must have been exposed to it.

Pug moved behind his desk and motioned for Amirantha to take a seat opposite, while Magnus remained standing near the door. Pug said, 'You are welcome here, Amirantha.'

The man smiled, though it was clearly not a genuine sign of pleasure, but a social concession. 'I came with a friend, who I believe is being held hostage somewhere against my good behaviour?'

Pug glanced at Magnus who said, 'Your friend is hardly being held hostage, but I didn't feel the need to drag both of you along to find my father. I brought you with me in case he was unable to return here. If you'd like, I'll send for Brandos.'

'I'd like that very much, thank you.'

Magnus left the room, leaving Pug and Amirantha alone. 'Why don't you tell me why Kaspar thought it important to bring you here?'

Amirantha smiled and this time it was a genuinely amused smile. 'And thereby betraying his relationship to another authority besides the Maharajah to whom he's sworn fealty?'

'Hardly a betrayal,' said Pug. 'Kaspar's relationship to the Conclave of Shadows predates his taking service with the Maharajah. His service to his lord and to us is not in conflict. Our interests and the interests of the Kingdom of Muboya are never in conflict and occasionally overlap.

'Now, again, why did you come here?'

Amirantha paused, framing his response, then began recounting his experiences since the surprise summoning of the battle demon. Pug listened silently, asking no questions nor offering comment. When Amirantha recounted his relationship with his two brothers, Pug stiffened in his seat and his eyes narrowed, but he stayed silent.

'So, we rode out at sunrise prepared for a long overland journey, but once we were out of the city and in a small wood-land thicket, we were told to dismount, and for a brief moment I was convinced that Brandos and I had been brought to that out-of-the-way place to be murdered.

'Of course,' he quickly added, 'that was merely my suspicious nature. The General could just as easily have tossed us into the dungeons of Maharta.

'Then your son appeared out of nowhere and we vanished. I assume the soldiers will camp out until Kaspar returns, then they will all ride back to the city together.'

'Something like that,' said Pug, his eyes fixed on Amirantha.

'Where is Kaspar, by the way?'

'If I know Kaspar, he's fishing on the north beach. He takes these little holidays when he can. If he returns to Maharta too quickly, people start asking questions. He'll guest with us for another three days, then head back.'

Amirantha seemed amused by that, just as Magnus returned with Brandos, with Caleb trailing behind. Introductions were made, and the old fighter sat down in a chair in the corner, content to let his friend do the talking. Pug said, 'I need to ask you about your brother.'

'Which one?' asked Amirantha.

'Sidi,' replied Pug.

'Ah, I take it that you've encountered him, then.'

'Several times, never with a good outcome.'

'Kaspar informs me he is dead. Is that true?'

'An absolute certainty,' replied Pug. He seen the report from Jommy Killaroo, that a Tsurani great one had been heard singing a Kingdom tavern song as he walked towards the Dasati's magical beachhead on the world of Kelewan. His description matched with Miranda's of the body inhabited by Varen, or Sidi, who had the ability to jump from body to body. Either he had been on Kelewan when the planet was destroyed or stranded on the Dasati home world, where Pug had no doubt he would eventually perish. Despite his considerable power, Sidi would not have the time to adapt to that environment before death overtook him.

Amirantha sighed. 'Good. He was a murderous bastard, and he slaughtered our mother for the sheer fun of it.'

Brandos had heard the story before, but shook his head anyway. Seeing the gesture, Pug gave the old fighter a quizzical look.

'Just, well, it's an interesting family.'

Magnus was forced to chuckle and decided he liked the old fighter.

Amirantha looked slightly annoyed, but remained calm as he said, 'I am not like my brothers.'

'Apparently,' said Pug. 'Had you been like Sidi, I doubt you'd have come looking for someone in authority to speak with.

'Now, as we understand very little about the demon realm, what exactly do you think we should know?'

Amirantha looked uncomfortable for the first time. 'I've heard about your Academy at Stardock, Pug; no magic user hasn't. I first became aware of it fifty years ago, or so.

'I even visited near there when travelling in Great Kesh, and soon realized that my sort wouldn't be welcome. I noticed the self-congratulating smugness of a few magicians I spoke with at an inn in Shamata, then went about my business.'

Pug nodded. He knew the students and instructors who had been around at that time were a conservative group of Keshians who would not have considered any summoner of demons to be a 'proper' magician.

Amirantha continued. 'I was hardly surprised, you understand, even if I was slightly disappointed. I do not know who trained you, if you were an apprentice or how such things were done on the Tsurani world. I did hear that is where you came upon this Greater Path of Magic, as some call it; but my brothers and I were raised by a mad witch, and we learnt our craft the hard way. I hear you have many volumes of lore in Stardock, tomes, books, scrolls, epistles, and even a fine collection of stone and clay tablets, allowing magicians to learn from others who came before them.

'My brothers and I had none of that help. And we were influenced by a mother who I am certain had made a pact with dark powers. The madness, if you will, seemed to dilute with each child she bore. Sidi was insane before he was out of boyhood.

'Belasco is different, but his rages are uncontrollable and he hates easily.

'I have had my . . . difficulties, and it would be fair to say I have made a fair number of mistakes. However, I have learned that to battle for no good cause, to be angry without reason, harms myself more than anyone else. In the end, I have endeavoured to find my own little place in the world and live there contentedly.'

'By tricking the gullible out of their gold?' asked Pug.

'Ah, that,' said Amirantha. 'My reputation precedes me.'

'To be truthful, few Demon Masters live. It's one of the problems we face.'

'Problems?' asked the Warlock.

'Later. Continue telling us about this event that caused you to seek us out.'

'Can I presume that while you are a master of many arcane arts, you know little of demons?'

'A fair assumption for the moment,' said Pug, 'though I have encountered and destroyed a fair share of them.' He thought it best for the moment to forgo mentioning that one had almost killed him.

'I don't know what sort of child you were, Pug, but I was curious. I'd sit over an anthill and prod it with a twig to see how the ants reacted. My eldest brother liked to see things die, and my middle brother like to hurt things. In my defence, my fascinations were the most harmless, except perhaps to the ants.' He smiled, and seeing no reaction, continued. 'We spent a great deal of time alone. Our mother had little use for us once we could be set aside to fend for ourselves, she had her own interests.

'Looking back on my childhood, it's surprising that any of us survived. Mother provided charms and potions, wards and minor enchantments for local villagers, who endured her proximity because they occasionally found her useful. At a very early age, we boys were shown that our presence in the village wouldn't be tolerated. Each of us wandered into the village. Each of us in turn was beaten and chased away. I had the dogs set on me.' He rolled up the sleeve on his left arm, showing old bite marks. 'I've had this scar all my life. I was only seven years of age.'

Magnus said, 'Harsh.'

'In a way, yes,' said Amirantha. 'But I was also tempered to endure a great many hardships. It's why I'm still able to sit here and speak with you, rather than having had some demon decorate a cave with my entrails years ago.

'My curious nature led me to a cave a few miles from my mother's hut, and there I found ancient runes cut into the stone by some primitive shaman. Even at the age of ten I could feel the power behind them. I had learned some lessons from my mother by then, minor cantrips and spells, things that would hardly impress, still I was something of a prodigy, or at least my mother said so. My brothers hated me even more for having shown talent at an earlier age than they.

'I stood alone in this cave, and suddenly something on the wall seemed to make sense to me. I don't know if there were ancient powers still abiding in the runes, or if my native ability had seized on their meaning, but I remember thinking that here was something I could play with.

'I conjured Nalnar, and we had a very rocky introduction. He's not malicious, at least not compared to his brethren, but like all manner of demons he can be unpredictable and combative. Fortunately, he was also very young, and while he managed to singe my hair a little, I eventually beat him into submission.

'We then spent a good month learning to speak with one another – the demon language is almost impossible for humans to manage, without magic, and at that time I had little power to speak of. I would bring him here once or twice a week over two years, and learn what I could of him.'

Pug and Magnus now looked thoroughly fascinated.

'When Sidi slaughtered our mother, Belasco and I went our

separate ways. At our final parting he accused me of being complicit in our mother's death, though I'm certain he knew that to be false; he just liked having other people to blame.

'I've encountered him on a number of occasions over the years, and despite two civil conversations, he tries to kill me most of the time. I've been avoiding both my brothers for over a century now.'

Both Magnus and Pug were unfazed by this revelation. Given how long Sidi had been a thorn in Pug's side, that his younger brother was also long-lived came as no surprise.

'After fleeing my brothers, I wandered and Nalnar, my little demon friend, became instrumental in keeping me alive. He's nimble and clever, and for nearly two years stole things for me, like a pie from a window, a new pair of trousers from a wash-line, or a coin from a beggar's bowl. And while I was lonely, at least I had him to talk to.

'I learned more of the demon realm.'

Pug said, 'Please stop. I think there are things here I wish for others to hear, as well.' To Magnus he said, 'See that our guests are comfortable and let me know when—'

Amirantha sat bolt upright in his chair and said, 'Demons!'

'What?' asked Magnus.

'Where?' asked Pug.

'Here, close.' He stood, turning his head as if he was listening for something. Then he pointed to the north. 'There. Not far away. More than one.'

'How do you know?' asked Caleb.

Flashing an angry expression, Amirantha said, 'Trust me.' To Pug he said, 'They are powerful. We must go and meet them, now.'

'North?' asked Pug.

Then Magnus said, 'Kaspar. He's fishing on the north beach.'

'Take us there,' said Pug.

Brandos said, 'I should come. I'm the only sword you've got that knows how to fight demons.'

Pug glanced around the room and said, 'We all go.'

Magnus reached out and Pug took one of his hands; Amirantha and Brandos understood and extended theirs, Caleb standing between them. When the circle was complete, Magnus incanted his spell and suddenly they stood on the cliffs above the beach on the northern shore of the island.

Kaspar of Olasko was giving a good account of himself as he confronted two red horrors. They had bat-like wings, which they were using to avoid Kaspar's sword. It was clear that the struggle had only been taking place for a few moments, as the two winged monsters were being kept effectively at bay.

Pug shouted to Amirantha, 'Can you do anything?'

'I've never seen their like,' answered the Warlock. 'But I have something that might help.' He reached into his belt pouch and withdrew a stone that he tossed at Kaspar's feet. 'Run towards us!' he commanded.

Kaspar was no stranger to military obedience and recognized a battle command when it was issued. He swung hard, and as the two creatures withdrew, he turned and sprinted towards Pug and his companions.

The demons hesitated for a moment; then energy pulsed from the stone in a barely visible sphere. The two creatures were hurled back, over the edge of the cliffs.

Kaspar reached them, and almost out of breath said, 'That was timely.'

Amirantha shouted, 'They're not done!'

Pug nodded, waved the others back and took three purposeful steps towards the cliffs.

The two red-winged horrors, looking like smaller versions of the monster that attacked the Oracle, save for their curling horns, like those of bighorn rams, rose from the edge of the cliff. Pug thrust out his left hand and a wave of force slammed into the left one, driving it back again, while from his right hand a lash of pale silver energy sprang and wrapped itself around the other demon. The creature howled in agony as the energy leeched the life from its body.

Magnus came up behind his father and cast a bolt of blackness, which engulfed the demon on the left. It convulsed within the sphere and tried to howl, but seemed unable to utter a sound. Amirantha hurried up to stand behind them and said, 'These are elementals, air or fire creatures. They do not like the touch of land.'

'How do they feel about water?' asked Magnus, and with a flick of his hand he launched the demon into a high arc over the beach below, to slam into the water. The creature vanished beneath the waves in an eruption of green flames and hissing steam.

Pug did the same with the one he held and in a moment all was quiet. 'I should have recognized them,' said Pug. 'I faced their like outside of Stardock, many years ago.'

Kaspar said, 'I was coming back up from the beach, and had just cleared the top of the rocks when they appeared, out of the air.' He said, 'I almost left my sword in the room you set aside for me.' He laughed. 'I don't know how long I could have held them off with a fishing stick.' He carried a long surf pole, but it hardly looked equal to the task of being a cudgel.

Pug looked at Amirantha. The Warlock said, 'This was no coincidence.'

'I didn't think it was,' said Pug. 'Your brother?'

'I don't know,' said the Warlock. 'I used a stone I've prepared to repulse any demon. I didn't engage them with magic, so I have no feel for it . . .' He closed his eyes as if trying to sense something and said, 'No, I only feel the lingering presence of those two demons.'

'How did you know they were there?' asked Magnus.

'The more I deal with demons,' said the Warlock, 'the easier it is to sense them. There was a time when I wouldn't have known if there was a demon in the next room. Now I can feel them miles away. Comes from having dealt with them for over a hundred and twenty years.'

Kaspar said, 'Well, I'm glad you did. They were giving me hell and truth be known, I'm not as quick on my feet as I once was.'

Pug looked out over the water, it was growing dark as dusk approached. 'So, who is sending them?'

Amirantha said, 'I don't know, but whoever it was isn't very adept at mastering demons.'

'Why do you say that?' asked Magnus.

'Those two were minor demons, little more than elementals of the air. Not intelligent, not powerful. Sending them to an island that's home to magicians as powerful as you two is like turning two attack dogs loose on an army.' He looked around. 'It was an exercise to get your attention, I think, or to let you know that someone knows you're here.'

'Let's go back to the house,' said Pug. 'There's a bottle of wine we can share before supper and,' he looked at Magnus, 'before your mother gets home. Where is she?'

'Still at the Academy.'

Pug shrugged. 'She's been there longer than I would she would be.' To the others he said, 'If you don't mind, let's walk. The way is short and fresh air clears the head, and I've been jumping from place to place so much over the last few days I could use a small dose of the familiar.'

No one objected, and they started to walk back to the house in the middle of the island.

CHAPTER FOURTEEN

Bargains

*T*OMAS LOOKED OVER THE FOREST.

Spreading out below him was the home he had known for most of his life. From the royal couple's private balcony, the view was stunning. The great trees of Elvandar were laid out in a fashion that at first glance appeared chaotic, but there was a pattern, and once the eye became accustomed to it, much was revealed. From here, Tomas could see the great meadow where children played as their parents watched over them while they repaired bows, made arrows, loomed cloth or prepared food. In the distance he could see the top of a hill where an ancient watch fire waited to be lit should trouble breach the outer forest. On this side of the River Boundary, no warning was needed, for only powerful magic could allow the uninvited to enter the inner forest at the heart of Elvandar, and the intrusion would be felt by all who lived within the glades.

Growing up in Crydee he had imagined heroics and great feats for himself as a warrior in service to the king, but fate had bestowed something far greater than his boyish flights of fancy. He was the heir to the white and gold armour of the Valheru, and with that came all of the knowledge of a being long dead. He had seen a thousand things in his memory that he had not witnessed in life, yet they were as vivid to him as if he had seen them first hand.

His old companion, there when he found the armour, stood at his side regarding the vista silently with his friend. The dwarves and elves had always maintained a cool but civil relationship until Tomas had gained the armour of the long-dead Valheru, Ashen-Shugar. As a battle companion he had saved many dwarves during the war with the Tsurani and as the avatar of a long-dead Dragon Lord, he had commanded nearly blind obedience in the elves. During the Riftwar a bond had been forged between the elves of Elvandar and the dwarves of the Grey Towers and Stone Mountain that had led to a far more cordial relationship than before the war.

Dolgan had remained Tomas's friend for over a century, always a calm source of counsel with a very practical view of the world around him. Tomas welcomed his friend's presence, though not the reason that had brought him to visit.

After delivering his warning to the Elf Queen, Alystan of Natal had departed, for he had many duties, but Dolgan had decided to linger. It had been almost six years since he had visited his elven friends in the north, and he felt the need to stay a while.

He knew Tomas nearly as well as Aglaranna or Tomas's boyhood friend Pug did, and so the dwarven monarch knew his friend was as disturbed by the arrival of this alien elf as he had been. 'It's something to ponder, isn't it, lad?' he finally said.

Tomas always smiled at being called 'lad' by Dolgan. 'That it is, Dolgan.'

'I knew there was something afoot that day in the mines of Mac Mordain Cadal, when I found you eating fish with a dragon.' The old dwarf laughed, and said, 'That was a tale worth a hundred nights of stories by the fire. But what came after, Tomas. The Tsurani and what changed in you and who you became . . .' He gave an emphatic nod, and then said, 'But it has all turned out for the best.'

'Has it?' the tall, blond-haired warrior regarded his old friend with blue eyes filled with concern.

'You've done a fair bit beyond your pledge to protect your adopted home, my friend. You've raised a fine son and you've given a wonderful woman all the love a man can give. That alone merits praise. But more, you've been a redoubt to your people. It's been pretty peaceful up here in Elvandar while the rest of the world has endured some pretty nasty times.'

Tomas nodded. Elvandar had been left untouched when the Emerald Queen's army had ravaged the Kingdom.

'Well, I've given you plenty to ponder, and not near so much as our new friend,' he said with a nod to where Gulamendis was being housed. 'He's a queer one, that's for certain, and if it weren't for the ears and all his elvish ways, I'd take him for a tall human, that's a fact.'

Tomas smiled. He enjoyed his visits with Dolgan, as infrequent as they were becoming. The dwarf would probably live another hundred years with luck and good care, but nothing was forever and even the most robust of the long-lived races was mortal.

Lately Tomas had been filled with a sense of foreboding, he could not shake the feeling that something was coming, something very powerful, and that the world as he knew it would change as a result of it, and not for the better. That feeling had deepened with the arrival of the alien elf.

Looking at Dolgan, Tomas said, 'So you're leaving, then?'

'Aye, lad. I think I'll wander up to Stone Mountain and visit old Hathorn. He's a bit elderly now and doesn't get out much. Need to chat a bit with his son, Locklan, about this and that. Dwarven business, you know.'

Tomas nodded. 'I understand. Would you like some company along the way?' Tomas didn't want to insult his friend by suggesting he needed bodyguards. After all, the dwarf had run all the way from the Grey Towers with only Alystan for company.

'No. It's a short run and I could use some time to think. Besides, it's been very peaceful these days since you chased the Dark Brothers north. The goblins around these parts may be stupid, but they're not stupid enough to trouble me.' He patted the legendary hammer at his side.

Tomas grinned. Dolgan had found the Hammer of Tholin, the sign of his kingship, in the same cavern the then boy from Crydee had found the armour of white and gold.

The powerful armour that provided him with the link through time was safely stored in his quarters, next to the ceremonial gowns and jewellery owned by his wife. Yet no armour was needed to see the power in him. He was arguably the most dangerous being on this world, perhaps only rivalled by his friend Pug, whose magic almost made him a force of nature. But Tomas's great strength and Valheru magic didn't give him the ability to see the future.

'Then fare you well, my old friend,' said Tomas.

'Fare you well, lad.'

Just then Aglaranna appeared and Dolgan said, 'Ah, lovely. Saves me the trouble of tracking you down to say goodbye, my lady.'

'You are leaving, Dolgan?'

'Aye, off to visit kin in Stone Mountain, then home before my boy makes too big a mess of things.'

'Then travel well and visit again soon, my friend,' she said.

He bowed and departed.

Tomas stared out again over the forest below, and his wife regarded him for a moment. She knew his moods and loved him so deeply she barely believed it was possible. She had loved her first husband, the last King of the Elves, but it had been a slowly built affection, a comfortable love that sprang from necessity, for it had been her fate since birth to rule at his side. But the first time she had seen Tomas as a man, no longer the boy she had first beheld, passion she had never imagined had sprung into her heart. Since then they had been as one, and she knew that now he thoughtfully considered the new elf who had come among them.

And she knew he was troubled.

Aglaranna, Queen of the Elves and Tomas's wife for over a century, came to stand behind him and put her arms around him. The gesture never failed to give him comfort. 'What troubles you, husband?' she asked softly.

He turned with a smile, gazing into the most marvellous sight he had ever beheld. 'Have I told you how beautiful you are?' he asked with moisture in his eyes.

She couldn't help but smile. 'Only every day, my lord.'

He grimaced and said, 'Well, if it grows tiresome . . .'

'No,' she interrupted. 'I'll endure you saying so if you must.'

The banter was just what he needed to relax. 'I'm concerned,' he said.

'I know. You are concerned over our guest.'

Tomas nodded. 'My recollections of Ashen-Shugar are not complete. Many have come to me over the years, but still there are holes. Of all my memories of the edhel, I cannot remember anyone like this Gulamendis.'

'He is very strange,' agreed the Queen. 'The moredhel resemble us, but this . . . elf, he is different.'

'Dolgan said but for his ears, he seems practically human.'

Aglaranna laughed, a musical sound that always delighted Tomas. 'My love, have you been with us so long you've forgotten you are human too?'

He smiled and folded her into his arms, her head resting snugly under his chin. 'I am what I am. Yes, I was born human, but that was many lifetimes ago. Only our son, Calis, understands what it is to live half in one world and half in another.'

'I thank our ancestors he found Ellia and her sons.'

Tomas said, 'Yes. A family can save a soul.' He was thinking of his own, and how he had nearly succumbed to the madness of the Dragon Lords. His wife and son had given him an anchor to hold steady in the teeth of the rage that swept over him in battle or the burning desire to dominate that was never entirely gone. Now his son had the same reason to live beyond mere survival, a foster family he had grown to love deeply.

Tomas was silent and Aglaranna was content to wait. After a few minutes of just enjoying one another's closeness, Tomas said, 'You rule in Elvandar, my love, so all decisions are yours. Still, as Warleader, it is my duty to be wary.'

'I understand and always welcome your counsel.'

He smiled. 'Now, always?'

She returned the smile. 'Most of the time.'

Acaila appeared at the edge of the royal couple's private balcony, seeking admission, and Tomas waved him over. The ancient elf was the leader of those who had returned to Elvandar from the world of Kelewan. With the death of Tathar, the Queen's closest advisor and senior spellweaver since the time of her father, Acaila had become the leader of the Queen's Council. He bowed and said, 'Majesty; Lord Tomas.'

The Queen waved him over and asked, 'This Gulamendis, what do you make of him?'

Acaila moved to a chair as indicated by the Queen. Sitting on the wooden seat – two large 'u'-shaped pieces of wood cleverly joined and padded with a down-stuffed cushion – the ancient elf smiled thankfully. 'It is most difficult, my Queen,' he began. 'There can be no doubt he is of the eldar. He knows not of our ancient lore, but that is to be expected of one who was not raised as a Lorekeeper or spellweaver; but to discover he is a Master of Demons . . .' He put his right hand to his face; his index finger tapped his bony cheek. Acaila's age was incalculable, he was the oldest living elf. His hair was now as white as snow but his blue eyes were still alight with curiosity. 'What troubles me is not the matter of his dark studies, for he would not be the first among the eldar to find such practices fascinating, it is his other . . . attitude.'

'What attitude?' asked Tomas.

'He hides it well, but he feels superior to us. He counts his "Star People" to be a superior expression of the Eldar tradition.' The old man sat back and sighed. 'He considers us primitive, rustics at best. Wood lore is as alien to him as it was to many of the ocedhel who came to us from across the sea.'

'What else troubles you?'

'There are many mysteries within this elf,' said Acalia. 'He is here for more than he admits. I sense he desperately wishes us to aid his people, but that he despises himself for asking for help.'

Tomas was no stranger to feeling conflict over difficult decisions, so he asked, 'Is his disdain dependant only upon our inferiority?'

'No, it is more than that. While talking of our lore and how it differs, I could tell he is an academic in many ways, like all the eldar; he loves knowledge for its own sake. But it's how that knowledge is used that is at the heart of his troubles.' Sighing, the old elf said, 'I do not know, but I suspect he has his own, personal agenda, and that is what we must uncover before we trust him.'

Tomas and the Queen said nothing and waited.

Acaila said, 'These elves, these taredhel . . . they are unexpected?'

Tomas merely nodded.

'Sire, you know our origins more intimately than anyone alive; can you imagine that any eldar took the path these taredhel speak of?'

Tomas was quiet as he considered the memories he had inherited from the Dragon Lord, Ashen-Shugar. Finally he said, with a slight sigh, 'No, but the Valheru were arrogant beyond any other race's imagining. They would not have understood the differences between those who served and those who laboured in the field.'

The old eldar nodded his agreement. 'We were Lorekeepers and among the most trusting. When the Dragon Host abandoned my ancestors in Kelewan, we assumed others would do the same: abide and hope that someday we would be found, as we were.

'When we returned here, and discovered the division between the eledhel, moredhel, and glamredhel . . . even discovering the ocedhel . . . well, all seemed logical, as if our basic nature was fashioned by circumstance, but these taredhel . . .' The old elf shrugged. 'They are strange.' He fell silent.

A patient race, elves thought in terms of years where humans worried about days. 'We have time to uncover these things,' suggested Tomas.

'That is where I must disagree, Lord Tomas,' said the leader of the eldar. 'There is an urgency about this Gulamendis, that leads me to believe we shall see the heart of this matter sooner rather than later.' He sighed. 'What I don't know is if we will like what we see. I don't think we will.'

'Are these taredhel more similar to the moredhel, than ourselves?' asked the Queen.

Acalia shook his head. 'No, different from both, Your Majesty, different from any of the eldar.' He looked out and waved his hand. 'This is the place of seeds, from where we sprang at the dawn of time, before the war in heaven and the freeing of the People. Like seeds, if you move them to different soil, the tree that grows will take on a different character. Some will grow strong and straight, others will be stunted and bent, while still others become something far different than what they were before.' It was clear to Aglaranna and Tomas that he was speaking of the differences between the eledhel, moredhel, and taredhel. 'Those who lived to the north came to abide with us and some have moved on to Baranor. Others, from across the sea, have returned to us. Is it not reasonable to think that those who have lived centuries on other worlds would be any less different than those who merely lived on another part of this world?'

Tomas nodded. To those who had always lived in Elvandar, the elves who lived to the north of the Teeth of the World, the glamredhel, were barbaric, almost primitive, while the ocedhel, who lived across the ocean, were almost too human in their ways. 'I can see how they would become alien to us.'

'Yet they are still a part of us,' said the old eldar. 'They have lore that is lost to us, as we have lore lost to them. For us to join with them in some fashion would benefit us both.'

Tomas looked dubious. He knew much of what that lore contained from his memories of the ancient Dragon Lord, and some of it deserved to remain lost. This caused him to consider something else and he asked, 'Is he concerned by my presence?'

'Perhaps,' said Acaila. 'Gulamendis asked questions about you, but no more than any newcomer. His fear and curiosity are balanced. No, there is something else he fears more than the prospect of your Valheru nature asserting itself and establishing dominion over his people.

'In fact,' said the old elf with a wry smile, 'though he tries to hide it, he believes that you would fail if you tried. These people, I think, are arrogant to the point of believing themselves to be the supreme race.'

Aglaranna said, 'That has never been our way.'

'Not your way, Majesty, but it is the way of the moredhel.'

Tomas nodded and the Queen said, 'I must admit that is so.'

'The moredhel were menial house slaves forced to build the abomination that was Sar-Sargoth, for their masters, and its twin, Sar-Isbandia for their own glory, ages ago,' Acaila reminded.

Tomas shook his head. 'You lead me to think we have encountered a race of eldar with the ambitions of the moredhel.'

'Not quite,' said Acaila. 'That would be too simple; these elves, these Star Elves, have become something even more dangerous. From what he has said, Gulamendis is representative of these people. They are physically bigger, and I think have strength far in excess of our own.' He smiled and nodded at Tomas. 'Your own being the exception, my lord.'

Tomas nodded, his expression indicating it was of no importance. Despite his majestic abilities, he was without vanity. He had endured too much and caused too much pain to others coming into his power to consider himself anything other than the luckiest of beings. Finding forgiveness from those he wronged had made him profoundly humble.

'More,' said Acaila, 'his magic is . . . dark.'

'How so?' asked the Queen.

'I have not seen him employ any spellcraft, yet there is power in him. It's hidden well, but it is there. He asks questions. He is insightful, perceptive, and has a keen mind, yet there is something about him that troubles me.'

'Me, as well,' said Tomas. 'He brings danger.'

Both the Queen and Acaila looked at the warleader. Tomas said, 'I don't think he is a danger, but there's something he's hiding, something that will be a danger.'

The Queen said, 'He is strange.' She paused, then added, 'There is no sense of kinship when he is before me.'

Acaila nodded. 'The taredhel have changed far more than any of our kin during their time out among the stars.' He looked thoughtful. 'Although he does seem enthralled by our great trees; he calls them "the stars" at times. When he is not with the Spellweavers he wanders the forest floor, touching the boles, almost as if he doesn't believe they are real.'

Aglaranna said, 'We may be as strange and unexpected to him as he is to us. We think of ourselves as unchanged since the time of the Chaos Wars, but that is probably not true.' She looked at her husband, knowing Tomas had memories of those days.

'You are a stronger, more noble people, more at one with the world around you. You have risen.' He looked back over the forest below. 'These taredhel have risen, too, but in a very different fashion.'

'He talks of cities,' said Acalia. 'Great cities of stone and glass, with massive walls and sky vaulting towers: elven cities.'

Aglaranna said, 'That sounds strange to my ear.'

'He hides things,' said Acalia, 'but also speaks of things he assumes we already know, like their Spellweavers who work with rock, stone and mud as ours work with the living magic of our forest; others who command fire, water, and air.'

'Elementalists,' said Tomas. 'I remember.' He looked out over the forests again. 'When the Valheru were gripped by the madness of Drakin-Korin, and built their first city at Sar-Sargoth, they gave that magic to their chosen builders.' He turned to see the Queen and Acaila looking at him intently. He smiled. 'You don't think the Valheru dirtied their hands by helping to build that city, do you?' he asked wryly.

Acaila said, 'What happened to those who build Sar-Isbandia?'

Tomas shrugged. 'Those who remained here, those who became the moredhel, lost their arts. Their magic users have never been a strong presence, or a threat to us.' Tomas paused, then said, 'What this says to me is the taredhel may be more moredhel than edhel.'

Aglaranna said, 'We are all edhel.'

Acaila inclined his head in a gesture they both read to mean *I wish it were so.*

Tomas spoke, 'Yes, it would be a noble thing if all the tribes of the edhel were as one.' He looked at his wife. 'For every moredhel who finds his way here, who returns to us and forsakes the Dark Path, we have slain a dozen more. It is in their nature to seek out power.' He looked at Acaila. 'And it appears the taredhel have found that power.'

Aglaranna said, 'What do you propose we do, husband?'

'I think it is time for me to have a private discussion with our guest.' He turned to Acaila and said, 'Ask Gulamendis to meet with me at the entrance to the Holy Grove.'

The old eldar bowed slightly, then bowed more deeply to the Queen, and departed. After he was gone, Aglaranna said, 'Why the Holy Grove, Tomas?'

'This Gulamendis seems to be struggling with something. I don't presume to know what it is, but I do know that there's no place on this world that gives an elf more strength to make difficult choices than the Holy Grove. Acaila says Gulamendis is almost consumed by wonder over these ancient trees.'

She nodded. 'I understand.'

Tomas sighed deeply. 'And I think I need to provide one more, additional prod.'

She watched silently as her husband went into their quarters to don his white and gold armour.

Gulamendis followed the elf detailed to escort him to his meeting with Lord Tomas. He found her a fair example of the females of the edhel, though their women were generally too dainty for his taste. Most of the taredhel women stood as tall as the men and were very striking, although he considered it was mostly a matter of taste. This female was attractive in a rough-hewn fashion.

They passed down a path in the woods that took them some distance from the heart of Elvandar, away from the majestic trees the Demon Master thought of as 'stars'. When they reached a clearing, she halted and said, 'Lord Tomas will meet with you shortly.'

He said, 'Thank you,' and she left him alone.

At first glance, there was nothing remarkable about the area, but he did feel a faint, gentle flow of energy. It was nothing he could identify, yet it did feel familiar, as if he heard the echo of a song he couldn't quite remember. The familiar feeling of conflict arose; his agenda was anything but simple, but it was straightforward, establish a relationship with these primitive elves and use them as a means to recruit allies against the Demon Legion, should they follow the taredhel to this world. He had no doubt they eventually would.

The blame placed upon him and others who explored demon lore was unfounded; neither he, nor any other taredhel magic user was responsible for the demons reaching the first outpost colony on the world of Estandarin. It was certainly no Demon Master's fault that the colonists had failed to destroy the portal before the demons reached the translocation hub in Shadin City on Dastin-Barin. From there they had spread like a cancer, infecting four other taredhel worlds.

At first, the taredhel were confident they could crush the attackers, for they had never known defeat in any conflict. But the number of demons appeared endless. Despite taking innumerable casualties, the creatures were relentless.

The Demon Masters knew the truth, but no one in the Regent's Meeting would listen to them. Somewhere, perhaps on Estandarin, there was a gate through which the demons poured into this realm. Gulamendis had tried to find other Demon Masters with whom to confer, but after their years of isolation and persecution, there were so few of them it was impossible for any coherent picture of the demon realm to be drawn.

He only knew what he'd discovered from his years of studying a handful of trained demons. But whatever the truth behind the demons' reach into this realm, he was certain that somehow they would follow the taredhel to Midkemia. Even if he was wrong, there was no harm in gulling these elves into an alliance; they would be allowed to serve. Yet there was something about their Queen, this Aglaranna. She might truly be of the ancient line, for when he beheld her for the first time, Gulamendis had felt something deep, basic, and . . . right. This woodland was new to him, yet she felt profoundly familiar.

As if reading his mind, a voice from behind said, 'It is the ancient Home.'

Gulamendis turned and experienced a shock close to a physical blow. Tomas, Warleader of Elvandar, stood behind him wearing a suit of white and gold armour. The golden dragon on his tabard captured the Demon Master's eyes, and when he finally looked Tomas in the face, he saw behind his eyes something he had not seen at the Queen's Council. Within this being resided an ancient power and now he let it show through.

The Demon Master trembled; instincts long stilled in his people awoke and he found himself terrified and in awe of another being for the first time in his life. Generations of arrogance and superiority fell away. His experience with the Demon

Legion had given him doubts about his people's supremacy, but one look at this being, this avatar of an ancient power, humbled him.

Almost whispering, Gulamendis said, 'Ancient One . . . .'

Tomas held up his hand and the Demon Master fell silent. 'Let us cut to the heart of the matter, Gulamendis.'

'Master,' whispered the taredhel. Even though he stood nearly six inches taller than Tomas, the Demon Master felt dwarfed by the presence of this icon of the ancient race that ruled over all elves.

Tomas said, 'This is the Holy Grove. This is the heart of Elvandar and the fundamental essence of your race springs from here.'

Gulamendis turned to regard the young trees and then he realized that this grove was where the sapling Stars were tended and nurtured. He had seen the majestic boles of the mature trees, but this was the first time he had seen them cultivated. He was certain that his ancestors had uprooted the Seven Stars from this place before carrying them to Andcardia.

'Yes,' said the Demon Master.

'This is where the edhel began,' said Tomas.

'Yes,' repeated Gulamendis.

'It is time for plain speaking. Why are you here?'

The taredhel looked away from Tomas and back to the grove. He said, 'I have reasons for what I do, Lord Tomas.' As he spoke, his feeling of being overwhelmed by the presence of the man in ancient armour diminished, though it never fully left. He took a deep breath. 'We are fleeing a horde of demons who have swept across every world we have colonized.' He looked at Tomas. 'How many live here?'

Tomas thought for a moment and said, 'Within the heart of Elvandar, at least ten thousand.'

'And throughout the world?'

Tomas said, 'We can only guess, but the moredhel to the north are likely to number more, perhaps twice our count.'

'Are there others?'

'Across the sea, perhaps four or five thousand ocedhel; in Baranor, another thousand, most of whom migrated from here.'

'There are fifty thousand among the scattered tribes of the edhel,' said Gulamendis. He reached out and gripped Tomas's tabard as if needing to hang on to something. Hoarse with emotion, he said, 'We were millions! We were the eldar! We *were*; but we made ourselves so much more than you can imagine, Dragon Lord.'

He let go of Tomas and turned away. There was moisture in his eyes as he looked around. At last he said, 'This is like looking into the past for me.' He turned, hands outstretched. 'We can never be this again.' He made a sweeping gesture. 'We can never return to living in trees.' Tears ran down Gulamendis's face. 'No matter how beautiful, or venerated those trees are. We have become something else.'

Looking directly into Tomas's eyes, he said, 'We will never wander into this wood to ask to be taken in, to be "returned". The moredhel were the least of us; we call them the Forgotten, for they were the servants who were permitted to serve *us*, the eldar! They envied us, their betters. *You* remember!'

Tomas nodded. Since donning the white and gold armour of a long-dead Valheru, memories came unbidden, sometimes triggered by certain circumstances or a word, other times at random. His memories of the long-dead Ashen-Shugar were not complete, but he knew many of the things Gulamendis said were true.

Gulamendis made a sweeping gesture with his hand. 'You permitted this, Lord; you and your brethren. This was where the elves arose to serve the Valheru! Without this, we are nothing.' He turned and again looked directly at Tomas, his expression defiant. 'We took this with us! We uprooted seven saplings from this grove, bound their roots as a mother wraps a child, and we carried them across a bridge to another world.

'That journey became the foundation of our history. Before that—' he again waved at the grove, '—may as well be myth, for we arrived on Andcardia with what we carried: seven saplings, a few tools and our knowledge.

'We planted those seven trees, our Stars, and we built our home around them. The first were hovels made of wood and animal hide, but we mastered our new world, and now our cities make those of any other world look like rude huts. We are a prideful race, Lord, but we have *earned* that pride.'

Tomas nodded. 'I take no issue with who you are, Gulamendis. I need only know your purpose in coming here. If it is not to take refuge from the Demon Horde, what is it?'

'To find a way to save what is left of the Clans of the Seven Stars.'

'Explain,' said Tomas, crossing his arms.

'We cannot survive if the Demon Legion follows us to Midkemia. None of us.'

Tomas said nothing, regarding Gulamendis coolly.

'We need you, and the humans and the dwarves. We need anyone who will resist the Demon Legion.'

Tomas said nothing for a long moment, then asked, 'Why not simply explain this when you first came to us?'

'I needed to . . .' He paused, looked completely around the

grove, then said, 'This calls to me. It's . . . powerful. I see you, Valheru, and fear, hate, and a dread all echo through my being. I thought . . .' He paused, gathered his thoughts and said, 'When my brother and I, and a few others, conceived of our plan, we knew we must quickly find those already on this world, our Home, who would unite with us should the Demon Legion come.

'So you understand clearly, when you remember the days before the time of chaos, when the gods raged across the sky, and the Dragon Lords rose to challenge them, in that time the taredhel stood first among your servants.'

Tomas closed his eyes for a moment and then opened them to look at Gulamendis. 'The eldar were our most trusted servants.'

The use of the word 'our' was not lost on the Demon Master. He said, 'Acalia and his brethren are descendants of the librarians. They were stranded on . . .'

'Kelewan,' supplied Tomas

'Kelewan,' echoed Gulamendis. 'One of the Dragon Host abandoned them there. What they achieved was remarkable given their limited resources.

'But we are the true Eldar. We were your housecarls, your ministers, your emissaries when you needed to negotiate with one another, and we were your lovers.'

Tomas closed his eyes once more and memories of the astonishingly beautiful elven females Ashen-Shugar kept near his throne returned. He nodded. 'Yes, you were first among our slaves.' There was a hard edge to his voice, and he didn't fully understand why he felt the need to emphasize the elves' position in relation to the Valheru.

Gulamendis's eyes narrowed and his expression was even

more defiant. 'We are more than what we were, Tomas,' he whispered with a tone full of menace. 'I have no doubt that you could cut me down with your golden sword before I took a step. I will not contest that, but should you face a dozen of us in the field, you would be challenged. And we number in the thousands.'

'A threat?'

'No, a warning, perhaps not even that; let's call it a courtesy. We do not come to you as lesser beings. We come to you as equals.' He looked back at the grove and said, 'We venerated those who had been granted responsibility for these groves. They were the most fundamental of us, those closest to the soil of this world and the very life-giving things nature offered.

'But they were gardeners. Your Queen's ancestors were gardeners, nothing more.'

Tomas said nothing for a moment, now fully understanding. 'You view them as your inferiors.'

'They are rustics. They are farmers and hunters and fishers of the sea, nothing more. Those are honourable crafts, but they do not define my people, or who we have become.

'We were the scholars, the academics, the explorers, the crafters and weaponmakers.' He pointed at Tomas's chest. 'That armour, that sword: my ancestors forged them for you. The devices that let you fly to other worlds: they were our invention.

'How do you think we were able to flee during the time of madness and find safe haven on Andcardia? We built the trans-location portals and we were the ones who took the tools and tomes, scrolls and books. The dragons carried you across the void to other worlds. We bowed to your might, because we could not command dragons to carry us, but we found ways to achieve what you achieved, and we did it without you!' He looked back again at the grove. His voice softened. 'And we took from here that which reminded us of our roots.

'But we are not who we once were, and we have only returned here out of need. But we will take what is ours, without asking your leave.'

'You present a troubling attitude, Gulamendis, if it is shared by all of your people.'

With a wry smile, the Demon Master said, 'I am moderate in my views. The Regent Lord will look upon your wife as a threat.'

Tomas's eyes narrowed as his anger rose and he said, 'You do your cause little good. Let any threaten my Queen and they will know the extent of my power, Gulamendis.'

'I am no threat. But you should know that there are others among my people who will see *you* as one.

'We thought it would be fairly simple. We assumed the elves remaining on this world would ascend, as we have for thousands of years, and that any other race we chose to deal with would be of little consequence. Then my brother spent months exploring this land.'

Tomas said, 'It was your brother who was seen in the valley north of Dolgan's holdings?'

'He was seen?'

'Humans have some gifted trackers and your brother was not adept at hiding his passage. A Ranger of Natal came across his tracks and was curious enough to follow them, even though he could not recall who made them just moments after seeing your brother. And when he saw your brother establish a rift—'

'Rift?' said Gulamendis.

'His way home.'

'We call it a portal,' said the Demon Master.

'Ah,' said Tomas. 'That is when your brother revealed himself.

Alystan was already near King Dolgan's village, and from there he came to see my Queen. You can imagine the concern the appearance of an elf such as yourself might provoke.'

At the mention of Dolgan, Gulamendis's features darkened. 'We've had issues with the dwarves in the past, and they have never come to an easy conclusion.'

Tomas's eyes narrowed. 'Dolgan is among my oldest friends, a dwarf of gentle heart and iron resolve. I have placed my life in his trust on more than one occasion and he has proven stalwart. I trust him as I trust few others.'

Gulamendis inclined his head slightly as if to say it was of no serious concern.

Tomas said, 'So, to the heart of it then ... Why have you come here?'

'To seek an alliance should the demons arrive and to help you understand that while you and your lady command our respect, that is all; obedience will not be offered.'

It was Tomas's turn to indicate that this was not important to him. 'Your ancestors fled before the one whose armour I wear took to the skies and told all below that they were now free.

'We seek dominion over no one. For reasons lost in antiquity the moredhel have declared us their enemies, so we defend ourselves when they venture south, but any among them who choose to return to their ancestral home are always welcome. Many among us spent their youth in the north. We welcomed the ocedhel from across the sea, yet many remained, unwilling to join us. We have no issue with them. And when we discovered the anoredhel endured to the south, again we claimed no sovereignty.'

'The Sun People?' asked Gulamendis. 'I have not heard of them.'

'The protectors of the Quor and Sven'gar-ri.'

Again he gave Tomas a questioning look. 'I should know these names, but I do not.'

'A matter for another time,' said Tomas. 'Very well, your position is clear. You seek our help but do not wish to serve anyone. As we have no wish for your service, we are in accord.' His expression reinforced his next utterance. 'But any attempt by your Clans of the Seven Stars to assume dominion over others will be thwarted.

'Not only will I draw my sword, I will call upon my allies.'

'Dwarves? Humans?'

'Stout warriors and powerful sorcerers, Gulamendis. Do not let your history blind you to this fact that they are your equal in many ways,' he thought of Pug, 'and some will prove your betters.

'Consider this a caution. Midkemia may be your ancestral Home, but it is home to many others, descendants of those who came here during the Chaos Wars and their claim is perhaps more enduring than yours. Your ancestors left, while theirs stayed.

'But any differences between our people must be put aside until after the Demon Legion has been dealt with. We will not trouble you so long as you do not trouble us, but should the day come when we are opposed, then I will be without pity.' His expression left Gulamendis' in no doubt that it wasn't an idle threat. The Demon Master said, 'I, and a few others, knew this world would be different than what we might wish it to be.

286

But the Regent Lord and those priests, magicians, and soldiers who make up the Regent's Meeting, will not so easily come to understand that accommodations must be reached. Were you to bring them here, as you have had me come, they would see it as a challenge, a threat, and one to be answered and swiftly.

'The Clans of the Seven Stars cannot endure here unless we make changes and reach agreement with the other races on this world. We need a change in leadership to achieve that goal.'

'Treason,' said Tomas.

'Reason,' said Gulamendis. 'The strengths of our race are also weaknesses, for we had never been vanquished until we met the demons. It is inconceivable to us that another mortal race might be our equal, let alone our superior.

'It would be better if we were able to consider a different perspective when the time came for us to seek aid.' He looked one more time at the grove. 'We must return here and take what lessons we have forgotten, Tomas.' He then looked at the warleader and said, 'Just as some of your people must come and learn from us. Only that way can conflict be avoided.'

'That sounds promising,' said Tomas. 'Little else of what you said does.'

'I understand.'

'Come,' said Tomas, 'we must travel.'

'Where?'

'There are others you must meet, humans, who are my friends, and who hold the safety of this world paramount. Perhaps after you've met Pug and his associates you'll rethink your feelings of superiority.'

Gulamendis looked dubious but said nothing.

Tomas closed his eyes and spoke softly, but the words were

powerful and Gulamendis felt magic forming. They stood motionless for nearly five minutes, then came the sound of gigantic wings and a shadow passed over them. Gulamendis looked up; if his first sight of Tomas had shocked him, what he now beheld nearly forced him to his knees.

A great golden dragon hovered above them, lazily beating its wings. In some speech only Tomas could understand, it seemed to question the human-turned-Dragon Lord, and Tomas spoke aloud in the same language.

'He's agreed to carry us.'

'Carry us?' said the Demon Master.

The dragon touched down as gently as a falling feather, lowering his head until it rested on the ground. 'Come,' said Tomas, walking over to a portion of the neck where he could climb aboard. 'Sit behind me and behold more of this world you call Home.'

Gulamendis was mute. He could barely nod and it took all his resolve to meekly follow Tomas and climb aboard the dragon, behind him.

CHAPTER FIFTEEN

Plotting

S ANDREENA AWOKE.

Her hand had reached for the haft of her mace before she was fully conscious, to attack whoever stood above her. A strong hand grabbed her wrist and prevented her from finding her weapon and she found herself too weak to break that grasp. A voice spoke softly, 'None of that, now. You're safe.'

She blinked and realized there was no mace next to her. It had been taken by whoever those Black Caps had been. She had had a sword, but now it was gone. She blinked again, trying to focus her eyes and remember where she was.

She lay in a simple bed of wood, on a straw-stuffed mattress suspended on a rope lattice, in a small monk's cell. Her memory returned. She was in the Temple in Ithra. She had arrived almost dead on her feet, her horse in little better condition . . . she didn't know when. She tried to speak, the face above her indistinct in the dim light of the room. 'How long?' she managed to croak.

'Almost a day,' said the voice. Now she could tell it was a man. The hand released her wrist and a moment later slipped behind her head, helping her to sit up a little as a cup of cold, clean water touched her lips. She sipped and as moisture awoke her thirst, started to drink. After she'd drained the cup, she could speak more clearly. 'More.'

The man stood up. He had been kneeling by her bedside, and she now got a good look at him. He was a dark-haired man, somewhere in his mid-thirties. Heavy set, but not fat. He wore a deep plum-coloured tunic and simple black trousers of fine weave, and his boots were also finely crafted. He appeared unarmed. His features were plain, even unremarkable, but there was something about his dark eyes that said he should not be underestimated.

'Who are you?' she asked weakly.

'I'm Zane.'

After another drink of water, she said, 'Just Zane?'

He shrugged and smiled. It was a simple expression, but without guile. That made him either straightforward or dangerous. She'd assume the latter until the former proved its worth. 'Well, if you care to use them, I've a couple of titles, one from Roldem, another from the Kingdom of the Isles, and I may be entitled to some honorific from Kesh, but I'm not entirely sure. Zane will do.'

He turned to indicate the figures outside the door. 'The monks tell me you're called Sandreena and that you are a Knight-Adamant of the Order of the Shield of the Weak. Is that correct?'

'Yes,' said Sandreena. 'I'm assuming you're harmless, or else the brothers would never have allowed you into my quarters while I was unconscious.'

He feigned a look of injury. 'Harmless?' He shook his head slightly. 'I'm no menace to you, certainly, but harmless?' He sighed as he sat back down next to her. 'You need your rest, but before you fall asleep again, there are a couple of things I need to know.'

Feeling herself slipping back into unconsciousness, she said, 'That may have to wait ...'

Zane was still there when she awoke again, but he was dressed differently. She could see that the light from the high window above was different, too: grey. 'Ah, there you are, again,' said Zane. He had been standing near to the door, watching her, and now came to sit on the edge of the bed.

'Water?'

'Yes, thank you,' she said and allowed him to help her drink. Gathering her thoughts, she asked, 'Who are you again?'

'Zane,' he replied.

'I mean, who sent you?'

'Ah, that,' he said, standing up as she appeared more lucid this time and able to drink without aid. 'I am presently a friend of the Father-Bishop Creegan. Well, associate is perhaps a better choice of words.'

'But you are not of the Temple?' she asked.

'No,' he said with a regretful smile. 'I tend to pray to Ban-ath or Ruthia more often than not.' He looked at her. 'I try to avoid ending up on the side of those needing Dala's intervention.'

'And as an associate of the good Father-Bishop,' said

291

Sandreena, elbowing herself upright, 'I assume you're here to ask me what I've uncovered?'

He reached under the bed and pulled out a folded blanket. He put it behind her as a makeshift pillow and said, 'Yes, straight to the heart of it. If you feel up to talking?'

'I'm a little hungry, but I could talk before I eat.'

He nodded and moved to the door to speak to someone outside. While sitting up, Sandreena took stock of herself. Someone had bathed her and redressed her wounds, which now itched as they were almost fully healed. She was wearing a simple white shift of bleached linen, and even her hair smelled clean.

She had been near dead when she rode into town. She had endured a week on the road with no food, and water from the few creeks she could find. She vaguely recalled finding a stand of berries along the way, but they had made her sick to her stomach.

Her exact recollection of her journey south was hazy. She remembered reaching a hillside overlooking the town of Ithra, and then nothing until she was spoken to by someone at the town gate, perhaps a warden or town watchman. Then she remembered being at the entrance to the Temple and trying to speak to someone, and then awaking today.

The last week on the road had been a blur. Her wounds had stiffened, as she had suspected they would, as she hardly had time to recuperate in that damp cave, and she was woefully malnourished. Somewhere along the way time became meaningless. Training had evidently taken hold, for she had somehow managed to keep her horse watered and find grazing along the way. Perhaps she had slept while the animal had cropped grass.

In any event, it was clear to Sandreena that the Goddess had been watching over her.

'So, you work for Creegan,' she said as she pushed herself upright. Every part of her ached and she felt shockingly weak. It was a feeling she didn't like.

'Work with him, is more the case,' said Zane. He looked over his shoulder at her as they waited for food to arrive. 'Or rather, I work for people who work with him.' He saw a monk approaching and said nothing while a tray was placed on Sandreena's lap. While she ate, Zane said, 'Your Order's resources are spread thinly right now, and you were the only high-level Temple Knight around, apparently. So the Father-Bishop asked us to keep an eye out for you.'

'You just happened to be in Ithra?'

'This was where they sent me. We have other people in Dosra, Min, and Pointer's Head just in case you showed up there. If none of us heard from you in another week, someone else would have been sent north. There's a strong suspicion something important is taking place in that very isolated village you went to . . .'

'Akrakon,' she supplied. She said nothing more, concentrating on eating the vegetable soup and coarse bread in front of her. She didn't think this man would be standing around in the middle of the monastery if he were any sort of risk, but his claim to affiliation with the Temple in Krondor didn't make it fact. As he observed, there were no other highly-placed members of the Order nearby; the monks and lay brothers of the Order in this little place of worship were far removed from Temple politics and intrigue.

When she said nothing for a while, Zane smiled and said, 'Fair enough. You can report directly to the Father-Bishop if you wish. I was given no instructions about learning what you know, just to see that you got safely home, so you had a better chance of delivering the intelligence . . . we need.'

She wondered which 'we' he spoke of, the Temple, the Father-Bishop, or whoever his masters were. 'Good,' she said. 'You're going to ride with me to Krondor?' she asked between mouthfuls of soup and chewy bread.

'Something like that,' he said with a smile. 'I'll wait until you're done.'

She said nothing while she finished her food, then watched him take away her tray. When he returned she was standing on wobbly legs. 'I'm weak as a kitten,' she supplied.

A monk arrived with some clothing, and Sandreena was annoyed to see that it was a dress. Seeing her horrified expression, Zane shrugged. 'It was the best we could do on short notice. I had to buy it off one of the shopkeeper's wives.' Lowering his voice as the monk departed, he said, 'And I think the brothers never considered that you might prefer tunic and trousers. I think you may have been the first Knight-Adamant they've seen in recent memory.' Lowering his voice even more, and looking over his shoulder as he handed her the dress, he added, 'Certainly the first woman.'

She pulled off the shift and donned the dress, ignoring Zane's presence. 'There aren't many of us,' she acknowledged. 'It's thankless work and not for those of weak constitution. It doesn't appeal to many men or women.' She held out the sides of the dress, which was obviously several sizes too large for her and said, 'How am I supposed to ride in this?'

'Ah, no,' said Zane. He drew an object from his belt pouch and said, 'Stand next to me.'

She moved a step closer and he said, 'This way is a bit faster.'

Suddenly they were in another room somewhere else. It was earlier in the day, judging from the brightness of the light, and noticeably warmer. There was a trio of men in the room.

Sandreena looked around, then her eyes widened. She stepped towards one of the men and drew back her fist. Before anyone could react, she delivered him a punishing blow to the jaw. He went backwards, skidding across the floor and slamming into the wall.

Shaking his head and blinking his eyes for a moment, Amirantha looked up and said, 'Why, Sandreena. Good to see you again, too.'

Pug stood dumbfounded. Few things could surprise him at his age, but the sudden appearance of Zane and the woman, who immediately knocked Amirantha across the room, managed to.

Brandos grinned. 'You're looking a little off, girl. Normally, you would have broken his jaw.'

Seeing the old fighter she returned his smile and came to hug him. 'You old fraud. How are you?'

He hugged her back and said, 'Well enough. I wonder how you are from time to time.'

Pug said, 'Obviously, I don't need to make any introductions.'

Sandreena said, 'Only who you are.'

'My name is Pug and this is my island.'

She frowned. 'The Black Sorcerer?'

He smiled slightly. 'It's a long story. Let's say for the moment that we all represent interests that have a common goal.'

'Which is?'

Getting off the floor, rubbing his sore jaw, Amirantha said, 'Discovering where some of the demons are coming from.'

She fixed him with a baleful look. 'This another of your confidences?'

He held up his hands, palms outward. 'No. In fact, an unexpected demon nearly gutted me a few weeks ago.'

'Too bad,' she said.

Brandos grinned. 'I've missed you, girl.'

She gave him a dubious expression. 'You're a good man, Brandos, but I can't say much for the company you keep.'

'If we can put aside the personal animosity for a while, we have others coming to meet with us,' Pug said.

'Who are you?' asked Sandreena, again. 'I mean, who are you to bring me here?'

Pug knew an exasperated tone when he heard one. 'Father-Bishop Creegan will be here shortly. I think I'll leave it to him to explain your role in this. However, before he arrives, perhaps you'd care to brief us on what you encountered up in the Peaks of the Quor.'

'No,' she said. 'I wouldn't care to.'

Pug shook his head slightly and said, 'Zane, if you would show Sandreena to her quarters, we'll wait for the rest of our guests.'

'Yes, Grandfather,' he said, and motioned for Sandreena to follow him. She cast another baleful glance at Amirantha as she left the room.

As they walked down the hallway, she took notice of her surroundings. The building was low and had doors that opened on gardens. She said, 'Grandfather? He doesn't look any more than ten years older than you.'

'Appearances can be deceiving,' said Zane. 'Pug is my step-father's father and he's old enough to be . . .' He shrugged. 'You'll see.' He led her to a room and said, 'You can rest here and if you get hungry, just pick up that bell and ring it. Someone will escort you to the dining hall.' He pointed to a small tulip-shaped bell that rested on a table next to a bed. 'Is there anything I can do for you in the meantime?'

Reaching down she tugged at the ill-fitting dress and said, 'Yes, if you could find me clothes that fit, I'd be grateful. Trousers and a tunic, please?'

He said, 'I'll see what I can do. I'll be back shortly.'

She sat on the bed after he left and put her elbows on her knees, burying her face in her hands. 'Oh, Goddess,' she said softly. 'What have I done to deserve this? Amirantha, again?'

By the time Zane returned with clean clothing, she was asleep, curled up on the bed like a child, and he could tell from the dried tear tracks on her face that she had been weeping.

Pug sat at a table near the door to the kitchen, dining with his wife, two sons, and Amirantha and Brandos, at a table large enough to accommodate twice their number. A large kettle of stew sat steaming in the middle, with platters of hot bread, cheeses, meats, fruits, and vegetables placed around it.

The Warlock observed, 'This is a . . . fascinating place. I always assumed your work was done at Stardock.'

Pug inclined his head slightly as he said, 'That's what we want people to think. My predecessor here on this island, Macros, created the legend of the Black Sorcerer to maintain privacy. We have continued the illusion to keep that privacy. Moreover, the Academy at Stardock is a busy place, and although much is accomplished there, this is where the real work, research and education of the exceptional students takes place.'

Around a mouthful of bread and cheese, Brandos said, 'I assume that either you've decided to trust us, or you're going to kill us.' He pointed to his bowl of stew. 'This is very good, by the way.'

Miranda smiled. There was something very unselfconscious about this veteran fighting man that appealed to her. 'If we wished you dead, Brandos,' she said, 'you wouldn't be eating up cook's good stew.'

'That's a relief,' he said. 'Though, as last meals go, this wouldn't be bad.'

Magnus and Caleb both laughed, and Amirantha said, 'Well, then, if we're not to be killed, are we to be trusted?'

Pug regarded the Warlock and said, 'I'm not sure "trusted" is the word I'd employ, rather consider yourself accepted for the time being. Demons are an issue for us, at the moment, and we have little knowledge of them here or at Stardock.'

Magnus said, 'The monks at That Which Was Sarth weren't especially helpful either; most of their records are pretty straightforward: "on this date a demon appeared, Brother Iganthal or Father Boreus banished it," or was eaten by it and someone else did the banishing. But as to the nature and ways of demons, they were surprisingly vague.'

'Not really,' said Amirantha. He looked at Pug as he spoke, as if addressing him specifically. 'It's difficult to negotiate with demons, and the power they bring is intoxicating, addictive even. But there's a price, and it's a price I was never willing to pay.'

'Your life?' asked Caleb.

The Warlock shook his head. 'My soul, for lack of a better

term. I may not be a particularly good man, but I'm willing to stand before Lims-Kragma when my time comes, and account for all I've done, good or ill. I'll take whatever passes for justice among the gods; I won't give up my place on the Wheel of Life for eternity in order simply to gain in this lifetime.'

'It would have to be an amazing deal,' agreed Magnus.

'It's not so simple, is it?' asked Pug.

Amirantha shook his head as he put down his large spoon, apparently finished eating. 'If some agency of evil came to you and offered you a bargain, the outcome would depend on your strength of character, but the agencies of darkness are far more subtle than that.

'There's a force out there,' he continued, picking up his cup of wine and sipping, then setting it down, 'that is hardly overt.

'I'm convinced that my brother, the man you knew as Leso Varen, was already more than half-mad when he killed our mother. Something had already reached out and touched his heart and found a willing minion. I knew my brother well; his vanity would never allow him to bend his knee to another, but that vanity could lead him to be manipulated easily.'

Remembering a conversation with the God of Thieves, when Ban-ath had revealed that Macro's vanity had been his biggest ally in manipulating the otherwise crafty sorcerer, he could only nod agreement.

'While my brothers and I were disinclined to speak, we did have mutual acquaintances. As you may already understand, those of us who practise what are called the "dark arts," often find our needs drive us to deal with a more unsavoury type of fellow: thieves, bandits, renegades, and their like. People who can secure goods that would otherwise be impossible for us to obtain.

'This is less true in my own calling, for I make most of what I need: wards, stones of power, and other items that over the years have proven useful in following my interests.'

'Having your head ripped off,' inserted Brandos.

'I was about to say something else, but he makes my point.' Idly picking up his spoon and poking at what remained of the food before him, the Warlock said, 'Those who need living human subjects must deal with slavers and those who need death – such as my brother – must also associate with slavers, warlords or others guaranteed to engender mayhem. Cults become particularly useful.'

At the mention of cults, Pug asked Caleb, 'Did Zane . . . ?'

'No,' said Caleb to his father. 'He said Sandreena preferred to wait until Father-Bishop Creegan arrives.'

'Creegan here?' asked Amirantha, his eyebrows rising as his only sign of surprise.

'We have many friends.'

'Indeed,' said the Warlock.

'You know him?'

'We've met,' said Amirantha.

Brandos said, 'Not to worry. Creegan might have Amirantha burned as a heretic, but he won't punch him in the jaw. He's far too well-mannered for that.'

Amirantha smiled ruefully. 'He's a practical man. He disapproves of my interests, but he's never tried to interfere with them.'

'It helps that we live on different sides of the world,' observed Brandos. 'Big ocean between us, and all.' He winked at Pug and his family. 'Keeps things civil.'

Magnus smiled and shook his head, and Caleb laughed.

Miranda asked, 'So, why the punch to the jaw? I'm sorry I wasn't there to see it; sounds like it was entertaining.'

Brandos said, 'Well, it's a long story—'

Amirantha interrupted. 'It has to do with the Father-Bishop, as well. I was travelling through the Principality about four, no five?' He looked at Brandos, who nodded. 'Five years ago. There was a story making the rounds, about a demon being sighted up the coast from the city of Krondor, near a village with the unlikely name of Yellow Mule.'

'Good tavern,' observed Brandos.

'Good tavern,' agreed Amirantha. 'We were in residence there, attempting to discern the validity of the rumour when we encountered Sandreena, who had also come looking to rid the region of this demon.

'Our interests seemed to overlap—'

'And Sandreena is a very good looking young woman; my friend here is particularly fond of them.'

Amirantha frowned at his companion who tried hard not to look smug as he continued to eat. 'So we joined forces.'

Pug looked thoughtful, then said, 'I'm usually aware of something as unusual as a demon sighting, especially that close to Krondor.' He glanced at Magnus and Caleb, who both shrugged, then looked questioningly at Miranda.

'I read the report; it came from our friend at the prince's palace.'

Pug's eyebrows raised and he said, 'Oh?'

'It seemed nothing worth bothering you about. A demon was sighted, some locals disposed of it, nothing further.'

Brandos and Amirantha exchanged a look of surprise and Brandos said, 'Locals?'

Amirantha said, 'Father-Bishop Creegan probably left our names out of any report.'

Pug smiled. 'Not unlike him. He's ambitious. But, please, continue.'

'Not much more to tell,' said Amirantha. 'A . . . strange man, a little mad I think, had wandered into the village and claimed he was a prophet of some sort and had done some fairly impressive things: at least they were impressive according to the villagers.

'He healed some wounds, rid a small orchard of a blight, and he did a fair job of predicting the weather. He gathered together a little group of followers and after a year or so had them convinced he was an avatar of a god.

'Then it got nasty, according to what we heard.'

'Yes,' agreed Brandos. 'People who didn't fall in with this bunch were suddenly struck by illness, their cow's milk soured, or their crops got blight.'

'Curses,' said Pug. 'Witch work.'

'Maybe,' said Amirantha. 'My mother was called a witch more times than I can remember. My title, Warlock, literally means "caller of spirits," in the ancient Satumbrian language, but it's used to mean "male witch" now.'

Brandos said, 'Never could quite understand all these names; you either use magic or you don't, right?' He addressed that question to Pug.

Pug couldn't help but laugh. 'You have no idea how many conversations I've endured on that very question over the years, my friend.'

Amirantha returned to his narrative. 'Over the course of a week we discovered there were others involved with this cult, men who would mysteriously arrive in the middle of the night then vanish.'

'Magicians?' asked Magnus.

Amirantha shrugged. 'Or renegade priests of some order, but they were a conduit for information or instructions between this false prophet and whoever was directing the goings-on in Yellow Mule.'

'The locals were a happy lot until they started dying,' said Brandos. 'This prophet, calling himself Jaymen, he blamed us! Can you believe that?'

Pug nodded. 'Go on.'

Amirantha said, 'So, as I said, by then Sandreena and I had joined forces. She was trying to save the villagers; apparently the reports to the Prince of Krondor's Coastal Wardens Office were being ignored, and I was very interested in the demon scent.'

'Scent?' asked Pug.

'Yes,' said Amirantha. 'You've encountered demons, right?'

'Yes,' said Pug with an emphatic nod. 'Not with the best results, I might add.'

'Did you notice how they smell?'

Pug recalled his encounter with the demon that had disguised itself as the Emerald Queen and yet the memory was a blur. He had been full of vanity and his own sense of power, and had flown in, only to be blasted from the sky in a scorching ball of flames that had almost ended his life.

'I can't say as I had the time to notice any smell,' said Pug. He looked at Miranda and Magnus.

'I've run into several demons over the years, and except for one who smelled of burning brimstone, the rest were . . . sweaty? It was a pungent, musky odour.'

Amirantha laughed. 'I'm sorry, I didn't literally mean their odour. I mean, how their magic smells.'

Pug's eyes narrowed and he said, 'This sounds a lot like a conversation I once had with a tribal shaman down in Kesh, many years ago. He claimed he could tell whose magic had fashioned a ward or cast a spell.'

Amirantha's eyes grew wide. 'You can't?' He glanced at the others, then at Brandos, and said, 'But I thought every magician could ... sense whose spell it was, I mean, if they knew the other magician and had encountered their spellcraft before.'

Magnus exchanged glances with his mother and father, and then said, 'An assumption based on limited contact with other practitioners of magic.' He thought on this for a moment, then said, 'I believe I can, as well.'

'Really?' said Pug.

'You've never said anything,' added his mother.

'I never really gave it much thought,' said Magnus. 'It's not something I do consciously. If you or Mother translocate into or out of the next room, I always know which of you it is.'

Pug's eyes widened slightly.

'If I'm in my quarters, I know who's teaching the students most of the time, just from the way the magic feels in the background.'

Miranda shook her head slightly. 'I had no idea.'

Pug said to Amirantha, 'After the current problems are concluded, perhaps I could persuade you to stay for a while, for I would like to know more of this ability you and my son speak of.'

'I don't know if it's an ability in the sense that it could be taught.'

'Maybe it's a quality that can be recognized, then,' said Pug. 'Something we do and give no thought to, like blinking or breathing.'

'Actually,' said Brandos, 'I give a fair amount of thought to breathing, usually when something is trying to keep me from doing it.'

Amirantha's gaze narrowed but he withheld comment. To Pug he said, 'Brandos must return home soon, else his wife Samantha will have my head on a stick, but I will stay for a while if I can help.' He smiled. 'Besides, there's a great deal here that piques my curiosity, for you've codified magic I've barely heard of. As I said, for those of us who practise the so-called dark arts, there's little social opportunity to meet with other magic users.'

Pug said, 'Agreed.'

Sandreena appeared, guided by one of Pug's students. The Knight-Adamant of the Order of the Shield of the Weak wore a man's tunic, trousers and sandals. Pug indicated that she should join them at the table, and she took a chair next to Miranda, on the opposite side of the table from Amirantha.

'Did you sleep well?' Miranda asked in neutral tones.

'Yes,' said the still-exhausted girl.

'You should have one of our healers look at those wounds.'

Sandreena took a bowl and helped herself to the stew. 'They are fine. I've sewn up enough of them to know if they're festering. I'm just going to have some new scars.'

Miranda said, 'There's a priest of Killian who can make those scars fade, if you care to visit his Temple.'

'Why?' said Sandreena. She looked directly at Amirantha as she said, 'Scars remind me that carelessness is a route to pain.'

305

Amirantha inclined his head slightly as if in agreement, but said nothing.

Brandos said, 'Well, that was fine, but if you have no more use for me, I think I'd like to get out and stretch my legs; otherwise I'll be napping and I find that a bothersome habit; it makes me feel like I'm getting old.'

Miranda smiled and said, 'I'll have one of the students show you around; there are a few places that wouldn't be safe to blunder into.' She signalled and a young man in a dark robe approached. Miranda instructed him to show Brandos the rest of the community he hadn't seen so far, and they left.

Pug asked Amirantha, 'Would you care to look around, too?'

The Warlock said, 'If it's all the same to you, I'd just as soon wait here for Creegan to arrive and get that out of the way.'

Pug and Miranda exchanged brief looks, but said nothing. Magnus said, 'We sent word to all of our agents that Sandreena had turned up safe and was here, so he should be along any time now.'

Amirantha said, 'Well, then, if you have no objections, might I inquire into your stock of wine?'

Pug laughed and motioned another student over and said, 'Do you prefer red or white?'

The Warlock said, 'Yes.'

Miranda laughed with her husband and Pug said, 'Fetch a bottle of wine from the cellar – and see if we still have some of that old Ravensburg red; I think there are a few bottles left. Bring it up and fetch some goblets.' He looked around the table. Magnus, Caleb, and Miranda indicated they were fine, so Pug said, 'Two goblets.'

Sandreena held up a hand with one finger extended, and Pug said, 'Make that three.'

The student hurried off and Miranda said, 'I've been organizing some old documents that have been languishing in the cellar at Stardock, on so-called "demon lore". Amirantha, if you'd like to look at it later I'd appreciate your appraisal of its worth. There isn't much, so it shouldn't take very long.'

The Warlock inclined his head indicating he was willing.

Magnus said, 'Well, I have a lesson to conduct after lunch, which is now, so I'd better be getting along. I will see you all later.'

Caleb also stood up as his brother departed and said, 'And there are household accounts and other matters which also need attention.' He took his leave of the guests as well.

The wine appeared and Amirantha was impressed at the quality of the vintage. As they sipped in silence, Pug's expression caused him to turn.

From a door across the room he saw a tall, redheaded man enter with Father-Bishop Creegan behind him. Amirantha muttered, 'There goes a pleasant moment.'

Sandreena began to rise, but the Father-Bishop waved her back into her chair. 'Finish eating, girl,' he said. Looking at Amirantha he said, 'I thought you were dead.'

'Hoped, you mean,' said the Warlock. 'Creegan,' he said in greeting.

Pug rose and said, 'Wine?'

Glancing around the table, the Father-Bishop nodded and pulled out his own chair.

Pug looked at the redheaded man and said, 'Jommy, wine?'

Grinning, and suddenly looking much younger, the man said, 'Of course.'

Pug motioned for two more goblets and Father-Bishop Creegan said to Sandreena, 'What did you find out?'

Sandreena began her tale slowly, starting with the assault on the innkeeper's wagon on the road to Akrakon. She omitted nothing she could remember, concerned that any detail might prove critical to the Father-Bishop and his companions. Occasionally she let her eyes drift to Amirantha, who sat motionless, listening as closely as everyone else at the table. Finally she recounted visiting the cave to find the old hermit dead.

When she was finished, she added, 'Most of the journey from Akrakon to Ithra is still a blur to me. I was fevered and passed out several times. My horse was stalwart and saw to my protection when I lay at her feet. I recall a little about entering Ithra and finding the monks at the Temple. After that, well, it is nothing to do with this mission, anyway.'

Father-Bishop Creegan looked at Amirantha. 'What do you draw from the summoning and the murder of the magician?'

Amirantha shrugged. 'It is obvious the cultists weren't happy with the results.' He fell silent for a minute and then said, 'I can only surmise, but the sacrifices were designed to call forth something, but from Sandreena's description they instead invoked a series of minor demons. I think I know their ilk; a particularly nasty little thing I call a ripper: bat-wings, huge talons on its forefingers . . .' Sandreena nodded. 'Whoever that unlucky magician was, he was attempting craft far beyond his ability and paid the ultimate price. He was fishing in unknown waters, using bait that could have landed him a shark as easily as a mackerel.' He was silent a moment longer, then asked Sandreena, 'All the demons, they were identical?'

She nodded.

'They vanished after they killed the sacrifice?'

Again she nodded.

He sighed. 'Murderous fools. Somehow, they managed to get their hands on a summoning ritual, and probably thought they could amend it somehow to call forth something else. Those who don't know demon magic . . .' He looked at Pug. 'It would be as if you were trying to call down rain, and decided to substitute the word snow.'

Pug said, 'I'm not a master of weather magic; that would be Temar, but your example holds. The entire structure of the spell would have to be crafted differently.'

Amirantha nodded in agreement. 'So it is with a summoning. If I could contrive one spell of summoning and just change the name of the demon, my life would have been a lot simpler.'

'Or shorter,' said Sandreena wryly. Pug and Father-Bishop Creegan looked at her and she said, 'I've seen him work. He can take liberties and often puts himself, and *others* at risk,' she added with emphasis. Letting her voice return to normal, she looked at the Warlock and added, 'You're an arrogant bastard, Amirantha.'

Amirantha inclined his head slightly as if conceding the point. 'But I know more demon lore than any man I've met.' He looked at Pug. 'Someone is attempting to master in short order what takes years to master. I suspect that means they feel there is an issue of time involved.'

Pug was silent for a moment, then said, 'Jommy, tell Amirantha and the others about that encounter you had when we first discovered the Sun Elves and the Quor.'

Jommy was unknown to Sandreena and Amirantha. He looked at them and said, 'Ten years ago I was still a lad in training and

had been given over to the less than tender care of one Kaspar
of Olasko.'

Amirantha laughed. He said, 'He's here, you know.'

Glancing at Pug he said, 'Fishing?'

Pug nodded. 'Even the demons couldn't stop him.'

Jommy looked uncertain about what that meant, but continued
on. 'In any event, the General trained myself and some other
lads while we were undertaking a mission for . . .' not knowing
if the newcomers were aware of the secret organization behind
this seemingly straightforward school for magic, he said, '—Pug,
and well, we were having a miserable time sitting in the rain
waiting for pirates.'

'Pirates?' said Amirantha.

'Well, that was the report.' He gave Pug a narrow look. 'Sometimes we lads at the front only get to hear rumours. Anyway,
this ship lay off the west coast of the peninsula where the Peaks
of the Quor sit, and three boats came ashore. They looked like
pirates, save they all wore these black headscarves.'

Sandreena glanced at the others around the table. 'Black
Caps?'

'Could be,' said Father-Bishop Creegan. 'If so, they've been
keeping to themselves for quite a while.'

'Even the level of magic Sandreena observed doesn't come
easily. If magicians are trying to learn demon summoning, ten
years is not an unreasonable amount of time to hide and study.'

Jommy said, 'They had this magician, and he . . . he summoned
this . . . this thing.'

Now interested, Amirantha said, 'Describe it.'

'Big and mean, it had a hazy outline like a man, only bigger,
maybe seven, or eight feet tall. It had smoke all around it, like

it wore a cloak or mantle over its shoulders. It spoke some language the magician understood and its voice was hollow, distant. It took shape and it was . . . hard to describe. The skin rippled, like thick cream when you tip the pitcher, or like a banner waving in a breeze. If that makes sense?'

Amirantha nodded. 'Yes, it does.'

'It had eyes like burning embers, bright and red, and then the skin got hard, like dark smoking rock. I can't tell you much more after that, because General Kaspar ordered a charge and all hell broke loose around me.

'I do know that the thing got bigger as it fought, and when it hit something, it burned them. After a minute, it was covered in fire, flames of yellow and white covered it from head to foot. I saw a shield get scorched and a man's tunic catch alight. Smoke came off it like a campfire. I don't know if we had a prayer until the elves showed up and banished it.'

'How did they do that?' asked Amirantha, keenly interested.

'I don't really know,' said Jommy. 'Didn't think to ask. One minute we were scrambling to stay alive, the next there was this bright shaft of light and the thing just froze; then the fire went out. It was raining, did I mention that? Anyway, as soon as it froze, and the fire went out, the rain started steaming off its skin, and then all of a sudden it just fell apart.'

Amirantha said, 'That was not a true demon. That was a bound elemental servant.'

Pug said, 'What is the difference?'

Amirantha said, 'I knew a magician by the name of Celik, who was fascinated with the properties of the elements of earth, air, water and fire.

'He contended there was an essential part of each element,

an aspect that was akin to life, but not true life. He called these creatures elemental servants. They came from some place ... not the demon realm, I am certain, but some other place, some plane of existence unknown to us.'

'Fascinating,' said Pug. His experience on the next plane of existence, with his son and Nakor, the little gambler who had been a friend for many years, when they had confronted the Dasati invasion of Kelewan, had fuelled Pug's curiosity about the existence of yet more realms. To his continuing frustration there was as little information on those realms as there was on demons.

'Well, whatever it was, it was one very scary thing to have bearing down on you,' said Jommy. 'But I'm not sure what it has to do with what you were investigating back in the Peaks of the Quor.'

'Neither do I,' said Pug. 'These Black Caps serve someone, or something, and for over ten years they've been interested in the Peaks of the Quor.'

Father-Bishop Creegan said, 'The Sven'gar-ri. While we still know nothing of their nature beyond the sheer beauty of their being, we know they are beings of power, and that they drew those wraiths—'

'Wraiths?' interrupted Amirantha. 'You've encountered wraiths?'

'I did,' said Jommy. 'Or something enough like a wraith.'

Amirantha said, 'Tell me.'

Jommy spoke of being harried by strange humanoid creatures that rode on the backs of wolf-like mounts, and who were almost impossible to see as anything other than dark spaces in his field of vision.

Miranda had been silent for the entire narrative, but she said, 'I helped obliterate them.' She described their camp and turned to her husband.

'As best we can tell, they are creatures of the void, something akin to the Dread, like wraiths or spectres,' said Pug. 'I've encountered the Dread on two occasions and their lesser kin a few more times.'

'My respect for you is now without limit,' said Amirantha with no humour or irony intended. 'No man living, to the best of my knowledge, has encountered the Dread.

'Wraiths and spectres are also not of the demon realm. They are . . . something else.'

'What?' asked Jommy.

'We don't know,' said Pug. 'We only know that they come from somewhere beyond the Seven Hells or Heavens.' He looked at Amirantha and said, 'They are creatures of the Void.'

Amirantha said, 'I have a feeling there's more to this than I'm being told, which is certainly your prerogative.' He narrowed his gaze as he studied Pug. 'And you already know a great deal about the demon realm, I warrant.'

Pug was silent as those around the table studied him. Miranda asked a silent question, but everyone else had an expectant look. Sandreena put down her spoon, as Father-Bishop Creegan did with his goblet. Pug saw two students standing ready to serve, and a pair conducting some independent study on the other side of the dining hall while they snacked on fruit and cheese. Pug called to them and said, 'You may leave us, and ask them to find another place for their studies, as well. Thank you.'

The two students hurried across the room, and soon the dining hall was empty save for those at Pug's table.

Miranda finally said, 'Tell them. Tell them all. They deserve to know.'

Quietly Pug began. 'You all know of the invasion of the Kingdom of the Isles by the armies of the Emerald Queen. To most of you, it's ancient history; Miranda and I, however, lived through it.'

Amirantha remained quiet; he had witnessed the devastation wrought by the Emerald Queen's armies in his homeland, too, when he had been a young man.

'There are things about those times, of which I will not speak. There are questions I will not answer. But what I will tell you is truth.' No one spoke, but there was a general acceptance of those statements in their expressions.

Miranda knew what he referred to, for she had been there. She remembered everything Nakor had said about the Fifth Circle and what transpired as they stood on the devastated world of Shila, how she had seen her father, Macros, battle the Demon King Maarg, and how she had spoken with the possessed demon controlled by the Saaur lorekeeper, Hanam. Only Miranda, Pug and Magnus knew that although Nakor had been one of their closest confidants, he had also been a tool of Ban-ath, also called Kalkin, the God of Thieves and Liars.

Pug said, 'One of the reasons your high priest in Rillanon introduced us, many years ago, Father-Bishop, was because much of what occurs here is in service to a much higher order, a fact not known by the majority of those who labour here.' He looked from face to face, seeing his wife, the Warlock, the prelate, his foster grandson, and the Knight-Adamant. 'You have all come into this for different reasons, or so you assume.' He looked for a long moment at Amirantha and said, 'Your role is not yet clear to me, but I suspect it is vital that we found you.

'Demons have begun appearing in unexpected locations, without being summoned.' At that Amirantha's eyes widened slightly, but he said nothing.

Pug fell silent for another moment, then said, 'Father-Bishop Creegan, Jommy, and Miranda, know this, but you two do not.' He pointed to Amirantha and Sandreena. 'Within the community of this island some of us serve a higher calling, through an organization called the Conclave of Shadows.

'We are by necessity a highly secret organization that has a very special relationship with the rulers of the three mightiest nations here on Triagia.'

Creegan added, 'Which also means they have influences in all the lesser kingdoms as well.'

'And given Kaspar's role in conducting me here,' said the Warlock, 'its influence stretches as far as the Kingdom of Muboya on the other side of the world.' He sounded impressed.

'We are also well established with other groups, including several of the major Temples. Our purpose is not to subvert or even influence these entities, political and secular, but rather to keep open our lines of communication, to serve a greater good.'

'And that greater good would be?' asked the Warlock.

Jommy barked a laugh, then said, 'The survival of the world.' He leaned forward and all mirth vanished from his expression. In that instant Amirantha could see a hard-bitten veteran of some terrible struggles under the affable expression of this young man. 'I've seen things. I've lived through things no man should have survived, and I've watched people I cared about die.' He paused and then said, 'There is no one in the Conclave for whom

I wouldn't lay down my life, and I'm certain that each of them would lay down his or her life for me.

'It's not blind loyalty either. These people make a difference.'

Pug said, 'Enough, Jommy. We're not here to convince Amirantha that we're an agency of good and all those we oppose are servants of evil.'

The Warlock smiled. 'No need. I already know that. At least I know you believe you're serving good.'

'Adroit comment,' said Miranda.

The Warlock smiled. 'Many of the people who've tried to kill me over the years thought they were serving a greater good.'

Jommy laughed. 'I've had similar experiences.'

Sandreena looked impatient as she said, 'The demons?'

'Yes,' said Amirantha. 'What do you know about the demon realm?'

'There are graduated levels of reality,' began Pug. 'This is what would be considered by some to be the first level of Hell.'

Jommy laughed. 'At times I think that's too generous.' He saw Miranda's expression darken and said, 'I'll be quiet now.'

'We fought demons on the world of Shila, home to the Saaur, and found our way to the passage from where they came. We destroyed the rift between Shila and here and escaped.' He neglected to mention that Macros, Miranda's father, had died holding the most powerful demon of the Fifth Circle at bay long enough for them to succeed.

'We know the demons are ruled by a creature named Maarg, and that he has captains. Of these we know little, save that a hundred years ago his first captain was named Tugor.

'They have intelligence after a fashion, but it is very unlike our own.'

'Agreed,' said Amirantha. 'So far my experience confirms they can be cunning, even clever, but there is a limit to their creative abilities.'

Pug nodded. 'They seem drawn to the higher planes as moths to a flame.'

Amirantha said, 'Such is the case. That is why any summoning must have a containment spell or ward accompanying it, or else the creature will devour everything in sight.

'Even the tiny imps, like my Nalnar, would run rampant if unhampered.' With a smile he said, 'He has a particular fondness for baked goods.'

Miranda didn't seem amused by the image. 'Most of those we encountered were meat eaters,' she said coldly.

'Again, such is the case,' said Amirantha. 'But I believe those of the highest level can also draw life-energy directly out of living beings using their own particular brand of magic.'

'We know they have magic,' said Pug, 'for a demon convinced all who saw him he was the Emerald Queen, using an illusion.'

Amirantha said, 'I would know nothing about that, as I have never encountered a demon with the power to create such an illusion. That the demon could perform such a feat surprises me. They tend to be fairly direct in their use of magic.

'From what the few demons I can trust have told me—'

'Trust?' interrupted Miranda. 'You have demons you trust?'

'Trust, perhaps, is the wrong word. They are reliable in that they will do what I wish and tell me what I want to know because they see me as powerful; they know I can destroy them as well as banish them back to the demon realm.'

'What have they told you?' asked Pug, shifting the topic back.

'They have cities, or something like social organization,' said

Amirantha. 'Not cities such as we would recognize, but warrens in the caves of mountains; hives might be a better analogy.

'They feed on one another constantly, but I have the sense there is something about that I don't fully understand.' He paused, and looked at Pug, Miranda and the others and said, 'I have no certain knowledge, but I have an intuition that they never really die. I think their essence is consumed either by another demon or that it somehow returns to some fundamental state in their realm.'

'Otherwise,' said Jommy, 'why haven't they run out of food already?'

'Yes,' said Amirantha. 'They do not farm or fish, and judging from what I've been told, their realm is devoid of any life other than demon life, as we understand it.'

Pug considered how alien the Dasati realm of the second plane of existence had been, and how the demon realm was even further removed, and said, 'Perhaps it is something we shall never understand.

'Let us go back to our present concerns. The Saaur are a race of warriors and magic users that are the equal of any I've encountered, and the demons crushed them after seventeen years of struggle. The Saaur's empire encompassed an entire world and millions died fighting the demons.

'Our concern of course is, why are demons now appearing with increased frequency here in Midkemia?'

Amirantha said, 'There are several possible theories.'

'I'd like to hear them all,' said Pug, 'but for the moment, I'll have your most likely, please.'

'Someone is bringing them here.'

'Your brother?' asked Pug.

Amirantha nodded. 'At least the one that tried to kill me, the event that had me off looking for Kaspar to tell someone something bad was occurring. And if he's able to subvert my spells and . . .' He sighed. 'He's either grown far more powerful than I thought possible, or he's allied with others. Either way, it's to no good end.'

Father-Bishop Creegan asked, 'Who does he serve?'

'Himself,' said Amirantha.

'Runs in the family, I see,' said Sandreena.

Ignoring the barb, Amirantha said, 'Belasco is not mad the way Sidi was, but he isn't entirely rational, either. He flies into rages that cause him to do things . . .' He shrugged. 'Sidi was completely irrational, and as a result unpredictable. I'm not sure if he even knew why he did half the things he did. Since childhood he was driven by strange impulses, needs and desires that I can only begin to imagine.

'Belasco, however, is driven by hatred. He hates whatever he cannot have, whatever he cannot control, or whatever he cannot understand.'

Jommy sighed. 'That's a lot of hate.'

'Indeed,' said Amirantha. 'If someone or something, an agency we have encountered before or identified, perhaps this organization of Black Caps as you called them, Sandreena, has offered him greater power, greater wealth, or greater understanding, in other words appealed to his vanities and desires, then he would serve.

'And I am certain that, if he is in service, eventually he will plan to surpass and supplant whoever or whatever he serves, but that's another topic. For the moment, he is either working on another's behalf, or for himself, but either way he seems determined to facilitate bringing some very nasty creatures into our world.

'The demon I encountered, the one that began this adventure for me, he was unlike anything I've run afoul of before; he was a battle demon *and* a spell caster. I can't emphasize how unprecedented that is. In no tome, nor during my own personal experience, have I seen or heard of such a creature.

'Demons tend to fall into two groups, with the magic users being the smaller. Their race is dominated by raw power, and often magic is more subtle. Those that use magic tend to be cleverer, more manipulative, even seductive with their arts.'

Sandreena said, 'Which reminds me, how is Darthea these days?'

Amirantha hesitated a moment, then ignored the comment. 'I've often wondered how the little creatures like Nalnar survive.'

Pug said, 'We think it's a system of fealty, being useful, buying protection from more powerful demons further up the hierarchy. Maarg rules through his captains, and they in turn have minions. We assume those like your imp serve a useful purpose, probably as intelligence gatherers, but perhaps nothing more important than carrying out the waste.

'Whatever the truth, we do know that we are confounded by ignorance and need more intelligence.' Looking at Amirantha, he said, 'What can you do to help us?'

The Warlock said, 'Whatever I can. Even were my brother not involved somehow, I would find this entire prospect fascinating. I don't believe there's anywhere else I'd rather be at this moment.'

A student stuck his head around the door and said, 'Sir!'

'What is it?' Pug asked.

'Sentry reports a dragon heading this way.'

Pug rose quickly and said, 'Dragons do not cause us trouble. It can only be Tomas.'

'Tomas?' asked Amirantha.

As he, Miranda, Pug and Jommy made their way towards the door, Father-Bishop Creegan turned and said, 'Why don't you two come along. This is something you may never see again in your life.'

They hurried outside where Pug and his family had quickly gathered. Amirantha saw Brandos had joined them, as well as the young man named Zane. In the distance they could see a speck in the sky, slowly growing larger, becoming bird-like, and then resolving itself into something akin to a wyvern or drake on the wing.

But it kept growing in size and each time Amirantha thought it now close enough to begin landing, it grew some more. Finally, it loomed above them, its massive wings impossible to measure, cracking like thunder as it halted its descent.

'Amazing!' said Sandreena, and Amirantha could only nod. He felt pain and looked down and saw she was clutching his arm, squeezing it tight enough to leave a bruise.

Kaspar walked over from a dell to the north of the landing site to join them. To Jommy he said, 'I never thought I'd see this again.'

'Me neither, General,' replied the redheaded young man.

The dragon lowered itself gently to the ground and bowed its massive head. Pug was surprised to note that two figures climbed down from its back. He was expecting Tomas, but the second visitor was a figure completely new to him.

It looked like an elf, but stood seven feet tall, with hair the colour of a red rooster's comb. It wore robes that appeared to be woven from fine satin, with embroidered edges of purple and gold, and across its back it carried a staff that reeked of arcane energy.

Tomas embraced Pug, who said, 'Welcome, old friend.'

The Warleader made his greetings to Miranda and the others, then turned and said, 'Pug, Miranda, may I present my companion, Gulamendis, Demon Master of the Clans of the Seven Stars, the taredhel, or Star Elves in our tongue.'

Amirantha turned to Father-Bishop Creegan and Sandreena and said, 'Now I am certain that there is nowhere else on this world I'd rather be this moment.'

• CHAPTER SIXTEEN •

Allies

*T*HE DRAGON LEAPT INTO THE SKY.

    Tomas bid it farewell and said he would call it again if needed, though more often than not when he visited Pug, one of the magicians transported him home in a much swifter, if less dramatic, fashion. Everyone watched in silent awe at the spectacle of a great golden dragon winging its way into the blue vault above.

Pug glanced at those standing near him and felt a pang. Here were some of the people he loved most in the world, his wife, his surviving children, and his oldest friend. As it had in the past, the sense of foreboding threatened to overwhelm him. Only Nakor, now dead, had known what Pug knew. Miranda had learned most of it, though he held back one painful and terrifying thing: he was doomed to watch everyone he loved die before him.

He had told Tomas some of the truth behind the manipulations of the god Ban-ath over the years, and even less to Father-Bishop Creegan, that most of his life had been spent as a tool for the Trickster to ensure the survival of this very world. He had no doubt that if it was not the God of Thieves and Liars behind what was occurring now, he was certainly involved somehow. He pushed aside his rising sense of sadness, realizing that part of what triggered this was his need to communicate some of the truth, but again, only a part, to someone. There was no one alive who knew the full burden of what Pug carried every day of his life.

He motioned to Tomas and his companion and said, 'Come, we have much to discuss.' He turned to Father-Bishop Creegan and said, 'Join us, please,' and then with a nod indicated that Amirantha was to attend as well. To Sandreena he said, 'I believe you could use new clothing and some arms?'

She nodded, still agape at what she had just witnessed. Pug motioned for one of the students standing nearby and who had observed Tomas's arrival and instructed him to take Sandreena and find her what she needed.

Pug said, 'Excuse me for a moment,' then went to speak privately with Miranda. They conferred quietly, then she nodded and departed, hurrying off to another part of the house.

Pug motioned for his guests to join him, and led them to the quarters set aside for himself and his family. An open garden with several benches served as a casual meeting place, and while this gathering lacked any aspect of social enjoyment, the privacy it afforded was needed. There was no one on the island Pug didn't trust, but many of his students were young, excitable and prone to gossip.

'If anyone wishes for refreshments,' said Pug, 'I'll send for some.'

As Amirantha and Father-Bishop Creegan had just enjoyed a repast, it fell to Tomas and Gulamendis to decline.

'Very well,' said Pug. He glanced from face to face, then said, 'Too many times in my life I have assumed coincidence, only to find later that some higher agency was at work. I may say things now that either surprise or alarm you, but it will be not conjecture, only truth. Something has brought us all to this council, something of the gods, or perhaps fate.' He looked at the strange elf from another world and said, 'Let us begin with our newest guest. Tell us your tale, Gulamendis.'

The elf studied the three human faces before him, his own an unreadable mask, but he did glance at Tomas who subtly nodded that he should cooperate, and the elf began to speak his tale. He started slowly and began with the history of his people as it obtained to this current crisis.

Time seemed to halt for Amirantha, Father-Bishop Creegan and Pug as the elf painted images with his words. He spoke of a struggling band of refugees, fleeing this world for another and the few thousand survivors who mastered the land around them. The images he evoked, of the reverent elves planting the saplings of the great trees they called the Seven Stars and building their first city around them, then expanding their control over the entire world.

His tale became epic as the elves who had fled to the stars became masters of all they beheld. Arts flourished, music, healing and scholarship. They encountered other races, and Gulamendis was unapologetic in recounting how those encounters became conflict and how relentless and unforgiving the taredhel were. Those who would not yield were destroyed. And few yielded.

Their client races withered and died out so that after five

centuries, on all the worlds of the Clans of the Seven Stars, only the elves endured.

Pug remained stoic during the narrative, but Tomas, his oldest living friend, could see his subtle signs of worry as the tall elf spoke. They were a harsh and unforgiving people, as relentless in nature as the moredhel, but so much more powerful.

'For nearly a millennium, we had peace and we flourished,' said Gulamendis. 'Then we came to a new world. It was devoid of life, but life had once abided. We saw the rubble of structures and the remnants of civilization. We investigated and discovered another portal, one not of our fashioning. Our aremancers studied it while others scoured the world, seeking clues as to what had happened. Those who worked with the portal unravelled its secrets and we opened it to yet another world. And there we met the demons.'

He looked from face to face and asked, 'Have any of you not faced a demon?'

Pug said, 'Of one stripe or another, all of us at different times.'

Looking at Amirantha, Gulamendis said, 'You are a summoner, yes?'

Amirantha nodded. 'I am.'

'You understand then, better than these others, what is required to bring a demon across the realms to our own dimension.'

'Yes,' said Amirantha. 'The magic is complex and difficult to master.'

With a smile that could only be called ironic, the elf said, 'That is why there are so few of us. Those who lack talent do not survive the learning process.'

He paused, and said, 'We are explorers, and for centuries we used our translocation portals, what you call 'rifts', to reach other worlds.

'Explorers died and most worlds we found were uninhabitable, but over the centuries we moved through the stars.

'For two hundred years or so, some have spoken of finding this world, our Home, the world from which we sprang. Some were against it, thinking it likely that this world had been destroyed by the war between the Valheru—' He glanced at Tomas '—and the new gods.

'Others dreamed of finding this world free of strife, as it was in our oldest myths.' Again he glanced at Tomas, 'Though they judged it likely we might again face our former masters.' He took a deep breath. 'Until I met Tomas I, like most of my people, thought we had risen so high, that we could vanquish the Valheru should they endure.' He lowered his eyes. 'I fear that our pride is why we fall before the demons.'

'Tell us of the demons,' urged Pug.

'One of our explorers found a world, desolate beyond measure. Barren rock and empty oceans, but once lush.'

'How could you judge that?' asked Father-Bishop Creegan.

'The world had been inhabited; we found the ruins of great cities. We found artefacts belonging to the people who had lived on that world. Within the cities were sprawling gardens with cleverly designed irrigation. Given the volume of water employed, we assumed that this hot dusty world was once verdant. Vast plains of farming land, again with miles of irrigation systems still in evidence, lay exposed to relentless hot winds, stripping them down to rock and sand. From the age of the artefacts and buildings, we judged the world depopulated less than a century before.

'Yet there was not a hint of life. Of the great race that once inhabited this world, we found nothing, not even bones; little remained to give us any hint of who they might have been. They were physically small, we think, because their doorways were short and their rooms tiny by our measure, yet they built majestic monuments, great pyramids of stone. We found art, paintings and tapestries, though few showed any hint of their maker; they tended to abstract designs of rich colour. We found a few like-nesses, and we think they may have been a race akin to the dwarves.

'They may have had libraries or great schools, but we found nothing but ash. Fires raged throughout their cities, across every vista, and we wondered who or what had caused this planet-wide catastrophe.

'In the deepest vault of one of those great stone buildings we found words, hastily scrawled over murals on a wall. Words painted with the most indelible paint they possessed, so that this tiny legacy might endure.

'It took our Lorekeepers years to unravel their meaning, but they simply said, "Why have our gods deserted us? Why are we to perish?" And then a word that we could not translate followed by "are without this hall. So we will end. Should any read this, cry for the . . ." and another word we could not translate.'

'Demons?' asked Amirantha.

'Later experience led us to believe so.'

Pug said, 'If demons somehow came to that world, and ran free, eventually all life as we know it would end. Once they ran out of prey, they would turn on one another, and eventually one would survive. The last would finally starve to death.'

Amirantha and Gulamendis exchanged questioning looks, and

the Warlock said, 'I've never conjured a demon that remained long enough to starve to death.'

The elf smiled as he nodded agreement. 'I have fed a few, along the way, but as with you, when they have done my bidding I banish them back to their own realm. Until we encountered the Demon Legion I had never even considered how a free demon would behave in our realm.'

Amirantha said, 'I have encountered a few.' He glanced at Father-Bishop Creegan and said, 'Not everything I do is a confidence trick. I have rid this world of several serious evils over the years.'

'No doubt,' said the cleric dryly.

Amirantha turned his attention back to Gulamendis. 'If one weak-willed, would-be Demon Master oversteps his limitations, a demon could easily run loose. I have hunted down and dispatched at least a dozen over the years.'

Jommy appeared at the doorway and entered the garden. Pug motioned him over and the redheaded noble said, 'Miranda is gone, she asked me to tell you. She'll be back soon.' He glanced around, and said, 'Should I leave?'

Pug shook his head and said, 'No, stay. You'll be involved deeply in whatever we run into as much as the rest of us.'

Jommy moved off to one side and took a seat on the bench near where Tomas stood.

Gulamendis said, 'Among my people, I am considered something of an outcast.' He noted Amirantha's slight smile in acknowledgement. 'Many of my people mistakenly blame me and others who are students of demon lore for the assaults.'

'Even though you found proof of demon incursion into other worlds decades before you encountered the Demon Legion?'

Gulamendis nodded sadly. 'It is the nature of things that many people are more interested in affixing blame than fixing the problem.'

Amirantha said, 'We hadn't encountered any of the problems you've mentioned on any significant scale until recently.' He sat back. 'I'm not sure we are, even now. It is almost certain that much of what I've recently seen with unexpected demon encounters is the work of one agency, a summoner who has the ability to wreak havoc for his own reasons.' He shrugged.

'How certain are you of this?' asked Gulamendis.

'Absolutely, for he interfered with one of my summonings and almost got me killed. I tried calling forth a familiar demon and instead got the most aggressive battle demon I've ever encountered.'

'Fascinating,' said the elf. 'I've never heard of a summons being distorted that way. I've had them interrupted, abruptly at times, but never ... perverted in such a fashion.' His eyes narrowed. 'It would involve magic of extreme power ...'

'And subtlety,' added the Warlock. 'Changes in the summoning would need to be introduced at key times.'

The two demon experts seemed on the verge of discussing the specifics when Pug interrupted. 'I'm as fascinated by this as you, but we need to consider the larger question: Why?'

'Why?' repeated Amirantha. 'Well, as I've said, my brother has been trying to kill me for years.'

'Your brother?' asked Gulamendis.

'I'll explain,' said Amirantha. Then to Pug he said, 'I'm surprised he has developed the skills needed, but not that he's trying to kill me.'

'Why now?' asked Pug. 'Why after all these years, and in a

way that would be most likely to create chaos? If he's as powerful as you say, and he has knowledge of your whereabouts, why not just drop a ball of fire on your head?'

'Fire wards are part of the proactive spells,' said Amirantha while Gulamendis nodded in agreement. 'But I see your point. He could easily have dropped a very large rock on my head while I walked to the cave.'

'Unless he couldn't see you,' added Jommy. When all eyes turned to him, he said, 'Sorry.'

'No need to be sorry,' said Pug. 'That is a good point.'

Amirantha said, 'It means he sees me with magic, not sight.'

'So he could be anywhere,' added Gulamendis, 'but he needs you to be working your arts to know exactly where you are.'

Pug said, 'My thought, entirely. But how is he able to spy upon you, or know when you're actively conjuring a demon . . . ?' Pug shrugged.

Gulamendis slowly shook his head. 'That is very subtle and very powerful magic craft, even for my people.'

Pug said, 'I have been a student of magic for most of my life, and am well into my second century of study, yet there is so much we do not know.

'I also have difficulty imagining how your brother is able to do this,' said Pug.

'My magic signature, for lack of a better term, would be as familiar to Belasco as his is to me,' said Amirantha. 'As yours and your wife's is to your son, Magnus.'

'But how is he able to know where you will be when you actually begin to conjure?'

'That,' said Amirantha, 'is the question.'

'Spies?' offered Jommy.

Amirantha said, 'Only Brandos, and perhaps his wife Samantha, know where I'm going to be when next I conjure. I trust them as family.'

'What about demon spies?' asked Jommy. 'I mean, I don't really know how this conjuring of demons works, do I? But maybe he's got a demon somewhere whose job is to alert him when you're calling up some other demon.'

Amirantha and Gulamendis both looked thunderstruck. The human Demon Master spoke first, 'I don't know . . .'

'Is that possible?' asked the elf.

Jommy shrugged. 'You two are the demon lore experts. You don't know?'

Gulamendis seemed insulted by the remark, but said nothing. Amirantha said, 'As Pug observed, there is so much more to know.'

Jommy shrugged. 'So, why don't you ask?'

'Ask whom?' Gulamendis's tone was cold.

Jommy grinned. 'Ask the demons.'

Amirantha looked stunned. Then he laughed aloud. 'Oh, gods and fishes,' he exclaimed. The star elf also looked astonished at the suggestion, then he started to chuckle.

Amirantha said, 'I suspect my new friend here has fallen prey to the same failing as I, to wit: we are so focused on mastering our particular arts – which is part of staying alive – that we neglected to be more curious about the smaller creatures we employ to do our bidding.'

'What do you do now?' asked Creegan.

Amirantha stood, said, 'Why, we summon a demon and start asking questions!'

With a single gesture and a word, he executed a spell. Pug and Jommy both felt the familiar sensation of hair rising on their arms. Tomas remained standing, but his hand fell to the hilt of his sword as the powerful spell was cast.

Creegan stood reflexively and stepped back as a puff of black smoke revealed a small, blue-skinned imp. 'Nalnar!' shouted Amirantha. 'You are summoned.'

'Master,' said the creature, looking around the group.

Gulamendis laughed in obvious delight. 'It's Chokin!'

'Chokin?' asked Pug.

'I have an imp that serves me, two actually, Choyal and Chokin. This one looks like Chokin.'

Hearing that name, the imp regarded Gulamendis. 'Chokin?' he asked, in a high-pitched voice.

'Do you know Chokin?' asked Amirantha.

Nodding vigorously, Nalnar said, 'We be of blood, and he is my elder. Choyal is my younger.'

'Brothers?' asked Gulamendis.

'What is brothers?' asked the imp.

'You are of the same mother or father,' said the Warlock.

'Mother? Father? Not understand, Master.'

'Apparently they don't have parents,' said Jommy, fascinated by his first look at a creature from the demonic realm that wasn't trying to kill him.

'What do you mean he's of your blood?' asked Amirantha.

'We spawn together. Choyal, Chokin, Lanlar, Jodo, Takesh, Tadal, Nimno, Jadru, and Nalnar! We nine. Jodo and Lanlar no more. Seven only now.' He lowered his head, an expression of sadness totally unexpected on a face that alien.

'What happened to your . . . brothers?' asked Amirantha.

RAYMOND E. FEIST

'Eaten,' he replied. Looking from face to face, the imp asked, 'Master needs Nalnar?'

Amirantha looked at Pug. 'Could we have something for Nalnar to nibble on? He's more cooperative if we feed him.'

'Certainly, what do you require?'

Looking at the imp who now had an eager expression on his blue face, he said, 'I think a plate of cheese and bread, perhaps a small slice of sausage, and any fruit would keep him occupied.'

The imp looked positively thrilled at the prospect of food. Pug used his arts to summon a student, and then sent the young woman to the kitchen to fetch the food.

While they waited, Sandreena appeared, now wearing a new suit of clothing and fine, highly polished armour. She even sported a new tabard with the symbol of her order on it. Father-Bishop Creegan looked at Pug and said, 'Impressive. How did you happen to have the tabard?'

Sandreena said, 'More, how did you happen to have an entire suit of armour that fits me perfectly?'

Pug smiled. 'We have resources.'

The imp began jumping up and down excitedly. 'Sandreena! Nalnar love Sandreena.'

The female Knight-Adamant of the Order of the Shield of the Weak looked on the imp with widened eyes. 'Nalnar?' Looking at Amirantha with hooded eyes, she said, 'Putting on a show, are we?'

Amirantha chose to say nothing.

Pug said, 'We have discovered that despite Amirantha and Gulamendis's experience with demons, we are still too ignorant of their realm. We thought we might begin by interrogating one of its more tractable inhabitants.'

Sandreena sat, saying, 'Well, my experience with this little monstrosity tells me it's a little more intelligent than a dog, less reliable, and prone to very rude and inappropriate behaviour at inopportune times.' She looked at Amirantha. 'Why not Darthea? I'm certain you and she have had many quiet conversations.'

Amirantha looked uncomfortable, but said nothing.

'Darthea?' asked Jommy.

Sandreena's expression was poisonous as she glanced at Amirantha, and the Warlock seemed genuinely embarrassed. She said, 'Not all the residents of the demon realm are hideous. Some are . . . beautiful.'

Jommy closed his eyes in sympathy for the Warlock, while Father-Bishop Creegan looked appalled. 'A succubus?'

'Succubi?' asked Jommy, his eyes wide with fascination.

Father-Bishop Creegan said, 'We scarcely believe the lore, but the succubi are female demons of incredible beauty who seduce the righteous into acts of depravity and worse.'

Amirantha took a deep breath and said, 'Those legends are vastly overstated.' He looked at the faces now regarding him and said, 'Each demon survives as he or she must, with whatever gifts they have. The succubi are . . . gifted with the ability to resemble a female of great beauty of many races. It's just an illusion.'

Gulamendis smiled, and said, 'My brother would be fascinated by such illusion. That is his area of expertise.'

Amirantha said, 'Enough. I'm over one hundred years old and have put any embarrassment over my personal proclivities behind me; I've outlived a dozen lovers, so if I choose to seek comfort with someone who I know will be around in another hundred years, that is my affair.'

Sandreena flushed and her anger was visible, though she was silent.

He turned to her and said, 'Again, as I have said on three other occasions, if I hurt you, I am deeply sorry.' Then his expression turned hard, and his voice firm as he added, 'But I made you no oath. If you cannot forgive me, that is *your* burden to carry, not mine.' Looking at Pug, he said, 'May we please return to the matter at hand?'

Pug had lived too long to find this sort of discourse anything but banal. He nodded and said, 'Please, speak to your minion.' Seeing the refreshments for the imp were at the door, he waved in the student carrying the tray and indicated that she should put it before Nalnar.

Without leave, the imp began devouring the cheese, bread, and fruit. Amirantha sighed, and with a slight inclination of his head, indicated he understood Pug's impatience with Sandreena's anger. He said, 'Nalnar, tell me of those with whom you were spawned.'

'Yes, Master?' said the imp.

'Perhaps if you were more specific?' suggested Gulamendis.

Nodding, Amirantha said, 'Tell me of Choda, Nimno . . .' he struggled to recall the other names '. . . and the others with whom you were spawned.'

'Tell?' asked the imp. He said, 'Tell what, Master?'

'Tell us of your life, what you do when you are not summoned here.'

'We live, we die, we fight . . .' A light seemed to enter the creature's eyes, and he said, 'We began. We were not, then we were. Hundreds of us swimming in the beginning place. We fought. We ate, we grew. Of the hundreds, fifty endured. Fifty crawled out of the beginning place, and we fought those bigger and hungry. We were the clever ones, we nine. We banded together and killed those who waited, and devoured them. We became strong, and we were nine together. Those who waited ran from us and sought out those weak ones who didn't band together.' He shrugged. 'We left the beginning place and hid.'

'Hid?' asked Amirantha. 'From whom did you hide?'

'All who were bigger, stronger, and hungry,' answered the imp as he impaled a piece of cheese on a talon and devoured it. 'Nalnar thirsty!' With a narrowing gaze, he looked at Amirantha and asked, 'Wine?'

'No!' said Amirantha. He looked at Pug and added, 'You do not want to see him drunk.' To the imp he said, 'Water.'

'Water,' the imp repeated.

Pug motioned for the student who stood watching with fascination and had to wave vigorously to get her attention. The young woman nodded vigorously and hurried off, returning moments later with a goblet of water.

The imp drank greedily, then dropped the cup. He looked around the gathered onlookers, then howled in glee. Amirantha sighed and with a wave of his hand, banished the creature.

'Why?' asked Pug quietly.

It was Gulamendis who answered. 'They grow intoxicated on our food, even water, and then become bold. We only usually feed them as a reward, after we're done with their service. It's why he banished him.' He nodded approval to Amirantha.

Amirantha said, 'He was of no further use as he would become fractious and start to lie; he needs to regain his sobriety in his own realm.'

'I have had similar difficulty with imps,' said the elf.

'We need more information,' said Tomas quietly.

Gulamendis inclined his head respectfully and said, 'Yes, Ancient One, and I have seen the error of my lack of curiosity.'

'As have I,' added Amirantha. 'But in your case, I wonder,' he said to Gulamendis. 'When your people ran afoul of demons, did it not occur to you to seek information?'

Gulamendis said, 'How reliable are your sources among the demons?'

Amirantha shrugged. 'I have not had the need to establish that.'

'Precisely,' said Gulamendis.

Pug observed the star elf and thought he detected a slight bridling at the implication that he should have done more. 'I'm certain Gulamendis had his own pressing concerns.'

Showing the self-restraint Pug had observed with Aglaranna's people, Gulamendis merely nodded slightly. 'Indeed. My standing with my people has never been high, and once the nature of the Demon Legion was established, let's just say we were not given opportunity to help.

'Some were executed outright—'

'Executed?' interrupted Tomas. 'How is that possible?'

Gulamendis seemed thrown off balance by the question. 'By order of the Regent Lord. Some of us were imprisoned, questioned and tortured, while others were summarily executed. The Regent's Meeting, or at least the majority of it, believed that we were responsible for this invasion.'

Tomas's expression was a mix of disbelief and outrage. 'Executed,' he whispered. 'Elf killing elf.' He lowered his eyes as if overcome by sadness for a moment. Then he looked at the taredhel Demon Master. 'I think that in days to come I may have to speak to your rulers, to this Regent Lord.'

Gulamendis did not like the direction that remark was taking them in, so he said, 'I did try to ascertain what I could of the Demon Legion from my summoned demons, but time was not my ally. I was imprisoned and confined under guard. The best I could do was summon Choyal, one of my imps, for a brief time at night, and send him to the kitchen to steal food and drink so I wouldn't perish in my cage.'

Pug asked, 'Why were you spared?'

'To guarantee my brother's good behaviour.'

'Explain, please,' asked Pug.

'As the Demon Legions pressed us, the search for a safe haven became more pressing. Our primary world, Andcardia, would eventually fall; the Regent Lord and the Regent's Meet knew this long before it was apparent to the rest of the population.

'Great meetings were held in the squares of our cities and glorious banners were unfurled and flowers rained down on the warriors marching off to fight the demons. Every type of elven magic was unleashed – we have spell-shattering weapons that cause demon magicians to falter so our armoured fighters can close in and kill them; we have death towers that unleash massive bolts of foul energy that destroys demon flesh on contact. Terrible war machines were erected and unleashed on them.

'And still the demons came.'

Pug said, 'Let us go back to that world your people discovered, the one devoid of life. If that wasn't where you first encountered the demons, where did you?'

'Our translocation portals work with a tiny degree of imprecision. I do not understand the problem, as its magic is alien to me.' He inclined his head towards Pug. 'You would most certainly understand what the portal masters speak of; I can not.

'I only know that in years past, it was decided that a hub would be constructed, one that all worlds would connect to, a centralized hall of magic through which anyone wishing to travel between the worlds of the Clans of the Seven Stars could easily find passage.

'So, one need only step through a gate to the hub world, called Komilis, and from there reach any destination.'

Pug nodded slightly as he mused, 'It would forestall the need for dozens of rifts, for each world would only need one, and only the magicians on Komilis would need to tend to multiple gates.'

'Precisely,' said Gulamendis. 'But when our exploration team found the world of the demons . . .'

'They overran the gate and gained access to your hub world,' said Sandreena. Her tone left no doubt she thought this was a military blunder of unforgivable proportion.

Gulamendis said nothing, but his expression showed that he agreed with her. Then he said, 'The struggle over the central city of Komilis lasted years.

'The demons took control of the hub long enough to find their way to all our worlds.'

'Didn't you try to destroy the gates?' asked Pug.

'Yes,' said Gulamendis, 'but it was too late. They had found their way.'

'And if they overrun the gate from Andcardia to Midkemia before you can close it,' said Pug, 'they'll be here.'

'Or they are here already,' said Amirantha.

'I think you'd know if they were here,' said Gulamendis dryly.

'Not necessarily,' said Amirantha. 'That demon I told you of, the one conjured by my brother, have you ever seen its like?'

Gulamendis said, 'I can't be sure, but I think not.'

'A battle demon that is also a magic user?'

'No,' said the elf. 'I have not seen its like.'

Amirantha said, 'I have a theory. It is only surmise, but it fits what we know so far.'

'I would welcome it,' said Pug.

'There is another agency at work,' said the Warlock.

'Your brother?' suggested Pug.

He shook his head. 'Perhaps, but unlikely. Belasco is many things, but he is not a fanatic. However, he would willingly serve those who are.

'Sandreena's description of the failed summoning means that someone is desperately trying to get demons into this realm, and is willing to risk making mistakes – even catastrophic ones – to achieve their goal.

'What I should have pointed out is that had the summoner been slightly more gifted, those demons he conjured would have remained in our realm a great deal longer.'

'And grown more powerful,' added Gulamendis.

'Which is beside the point, really,' said the Warlock. 'The point is that some agency knows this world exists and is trying to bring demons here, and is willing to unleash madness to achieve that goal.

'Moreover, it may be completely unrelated to the danger our elf friend has come to warn us of.'

'Why do you say that?' asked Father-Bishop Creegan, his doubts about Amirantha's presence set aside for a moment.

'Because if I have my time-line correct, these occurrences

preceded his people's arrival by a decade?' He looked at Jommy.

'Yes,' said the redheaded noble. 'It was about ten years ago when we ran into that bunch of Black Caps off the shore of the peninsula.'

'And your brother arrived here, what, less than a year ago?' said Amirantha to Gulamendis. The elf nodded. Looking around the room he said, 'The demons were trying to come here before he reached his homeworld.'

'I'm not convinced these are unrelated problems,' said Pug, 'but even if they are, they both must be confronted.

'We can't have lunatics running around trying to bring demons into our realm whenever they please.' Amirantha's expression revealed he was unsure if Pug put him in that category. 'And if the Demon Legion follows the star elves to this world . . .' He left the thought unfinished.

'Two problems, then,' said Jommy.

Tomas said, 'What do we do?' His question was directed at Pug.

Pug hesitated for a moment. As leader of the Conclave of Shadows he had been expected to give instructions for decades, but he still found it difficult sometimes to order men of vast power and experience, rather than let them suggest their best course of action. Finally he said, 'Father-Bishop Creegan, Amirantha, Sandreena, and whomever else they wish to recruit from here should return to Akrakon and start looking for any sign of who is trying to summon demons there.'

Jommy said, 'I'll go, too, if you have no objection. I saw that first monster come ashore ten years back and think it might be time to finally get to the bottom of who these Black Caps are.'

Pug nodded. Looking at Tomas, he said, 'I think you and I should travel with Gulamendis to greet the newcomers and assess the possibility of the Demon Legion following them here.'

Gulamendis said, 'There could be difficulties.'

Tomas said, 'You've made me aware of those possible difficulties. Still, we have no choice. We cannot ignore an incursion of this size. Moreover, the Kingdom of the Isles will not ignore it once Alystan of Natal's report wends its way to the prince in Krondor. A detachment of riders will certainly be dispatched to ride from Carse or Tulan to investigate. Dolgan's dwarves will also send someone up to keep an eye on your people.'

'That would be unwise,' said Gulamendis.

'Why?' asked Pug.

'Because the Regent Lord has issued orders than any who blunder across our valley are to be killed on sight.'

'What!' said Tomas. 'Your valley!'

Gulamendis said, 'We are a people facing extinction! We will dig in and we will fight if threatened, by humans, dwarves, or even our distant kin. It would be better if you let me approach the Regent's Meeting first, to let them know I've made contact and that you are interested in helping prevent the demons' arrival here.'

Tomas glanced at Pug who nodded slightly.

'Very well,' said the Warleader of Elvandar. 'I can summon a dragon and land you within a short distance of your outposts.'

'No need,' said the Demon Master. 'I can summon a flyer.' He saw Pug's expression, and quickly added, 'It will be completely under my control and dismissed when I arrive.'

Tomas said, 'Leave as you will, but tell your leaders that I will be along within three days. I will return to my Queen and then

I will come to your new home. I will bring members of my lady's council, and we shall sit with your Regent and discuss what we shall do should the Demon Legion come.

'But your leaders would be well advised to reconsider their attitude towards those who may approach the boundaries of your encampment in the mountains, Gulamendis. Despite your people's belief in their superiority, you are few in numbers, hard punished by a war seemingly without end, and you will need help. Those who come to you may do so inadvertently or out of curiosity, so treat them with respect.' Tomas left it unsaid that should his message go unheeded by the Regent Lord, he would not be pleased, and even a Valheru of such strange origin was still a being to be respected, if not feared.

The elven Demon Master nodded, and bowed to those in the garden. To Amirantha he said, 'We must sit down soon; we have much to discuss. There is much to learn.'

'Agreed,' said the Warlock, standing to bow slightly in respect.

As he made ready to depart, Gulamendis said, 'There are so many things I would learn from you and your companions, Pug. But I am not typical of my people.' He glanced at Tomas and said, 'Your old friend may tell you about a conversation we shared, and you will realize that I am being honest when I say we will not welcome your people's overtures until we know we are safe.'

He looked up at the sky above and said, 'Home. It is a myth, yet here I stand; under the same sky looked upon by my ancestors.'

Looking again at Tomas he said, 'And I am not the best interlocutor you could have chosen, Lord Tomas, for most of my people blame me and those like me for the demon invasion. No matter what we say, they will not believe there is a demon gate somewhere out there through which these creatures travel.'

'Demon gate?' asked Pug. 'You said nothing of this.'

'It's almost a myth; a rumour. It is said that one Demon Master, prior to his execution, pleaded to tell the Regent's Meeting that he knew the demons came into our realm through a demon gate. He never said how he knew this, though he may have gleaned the information from one of his summoned creatures. But it may present the hope that we who practise my craft hold to, that some day we shall be forgiven for this horror visited on our people.'

Calmly Pug said, 'I know there's a demon gate.'

For the first time Gulamendis's composure cracked and hope played across his face. 'How do you know?'

'Because I have been there.'

CHAPTER SEVENTEEN

Determination

*G*ULAMENDIS LOOKED STUNNED.
Slowly he asked, 'You've been there?'
'It's called Shila.'

'Shila?'

'The world from which the Saaur – a race now living on this world – were driven by the demons. It must be the location of the gate where Macros battled Maarg, the Demon King.'

Gulamendis sat down, now completely stunned. 'Maarg?'

Amirantha said, 'We've heard legends . . .'

Gulamendis stood, and conjured a spell. In a moment a twin to Amirantha's imp stood before him, wrapped in dissipating smoke. The creature looked surprised to be surrounded by so many onlookers, and spun around before acknowledging Gulamendis. 'Master?' he asked, looking meek and pathetic.

Gulamendis said, 'Tell us of Maarg.'

Instantly the imp shrieked in terror and spun, as if seeking a way out. 'No!' it cried in a shrill voice. 'No! No! No!'

The creature was obviously terrified, but Gulamendis held out his hand. 'Tell us of the Demon King!' he commanded.

The imp looked around, a crazed feral cast to his features, his eyes hooded as if he sought escape or a route for attack. He crouched with clawed hands extended as if he would rend anything that he could reach. 'No!' he shrieked, a sound of rage and terror. 'No! No! No!' he kept repeating.

Gulamendis's eyes narrowed and he said, 'He has never disobeyed me before.' He stuck out his left hand, palm up and incanted something in a language Pug and the others did not understand, but it caused a reaction from Amirantha, who seemed as shaken by the imp's behaviour as the others. 'Tell me!' said the taredhel elf, and in closing his hand enacted some magic, for the imp doubled over holding his stomach, suddenly in terrible pain.

'Master, no!' cried the imp, the rage and fear in his eyes now gone, his expression one of pleading.

'By ward and word, spell and will, *tell me of the Demon King!*' Again he opened and closed his hand and the imp shrieked in agony. Then with a wave he released his magic and the imp drew a deep gasp of air.

The creature cringed and whispered as if terrified of being overheard outside the room. 'The Demon King is greatest of all! He hears what is said; he sees what is done. He rends and eats, and no one escapes him. He rails at the gate, waiting for the final opening.' Suddenly the creature's eyes widened, and it stiffened as if struck from behind, then its eyes rolled up and it fell forward.

Amirantha stood and sweeping his hands in an arc, inscribed a dome of energy above the garden. 'Brace yourself!' he shouted.

The sky above them exploded, the calm blue of the afternoon instantly changed to a raging blast of yellow and white, blinding anyone who glanced upward. Even through the mystic shield, the heat swept down over them like waves of torment. Pug was but an instant behind the Warlock with his own counter-spell, and the heat vanished as he neutralized the inferno.

Gulamendis, Father-Bishop Creegan, and Sandreena were all just reacting, as Jommy dived for the ground, seeking to be as close to the cool soil as was humanly possible.

As the flames above vanished Pug swept his hand around him in a circular motion, incanting another spell of protection.

Then from another part of the building a massive silver bolt of energy sped into the sky, arching quickly out of view.

Amirantha said, 'What was that?'

Pug glanced around to make sure everyone was all right, then knelt to examine the fallen form of the imp. 'That would be my wife. Whoever sent that mystic comet down on our heads is about to be repaid. It's a nasty trick she learnt before I met her. If our attacker has no protective wards in place, he's about to get back worse than he gave. That energy bolt requires far more protection than mystic fire does. It could melt a house.' Dropping the arm of the imp, he said, 'It's dead.' Looking at Gulamendis he added, 'I think.'

'As dead as it can be here in this realm. It will slowly reform back in the. . .' He pointed. 'Look.'

The figure of the imp faded into transparency then mist, then was gone within a moment.

'It will reform, as I said, and I will be able to summon it once more.'

'With demons, there's dead and then there's dead,' said Amirantha. 'I was going to ask you later how your warriors have been killing them.'

'With every weapon and spell we can muster,' said Gula-mendis.

'There's one of your problems, then,' said Jommy.

Both Demon Masters looked at him and Amirantha said, 'Yes, he's right.'

Gulamendis nodded. 'No one believed me when I told them that, short of complete destruction through very powerful magic, the demons were only ever banished to their own realm.'

'And if they rested up a bit, they could come back through any open gate into this realm,' said Jommy.

'An army that cannot be destroyed, only delayed?' asked Tomas.

'Oh, demons can be destroyed,' said Sandreena. 'I've destroyed more than one myself. Completely and utterly.'

Father-Bishop Creegan indicated agreement. 'It's the magic of the gods that obliterates them. If you can stun one long enough to utter a specific oath or spell, the creature is utterly destroyed.' But he sounded worried. 'But those are rare cases, Pug. Most of our magic is banishment. We do not belabour the difference when we teach that magic, but the majority of demons we deal with are merely sent back to the demon realm.'

'How difficult will it be to deal with a host of them?' asked Tomas, pointedly.

The old cleric sagged visibly as he admitted, 'Impossible. Even if I should muster every priest, priestess, monk and nun of every god as well as all the martial Orders, each would only be able to destroy one or two each day. The magic is difficult and exhausting.'

Pug let out a sigh as Miranda came storming into the garden. 'What was that?' she asked accusingly. 'Half of the outer buildings are on fire and we have a lot of very frightened students, not to mention a few who were badly burned. It's a miracle no one was killed.'

Magnus also appeared and looked ready to do battle. When he saw his mother's mood he said nothing.

Pug glanced at his elder son and said, 'Caleb? The others?'

'Everyone is fine, as far as I can tell,' he answered. 'Whoever erected that barrier saved this building and this is where most of the heat struck. There are fires in the outer buildings, but they are being dealt with.'

'Good,' said Pug. Looking at his wife, he continued, 'That retaliatory bolt you threw back along the path of the incoming spell, do you have any sense of where it went?'

She nodded. 'To the southeast, to somewhere near the Peaks of the Quor I think.'

'Well, someone has just had a rude awakening if they've survived that,' said Pug. To Magnus he said, 'I want you to pass the word; we're now on a war footing. Send the younger students away, either back to their home worlds or to Stardock. Send messages to everyone to return here as quickly as possible. I want every master magician in council in the next few days.'

Gulamendis moved over to stand next to Amirantha. 'These human magicians are . . . impressive.'

'You would do well not to underestimate them,' suggested the Warlock.

'I don't take your meaning,' said Gulamendis.

Amirantha gifted the taredhel Demon Master with a slight smile. 'I think you do.'

The elf lowered his voice and said, 'I will not, but others of my kind . . . even the harsh lesson of the Demon Legion is lost on them. Arrogance is a relative term among my race.'

Amirantha saw Pug, Tomas, Miranda, and Magnus were in a deep conversation, while Father-Bishop Creegan was speaking intently with Sandreena, and Jommy seemed more intent on watching the pair of them than the two demon experts. The Warlock gently took Gulamendis by the elbow and led him a few feet away. In a low voice he said, 'Let me speak candidly, my new friend. You and I understand what is coming, that few people can imagine the nightmare approaching this world. And we've only had glimpses into that realm from which those nightmares come.

'Perhaps those you left behind have faced them, but until the Demon Legion arrives, we have much work to do.'

'What are you proposing?' asked Gulamendis.

'From chaos comes opportunity,' said the Warlock. 'You and I will never fully be accepted by our people, but here—' he waved his hand in a small circle '—this place is unique. I know you haven't had the time to socialize, but there are creatures from other worlds here, intelligent beings who are studying with Pug and his magicians.' He looked back at the sorcerer, who he saw was now watching him speak with the elf. 'These people have something here unique, and we could share in it.'

The elf said, 'I sense what you mean.' He also looked back

to see Pug watching over his wife's shoulder as she spoke to their son and Tomas. He nodded once, then said, 'In a very short time I have come to understand that my view of things, radical and even treasonous to my people's thinking, is perhaps not radical enough.'

'Think of it, people who wish only to seek knowledge. Isn't that why you began poking around in dark caves when you were a child?'

Gulamendis broke into a laugh, which caused others to turn and look. He held up a hand. 'It is just an unseemly jest,' he said to the others. Then to Amirantha, he said, 'Yes, that is exactly why I began turning over rocks, it was just to see what was under them. Pushing sticks into hollow trees to see what was inside. Never-ending curiosity that took me places no one else even imagined. You as well?'

Amirantha nodded. 'Over a century ago. One day, I will tell you about my mother, who was a mad witch, and of my brothers, two evil bastards if ever there were, but for the first time in my life I sense that here our kind may be welcomed, and I think we'd be fools to not take advantage. Think of being able to study without fear, and of having others nearby to support your work, to aid you if needs be. The knowledge we could discover . . .'

Gulamendis inclined his head as if thinking for a moment, then said, 'Perhaps, if time permits, I'll find my brother alive and bring him here as well. He would also enjoy this atmosphere.'

'Good,' said Amirantha. 'I know trust is hard earned, especially to those like us, but I vow, on my blood, that if you serve to forestall the Demon Legion, I will serve along with you, and should we prevail, I'll call you brother.'

The elf studied the human before him, seeing a steely resolve in his features. He said, 'Why do I get the feeling that you've found yourself in an unusual position?'

'Because trust comes hard to me, and I've spent my life watching people I have come to care for die. I find it easier to be aloof and to keep to myself; when I spend time with people, it is usually to rid them of their gold.'

'A frank admission.'

'I am not a prideful man, Gulamendis. I have vanity, but that is not the same. I have done little in my life for which I feel a sense of achievement.' He nodded towards Sandreena. 'That young woman was someone who came to feel something for me, and I repaid her affection with callous abandonment.'

'Ah, that would explain her attitude when she looks at you,' said the elf.

'In many ways she's as strong a woman as one can imagine – certainly the better of most men when it comes to skill at arms – but strong of mind and will, too. What is not so apparent is that she's easily hurt.' His voice trailed off at the end of his remark and the elf remained silent. Amirantha eventually went on. 'Her strength hides the vulnerable nature of her heart. She was ill used by men as a child, and I assumed that would have made her callous; quite the opposite, in fact. I do not know how it is with your race, Gulamendis, but with us such matters are often confounding, and out of all the goals my race pursue, finding love can bring the most harm.'

'It is not that different, though we have much more time than humans to discover what we should truly value. My brother and I are both counted young by our people, barely halfway through our first century of life. And like you we live on the fringe of our society, so finding a woman who will bear that social stigma is even more difficult.' He glanced over to where Sandreena stood and said, 'Perhaps all of this will help you heal the breach between you?'

'I will never repair that breach,' Amirantha said quietly, 'but I can choose to live a better life.'

'Upon that we can agree,' said the elf. 'All should wish to live a better life.'

'Come, let us return and make plans to help where we can.'

They returned to the discussion taking place and found Pug giving detailed instructions as to what must be done and how quickly. He turned to Gulamendis and said, 'Return to your people and let them know of Tomas's arrival, for he will come within three days and speak to your council. We will not wait upon your leaders to act, but we will welcome them as allies should they choose to join with us.' To Amirantha he said, 'I have a difficult task for you, should you be willing.'

'I'm not prone to taking needless risk, but under the circumstances, I am willing to serve.' He glanced around. 'I like what I see, Pug, and would gladly linger here to study, and share what I know.'

'After,' said Pug, and Amirantha did not need to be told what that meant. To his wife, the sorcerer said, 'It would be valuable if you took the Warlock with you, as well as Sandreena,' Amirantha tried hard not to wince, 'and discover what you can of where that bolt of fire came from. Whoever sent it here knew we were questioning the imp, and that worries me in several ways.'

Miranda said, 'Who can overhear what is said here?'

'Someone who has links to that imp,' said Amirantha. 'You may not understand fully, but those like Gulamendis and myself who master demons, have always believed we were utterly in control; for another entity to be able to eavesdrop on what is said by a demon under our sway is most disturbing.'

'Very well,' said Miranda, hugging her husband. 'Do I dare ask where you and Magnus will be?'

'I must return to Shila,' said Pug, and the colour drained from Miranda's face. She had stood alongside her husband and watched her father battle the Demon King on that world. Macros had held Maarg at bay just long enough for Pug to destroy the rift that led to the demon realm, or so he had thought.

Strange alien creatures, the Shangri, had constructed the rift in the ancient city of Ahsart, the Saaur holy city. Pug and she had entered the rift, collapsing it from within. But something Pug had said to her years ago on that world returned now: if the rift somehow survived, it could be reopened. She said, 'What if the rift to Midkemia closed as we planned, but the one to Shila from the demon realm did not?'

Pug closed his eyes and said, 'I have feared the same. When I first saw that rift I did not understand how unique it was. Since I've visited the Dasati world on the next plane of existence, I now realize what a feat it was to create a rift to reach down to the Fifth Circle. I underestimated the nature of that invention, I fear.'

'Still,' said Magnus, who had listened to his parents' discussion, 'even if the rift between the demon realm and Shila existed, how did the demons leave that world to raid the elves' worlds?'

'What if Shila was the world they reached, the one where the demons swarmed into their rift, reaching their portal hub?' said Miranda.

'We'll know soon enough,' said Pug. To Magnus he said, 'You are coming with me. Pick two others who are adept at keeping their wits about them.' He kissed his wife on the cheek and said, 'I've got to see what damage has been done before I leave, and speak to a few others, but we shall be gone before night falls. I suggest you do likewise.'

She watched him walk away and Miranda said to Magnus, 'Now he will miss Nakor like he hasn't in ten years.'

Her son could only nod silently.

Gulamendis approached the northern end of the valley containing his new home, E'bar: Home. He knew the sight of a winged demon speeding towards the city walls would earn him a harsh welcome, so he directed the creature to land in a small clearing some distance from an outpost to keep from being filled with arrows or, worse, incinerated by a magic blast of flame.

He dismissed his winged horror, which despite its appearance – mostly drooling jaws and massive claws under gigantic raven's pinions – was a reliable, if bony, steed. The Demon Master looked around to see if anyone noticed his approach, and decided if they did they were slow in coming to investigate. Given the level of alertness that became a way of life for the taredhel, that was unlikely. Coming in low over the treetops for the last few miles had proved a wise choice.

He worked his way down the hillside until he approached the first outpost on the trail, and he halted within sight of the walls. He waved his hand back and forth and waited to be hailed by the sentry. When a question was called out in his native tongue, he replied and was urged to walk slowly forward.

He paused at the gate while they opened it, and when he stepped inside he was impressed. While the city below was growing at prodigious speed, by magical means, here in this former moredhel village, only the sinew and sweat of those detailed to it had been resurrecting the place. Yet it looked as if the work was almost done. Walls had been repaired, roofs re-thatched, streets cleared of brush, and a new well had been sunk in the village square.

A guardsman in the uniform of the Starblood Host said, 'Your name?'

'Gulamendis, on the Regent Lord's business,' he answered.

'Proceed, but halt at the last hut and see Lacomis.'

He moved through a very busy village and noticed that even the children were helping with the final clean up and repair. Taking note, he judged fifty warriors and their families were now ensconced here and would soon be getting on with the business of hunting, fishing and farming. Should the Demon Legion not arrive, which he judged unlikely, or should they be defeated – again unlikely – this quiet little village might not be a bad place to settle.

He reached the last hut and knocked on the side of the door. A voice said, 'A minute,' then an elderly elf stuck his head out. 'Who are you?'

'Gulamendis. On the Regent Lord's business. The guard told me to announce myself to you.'

The elf stepped out of the hut and from his robes, the Demon Master could see he was a magic user. Gulamendis had little to do with members of the Starblood clan over the years so didn't recognize him. 'Stand over there,' said the old elf.

Gulamendis moved to the indicated spot and the old elf closed his eyes; he waved his hand and the Demon Master felt a mild magic gathering in the air around them. After a moment, the old elf opened his eyes and said, 'Yes, you're who you say.'

'Worried about infiltrators?' asked Gulamendis.

'Worried about everything,' said the old magic user. He smiled. 'So far we've only encountered squirrels, mice, and a few foxes, but until we completely secure this valley, we have orders to be wary.'

'Understood,' said the Demon Master. 'I must go.'

'Walk with the Stars,' said the old man, returning to his hut.

Moving down the hillside from the village, Gulamendis was impressed by the work that had been done in his absence. The road a mile south of the village was now being paved with stone. A pair of young geomancers directed labourers who dumped baskets of stone into piles across the road. The magicians would then use their craft to reform the loose pebbles and rocks into flat pavements that provided easy travel for wagon and mounted rider.

Gulamendis nodded in greeting as he passed the work crew. Another mile on and he encountered a lone galasmancer, a master of plants, who was digging a small hole beside the road, using a simple wooden stick. He placed a seed in it and closed his eyes. Waving his hand, he called forth a small plant that rose up before Gulamendis's eyes. It was a glow tree, native to the world of Selborna. Midkemia might be Home, but the taredhel were returning with the best they had found on other worlds. The tree would grow to a height of ten or twelve feet above the roadway and illuminate it in a soft, bluish glow, making night travel safe and easy. Gulamendis realized that such discoveries had robbed his people of the legendary woodcraft they had once possessed. He had no doubt those elves he had encountered in Elvandar had no need of light to move effortlessly though the woods at night.

The magic used by the galasmancer would cause the tree to grow at a furious rate, reaching maturity in months instead of years. At this time next year, there would be a line of trees along every highway out of E'bar, magically lighting the night. He thought it would make quite a view from the hills above the valley.

Now that he was on paved road, the journey passed quickly. Cresting a rise, the city came into sight and he stopped. His people might prove to be many things in the days to come, but they were incredible artists. The city was already breathtaking, one to rival Tarendamar when it was completed.

The outer wall was nearing completion, its massive gates being erected at the entrance. Beasts of burden and magic would lift the huge wooden gates into place, securing them on balance so perfect a child could open a side with a single hand, yet once secured, only the rams of the most massive force could breach them. They were painted white, as were the walls, which had been faced with limestone or some other material that made the city sparkle in the afternoon sun.

Spires rose from the central palace, and outer buildings were being worked upon. Gulamendis considered that there was enough room here for every surviving elf from Andcardia, and quite a few more. Cynically, he did not imagine that the Regent Lord was considering extending an invitation to their lost kin. He was simply anticipating a successful transition to Midkemia and the need for expansion in the future. He planned on seeing his people's descendants play in the streets of this city.

As he reached the gate and moved past guards who seemed unconcerned with another elf entering the city, Gulamendis wondered how wise it was to put so much energy into creating such splendour, when defence was paramount. Then he noticed an outer tower rising above the gate, and saw a black presence recessed within the white façade, under the golden roof: a crystalline form of baleful aspect. The Regent Lord was building death towers on the walls.

Sighing at how the ugly reality of their situation endured even under this beauty, he moved purposefully towards the city centre. The metropolis was manifesting as he had anticipated, with a great Pavilion of the Stars at its heart, with the Seven Stars planted around it. The trees of ancient myth seemed slightly less impressive to Gulamendis now that he had travelled to the Holy Grove in Elvandar.

To the south rose the new palace of the Regent, still under construction as most of the geomancers had been tasked to building the outer defences. Still, even as others laboured to erect massive walls and towers, some artisans were at work decorating the façades already complete. The palace – for no other word could do justice to the building – was white. Royal purple stonework, which resembled knot-work, twisted around each opening; the rooftops and the spires gleamed in the sun, constructed of some quartz or glass stone. And from this distance, the top of the structure looked to be topped in gold.

He walked up the broad steps of the main entrance, noticing guards detailed along the way. Already the Regent Lord was exercising his appetite for pomp and ritual, for these soldiers were among the best remaining, and could now have been struggling with the enemy on Andcardia, buying more time for more of the People to flee to Midkemia.

As he neared the portal, he saw several of the honour guards showed signs of recent combat: a bandage under a tunic collar, or a slight lean to one side to remove pressure from an injured leg or foot. With a sinking feeling in the pit of his stomach, Gulamendis knew that meant the struggle on Andcardia was over, or nearly so. These warriors were being rewarded for service, by being placed in the Regent's own personal guard.

As he crossed the vast marble floor, cleverly set off with borders of sparkling rose quartz between the massive slabs, he was hailed by a figure approaching him from the left. Tandarae motioned for the Demon Master to come closer. 'Fare you well, Gulamendis?' he said loudly enough to be overheard.

'Well enough,' answered Gulamendis.

The Lorekeeper motioned for the Demon Master to walk with him and in a low voice said, 'Before you see the Regent Lord, have a refreshment with me, please?'

Again Gulamendis recognized it was not a request. He followed the Lorekeeper into a small apartment overlooking a huge central courtyard. Tandarae motioned Gulamendis to the window.

Looking down, the Demon Master could see the construction of a device, a massive latticework of golden metal, with large spheres of polished stone and gears, topped by a magnificent crystal. 'The Sun Tower,' said Tandarae. 'Our leader has decided to employ the sun to provide energy for the defences of this new city.'

'The death towers?'

'You noticed.'

'Difficult not to if you glance into the cupolas on top of the towers. I've seen them up close before, in the battle of Antaria, and they are not easily forgotten.'

'I'll take your word on that. I have no desire to ever see one used.'

'Have they named the city yet?'

'No, but everyone calls it E'bar, so I expect that will be what it will become. So, tell me of what you've discovered.'

Gulamendis sat as the Lorekeeper poured two goblets of wine. He sipped and found the vintage reminiscent of what he had tasted on Pug's island. 'Very good.'

'Local,' said the Lorekeeper. 'We sent raiders to the east and brought back everything not planted in the ground – and some things that were.'

'Raiders!'

'A small town. We made it look as if the moredhel had returned from the north. Our soldiers wore dark cloaks and left survivors to carry the word that the Forgotten had fled northward, out of the region once more. Two of our trailbreakers even left miles of false trails leading away from here.'

Thinking of what he had heard and seen, and about his own brother being detected by a Ranger of Natal, he said, 'We should not underestimate these humans, Tandarae. They count able men in their ranks, and those trails may not conceal our presence here for long. And their magic users are not to be trifled with.'

'I know,' said Tandarae. 'I counselled caution, and almost lost my place in the Regent's Meeting.'

Gulamendis sat in a cushioned chair and sighed. 'It will be hard enough to convince these people to trust us, to ally with us against the Demon Legion, without pillaging their towns and villages.'

'The Regent Lord has little use for allies. Subjects perhaps,' said Tandarae. He glanced towards the window as he added, 'He is consumed with creating a new home for our people, and he will hear of nothing else. I am convinced he plans to move against our neighbours once this place is complete.'

Gulamendis said, 'I must report to the Regent Lord soon, but let me tell you what I have found.' Quickly, but in detail, Gulamendis recounted his experiences since reaching the Queen's court and then Sorcerer's Island. He omitted one detail, that of Tomas's nature, as he did not want the conversation to go off on a tangent. He did not want the full disclosure of facts to be overshadowed by the emotion that would greet his news of the Valheru living in Elvandar.

The Lorekeeper listened without comment, and when Gulamendis finished, he had questions. The exchange added another half an hour to the conversation, and at the end the lorekeeper said, 'They sound like impressive beings.'

'I saw little of the dwarven king, which was how I would have wished it, anyway.' His people's distaste for dwarves was almost inbred; of all the races they had proved the most difficult to conquer. 'But he was at ease with the elves in Elvandar, and has strong ties with the humans of the area.

'Our cousins are rustic, as you would expect them to be; at one with the forest, deeply imbued with a sense of nature we have long ago forgotten.' He lowered his voice, more out of habit than necessity. 'We would do well not to underestimate them, Tandarae. They may appear primitive, but their magic is strong if subtle. They have groves of trees that dwarf our Seven Stars, they are ancestors of our Seven Stars! And they are one with the land under their feet. I saw no overt wards or other magical barriers, but I could not bring myself to cross the river into their land until I was bid welcome. We could mount an army on the opposite shore from Elvandar yet never step on that sacred land.' He sighed. 'It worries me, fascinates me, and somehow, it pleases me. It's like seeing ourselves in the mirror of time.'

'I will go there, someday,' said Tandarae. 'If we survive.'

'The war?'

'Goes badly. You may have noticed that those who line the steps to this palace are recruited from the survivors of the last battle of Andcardia, those fit enough to stand watch. Many more linger at death's door, tended by the few healers we have left.' He sipped his wine and said, 'These humans make fine wine, do they not?'

'Indeed,' agreed Gulamendis. 'My brother?'

'No one has seen him,' said Tandarae, but then he laughed. 'Of course, he could be standing next to them and they'd never know.'

'A few would,' said Gulamendis.

'There's a reason your brother was counted first-most among the Circle of Light.'

Gulamendis frowned.

Tandarae held up his hand, palm outstretched to indicate no harm intended. 'This is not a secret, Gulamendis, even if we are expected not to speak of such.

'The demise of the Circle of Light is regrettable, in my

opinion.' He sipped his wine. 'It was foolish for the Meet to insist that all magic users fall under their purview. And when they stumbled across those like you . . .'

'My brother objected.'

'Indeed.' Sipping his wine again, Tandarae seemed to be choosing his words carefully. 'Had he not been so pre-eminent among the Circle, he might have suffered more harshly than . . . well, let's say despite his vanities and eccentricities, the Regent Lord and the Meeting recognize a valuable resource.

'They say Laromendis can create illusion so vivid that should his target be shown a knife plunging into his chest, his heart will stop as if the blade is real.'

'So they say,' replied the Demon Master noncommittally.

'Such ability is rare, and I suspect that once our new home is built and we turn our attention to dealing with our neigh- bours, we will give more credit to those of you who've been . . . let's say not properly recognized for the work you've done on our behalf.' He put down his wine for a moment. 'What do you think of these humans?'

'We are more like them than we are like our kin in Elvandar,' he replied flatly. 'They wear their emotions on their faces like the shirts on their back, but they have very keen minds among them, and talents to rival our own. I saw just enough of their magic to conclude that these are people we need to respect, for they are as endless as the sand on the beach and we . . .' He shrugged.

'. . . are but a shadow of our former might. Yes, I know all of this too well,' said the Lorekeeper.

'There is one among them, by the name of Pug, who may be among the most puissant magic users I have encountered.' He lowered his voice. 'He claims to have been to the world housing the demon gate. He claims he can return.'

Tandarae looked stunned. 'If that is true . . .'

'I think it is. I think he can provide the proof that no one among the taredhel brought the demon wrath down upon us. It was simply bad fortune that exposed us to the Demon Legion. And, moreover, he claims to have the ability to close the gate for all time.'

'Astonishing,' said the Lorekeeper.

Gulamendis continued, 'When we last spoke, I was uncertain of how to receive your comments, but now that I have been out and among the humans, our kin, and have even met a dwarf, I think nothing in our past can prepare us for this world. It is so different and holds many questions; with answers we may not entirely care to hear.

'Yet, it is also a place of opportunity and, perhaps, even evolution to become even greater than before.'

'What of this Queen?'

'I think she is of the blood. I think her claim valid. You would be better able to judge, but there is something about her that speaks . . . No, sings to your heart and mind. To see the Stars in their majesty, as they were before we fled to other worlds, to imagine what it must have been like here, at Home, when the world was young.' He sighed. 'Our kin in Elvandar are truly one with the land beneath their feet, which is something we have lost.'

'Those in Elvandar are more like we once were than any among people now,' began the Lorekeeper. 'We named the finest among them rulers, partially in secret defiance of the . . . Ancient Ones, but also to honour them as being more closely linked to the magic of this world. They were the grove guardians, the protectors of the Stars. Some among the fleeing eldar even venerated them.' He finished his wine. 'The reason they chose to remain was to avoid relinquishing their responsibility towards the sacred trees.

'I'm pleased to see they have endured.' He stood up and said, 'I intercepted the report that said you were approaching from the hills so that we might have this chat before you report to the Regent Lord. But we have tarried long enough. I'll escort you so there's no further delay. Is there anything else you need to tell me before we see our lord and master?'

Gulamendis stood. He had been weighing the possibility that he had found an ally in Tandarae, or if the Lorekeeper saw him only as a usable tool or weapon. He judged it time to test that. 'One thing. The Queen's Consort will be arriving in three days to speak with the Regent Lord.'

Tandarae's expression revealed volumes. 'Is he coming to establish a claim?'

'This Queen has no desire for sovereignty. She will affirm we are a free people. No, it's something else.'

'What?'

'Her Consort wears the armour of the Ancients.'

Tandarae's concern deepened visibly. 'That is both odd and disturbing. A likeness or an artefact?'

'More than an artefact,' said the Demon Master, perversely beginning to enjoy the mounting discomfort in the Lorekeeper. He might trust the elf, but that didn't mean he had to like him.

'More?' Tandarae's eyes narrowed.

'Her Consort is named Tomas; he is Warleader of Elvandar. He is Valheru.'

Tandarae was visibly shaken. 'How can this be?' he whispered. 'If the Ancients still ruled, we would have been greeted by fire and sword; the humans, dwarves, goblins, all would have been obliterated.'

'There is much to explain,' said Gulamendis. 'He is Valheru and he is human, and I only know part of his story, but when he arrives, you will see without a doubt that he is a Dragon Lord.'

'And he comes to us as an envoy?'

'Yes,' said Gulamendis. 'Now, may I suggest you keep that part of the report for later, because I do not know how our coming envoy would react to being greeted with magic and fire.'

Tandarae took a deep breath, and then he began to chuckle. 'Your levity tells me I need not worry, though I will need more reassurance. Still, it might be worth risking a quick death from the Regent's personal guards to see the expression on his face when the Queen's Consort arrives.'

'For you, perhaps, not I. If you don't tell him eventually, I most certainly will. It is part of my charge to him, and my brother's life and my own hang in the balance.'

'I wonder what has become of your brother?'

'He is almost certainly here,' said Gulamendis. 'And if he's here, he's out looking for me.'

'What are the chances he'll find you?'

'Good,' said the Demon Master. 'We have the knack for tracking each other down. He thinks as I, and will trace my route, but once he decides it's time to return, he will come back.'

They left the private room and the Lorekeeper said, 'Let us

get this over with. The Regent Lord will be . . . unhappy, with much of what you have to tell him.'

With a hint of foreboding in his voice, Gulamendis said, 'A fact of which I am painfully aware.'

CHAPTER EIGHTEEN

Exploration

S ANDREENA HELD UP HER HAND.

She had not been comfortable with the sorcerer's selection, with the Father-Bishop relegated to what looked to be, at best, an advisor. Yet, these people had treated her well, seen to her care, and provided her with everything she needed without question or obligation. She had been transported by the woman, Miranda, who seemed a magic user of significant power and ability, along with Amirantha, who was the last person in the world she ever wanted to see again.

Now they worked their way up the trail towards the site of the sacrifices she had observed less than two weeks before, though it felt like ages. Something ahead moved, which is why she had signalled a halt. Brandos brought up the rear, for despite Amirantha's and Miranda's significant magic, a second sword was welcome. And despite her reservations about Amirantha, Sandreena had a fondness for the old fighter, who was steadfast and honest, or as honest as any companion of Amirantha was likely to be. She gave him credit for at least attempting to warn her that Amirantha was not a man to grow close to. More than once in the last five years she had wished she had listened.

The sounds were furtive, either an animal in the evening brush or someone hiding badly. She indicated she would scout ahead and not for the first time, wished she had chosen less cumbersome armour and arms. Still, with practice she had learned to move in a relatively quiet fashion.

She moved in a low crouch, until she could raise her head enough to see what lay ahead. As she suspected, there was a sentry who was not being particularly attentive, but who was showing no sign of being sleepy or easy to approach. She slowly retreated.

Reaching the other three, she whispered, 'One lookout. He's too far away for me to approach without giving too much warning.'

Miranda said, 'I'll deal with him.'

She moved forward without employing much stealth. Although her dark dress served effectively as camouflage against the evening shadows inside the narrow canyon, her passage still caused a significant amount of noise and enough movement that the sentry noticed her when she was about a dozen yards away.

'Huh?' was all he managed to get out.

With a single wave of her hand, Miranda sent out a bolt of energy that compressed the air before it, to deliver a punishing blow to the man's face. He somersaulted backwards to land on the rocks behind him, smacking his head hard enough to render him motionless.

They hurried forward and Amirantha asked, 'Is he dead?'

Kneeling, Sandreena inspected the fallen guard and said, 'No, but he's not going anywhere for many hours.'

'Scout on ahead,' said Miranda.

Sandreena did as she asked and in less than five minutes she returned, her face drained of colour. 'We have to move, now!' She motioned for the others to follow and hurried forward without any attempt at concealment.

They reached the rise from which Sandreena had been able to watch the ritual the last time she had been here. She motioned for them to follow and when they neared the top of the ridge, they understood why she had abandoned silence.

Voice chanted in unison, and when they cleared the rise, they saw that there must have been a hundred of them. A huge fire was burning, flames leaping thirty feet into the air, and around it stood a dozen robed men and women. The others were gathered in a semi-circle around them; men and a few women, dressed in a variety of fashions, from all parts of the world, Keshian, Kingdom, Novindus, and the Eastern Kingdoms. But all wearing a black head cover. Tied scarves, flop hats, leather caps, it didn't matter; everyone had covered their head in black.

Miranda said, 'Well, there are your Black Caps and it looks like they've shown up for something important.'

'It's a summoning, but it's different;' said Amirantha.

'How's it different?' asked Miranda.

'I don't know. It's just . . . different,' He whispered, yet there was an urgency in his voice. 'Something very wrong is about to happen.' He looked at Miranda. 'Be ready.'

'For what?' she asked.

'I'm not sure, but whatever is it, it will be very bad.' His skin crawled, and he felt dark powers gathering, more terrible than anything he had ever encountered in his long life of dealing with infernal beings.

Three men appeared from the other end of the canyon, one wearing bright red robes trimmed in black and silver piping. The other two stood on either side of him; they wore black like the others. The two black-clad figures were hooded, their features obscured by the deep shadows. The red-robed man had his head uncovered, and he smiled broadly as he came to face the semi-circle of gathered adherents. He stepped up on to a large rock and held up his hand for silence. Instantly the chanting ceased.

'Servants of Dahun . . .' he began.

'Damn,' swore Amirantha.

'What?' asked Miranda.

It was Sandreena who answered, 'Dahun is a demon prince.'

'One of Maarg's captains,' said Amirantha, 'if I understand everything told to me in the last few days, correctly.' He pointed. 'But even if I don't, I know that man and I know that anything he's involved with is going to be very bad.'

'Who is he?'

'That,' said Amirantha, 'is my brother, Belasco.'

'Evil-looking bastard,' said Sandreena. 'I can see the resemblance.'

Miranda shot her a dark look, then realized it was only the young Knight's manner of dealing with fear. Miranda had neither Sandreena's, nor Amirantha's experience with demons, but she had faced enough dark magic in her life to sense this situation was verging on becoming something terrible.

'In four nights,' shouted Belasco, 'we shall greet our master and begin the transformation of this world into his domain, and we, his blessed servants, will be his first chosen, ruling at his side.'

'First to be eaten, most likely,' said Brandos.

'Well, I'm hardly one to condemn lying to the gullible, but I only took their gold, not their lives,' said Amirantha.

With a grudging tone, Sandreena said, 'For that small difference, you might find Lims-Kragma lets you return to life as something a little higher than a cockroach.'

Miranda said, 'We have four nights to decide what to do.'

Amirantha said, 'No, we have until that guard wakes up.'

Sandreena said, 'Will he know he was struck by a spell?'

Miranda said, 'Normally he'd wake up feeling like he'd been on a three-day drinking binge, but the way he hit his head . . .'

'Well,' whispered Brandos, 'we could finish the job on the way out and make it look as if he simply fell off his perch and broke his skull on the rocks.'

'Someone in that bunch will be a tracker and will see we were here,' said Sandreena.

'If there was some way we could convince that fellow he had just fallen asleep,' said Miranda.

'I have an idea,' said Amirantha. 'Come on, we must hurry.'

He led them back down the trail to where the recumbent guard was still sprawled across the rocks. Amirantha motioned for them to follow him a good thirty yards down the narrow trail. 'Just be silent,' he whispered. 'Can you wake the guard when I tell you?'

Miranda said, 'I believe so, though why would I want to?'

'Just wait and do it when I tell you, then all of you get down out of sight.'

He closed his eyes, reached inside his belt pouch and pulled out a crystal. Holding it tightly he muttered an incantation and suddenly a puff of dark, fetid smoke erupted from the ground.

Stepping out of the smoke was a tall woman, stunning in appearance and completely nude.

The newly summoned demon looked around with large, expressive brown eyes. Miranda was forced to admit she was probably the perfect male fantasy: long legs, round buttocks, a flat stomach, pert breasts and perfect skin. Thick brown hair tumbled down her lower back, and she had a flawless face. Her full lips parted in a delighted smile and she said, 'Master! I love you!'

Sandreena said, 'Darthea? Really, Amirantha, is this the time?' Her expression was venomous and her cheeks flushed with anger.

'Shut up,' said Amirantha impatiently. He held up his hand and said to the demon, 'Not now. I have a task for you.' He took the beautiful demon by the elbow and pointed to the unconscious man. He whispered a series of instructions, then said, 'Can you remember that?'

'Yes, Master,' she replied and with dainty steps, unmindful of the sharp rocks beneath her bare feet, she hurried to the sentry's side.

'When she reaches his side, wake him,' said the Warlock.

Miranda waited, then when the female demon knelt next to the unconscious man, Amirantha signalled it was time.

Miranda closed her eyes briefly, pointed her hand, and was rewarded with a groan from the sentry.

Amirantha waved the others out of sight and crouched down.

'Oh, you poor man,' said Darthea to the recovering warrior. 'I'm so sorry. I did not mean to startle you like that, making you fall off the rock and hit your head. Here, let me help you up.'

The stunning nude woman helped the man to his feet and as his visibility returned, his eyes widened in disbelief. Amirantha spoke a short, quiet phrase, and suddenly Darthea was gone, vanishing with a tiny puff of smoke.

The blinking, confused sentry looked around, then on wobbly knees, sat down and rubbed his tender head.

Amirantha crawled back to where the others waited and motioned for them to follow. When they were far enough away to transport without being detected, Miranda said, 'That was interesting.'

Brandos laughed quietly. 'He's certain now he slipped and hit his skull on a rock, because who in their right mind would think he was startled by a naked beauty in this gloomy backside of the universe? And I pity the man if he tries to tell the story to any of those cutthroats he's in league with.'

'He'll keep quiet,' said Sandreena grudgingly.

'You've bought us three more nights,' said Miranda. 'What now?'

'We return in four nights and see how much magic it's going to take to ruin a very powerful summoning.'

'We have as much as you'll need.'

'I have no doubt,' said the Warlock, 'but I'd like to see it done without you or I or anyone else dying in the process.'

'There's always a risk,' said Miranda.

'Let's go somewhere to talk about it,' said Amirantha.

'Grab his arm,' Miranda said to Brandos, who complied. She reached out and gripped Sandreena and Amirantha and suddenly they were back in the garden on Sorcerer's Island.

'I have got to learn to do that,' said Amirantha.

'It takes years,' said Miranda.

He smiled. 'I'm willing.'

'Well, if we survive this, maybe. Right now you need to decide who or what we need, and how we're best served to deal with this mess. I can manage perhaps a few more people when I transport that way.' She seemed distressed as she said, 'If Magnus was here, together we could get as many as nine or ten people to that spot. If he and Pug were here ... well, if Pug were here I wouldn't worry as much.' She fell silent.

Brandos said, 'Besides magic, there are a lot of swords and evil men willing to use them back there. I've been around magicians long enough to know you don't have time to cast more than that first spell if someone's busy trying to cut off your head.'

'We need two plans,' said Miranda. 'One if we have to do this alone, and one if Pug and Magnus return.'

'Are there others here that can fill in for your husband and son?' asked Amirantha.

'All the magicians I know who could help us in a fight like this are either dead or on the world of New Kelewan. Most of the students here have never been in a fight, let alone a battle.' She thought for a minute, then said, 'Sandreena, how many magic-using priests in your Order can handle demons?'

'Some. I know banishment spells, as well as most of them. It's part of our training.'

Amirantha agreed. 'If she has a weakness, it's to use her mace first, but when she's able, she can banish a minor demon as well as I can. I've seen her do it.'

Sandreena scowled, not sure if she was being complimented or insulted.

'You're coming with us, then,' said Miranda.

'I wouldn't miss it,' said the Knight-Adamant.

Miranda said, 'Rest, and get something to eat if you're hungry. I have more plans to make.'

She hurried out of the garden, and Brandos said, 'Well, food sounds good. Coming?'

'In a moment,' said Amirantha.

Brandos looked from the Warlock's face to the young woman's and nodded, turned and left them alone.

Expectantly, Sandreena said, 'What?'

He took a deep breath. 'I have no idea what will happen in four days, and I know I can't talk you out of coming.'

'Why would you try to?' she asked.

'I know things ended badly between us—'

'There was no "between us",' she interrupted. 'We spent some time together and you lied to me to get me into your bed.'

'It was your bed, actually,' said Amirantha. 'And I never lied. I just didn't tell you the entire truth.'

'A fine distinction, I'm sure, but we have other things about which to concern ourselves, don't you agree?' He nodded. 'Why would you try to talk me out of coming along?'

'You're the most resourceful woman I know,' said Amirantha, 'but you have a decided knack to rush in without hesitation.'

'I'm a Knight-Adamant,' she reminded him.

'A fact of which I am painfully aware, but you sometimes

underestimate risks. Look, you never told me what happened before you got here, but I've seen you look better. You almost got yourself killed again, didn't you?'

'I appreciate your show of concern, but it's too late.' She spun on him and poked him hard in the chest with an armoured finger. He winced but stayed silent. 'I was a whore, Amirantha, and no man showed me anything but contempt or lust until I met Brother Mathias. After that, it was bloodshed and mayhem, and I found a calling, but even then, men only looked at me with hate or with lust.

'Then you came along with your damned charm and funny sayings, and made me feel as if someone could actually see beneath the surface . . .' She took a breath as if to calm herself, and said, 'I can face your demons, Amirantha. I can face a room full of armed cutthroats. I just can't face your false-hoods.' She took a step and then turned to say, 'One thing, though. Darthea: you've done well in changing her looks. Though the goat's hooves and horns did add a certain exotic quality to her.'

Without saying any more she turned and left the Warlock standing alone in the garden. Amirantha had always been willing to take advantage of the passing generosity of women when it suited him, for often they repaid his kindness with the only currency they possessed, their bodies. But when he was ninety years of age, he happened to chance upon a lover he had known in his youth; she had changed into an old and faded grandmother, content to sit in the shade and card wool while her daughters and their families worked hard on a farm. She didn't recognize him as he asked for and was given a cup of water.

He had watched her, as she in turn watched over her grand-daughters, and he had realized that he would probably still appear unchanged when her granddaughters were old and at the end of their lives; perhaps he would watch them watching *their* granddaughters.

At that moment, whatever spark of affection he still felt for humanity was damped. The only woman he had truly cared for after that encounter was Samantha, but only because she made Brandos happy.

His feelings for Brandos were still a mystery to the Warlock, perhaps because he saw him as the son he would never have. But now when they were together, people mistook the fighting man as his elder and Amirantha knew the day would come when his companion would either die in battle or have to quit the adventurous life to sit at home, next to Samantha as she carded wool, watching their grandchildren.

He took a deep breath. Sandreena was a confusion he had no answer for. There was something about her that troubled him deeply, something that made him desperately want her to forgive his cavalier behaviour years earlier. Shaking his head in irrita-tion at himself, he turned to find Brandos and get something to eat.

Gulamendis knew his life was hanging by the barest thread as he spoke to the Regent Lord about Tomas's pending arrival. It had been clear from the first moment that the Regent Lord and the attending members of the Meeting were ready to declare war on their cousins to the north. As most of the current council members had been hand-picked by the Regent to replace those who had fallen to the demons over the last thirty years, Gulamendis knew he would get no support arguing against any position the Regent Lord took.

Even Tandarae would only be able to offer subtle influence, to shade how things were presented, but he too risked being swept away by the Regent Lord's unpredictable wrath. He was not yet the new Loremaster, first among the Lorekeepers, though it was rumoured the position would be his soon. Gulamendis knew that if it came to a choice between his ambition and supporting the Demon Master, Tandarae would happily light the fire around Gulamendis himself.

Slowly, step by step, Gulamendis recounted his journey: his frustration at not being able to locate the demon source, his ride up the Far Coast and his eventual discussion with the Queen and her Consort. He thought it best to omit his journey to Sorcerer's Island until he knew he was going to survive what he had to say next.

'The Queen is sending her Consort in two more days to greet you, my lord,' said Gulamendis.

'Her Consort?' He glanced around. 'There is no king?'

'Her King made his journey to the Blessed Isle many years ago, and to ensure his son inherits, her second husband rejected the crown. Prince Calen will rule in Elvandar after his mother.'

The Regent Lord said, 'Odd. One would expect any elf would aspire to rule in Elvandar.'

Gulamendis could already see the Regent Lord's mind turning. If he could somehow rid the world of this Consort, he would be the logical suitor for the Elf Queen's hand, after a suitable period of mourning, of course. Long before departing on this journey, Gulamendis has begun to suspect that the strain of the thirty-year war, of losing so many close companions, of watching his People being systematically obliterated, had taken its toll on the Regent Lord. Having seen the Elf Queen, Tomas, Pug, and others, he was now certain: the Regent Lord was unfit to rule, perhaps he was even mad.

The jest between himself and his brother, their subversive prescription, now seemed too light; an act of treason was closer to what the taredhel needed. Gulamendis generally lacked the nobility of spirit he had felt in Tomas, who he sensed would gladly give up his life to defend Elvandar, but at that moment, if he'd seen an opportunity to end his People's suffering and kill the Regent, he thought he would have.

But the wards already in place, to guard against the coming of the Demon Legion or others, were just as effective against Gulamendis's powers. Perhaps one of the human magicians could turn this hall into a fire pit before the Regent's guards reacted, but Gulamendis knew he would be dead before he was halfway through a summoning.

Mustering up the courage to say what needed to be said, Gulamendis spoke softly: 'He's not an elf, my lord.'

The Regent Lord blinked, as if confounded by his own senses. 'What?' he asked.

'I said the Queen's Consort is not an elf.'

With a tone bordering on outright revulsion, the Regent Lord said, 'What is he?'

Calmly, Gulamendis said, 'He was born human.'

Anger rose up in the Regent Lord and he said, 'Whatever claim she may have held to the most noble line in our ancestry is fouled by such a mating. A human!'

Taking a deep breath, Gulamendis said, 'I said he was born a human, my lord, but today he is far more than that. He wears the armour of an Ancient One.'

The Regent Lord looked as if Gulamendis had struck him a blow across the face. Almost whispering, he said, 'He *dares?*'

'There's more,' said Gulamendis, judging it time to give the full truth and hope that the Regent Lord continued to be stunned enough not to feel the need to affix blame to the messenger. Glossing over the very complex story Tomas had told him, Gulamendis said, 'He was gifted the armour by the greatest of the great golden dragons in reward for some great deed.' He knew it was false, but he needed to glorify Tomas as much as possible to prepare the Regent Lord for the shock of meeting him. 'The armour's magic transformed the human, and now he does more than carry Ashen-Shugar's shield, he carries his . . . his powers. In all but heart and spirit, he is Valheru.' He had at the last moment decided to omit the fact that Tomas held the Ancient One's memories.

The Regent Lord was reeling. He looked around the nearly completed meeting hall and moved to the large chair set on a small dais, and slowly lowered himself into it.

Of all the possibilities he had prepared for since Laromendis had discovered this world, this was one he never considered. They had feared the Valheru might have survived the Chaos Wars, but when Gulamendis's brother made no mention of them, that fear had vanished. But now, suddenly, it returned, yet it was tempered by the fact that the Demon Master was bringing greetings.

'Tell me of him,' whispered the Regent Lord, and Gulamendis knew his life was safe for the moment. He spoke about Tomas, changing the story of the boy lost in the cave – omitting any mention of the dwarf king – to the tale of a brave lad seeking to destroy an evil demon, which resonated well with the Meeting.

After Gulamendis finished, the Regent Lord asked, 'This human turned Ancient One, he does not seek to rule?'

'It is most strange,' said Gulamendis carefully, 'but he seems content to protect Elvandar and leave command to his wife, the Queen.' The Demon Master slightly emphasized her title, again reminding the Regent Lord that the old ties need never be forgotten. The elves of Elvandar might be rustics in the eyes of the taredhel, but they were blood kin, and after the losses suffered against the demons, they needed as many kin as could be mustered. After the Demon Legion had been confronted, then the Regent Lord could worry about ruling this world.

The Regent Lord continued to ask questions about Tomas and the Elf Queen for nearly half an hour, but then dismissed Gulamendis. As he and Tandarae left the Meeting, the Lore-keeper said, 'You acquitted yourself well, my friend.'

Saying nothing, Gulamendis thought, *A friend now, perhaps, but only so long as it suits you.*

Two days later, the assembled members of the Regent's Meeting stood in the central plaza of the newly christened city of E'bar, awaiting the arrival of the Queen's Consort. Gulamendis had been invited to attend, but had been relegated to one side by those of higher rank. From a short distance away, Tandarae nodded a greeting to the Demon Master, a faint acknowledge-ment of his part in forming this negotiation between the Regent Lord and his titular Queen.

Gulamendis had purposefully neglected to mention Tomas's most likely mode of travel, thinking it might serve the Regent's

Meeting well to be awed. They stood waiting for the signal from the outer garrisons that riders were approaching.

Instead a large shadow suddenly covered them as a massive flying silhouette loomed overhead. Most of the members of the Regent's Meeting stood motionless, though Gulamendis noticed a few flinch until they were certain that nothing was about to drop down upon them. Then he saw their reactions as the recognition set in: a gigantic golden dragon was descending into the central plaza.

With a thunderous beat of its wings, the dragon halted its descent, then landed gently. The size of a building, the enormous creature was nevertheless a thing of grace and beauty in its movement. A head the size of a wagon lowered from a surprisingly sinuous neck to allow two figures to dismount.

Gulamendis's eyes widened in delight as he recognized the second figure as his brother. Laromendis nodded ever so slightly in his brother's direction, acknowledging his presence, but stayed close to the Dragon Lord.

Arriving with Tomas guaranteed that Laromendis would avoid any rash punishment the Regent Lord might otherwise mete out for his absence. Gulamendis had inquired about his brother after parting company with Tandarae, but no one had seen him since he had been posted to the defence of Tarendamar, which meant either that he was dead or had deserted his post. Gulamendis was certain it had been the latter, unless his brother had been terribly unlucky.

If Tomas had shown restraint when confronting Gulamendis outside the Holy Grove, now he withheld nothing as he dismounted the dragon. He used his mystic arts to unleash the full power of his Valheru aura. Even though Gulamendis had already experienced this in part, and Laromendis had ridden with the Dragon Lord from Elvandar, both were moved.

The members of the Regent's Meeting were stunned. Several fell to their knees reflexively, some wailing and weeping. Others stood trembling, unable to move. Only the Regent Lord and two of his most senior advisors stood silently, waiting.

Tomas strode towards them, exuding power with every step, his left hand on the hilt of his sword. He wore golden armour, with a dragon-crested helm, its down-sweeping wings forming the cheek-guards. His tabard and shield were both white, with a golden dragon emblazoned on each, and his every movement was fluid and graceful.

He was beautiful and fearsome and a legend, come to life before their eyes. Whatever arrogance the taredhel possessed, whatever certainty they had of their own supremacy, fled before the magnificent power that was Tomas in the guise of a Valheru.

He came to stand before the Regent Lord and said, 'My lord,' and then waited.

Almost whispering, the Regent Lord said, 'How should I address you?'

Tomas smiled and it was as if a huge cloud passed and he said, simply, 'My name is Tomas. And before anything more is said between us, I must tell you this:

'In ages past, when war raged across the heavens, the wearer of this armour sat astride a dragon like my friend Sarduna, and he proclaimed to the world that all who had once served, all among the edhel, were now a free people.' With a slightly wry smile, he said, 'Your ancestors fled this world before that voice was raised, so I say to you now, you are a free people.

'Let it be clear that I make no claim upon you, nor are you

obliged to serve because I wear this armour and this mantle. I come to you in the hope of friendship, on behalf of my lady, Queen Aglaranna, who also bids you welcome to your ancestral home, and wishes for nothing but friendship and peace between us.'

There was silence for a moment, then the Regent Lord said, 'Fairly spoken . . . Tomas. You are welcome.'

Introductions were made and they then retired to the council chamber, where Tomas would discuss two things with the Meeting: the prospect of the Demon Legion following the taredhel to Midkemia, and an alliance with the established inhabitants of Midkemia.

Tandarae lingered for a moment as the brothers were reunited. 'You both did well,' he said quickly. 'I must attend our masters now, soothe things should tempers flare.'

Gulamendis said, 'Do you think they might?'

With as much of a smile as the Lorekeeper would allow himself, he said, 'Given Lord Tomas's presence, not until he departs. He is . . . impressive.' He glanced at the retreating gold and white back, which although shorter than every elf in the Meeting, still seemed to tower over them. 'Stunning, even.' Looking back at the two brothers, 'I have work to do, but remember that the sanctions placed against you in the past, are now abated.' He pointed to the north and said, 'Find housing. There is a magistrate up on that hillside who will ask you many stupid questions, give him this.' He handed them a token with the Regent's seal on it, and turned away.

As the Lorekeeper hurried to overtake the Regent and his guest, Gulamendis said, 'You made quite the entrance.'

His brother said, 'Yes, I expect I did.'

'How did you manage?'

'Come, I'll tell you as we go and find ourselves a nice set of rooms.' They left the central plaza and as they walked, Laromendis said, 'I managed to depart the battle at Tarendamar early; my command was obliterated and as we fell back, I was ushered into a company of refugees who were being escorted to the portal. I was not in uniform, everyone who might have recognized me was already dead, and my new superior officer was ordering me to go through the portal "with all haste", so who was I to argue?'

'You weren't disguised as an old woman, then?' asked the Demon Master dryly.

'No, I swear; no illusions. I didn't even get a chance to argue with him.' He smiled. 'Of course, I was rather disinclined to argue.'

'How goes the battle?'

'It's over, but for the closing of the portal.' He glanced up to the hillside to the west where refugees were still arriving and said, 'They'll close it soon, and whoever's left on the other side will die.'

Changing the topic, Gulamendis said, 'How did you contrive to arrive on dragonback?'

'I went looking for you, and after a few days wandering in the west, I decided that no matter what else you were doing, you had to see the Elf Queen in her court, so that's where I went. As I didn't wander around all that much, I managed to get there fairly quickly.' He slapped his brother on the back. 'Lord Tomas and the Queen said you'd been there, and said you'd most likely be waiting here; he offered me a ride and I said yes. Riding on the back of a dragon! Can you imagine?'

Laughing, very glad to see his brother, Gulamendis said, 'Actually, I've already ridden on one.'

'You?'

'Yes, and it's quite a story. The locals have some very fine wine; if I can secure us a skin or a bottle, we'll find a place to sit, drink, and I'll tell you of my time on a very special island.' Lowering his voice he said, 'I think it's a place you'll wish to visit, and very soon.'

As they walked north, seeking the magistrate who would supply them with living quarters, Laromendis said, 'I just realized; we are the only taredhel in history to ride a dragon!'

Gulamendis said, 'Ironic, in its way, especially if you consider how much the Regent Lord would likely want one for a pet.'

Both brothers laughed and began looking for a bottle of wine and a place to live.

A bitter wind blew across the plateau. Pug and Magnus stood motionless, accompanied by two other magicians. Randolph, a middle-aged man from a village near Tulan, was Magnus's best student of battle magic, and looked it. He was a bull-necked, broad-shouldered, brawler with a balding head and a barrel chest. If it wasn't for his ability to conjure spells of stunning power very swiftly, Pug would have judged him as unlikely a magician as he had ever encountered.

The other magician, Simon from Krondor, was his exact opposite in appearance; tall and ascetic looking, he was a little older, his blond hair now prematurely white, matching Magnus in appearance. He was a master of the far more subtle craft of detection. He and Pug both stood, attempting to sense any arcane presence.

'Nothing,' said Simon. 'If there has been any magic used in this area, it's not been for years.'

'I too am getting nothing,' said Pug. He pointed to the northwest. 'There, that's where we'll find Ahsart, the City of Priests.'

It had taken Pug the better part of a day to recalculate the rift to Shila. He had forgotten how difficult it was to redefine an ancient rift if constant contact hadn't been maintained. His efforts had resulted in two failed attempts and a serious headache before he was successful. He was thankful he had become rigorous about taking notes over the years and had recorded everything about Shila and how to get there.

Once the four magic users had arrived, it had taken a few more hours for Pug to get oriented. They had begun the slow process of using Magnus's ability to transport them magically to distant locations, moving in jumps across the planet to seek any sign of demon activity.

There had been none.

Pug's thesis suggested that if the portal from the demon realm was still closed, there would be no life on Shila. If this was the planet upon which the taredhel explorers had first encountered the demons, there would have been some movement between the original gate and wherever the rift to the taredhel hub world was located. There should have been a steady stream of demons flying and running out of Ahsart.

All was quiet.

Magnus used his arts and took them to a hillside overlooking the City of Priests.

The city had been an immense metropolis in its time, a sprawling home to millions. A high wall surrounded the ancient settlement, that had been the heart of Ahsar, but the foulburg spread out five times its distance, indicating that this region had been peaceful for centuries after the original city had been founded. Broad streets criss-crossed throughout and tall towers rose here and there. Pug indicated a path and they began walking towards it.

'In ancient times, before recorded history, a gate was created between the demon realm and this world. It had been sealed, which is how this place came to be settled. This was where the Saaur shamans and priests who had closed and protected the gate lived. Others came to study and it became a holy place,' said Pug. 'The Saaur were a race of noble warriors, and they numbered millions. They rode across endless plains of grassland and hunted.' Pug motioned for them to walk towards one particular avenue. 'Then something changed.'

'This must have been a remarkable place,' said Simon. 'It rivals the City of Kesh in size.' He glanced at Pug and said, 'What changed?'

'A mad priest, so the story goes,' said Pug, 'opened the seal admitting the first demon, and was devoured for his trouble. But before the other priests could reseal the breach, they were overwhelmed.'

Randolph said, 'Sounds like the demons were ready to launch an offensive as soon as it was opened.'

'Yes, it does, doesn't it?' agreed Pug.

As they entered the now deserted ruins, the only sound in their ears was the wind. In the hours they had been on this world, they had detected no hint of life. As far as they could tell, this planet was completely devoid of even the tiniest insect. At one point they had passed through a region just after a rain. Pug had remarked that the scent of wetness lacked something. Simon had replied that it was because life was abundant in soil:

moss, lichen, and spores of all sort, and water usually caused their scent to rise: none of that existed here.

The walked down desolate boulevards, immense by human standards. The Saaur were a huge race, and the scale of their city reflected that. Even their horses stood twenty-five hands at the withers. They were also a nomadic people whose concessions to city life were few. No rider of the Saaur would ever be caught far from his mount, so there had to be room to accommodate the massive beasts, too.

Pug paused, trying to get his bearings. Then he pointed. 'That way lies the main Temple.' As they walked, he said, 'As I understand it, the great hordes of the Sha-shahan, or ultimate ruler, rode throughout this world. It has smaller oceans than Midkemia and save for a few big islands, it's possible to visit every part of the globe on horseback.

'This city was originally a holy place, and so the hordes left it alone. Some of their shamans came here to study, I was told. But for some reason, the hordes changed their attitude; after centuries of respecting this city, the hordes decided it was time that they be paid tribute. When the hordes arrived here to demand it, the priests and shamans of this city were divided on what to do. Some wished to continue their work in peace and were willing to submit, but others refused, and before a consensus was reached, war erupted.' Looking at Randolph, he said, 'You're the battle magic expert here. Imagine five thousand magic-using priests and shamans confronting a hundred thousand mounted warriors.'

'Messy,' said the bull-necked man. 'If the magic users were really good, they might hold them outside those walls for a week or so. Then the attrition and fatigue would win out for the attackers. The perimeter would breach eventually, and once inside, the slaughter would begin.'

'Which is precisely what happened,' answered Pug. He pointed. 'Over there, somewhere, a gate was battered off its hinges, and the defenders were overrun. Priests and Temple guards were no match for the soldiers of the horde.

'Had they surrendered then, it would have ended well enough. After a few public executions to demonstrate the iron rule of the Sha-shahan, Jarwa by name, they would then have pardoned the rest to demonstrate his leniency, and then the horde would have ridden on, leaving little more than a garrison and tax collector behind.

'Instead, a priest unsealed the demon gate, in the mad hope that the demons would repulse the horde, and that he could seal it up afterwards.' Pug shook his head. 'He was the first to be devoured.' He sighed as they mounted steps leading up into the great Temple. There were fifty steps in the staircase; at each end of the broad expanse of carved stone, a pillar rose, on top of which sat empty stone cauldrons, where offerings to the gods and ancestors could be burned. 'Of course the demons drove back the horde, but they also destroyed the only possibility the people had of repulsing them – the now exhausted priests and shamans of the Saaur.

'A very courageous and intelligent shaman, by the name of Hanam, seized control of a demon through a brilliant ruse, and used his control to infiltrate the demons and reach your mother and me,' he said to Magnus. 'He was instrumental in defeating the demon captain, Tugor, as Macros, your mother, and I battled Maarg, keeping him on the other side of the rift.'

'Tugor was defeated?' asked Magnus. 'I thought one of those imps mentioned him . . . perhaps I was mistaken.'

'We'll ask Amirantha when we return. I have the suspicion that demons are more difficult to kill than we thought,' said Pug. He led them across a large pavilion, into an antechamber. Looking around he said, 'It looks so different.'

The stones of the city were now free of the soot and ash that had coated them the last time Pug had been there. Fires had still raged across the landscape, but a century of wind and rain had effectively erased the stains, everywhere but in the deepest recesses.

Pug recognized a hallmark, a massive stone bas-relief showing some legend of the Saaur, and moved towards a deep vault. Once they were inside, the gloom swallowed them. Magnus moved his hand reflexively and light sprang up around them in a comforting cocoon.

For reasons he couldn't explain, Pug felt the urge to whisper. He resisted and said, 'Over there.' He pointed to a cavernous doorway leading into the Seal Chamber, where the demon gate had been located. When he had last visited, along with Miranda, Macros, and the Saaur shaman Hanam, the alien race the Shangri had been trying to move a rift to Midkemia directly in front of the entrance to the demon realm. They had been disrupted and had fled. After that, Macros and Hanam had given their lives to stop the demon invasion. Pug had slain the Shangri who had created the rift and assumed the portal to the demon realm had been closed as well.

When they reached the site of the demon gate all four men froze in astonishment. A body lay sprawled out before the wall that had housed the gate. It was emaciated, barely larger than a human, but Pug instantly recognized it. Now he whispered, 'It's Maarg.'

When he had last seen the demon king, he had been a

mammoth, gross creature, nearly thirty-five feet in height. Massive jowls had hung down from his cheekbones, lending him an almost bulldog-like expression. Eyes of burning fire had regarded Pug with a hatred that came in waves; he was the personification of evil.

'Everything is so much smaller now,' said Pug softly. He turned Maarg over and found that his body weighed almost nothing. His face looked like parchment drawn across hollow bones, and showed evidence of being fashioned from the skins of living beings. When Pug had last seen him, every inch of his visage had moved and twitched, as if the souls he had devoured were attempting to escape. The nude body before him was a thing of tattered skins that looked sewn together like patchwork.

Pug stood up. 'He had wings that could spread right across this chamber, and—' He looked at the wall. 'Unbelievable.'

The stone was gouged with deep talon marks, as though, once the demon gate had closed, Maarg had tried to claw his way back into his own realm.

'How?' asked Magnus.

'When your grandfather died, I thought the gate was closed, but Maarg must have somehow slipped back into this realm moments before it shut. Your mother and I were already on Midkemia.' He shrugged. 'He must have devoured every life on this world and when hunger drove him even madder than before, he returned here and tried to get back . . .' Pug shook his head. 'I can't feel sympathy for a thing like this, but it must have been a terrible way to die.'

'There's one thing, Father,' said Magnus.

'What?'

'Amirantha's imp was terrified of Maarg. If Maarg is dead, who's pretending to be Maarg, and convincing the other demons that he's their king?'

Pug looked stunned by the question.

CHAPTER NINETEEN

Onslaught

MIRANDA SIGNALLED.
She had managed to bring Sandreena, Amirantha, Brandos, Jommy, Kaspar and Father-Bishop Creegan with her. The moment they appeared at the mouth of the passage leading up into the clearing where the summoning would occur, they were instructed to remain silent.

Kaspar still whispered, 'I don't care how many times I do that, I'll never find the experience pleasant.'

Miranda smiled slightly. 'It is, however, efficient.'

Kaspar glanced at her and smiled. 'This is true.'

Sandreena looked around to see if there was any sign remaining of the Black Caps. All appeared quiet. She relaxed and considered this undertaking. She was pleased the Father-Bishop was with them, for while he had never been a warrior like the Knights-Adamant, he was a magic user of significant power, especially in the area of banishing demons. She had known Brandos during her first encounter with Amirantha, years before in the village of Yellow Mule. Kaspar and Jommy were also brawlers if she judged them correctly, and would be useful standing at her side if they needed to protect the spell casters.

Sandreena also found herself wondering about Miranda. At first the woman annoyed her, and Sandreena couldn't quite understand why. Then it dawned on her, she shared the same expectation of obedience as the High Priestess of her Order in Krondor. The difference was, Sandreena suspected, Miranda had earned that attitude, whereas the High Priestess considered it her birthright.

Miranda looked around as if saying, 'If everyone's ready, let's begin.'

They had fashioned the plan over the last four days. If possible, they were going to try to gain a better idea of what was taking place, who the Black Caps, these Servants of Dahun, were, before the mayhem truly began. The agreement was they would all observe as best they could, no one was to launch an assault unless discovered or upon Miranda's command. Getting some knowledge of the enemy was vital.

Too many times Miranda and Pug had discovered darker forces behind the apparent troublemakers they faced. Ban-ath, the God of Thieves and Liars, had a hand in everything, and they were horrified to discover the so-called Dark God of the Dasati was actually a Dread Lord who had managed to insinuate himself into the Dasati culture, usurping the allegiance of the Dasati race, twisting and warping them into a tool of evil.

Miranda had tried to pry as much information out of Amirantha as she could, but he had not had contact with his brother in any meaningful fashion in over a century, and had no notion of what had brought him to his current position as the apparent leader of these Black Caps. After several long discussions, Miranda was convinced of only one thing about Amirantha: he wanted to see his brother dead and felt it could not come too soon.

Miranda's own childhood had been anything but conventional. Her father, the legendary Macros the Black, had vanished when she was still a child. Her mother, known by several names over the years, Lady Clovis, the Emerald Queen, and others, had been alternately loving and remote. After Miranda matured, the only thing they had in common was their love of magic. But Miranda had inherited, perhaps from her father, a fundamental distaste for the very things that drew her mother deeper into darkness: the pursuit of power and a fear of ageing. Ironically, Miranda never seemed to age, this was in part due to her long lifespan, but also because of her exposure to the energies of an artefact called the Lifestone.

Her experiences gave her a unique perspective, she understood how two brothers could become so different, and why Amirantha would show no hesitation in killing Belasco.

Belasco was the mystery. He was unknown to any of them, save Amirantha and Brandos, and what the old fighter new about Belasco came through Amirantha.

It wasn't so much that Miranda didn't trust the Warlock; not that she was particularly fearful of him. If Miranda had a critical flaw, it was of overestimating her ability. Should the demon summoner prove a danger, she felt certain she could deal with him. Her unease sprang from her uncertainty about his motives beyond dealing with a murderous brother. He said he was envious of the community on Sorcerer's Isle, and wished to return after this encounter to spend time learning from Pug and the others. Miranda only half believed him. She didn't know what he was hiding, but she knew he was hiding something.

Miranda also didn't care for the fact that Sandreena and Amirantha shared a past. One that was far from happy, by all appearances. One of the reasons she agreed to have Creegan accompany them was he might be a calming influence on the Knight-Adamant. Like most of those of her Order, Sandreena was used to working alone, unsupervised. She might be a powerful fighter, but she also might be as dangerous as loose cargo on the deck of a ship during a storm.

Jommy and Kaspar were people to whom she trusted her life, and Kaspar had worked hard to gain that trust.

Creegan she had reservations about. Not his character, though she generally tended to mistrust the politically ambitious type, and he clearly intended to be the head of the Church of Dala someday. It wasn't even a case of his dedication; Pug never would have recruited him for the Conclave had there been any doubt of that. It was the liability. He was not a brawler, not someone who had been tested in battle, in her opinion, though he claimed to have faced demons in his youth.

And, there was always the complication that the Conclave could encounter some serious issues with the Temple if she managed to get one of their Father-Bishops killed along the way. Had he known, Pug would have forbidden his coming, she knew. But then Pug wasn't here. He was on another godforsaken planet, who knows where.

She tried not to worry, but couldn't help it; she was a wife and mother.

Miranda signalled again and Sandreena, Jommy, and Kaspar took the lead, moving in a rough v-shaped formation, with Sandreena in the vanguard. As the heaviest armoured of the three, she was the most likely to survive any unexpected attack. Miranda and Amirantha were close behind, with Brandos serving as a rearguard.

Slowly, they made their way along the narrow trail, into the cleft that led into the clearing where the sacrifices had occurred before. As expected, they encountered another sentry, but this time they weren't concerned with stealth. Kaspar threw a dagger that took the man in the throat and he died before he could utter a sound.

From that point on, they crouched, and moved slowly to avoid alerting any second sentry. As Miranda anticipated, there were two additional sentries stationed, but ironically on the very ridge they had planned to watch from.

Miranda motioned to Jommy and Sandreena to follow Kaspar's lead. He was the most experienced soldier in the group. He knelt and whispered, 'Can you attract the sentries over here without alerting those on the other side of that ridge?'

'I have a trick,' she said, thinking instantly of Nakor. How that funny little man would have loved this sort of madness. It was exactly the sort of insanity that seemed to bring out the very best in him.

She whispered, 'I'm going to get them over here in a hurry, so you'll need to subdue them before they can alert anyone. Now, we need to wait until their attentions wander for a moment.'

The air was suddenly filled with chanting, more rhythmic and lower than the sound they heard four nights before. Miranda waited, patiently, watching as the two guards stood their post.

She would occasionally glance at Kaspar and the others, and was gratified to see that not one of them was losing focus or letting the tedium dull their readiness. There was too much at stake to grow lax even for a moment.

Time passed slowly, then a scream of absolute horror and agony caused the two sentries to look towards the source of the sound for a moment. Instantly Miranda was on her feet and with a short incantation she mystically reached out and seized both men by the scruff of their collars and brought them flying backwards in a high arc, to land at her feet. Instantly Kaspar, Jommy, Brandos, and Sandreena were upon them and they died without a sound.

'Now we go!' said Miranda and she led the way to the ridge from where she had plucked the two sentries.

They hurried, less mindful of the noise they made as the chanting had reached a crescendo of screams and chants. They breasted the rise, and Miranda instantly knew they faced obliteration.

This was no ceremony. Two hundred armed warriors stood ready, poised to charge, and behind them on a large rock, stood Belasco. The chanting was only an illusion, cast by a robed magician at his side, and at his other side was the nude figure of Darthea, clutching him as she would her love. She looked at Amirantha with contempt as Belasco shouted, 'Brother! You've brought friends! How considerate!' To his warriors, he shouted, 'Kill them!'

'Hold!' shouted Miranda to Sandreena and Brandos who readied themselves for a charge.

With a sweeping gesture, Miranda sent a wave of flame rolling towards the attackers. Men screamed as flames rolled over them, and several fell to the ground, only to trip others or be trampled on. Amirantha began to conjure, but Sandreena shouted, 'Don't!'

He paused and shouted back, 'Why?'

'Isn't that your lady love over there with your brother?'

Amirantha suddenly realized exactly what Sandreena meant: no demon he conjured could be trusted. They were all in thrall to whoever was behind his brother's plan.

Amirantha acted as much out of pique as self-preservation. He sent a punishing spell towards Darthea. The demon recoiled, almost pulling Belasco off his feet before he let go of her. The agony she felt was passed along to him for a moment, until contact was broken. He staggered, while she fell and writhed on the stones. She contorted in agony and her body shifted, smoke rose from her skin. Her features changed, becoming more demonic by the second as her illusion of human beauty faded. She stopped thrashing and lay quivering and twitching. The thing at Belasco's feet had the torso of a woman and her face was still beautiful, in an otherworldly fashion, but her legs were those of a black furred goat. Two long horns swept back from her forehead, and her fingers ended in black claws. Suddenly a burst of green flame consumed her, and Belasco scuttled backwards to avoid being burned.

The magician at Belasco's side began another conjuration, and Sandreena pointed her mace at him. A blast of energy, clear and colourless, rippled the air as it shot from her weapon, sped across the clearing and took the magician in the chest. He was slammed backwards in an explosion of white and yellow lights, to lie stunned on the rocks behind Belasco.

'Close your eyes!' shouted Miranda, and those warriors not

consumed by her wall of flame were blinded by an explosion of light.

'Now!' shouted Miranda. 'Fall back!'

'Back!' shouted Kaspar, lashing out to skewer a blinking Black Cap who stumbled too close.

All around them lay burning, screaming men. Others tried to see through eyes blinded by a flash so brilliant that they would probably remain blind for the rest of their lives. A few cried out in fear, and suddenly their angry resolve was replaced by rising panic. The stench of burning bodies and the screams of the dying only added to the terror.

Jommy saw an opportunity and shouted, 'We've been betrayed! Belasco lied to us! We're all going to die!'

No one among the Black Caps could see who had shouted, but as he hopped, the warning was repeated.

Miranda almost pulled him off his feet by grabbing his collar and hauling him away. 'Fall back now!' she hissed.

They retreated, seeking enough room for Miranda to transport them away. Across the sea of writhing bodies and smoking chaos, Belasco rose to his feet and shouted, 'No you don't!' He reached back and flung his arm forward, as if throwing a rock, and they all saw a flaming orange ball ripping towards them.

It was Creegan who reacted first, throwing up a mystic barrier that caused the flames to spread up and around the intended targets. It was still hot when it struck, and Jommy yelped as his hair singed. Brandos drew his dagger and with an impressive heave sent it speeding across the gap between themselves and Belasco.

With a maniacal laugh, the magician dodged to one side, shouting, 'That was too close! Time for me to bid you all farewell!'

He vanished.

'Damn!' shouted Miranda as she sent a bolt of searing red energy into the midst of a clump of warriors, sending most of them into the air as if thrown by some giant's hand. 'Back!'

Most of the warriors serving Dahun were either dead, or blinded, or confused and trying to get away from the struggle, but quite a few had gathered their wits, and soon Miranda and her companions would risk being overwhelmed. 'Back!' she repeated.

They hurried up the draw onto the narrow track that eventually led down to the sea. Brandos, Kaspar, and Jommy backed along the path, swords ready, but the few Black Caps who followed seemed less than eager to engage them. They had seen the damage the magicians had done, and their own magic users were nowhere to be seen.

When Miranda felt it safe to conjure, she said, 'We were led into this trap. Somehow they knew we were coming.'

'We can sort all of that out when we get back to Sorcerer's Isle,' said Jommy.

Miranda's eyes widened. 'We must go there now!' She reached out and grabbed Amirantha and Creegan and shouted, 'Grab on!' When everyone was secured, she willed herself to the island.

And they arrived in the middle of a holocaust.

Pug and Magnus finished examining what was left of the Saaur library at Ahsart. Most of the writings had perished at the same time as the shamans and priests who had gathered them, but a few older clay tablets and a handful of bound books locked away in a vault had endured. The language was unknown to them.

Simon said, 'I have a spell which would allow me to decipher these within a week, two at the most.'

'We don't have the time,' said Pug. The discovery that Maarg was dead and that someone or something else was using his name to mask his identity was troubling. This was not the first time in his life that he had discovered that what he assumed to be true was only a half-truth. 'With no one here, we can arrange for some students to collect and return it to Sorcerer's Isle. Then,' he said with a weak smile, 'you can study them at your leisure.'

Magnus came to stand next to his father and spoke softly. 'What is it?'

'Something is terribly wrong,' said Pug, not caring if the other two magicians overheard him. 'Every piece of information we received about the Demon Legion led us to believe that things in their realm were much as they had been when we battled the Emerald Queen.' A demon captain, named Jakan, disguised as Lady Clovis, the Emerald Queen, had engineered a war that had engulfed half of Midkemia. 'But now we see that Maarg is dead, a victim of his own gluttony, stranded here . . .' His eyes widened. 'Is it possible?'

'What?' asked Magnus.

'That everything that has happened to me from the day I was captured by the Tsurani, was part of a much larger plan. Your grandfather said so, Ban-ath said so, and I've always seen myself as a player in a larger drama. But like a player, I've only been concerned with my part. Oh, I'm aware of the roles of others, your mother, Tomas, Nakor when he was with us, even Ban-ath's to a lesser extent. But just because I understand my role, or think I do, and just because I know of the others', doesn't mean I can comprehend the complete drama.' He visibly winced. 'I am such a fool!'

'What?' asked Magnus, obviously not following his father's deductions.

'At first I blamed the Nameless One, because I was told he was at the heart of every evil that befell Midkemia. It was logical, even obvious, given that he is the God of Evil.

'But what if there's *another* agency, another cause of evil that is creeping into our realm using the Nameless One to prevent us from seeing his hand behind things.'

'The Dasati Dark God?'

'Perhaps he was a tool as well. Did he strike you as particularly subtle, though?'

'He gulled the Dasati into thinking he was their Death God,' reminded Magnus.

'True, but that is a simple deception compared to what I'm imagining.'

'What are you imagining, Father?'

'I assumed that Jakan, the demon playing the role of the Emerald Queen, wanted to reach the Lifestone, to seize its power for his own use. I was unclear about what that use was, to fortify his own role in our universe; to return and battle Maarg for supremacy of the Fifth Circle of Hell; or some other motive. I was so intent on stopping him, I almost got myself killed, and I really didn't care why he wanted the Lifestone.' He looked at Magnus and a rueful smile crossed his face. 'What if he was simply bait?'

'For what?'

'To lure Maarg here, to die of starvation, while someone, or something else, gains domination of the Fifth Circle. Jakan was on Midkemia, Tugor died fighting Hanam, and Maarg was left here to die.

'Someone else is ruling the Fifth Circle, but doesn't want us to know his identity.'

'Why?'

'Because understanding that identity might be key to defeating him; or else why guard it so jealously with all this misdirection?'

'Perhaps Amirantha can shed some light on this, or maybe the elf, Gulamendis?'

'We certainly will need to speak with both of them.' To the other two magicians he said, 'Come here and stand close.' To Magnus he said, 'Take us back to the rift, please.'

The four magicians gripped hands and Magnus used his power to take them to a position just before the rift, a short distance from the edge of the plateau overlooking the city of Ahsart. Pug started to step through and halted.

Instantly Magnus said, 'What is it?'

'We're being blocked!'

'What?' asked Randolph.

'We cannot go through this rift.'

'How is that possible?' asked Simone.

Pug looked around the hillside and saw a large rock. He threw it at the portal and when it touched the shimmering grey void that marked the rift, it bounced back. 'It wouldn't have killed you, but you'd have received a bloody nose from walking into that.'

'Who could do this?' asked Magnus.

Pug took a deep breath and said, 'The same evil bastard who's able to subvert Amirantha's summonings and use them against him, I think.'

'Belasco?' asked Magnus.

'Or whoever his master really is,' answered Pug. He looked around and pointed to another clear area. 'Come, let us begin. We're not going to waste time trying to overcome that barrier. I know enough rift lore to construct another that will follow this one to our home. It should only take an hour or so, less with your help.'

Randolph said, 'Tell us what to do.'

They began.

The heat rolled off the burning building like a wave, sweeping over Miranda and her companions as they appeared in the garden. 'Grab hold!' she shouted, choking from the heavy smoke. As no one had stepped away since they appeared, it took mere seconds for Miranda to will them a short distance away, on a low hillock overlooking the rear of the main building.

Everything was on fire.

Below, the main house burned like a bonfire and the outer buildings were either reduced to flaming wooden skeletons or little boxes with fire shooting out of their windows and doors. The ground around the compound was littered with the bodies of students and instructors. Miranda could barely contain her rage.

Then the first demon came into view, running around the corner as he chased one of the students. Miranda pulled back her arm and let fly a bolt of energy that should have reduced the creature to ash. Instead, the spell only stunned him long enough for the student to put more distance between herself and the demon, as it stood reeling for a minute. Then the infernal creature shook his head and looked for the author of the assault.

Spying Miranda on the top of the hill, the demon lowered its shoulders and charged. It was roughly human in shape, but with shoulders far broader than any human. Its head looked like a cat's skull, devoid of flesh, with exaggerated fangs, and its legs like they came from the back end of a horse; but while it appeared ungainly, it moved with uncanny speed.

Miranda's eyes widened in surprise when the demon weathered the blast she had sent and began another attack. Then her mind locked up, and suddenly she couldn't remember anything.

Amirantha incanted a spell and unleashed it at the charging demon, who stumbled and then stood motionless, trembling as if it had been seized by a monstrous hand that now shook it. 'If one of you would please kill this horror,' he said to Sandreena and Father-Bishop Creegan.

Both hurled their most powerful spells of destruction, especially crafted for demons, and the creature let out a howl of agony as it fell to its knees and was consumed by orange flames.

Miranda said, 'Thank you. I thought . . .'

'Demons are not like mortal creatures,' said Sandreena. 'Sometimes, brute force works—'

'Sometimes it doesn't,' finished Brandos. 'Look out!'

A flying nightmare, all wings and talons, came swooping in, apparently intent on ripping someone's head off. Creegan shouted a single word as he stuck out his hand, and a black shape, like a shimmering blanket of silk, suddenly enveloped the demon, smothering it. As it fell to the ground, the wrapped shape grew smaller and smaller, until it vanished completely.

Sandreena said, 'Look!' and pointed at a knot of demons surrounded by some of the island's magicians. The magic users were using a variety of spells and enchantments to keep the monsters at bay, and it appeared to be working.

'We've got to help them!' shouted Miranda, charging down the hillside.

'Oh, mercy,' said Brandos, half a stride behind her.

Miranda pulled up short and began to cast a spell, but Brandos dived and dragged her down, just as the demons unleashed a blast of blackness pulsing with purple lights. Each magician was shrouded by the dark energy. They fell to the ground, their screams muffled as if their faces were covered in cloth.

'When they gather like that in a knot, it means they're going to pull something like that,' shouted the old fighter. He got to his feet and helped her up as a demon from that small group charged them.

Amirantha, Sandreena, and Creegan all caught up, and Sandreena intercepted the charging demon, bashing it in the face with her shield, and swinging her mace in a wicked arc to crush the creature's skull.

Miranda allowed herself to be pulled aside by Creegan and Amirantha, as Jommy took up position beside Brandos. 'What do I do?' asked the young noble.

'Keep these bastards off the Spellcasters so they can do their work,' he said, slashing out at a demon that had ventured too close.

'What about Sandreena?' asked Jommy as he repelled another demon with a wicked slice of his blade that took the creature on its unprotected forearm.

'Don't worry about that girl,' said Brandos, holding off another demon who was leaping towards Amirantha, as if he knew where the real threat was coming from. 'She knows how to take care of herself.'

Sandreena was expert in avoiding the animal-like claws of the demons. This bunch was similar to those she had encountered before, mostly sinew and fangs with little intelligence, though they were cunning, as demonstrated by the trap they had unleashed on the young magicians.

Miranda tried to pull the smothering black fabric from one young magician, and then threw spells designed to dispel enchantment at it, but it resisted her every attempt to remove it. She felt her heart sink and went cold inside as the young magician, a bright young man named Patrick from Yabon, died. 'Do something!' she shouted at Amirantha out of frustration.

He recognized and ignored her frustration, concentrating as much as he could on dealing with the threat right before him. He could have easily gated in half a dozen demons of his own in this period of time, but he now realized he could not trust any of them to do his bidding. Instead he focused on the spells at his disposal that would either destroy them outright, or banish them back to the demon realm. But it took time. Each target had to be in his line of sight for nearly a minute as he enchanted it, and sometimes the break in his concentration forced him to start over.

Father-Bishop Creegan seemed to have different abilities at his disposal, more effective, but slower. He would single out a demon, chant, and after a minute, a bright light would envelop the target and it would freeze motionless. Then after another few minutes, it would simply vanish. Unfortunately, from Amirantha's point of view, he could only manage one at a time.

The wind shifted and suddenly they were choking from the smoke as it billowed from the flaming buildings and swept over them, a blinding wall of darkness that filled the lungs and caused the eyes to sting. 'This way!' shouted Miranda, coughing as she tried to lead them upwind of the flames.

Sandreena crouched as another demon tried to claw at her, its talons scraped her helm and she stood, bringing her helmet up under its chin as she held up her shield to block a second demon to the right. Then she spun, her mace held out, so that when she finished the circle, the mace head slammed into the second demon's side. The creature doubled over and fell on top of the stunned first demon; then Sandreena retreated after the others.

As they moved back and regrouped, a scene of horror before them unfolded. Of the hundreds of students and instructors in residence on Sorcerer's Isle, most lay dead on the ground. Many had been maimed or mutilated, or partially devoured. Also scattered around the area were demon corpses, mute testimony to the courage of the young magicians.

From their vantage point, they could see figures scampering in the fire as the main house went up in a tower of flames. Then they saw it.

In the middle of the inferno, where the flames reached highest into the sky, stood a figure of terror. It was nearly twenty feet tall. Its head was like that of a bull, but with an elongated snout, and its horns were impossibly wide, spanning at least eight feet. The creature had massive shoulders and enormous arms with muscles that looked like heavy cable under black silk skin. Its eyes were red flame and steam or smoke blew out of its flaring nostrils. As if challenging the very heavens, the creature threw back its head and bellowed so loud it was painful to listen.

Confusion and panic were mounting on all sides, and Miranda struggled to make sense out of what she could see through the blinding smoke. 'Amirantha! What is that?' she demanded.

'If I had to guess,' said the Warlock, coughing from the smoke, 'it's a demon captain, perhaps the Dahun those Black Caps were summoning. Right now—' he exploded into a fit of coughing, then swallowed hard '—I don't know if I understand anything about demons.' His tone left no doubt he was shaken by the day's revelations.

'Everything we saw over by the Peaks was simply a diversion,' said Father-Bishop Creegan. 'To lure us away so they could destroy the Conclave.'

'As long as I'm standing and Pug and my sons are alive,' said Miranda, 'so is the Conclave.' Her tone left no doubt of her anger. And she shot forth a bolt of searing energies that should have withered the demon where he stood. Instead, he turned and looked for the source of the attack.

Sandreena, Amirantha, and Creegan all reacted within moments, simultaneously unleashing three spells of banishment. The creature seemed stunned, staggering back, but didn't vanish as intended.

'It's tethered!' shouted Amirantha.

'Tethered?' asked Jommy.

It was Brandos who answered. 'Something's anchoring it here, in this realm. You do it to keep a demon from going home if it's unhappy with what you want it to do!'

'Look for anything that seems out of place,' shouted Amirantha. 'An icon, a pole, something that's not burning. That will be the tether. Destroy it, and we can banish that horror.'

Miranda said, 'I can't see a thing with all this smoke and flame.'

Then the monstrous demon recovered from their attack. With a bovine grin, it advanced on their position, a band of scampering and hopping smaller demons in its wake.

414

Brandos shouted to Jommy and Kaspar, 'Don't try to attack it directly. Kaspar, break to the left! Jommy, break right with me, when I give the word! Keep those smaller devils in front of you! Don't let any of them get behind you!'

'Amirantha, you have to protect Creegan and Miranda as best you can!'

'Understood,' shouted the Warlock. He shouted to the Father-Bishop and Miranda, 'Don't act until I give the word!' He reached into his belt pouch and withdrew a large gem. Crushing it in his hand, he shouted a single word, and suddenly they were engulfed in red smoke.

'Now!' shouted Brandos and he and Jommy ran right, while Kaspar took off in the other direction.

The large demon bellowed again and swung a massive claw through the space occupied a moment before by the three fighters, and then backhanded the cloud of red smoke. He shouted in pain and anger when his hand came away with red smouldering sores, as if he had touched acid. The unexpected wound distracted the creature for a moment, while the smaller demons rushed the fighters.

Inside the gas, Amirantha said, 'Back up slowly!'

His two companions did as they were told and moved back until they could see the befuddled demon captain standing over the roiling cloud of caustic gas. 'Whatever you have, Miranda,' said the Warlock. 'Now's the time.'

Her eyes were wide with anger and frustration and she reached into the depths of her power, using her will to focus the most destructive spell she could muster. A line of light extended from her outstretched palm to strike the creature, and down it flowed a brilliant white pulse. The demon captain stood stunned for a moment, then bellowed in pain and began to writhe.

'I see it!' shouted Jommy to Brandos. He pointed to a strange object, a black post with alien runes carved on its surface. It sat amidst the flames, untouched.

He stepped towards it, but Brandos grabbed him from behind and yanked him back just as a demon lunged at the spot he had just vacated. The old fighter swung hard with his sword, severing the creature's head from its shoulders. The body lay flopping on the ground while its features contorted and tried to scream. 'Unless you're fireproof, that's not going to work.'

'Look out!'

Another pair of demons leaped at them, each about the size of a large monkey. Jommy extended the point of his sword and allowed the creature to impale itself. The shock that ran up Jommy's arm almost cost him his weapon. He lifted his boot and kicked hard as he pulled back, sending the demon tumbling back. Brandos beheaded the other one efficiently. 'Point's useful, but not that way,' he said as he struggled to breathe in all the choking smoke.

Jommy was forced to agree and began slashing at anything that tried to approach them. 'What do we do about that anchor?'

'Wait,' said Brandos, looking around, as if seeking inspiration. The large demon seemed to be coming out of the shock induced by the three spells, and stood slightly shaking its head, as if clearing it.

'Miranda!' shouted Brandos. 'If you can destroy that totem over there, Amirantha and Creegan can banish—'

He stopped as he saw a figure in white and silver dash through the flames towards the carved pole. 'Oh, girl, no!' he shouted.

Sandreena had worked her way to the other side of the fire

and now was making a mad dash for the totem. She obviously understood the significance of the device as much as Brandos and Amirantha did. Her tabard was stained with soot, and was smoking along one side of the back. Mindless of the scorching heat, she raised her mace above her head, then brought it down in an underhanded sweep. She threw her complete weight into the blow and when her mace struck the wood, the shock reverberated throughout her body, but the wooden icon shattered, bursting into fragments that instantly went up in flames. She kept running, her tabard now alight.

'To me, girl!' shouted Brandos. 'To me!'

She turned towards the sound of a familiar voice, and saw Jommy slash at a demon that had turned to see what was coming up behind him. The blow cut the demon's throat and black blood gushed from the wound. Sandreena was blind from the smoke it gave off and started to run past Brandos, who reached out and grabbed her arm, shouting, 'Fall down!'

She did as told, and he lay on top of her, putting out the flames with his own body. Jommy kept his blade slashing in all directions as demons sought to swarm over the fallen Knight-Adamant and the old fighter.

A sizzling bolt of green fire sped out of nowhere to strike two demons from behind, causing them to fall to their knees then convulse, their red leather hides smoking and blistering as they writhed and then vanished in a blinding white flash.

Jommy searched for the origin of the bolt and saw Pug, Magnus, and two other magicians floating above the fray. Randolph and Simon were not the masters of destructive magic Pug and Magnus were, but they knew enough violent magic to inflict harm on the demons below.

'Pug!' shouted Jommy, and he felt reinvigorated as he hacked at the demons in front of him allowing Sandreena and Brandos to regain their feet. Whatever damage the young woman warrior endured, she ignored it as she joined the fray, using her mace to good effect and driving the demons back so the older fighter could catch his breath and continue the fight.

The massive demon was stunned by Sandreena's attack, and Amirantha and Creegan both seized the opportunity to begin complicated banishing rituals. Their chanting was almost in harmony, though they spoke different words. Then as one they finished, and the large demon simply faded from view.

The tide of battle turned, for with their captain gone, the demons now sought a means of escape. Several had the arts to will themselves back to their own realm, but others appeared to be abandoned to the less than tender care of those they attacked. Other magicians, many gravely injured, began to appear around the edges of the fire, and they did what they could to keep the demons surrounded.

'Remember that nasty trick of letting us surround them!' shouted Brandos.

Pug threw a massive energy bolt, but instead of striking the assembled demons, now down to about a dozen of them, it caused a huge compression of the air above them. The thunderclap caused everyone's ears to pop, and as if blowing out a massive candle, the flames dispersed and suddenly the fire was mostly out. A few hotspots still burned, but mostly the building was now smoking char.

Miranda ran down the hill to help finish the fight, when a prone demon suddenly leapt to its feet, and onto her back.

Pug shouted, 'No!' as the creature set its fangs to her neck and tore out the side of her throat, faster than she could react. Miranda's legs gave way and she collapsed.

Magnus's cry echoed his father's; he extended his hand and the demon withered to ash in a moment. The rage he displayed was incredible, and every demon that saw him turned to flee, only to be cut down by those nearby. Pug cut a charred path through demonic bodies as he struggled to reach his wife.

In less than a minute it was over. Pug and the others reached Miranda, and he knelt next to his wife. No one needed to be told she was dead. Her lifelessness and fixed gaze made it abundantly clear. The attack had been so sudden, the damage to her neck so severe, only the most powerful healing magic used instantaneously might have saved her. In the scant moments it had taken for her husband to reach her, she had bled to death.

Pug was motionless. Magnus came to kneel next to his father and both were still.

The struggle was over, and silence fell, punctuated only by the occasional crackle of flame and pop of cooling embers. Slowly they gathered around Miranda, save for a few who were trying to tend to the wounded.

Nothing was said for a long time. Pug reached under his wife's prone body and lifted her with the help of his son. His features were set, but wetness ran down his cheeks, as he softly said, 'I will see to my wife.' He glanced at Magnus and said, 'You must be strong. There's still work to be done.'

Magnus looked around and nodded. His face was ashen, but his features showed resolve. He looked at one of the injured students and asked, 'My brother?'

Unable to speak, the student merely shook his head in the negative, then pointed at the heart of the house, where the office used by Pug and his son had stood. Only smoking rubble now remained and the charred bodies that lay throughout that part of the building.

Magnus hung his head for a long moment, then with tears running down his cheeks said, 'Come.' He led the others away from where his father stood motionless, holding his mother.

Pug remained alone with his wife amidst the smoking ruin of what for had decades been their home.

Epitaph

*T*HE CROWD WAS SILENT.

Father-Bishop Creegan stood before a single stone marker as the sunrise lit the landscape with golden and rose hues. Up on a hill a pyre stood ready and Miranda's body, wrapped in white linen, lay upon it ready for cremation. Other bodies were also prepared for final rites, but most were burned beyond recognition so they were receiving group services.

Caleb and Marie were somewhere in that number. Over sixty bodies had been recovered and four were missing, devoured in the heat of the fire. The community at Sorcerer's Isle had been reduced by nearly two thirds. Of the teachers, only a dozen were left, and of the students, not even twice that number.

The entire population of the island was stunned from the events of the day before, and all duties and tasks had been carried out quietly, as if most were too numb to speak. Pug and Magnus had spent the entire night sitting with Miranda while she was prepared for this morning's funeral. Pug had let no one else carry her to the top of the hill and had placed her gently on top of the piled wood, himself.

Magnus's face had been set in a fixed expression all night, and he and his father barely said a word.

Creegan spoke: 'Our time on this world is short. Even for those like Miranda who lived longer than most. Some will count her life a full one, replete with achievements enough for a dozen others, yet we feel her time with us was too short.'

He fell silent for a moment then said, 'It is not the usual duty of my Order to conduct services like this for an outsider, but Miranda was not an outsider to me. Our work together made her my sister.' He looked at Pug and Magnus. 'Everyone here shares in your loss, even if we can only claim a small portion of the grief you feel, Pug, Magnus. We know a great injury has been done to you, and we mourn with you. We know that it seems as if something profoundly unfair has happened.

'We in the service of Dala believe in achieving balance, seeking the equitable outcome. The universe doesn't always permit such insight, and the ways of the gods are manifold and difficult to comprehend. Miranda served others and put herself at risk many times; she endured hardship and privation for the sake of others. There is no higher calling in life than service such as hers and I believe she is standing before Lims-Kragma at this moment and offered a better place on the Wheel of Life. I believe our Goddess, Dala, is standing at her side singing her praises to her sister.'

He took a breath, as if fighting back emotion. 'Caleb stands on her other side, I'm certain, with Marie, his wife, and so many others who served here at the island. They are all to be praised and they will be missed, for they were our brothers and sisters in struggle. Good men and women all, may the Goddess bless them, each and every one.' He turned and looked up at the top of the hill, and signalled. A torchbearer began the blaze, moving around the edges of the pyre to set the kindling at the bottom alight. Quickly the flames spread and the bodies atop the wood were consumed.

Magnus spoke quietly, 'There's been too much fire, Father.'

Pug could only nod.

Without another word, Creegan came to stand before Pug. He took his hands, held them for a moment, nodded once, and then moved down the hill towards the remains of the villa. Others followed suit and when it was over, the remaining community of Sorcerer's Island waited some distance away while the father and son said their goodbyes.

Time passed, then finally in a whisper, Pug said, 'We have work to do.'

'What first, Father?' said Magnus. 'I need to keep busy for a while.'

'You will,' said Pug, turning towards those waiting below. 'Your mother and I discussed many things, including what to do should such a terrible day visit us.

'We move to the castle, and we shall stay there for a while. Let those responsible for this think us in tatters and hiding. We shall send messages to all our agents around this world and the struggle shall continue.

'We will find Belasco, Dahun, and whoever else is involved,

and we will uncover who is truly behind this madness. We will also find the demon gate, and we shall close it down.'

He continued down the hill, determination in his step, and his son followed, swallowing his grief for his mother and brother. If his father could endure such a loss and press on with the work that needed to be done, Magnus was determined that he could as well. If only the pain would fade, even just a little.